Payment Deferred

Payment Deferred

Joyce Holms

ISIS
LARGE PRINT
Oxford

Copyright © Joyce Holms, 1996

First published in Great Britain 1996
by Headline Book Publishing

Published in Large Print 2003 by ISIS Publishing Ltd,
7 Centremead, Osney Mead, Oxford OX2 0ES
by arrangement with Headline Book Publishing

British Library Cataloguing in Publication Data
Holms, Joyce
    Payment deferred. – Large print ed.
    1. Detective and mystery stories
    2. Large type books
    I. Title
    823.9'14 [F]

ISBN 0–7531–6701–8 (hb)
ISBN 0–7531–6702–6 (pb)

Printed and bound by Antony Rowe, Chippenham

Dedicated, with gratitude, to my
husband John

Prologue

Hanover Crescent Mews may not be an ideal place to die but at least it affords a little privacy, which in Edinburgh, and particularly during the Festival, is not easy to come by.

A hundred years ago it housed the carriages and the coachmen attached to the terrace of Georgian mansions on the north side of the cobbled lane. For a hundred years before that it had rung to the clang of farriers' hammers and the clatter of hooves and the rattle of iron-shod wheels on granite setts. But these days the mansions were either hotels or retirement homes or divided into flats, and the mews buildings were occupied by small businesses — plumbers, exhaust-fitters and the like — all of whom shut up shop around five thirty, leaving the lane deserted.

There were three streetlights, which had come on just after ten, illuminating little more than the cobbles directly beneath them, but the reflected glow of sodium lighting from Princes Street managed to penetrate this far, tinting the darkness with a wash of sickly orange, and in that distorted spectrum of colours the blood running across the pavement looked as black as oil. It ran between the cracks of the cobbles, soaking into the

1

dust and debris of a hundred years, forming a long, dark delta from the railings to the gutter.

Three inches above the tip of the delta dangled a pair of feet. One wore a high-heeled shoe, the other was naked, small, narrow and curiously pathetic. Blood had flowed, unchecked, down both of them, clotting into strings that would soon appear to fetter them to the ground.

At first glance, only the feet identified the body as female. The white shirt and dark trousers could have been worn by either sex, and the hair was short and blood-soaked, hanging back from the destroyed face.

Like a crucified Christ the dying woman hung from the tall iron railings. One spike had gone straight through the left arm just below the elbow, the other arm was caught by the biceps so that both were held extended. The head, sunk low between them, was pierced by a third spike which had entered behind the angle of the jaw and could be seen protruding below the shattered socket of the left eye.

The moon lit her and passed on, while behind her, in the Hamilton House Hotel, people danced and drank and made love and slept, playing the game in which she no longer had a part. She was seen by more than one of the guests as they watched the firework display that signalled the end of the military tattoo at the Castle, but the possibility of violent death was so far from their thinking that they failed to recognise the foreshortened bundle of rags on the railings for what it was.

In the end — and much too late — it was a trainee barmaid who spotted her, from the kitchen extension

2

which verged upon the mews itself. At that distance there could be no mistake.

Before the news could spread beyond the manager's office the police had arrived, the lane was sealed off and the crucifixion was shielded from view by PVC sheeting and striped ribbon, as though it were gift-wrapped for the CID.

There was still much of interest to be observed from the hotel windows, however. Police cars came and went; personnel in overalls or in dark suits visited the tent; a middle-aged man with a black bag — clearly the police surgeon — arrived, and shortly afterwards the blue glare of an oxyacetylene burner could be discerned through the PVC. By the time the body had been discreetly transferred to an ambulance the press had closed in, further disrupting the sleep of the Hamilton House residents.

The trainee barmaid was in great demand by both newspaper and TV reporters, and at first she was not averse to being, for once, the centre of attention. She was not aware of affording the body more than that single cognitive glance, since she had instantly realised, as she told her interviewers, that the less she saw, the easier she would forget.

It was only later in the day that the excitement wore off and she discovered that she had, in that second, seen more than enough to make forgetting — ever — out of the question.

CHAPTER
ONE

Buchanan could see it clearly, in all its venomous detail: bright red, pulsating, growing in size and virulence by the minute, oozing a bile-green acid that burned a smoking scar across everything it touched.

He snuck through the lights behind a bus that was the third vehicle going through on the red and got stranded athwart the crossing, unable to complete the turn into Princes Street because the traffic had jammed again at the next traffic light. Contorted faces snarled at him through windscreens, arms gesticulated and fingers conveyed furious insults, undeterred by the fact that, even if he had not been blocking the road, nobody was going anywhere till the gridlock cleared.

Even with nearly a fortnight to go before the Festival the capital was choked with tourists, and by nine thirty a.m. Princes Street was jammed solid.

It didn't help Buchanan's frustration to know that he had only himself to blame for getting stuck in it. He should have (a) remembered to buy a new battery for his alarm clock; (b) put away his laundry when his cleaning lady brought it back instead of letting it slide down the back of the couch so that he had to re-iron a shirt every morning; and (c) filled up with petrol on his way home the previous night.

He was already seven minutes late for his first appointment, which would have annoyed him even if his waiting client had been a paying customer. The fact that he didn't collect a fee for these Monday-morning consultations made his lateness worse, lending it an element of contempt of which he was, in fact, totally innocent.

He was now absolutely certain he had an ulcer. As he waited politely for a white-haired woman in a Ford to notice that the lights had changed, it was as clear in his mind's eye as if it were stuck to the inside of the windscreen with suckers like one of those ghastly orange cats. He watched it swelling and sizzling, squirting pints of bright-green acid into his gut, and the pain skewered him to the seat.

At the West End the traffic thinned enough for him to accelerate away down Haymarket, but he met up with another jam in Dalry Road and it was after quarter to ten by the time he swung into the car park at the community centre.

The lift, naturally, was at the fourth floor and going up. Buchanan took the stairs two at a time, swearing under his breath. At the second landing, he ran into McGuigan, the administrator of the centre and probably the person he disliked most in the world.

"Tam, dear boy! Just the chap I'm looking for!" McGuigan spread wide his arms, blocking half the stairway. A pall of tobacco smoke surrounded him like an aura, pale blue in a shaft of sunlight.

Buchanan side-stepped him neatly and continued upwards without breaking his stride. "Can't stop now, McGuigan. I'll talk to you later."

McGuigan flapped a hand at him. "I've got you an assistant."

Buchanan executed an emergency stop. He peered over the banister at McGuigan's wide and yellow-toothed grin. "You're joking! After all this time?"

"Now, now. A little more gratitude, Tam. It's only been a couple of months. I told you I'd do my best, didn't I? Well, then." McGuigan's hand covered his entire jaw as he drew on the cigarette he held in the junction of his first and second fingers. Inhaling, he pulled down the corners of his mouth and sucked the smoke into his lungs with a sound like the last drops of Coke going up a straw. "By rights it's the day nursery I should be allotting her to. I swear to God, the little buggers are running rings round Mrs Hannay and Pam. But I promised you I'd do my best for you, so I told her it had to be the legal advice office."

"She has no legal experience, then?"

McGuigan's broad grin wavered only momentarily. "Don't look a gift horse in the mouth, dear boy. If she had any legal experience she wouldn't be offering her services here, would she?"

"What do you think *I'm* doing? And practically for nothing!" Buchanan resumed his upward charge while behind him McGuigan's voice asserted plaintively that she could at least type. "Well, that's something anyway," Buchanan shouted over the banister. "Send her up in about twenty minutes."

McGuigan's rejoinder was lost in the thunder of Buchanan's footsteps as he mounted the final flight.

Because his office was at the end of the corridor there was room for a bench and two chairs beyond the door. Mr Armitage, who had presumably been waiting for twenty minutes, was seated on one of the chairs, in earnest conversation with a plump girl of about seventeen who was a stranger to Buchanan. So intent were they that they didn't notice him till he spoke.

"Mr Armitage," he said, forcing himself not to pant. "I do apologise for keeping you waiting. I'm afraid it's been one of those mornings."

He could feel his shirt sticking to a line of sweat along his backbone, and the office keys had somehow burrowed under a litter of papers at the foot of his briefcase. Irritation may have lent an unintended edge to his voice as he addressed the teenager.

"You're waiting to see me, are you?"

She had a sweet, dimpled face and an expression of unassailable innocence. "Well," she said with a hesitant smile, "that rather depends on who you are."

The discrepancy between what his eyes saw and what his ears heard was so great that Buchanan was momentarily at a loss. It was like being savaged by a day-old chick, which was clearly impossible, so he had to assume that she had not intended the put-down but was merely trying to sound sophisticated, or some such rubbish.

"I do beg your pardon," he said, with exaggerated politeness, and then regretted it. She was, after all, just a kid, and besides, he should have had the common

8

decency to introduce himself before barking at her. "I'm Tam Buchanan, Legal Advice."

She gave him a shy nod and offered a small but surprisingly strong hand. "In that case I *am* waiting to see you. I'm your new assistant. The name's Fitzpatrick."

Buchanan's already low spirits plummeted to new depths. McGuigan's face rose before his eyes, wearing its Bechstein grin, and his hands itched to punch it. Two months he'd waited for the promised assistant: two months of answering his own phone, of making his own appointments, of taking his notes and letters back to his New Town office for his own staff to type up. And now he was expected to be grateful for this schoolgirl, who would take weeks to train and would disappear into limbo long before she became of the slightest use to him. Well, thanks but no thanks, McGuigan, he thought bitterly. You're not saddling me with this teenage bimbo. The day nursery can have her and welcome!

"Um . . . right," he got out, through clenched teeth, and turned away to unlock the door, his smile still adhering inadvertently to his lips.

When he had shown Mr Armitage to a seat in the inner office he stuck his head back round the door and nodded at her encouragingly. "We'll have a chat shortly," he said. "I'll be about quarter of an hour with Mr Armitage, but there's no one else till ten thirty."

"Fine," she said, settling herself behind the minuscule reception desk and peeking into the empty drawers.

"In the meantime," he said, making the most of having an assistant while he had the chance, "what about some coffee?"

"Not for me, thanks. I think I'll just pop downstairs and see if I can rustle up a typewriter, shall I?"

It was quite clear that she had misunderstood him. For a second he considered disabusing her but decided he didn't care about coffee anyway. Discovering his hand still indicating the cupboard where the cups were kept, he stuck it hurriedly in his pocket.

"Yes. Sure. You do that," he said. It would take days of negotiation and bargaining before McGuigan would allocate them a typewriter. He knew that. He also knew that it wasn't fair to let her start to settle in when he had already made up his mind that she'd be in the day nursery before the end of the morning, but, hell, it would keep her out of his hair for a while.

By the time he showed Mr Armitage to the door she had acquired a word processor, several notebooks, a collection of yellow pencils and a gangrenous-looking spider plant, and was engaged in moving the desk to make room for the two chairs from the corridor. Already the place was looking uncomfortably hers, and Buchanan could see that if he was going to give her the elbow he'd better not waste any more time.

"Bye-bye, Fizz," Mr Armitage said to her from the doorway. "See you next week."

"Bye-bye, Mr Armitage. You take care now."

Buchanan raised his eyebrows at her as the door closed behind his client. "You two have met before?"

"Just when we were waiting for you. We'd plenty of time to get acquainted."

He looked at her sharply but could see no sign that she was deliberately getting at him. Her expression was one of timorous respect and as guileless as a baby's. Still, he supposed he should have apologised to her as well as to Armitage. He said, "What did he call you? Fizz?"

She nodded. "Short for Fitzpatrick."

Great. It suited her down to the ground. The kids in the day nursery would love it. "Okay, Fizz. Let's take the weight off our feet and talk."

She followed him into the office and took in the view from the window before settling into the clients' chair across the desk from him. They smiled at each other; she with an assurance beyond her age, he with an unspecified foreboding which was far from easy to understand. There was certainly nothing to justify it in her appearance. Nobody could have looked more cherubic. Her hair was dark gold, pulled back into one of those elastic clasp things but escaping in curly, sun-bleached tendrils that dangled round her brow and ears. She was wearing no make-up, but her face and such other areas of skin that were visible were an even, biscuit-coloured tan that was quite foreign to Edinburgh even in the middle of summer. Her eyes were the colour of washed-out denim and held an expression of arresting innocence and absolute trust. While he was swithering about how to begin shattering that trust, she said:

"So, what's happening about Mr Armitage? What are you going to do for him?"

Buchanan waved a hand noncommittally. "We'll see, we'll see. It's a very complicated case."

"What's complicated about it?" she wanted to know. "He's got a loony lodger who won't pay his rent arrears, refuses to move out and has started putting the frighteners on his wife. Surely he has some recourse in law?"

"Well, it's not as simple as —" Buchanan stopped and looked at her closely. "He told you all this?"

It seemed highly improbable that Armitage should have unburdened himself to a perfect stranger. Especially this one. He was no blabbermouth; nor, for that matter, was he above kneecapping his lodger if the law failed to move fast enough.

"Sure," Fizz said with an insouciant shrug. "It's getting him down. I told him not to worry, that you'd put the skids under the mother, PDQ."

Several seconds passed while Buchanan stared at those rosebud lips as though they were being operated by an unseen ventriloquist. Unparliamentary language did not normally shock him; indeed, on the lips of someone like Mr Armitage, such a term, even enunciated in full, would, more often than not, pass unnoticed. But coming from a child with a face like a Botticelli cherub it had full-metal-jacket pungency. Finally, he drew a breath and said, "Well, I don't think you need concern yourself with Mr Armitage's problems —"

"Why not?" She pushed up the sleeves of her enormous baggy sweater, crossed her arms on the table, and gazed hopefully into his eyes, looking exactly, he thought, like his two nephews when they said, "Tell us a story, Uncle Tam."

"Well . . . because that's what *I'm* here for." He grinned weakly.

"Oh." Her eyes widened with mild curiosity. "And what am *I* here for, then?"

Buchanan chewed his lip wordlessly. He had a niggling feeling that he had lost control of the conversation and couldn't think for the world how to get it back on course. What was he thinking about to allow this kid to put him on the defensive?

What he *was* thinking about, in point of fact, was the way the soft wool of her sweater flowed around her breasts like draperies on a Greek statue. It was clear she wasn't wearing a bra, and the loose folds of material clung to her body seductively, making her look soft and cuddly and as boneless as a kitten. He had been lost in pleasurable contemplation for some time before he raised his eyes to her childlike face and instantly felt like some kind of a pervert.

She smiled at him with infinite kindness. "Because, you see, I'm not interested in just typing and making coffee. That's not why I volunteered my time."

"Ah . . ."

"No. I thought Mr McGuigan would have made that clear. I'm starting a degree course in law at the University in October and I want to begin familiarising myself as much as I can. I offered my services as an

13

assistant, not a dogsbody. To be honest with you, I wouldn't even have admitted I could type if Mr McGuigan hadn't said it would be necessary."

So much for McGuigan's generosity, Buchanan thought. If he could have shunted her into the day nursery he'd have done so, and to hell with the legal advice office. However, the legal advice office had enough to do without running foundation courses for embryo law students. He leaned back in his chair, smiling a little now that he spotted an avenue of escape.

"Well now, as you say, Fizz, McGuigan should have told me this, because, with the best will in the world, there's not really much I can give you to do. Virtually nothing, in fact. Not in the legal sense. You'd need a certain amount of experience to be of any use to me there."

"That's too bad," she said, marring the smooth curve of her brow with a tiny frown. "So what sort of thing would an *assistant* have to do? Other than typing and coffee-making, that is."

Buchanan knew he was going to have to waffle and resented it deeply. It was appalling to think that he was allowing this — this *child*, for God's sake! — to put him on the spot, yet he couldn't quite bring himself to be harsh with her, any more than he could slap down his nephews when they got too sassy. She was such a sweet, unsophisticated kid and it was quite obvious that some smartass had told her to act tough and hold out for a fair deal.

"What sort of thing?" he temporised, stopping himself only just in time from shuffling the papers on his desk. "Oh . . . taking messages, I suppose. Interviewing people. Helping them to fill in forms, there's a lot of that."

"But I could do that."

"Ah . . . but you see, er . . . Fizz, it's a matter of age. Maturity. In this business youth is a definite no-no. Clients have to have confidence in your judgement. Nobody wants to talk things over with a teenager."

"I'm twenty-six," she said flatly.

Buchanan had a hard time keeping his face straight, but when he saw the glint in her eye he was glad he'd tried. Incredible as it seemed at first, he could see she was perfectly serious, and that, moreover, she'd had her fill of sceptical rejoinders. Now that he looked at her closely he could see signs that she was telling the truth: nothing that would stand up in court, maybe, but an air of confidence, a certain knowingness, a faint look of calculation that was at odds with her bashful smile.

"Really?" he said, keeping his voice carefully expressionless. "I do beg your pardon. You look much younger."

She lifted her chin and straightened from the table, and for some reason he felt he'd passed some sort of test. "So I'm told," she said. "But Mr Armitage had no problem with that, did he? And, in fact, I've found it's an advantage rather than a drawback. People forget to be on their guard against me."

That's for damn sure, Buchanan thought, doing a rapid reassessment of the situation and not liking the result. It was obvious that she had been running rings round him since the word go, and the realisation merely hardened his resolve to get shot of her as quickly as possible. "Well, I'm really sorry, Fizz . . ." he started to say, but halted as he realised she was already speaking.

"I only have a few weeks before term starts, but it would be tremendously helpful to me if I could just fit in a little work experience in the meantime, and I'm sure I could be a help to you. Mr McGuigan said I could come in on a Monday morning when you're here and also do Tuesday mornings to catch up on the secretarial work."

"*Two* mornings a week?" Even to his own ears he sounded wistful. In two mornings she could probably keep abreast of the work, even if she were as inexperienced as he suspected.

That would at least take the strain off Beatrice, his own secretary, who had been flouncing around with a face like an Easter Island statue for weeks. And it was only till the start of term, by which time, with a little prodding, McGuigan might have come up with a more satisfactory replacement.

All of which, he discovered, counted for nothing when weighed against a gut feeling that he'd be cutting his own throat. It wasn't just the bruised self-esteem of somebody who'd been taken in and didn't like it. At least, not entirely. It was . . . he couldn't put his finger on it exactly but he was damn sure she would be more trouble than she was worth.

"I really like what the council is doing here," she was saying. "I bet a lot of people who need legal advice would find a solicitor's office quite off-putting, but when they can talk to someone here in the community centre it's so much less formal, isn't it? It makes it just like going to the t'ai chi class or the literacy project or whatever."

"It's only a pilot scheme," Buchanan said. "The council wasn't sure if there would be much response to the idea, so I agreed to give it one morning a week for six months. Unfortunately for me, the response has been enormous and I've been run ragged for the past two months."

That was a mistake. The admission was no sooner out of his mouth than she was in there like a shot. "Well, if you're so rushed I'm sure I could be a help to you, even if it's only till you find someone more experienced." She leaned further across the table. "All the other professionals appear to have volunteer assistants, the community artist, the well woman clinic and such like. And there are three paid typists in Mr McGuigan's office, none of whom appear to be particularly overworked. And yet you are, apparently, expected to operate efficiently without even a receptionist."

These were so exactly Buchanan's sentiments that, for a few seconds, he was almost swayed. Only the realisation that he'd be stuck with Fizz for good made him think twice. Once he had a helper of sorts McGuigan would be deaf to his pleas for a more qualified assistant. No, better to do without till a better applicant came along.

Those few seconds of hesitation, however, proved to be his downfall. Before he could assemble the words that would, firmly but gently, send Fizz packing, his next client was tapping on the door, and from then till lunchtime he didn't get a minute to draw breath. At the back of his mind as he worked was the realisation that things *were* running a little more smoothly, that he wasn't having to jump up in the middle of a consultation to admit clients or answer the telephone, but the best that could be said for his state of mind at the end of the morning was that he was seriously undecided. And he still couldn't put his finger on what it was about her that worried him.

It wasn't that he thought she had deliberately deceived him. That was rubbish. You only had to look at her face to know she wasn't that cunning. Yet every time he thought of her, installed behind that reception desk out there as though she'd bought the place, an alarm hooter started going *Woop! Woop! Woop!* inside his skull.

As he was throwing papers into his briefcase she stuck her head round the door and grinned at him.

"That the lot?" he said, knowing that it was. There were no more appointments, and he rarely saw anyone without one.

"Actually, no." She tipped her head, indicating the outer office. "I've got a friend of yours waiting to see you. A Mr Kingston."

Shock brought his teeth together with an audible click. *Murray Kingston*, for God's sake! The utter inconceivability of his turning up here — the downright brass neck of it! — left Buchanan dazed. He had to make a show of studying a sheaf of papers to hide his fury from Fizz while he decided what to do.

Had the irreplaceable Beatrice been in attendance there would be no problem. Beatrice's way with unwanted guests was firm, polite and totally final. Nobody, but nobody, got to see her Mr Buchanan without her say-so. In fact, had Marat had a secretary like Beatrice, Charlotte Corday would never have seen the inside of his bathroom. Unfortunately, Fizz was not in that class, therefore he'd have to do the eviction himself — an altogether messier procedure.

The fact that Kingston regarded him as a close friend, and had done so for near enough fifteen years, was also something that gave him pause. It wasn't easy to throw out somebody like that, even though theirs had been, from day one, a seriously one-sided relationship and had, besides, ceased to be a relationship of any description more than three years ago.

The sudden awareness that Fizz was already standing aside to allow Kingston to enter galvanised him into action. Dodging round the desk, he was just able to make it through the doorway first.

Kingston halted in mid-stride, his eyes wary. "Tam. It's good to see you."

Buchanan kept his face blank. "Something I can do for you?"

"I need to talk to you, Tam. I need a lawyer. If I could just —"

"You've got a lawyer. There's nothing I can do for you that he couldn't."

Kingston's face twisted. There was a film of sweat along his upper lip and his eyes clung to Buchanan's with dogged determination. "You've got to help me,

19

Tam. There's not a soul in the world I can turn to except you."

Buchanan didn't want to witness this. He hated himself for kicking aside the piece of shit that had once been Murray Kingston, and he hated that same Murray Kingston for forcing him to do it. The bastard just didn't know when to crawl away and die.

"You made your own bed," he said harshly. "Frankly, I wouldn't help you if I could."

He walked towards the door and held it open, glimpsing on the way a wide-eyed Fizz with a corner of her bottom lip gripped in her teeth. Kingston stood his ground, however, his spongy white hands plucking at the front of his jacket.

"It's not true, Tam. I swear to God I never did it. Christ, you've known me fifteen years! You have to know me better than that. How —"

"Let's not go through all this." Buchanan cut him off with a gesture. "You know damn well the evidence was irrefutable. The best advice I can give you is to put it all behind you and try to make a new life for yourself someplace well away from Edinburgh. Now, I'm sorry but you'll have to go. We're just locking up."

"Ten minutes," Kingston said, and to Buchanan's horror, his eyes filled with tears. "You owe me ten minutes, Tam, you know you do. You're my last hope. If you turn me down there's nowhere else to go."

Had it not been for Fizz's presence Buchanan would have relieved his feelings with a few choice phrases. As it was he could do nothing but grind his teeth as he turned and led the way into his inner sanctum.

20

CHAPTER
TWO

It was clear to Fizz from the start that Donna in main reception was the colleague to cultivate. As one of the paid staff, she knew her way around the community centre and, with a little encouragement, could be a big help with those areas of office administration where Fizz's expertise was a little shaky.

"The trouble with you, Donna," Fizz told her the following morning, "is that you are too honest. Know what I'm saying? Like, honesty's all very well in important issues, but you've got to know when to draw the line. If you really want something — and it's not doing anybody any harm — you have to be prepared to bend the truth a little."

She was engaged in reversing the orientation of her desk so that, with the cupboard door open, the word processor wouldn't be visible from the doorway. Donna watched her glumly, clearly undecided whether her response should be one of admiration or condemnation.

"But, saying that you could type . . ."

"I had no choice. That upright rodent . . . what's-his-face?"

"McGuigan?"

"Yes, McGuigan. He was for shunting me into the créche. When I told him I was only interested in the legal work he said I'd have to be able to type, so I thought, well, what's the big deal about typing anyway? Anyone can do it, it's just a matter of getting your speed up."

This did not go down too well with Donna, who had, no doubt, Fizz realised abruptly, spent months on a typing course before landing the job in reception.

"*Touch*-typing is something *else*, Fizz," she said stiffly, "as you'll very quickly find out — if you last that long. Mr Buchanan will soon catch you out."

Fizz waved the biscuit she was eating in the direction of the word processor. "Not as long as I have that thing. Now that you've shown me what to do and set up all the margins for me, it's easy. I've already got six letters typed and ready for you to edit."

"Yes, but there's more to it than that. You don't know a thing about setting up phrases or blocks, and we haven't even started on printing out." Donna swept back the curtain of long chestnut hair that hung across her face and sent Fizz a sideways glance. "And if anyone asks you where you got the computer . . ."

"I won't say who told me where to find it, don't worry. If McGuigan wasn't such a pustule he'd offer Buchanan the use of it, instead of letting it lie around unused for weeks on end."

Donna finished eating her chocolate biscuit and dabbed up the crumbs from the tinfoil wrapper with a licked fingertip. "I ought to get back," she said, without making any move to go. "I'm not supposed to pay social calls during my tea break, but I thought I'd just check that you'd settled in okay. What's Tam Buchanan like to work for?"

Fizz lifted a shoulder. "Could be worse. A bit of a fuddy-duddy. Can't for the life of me see what it is about him that turns you on."

Donna tipped her head to one side and went all dewy-eyed. "Mmmm. He's gorgeous! Did you see how blue his eyes are? And those eyelashes? Honest, Fizz, when he smiles at me on his way past reception I'm spaced out for the rest of the day!" Her face sobered. "You really think you can sort of . . .?"

"Bring you to his attention? No problem. Like I told you yesterday, Donna, all Buchanan needs is a gentle shove in the right direction. If I can't open his eyes to you my name's not Fitzpatrick. Give it a fortnight, we don't want to rush things."

"God, no! Don't be too obvious, for heaven's sake. I don't want him to —"

Fizz held up a hand. "Trust me."

Donna's worried face broke into a sudden smile. "I do, actually!" she confided, with rock-solid but totally misplaced confidence. "And if you can do that for me, the least I can do in return is to help you with your typing. I'd do it for Tam anyway if McGuigan allowed me to."

"I take it there isn't a particular lady in his life right now?"

The smile died a sudden death. "Well, actually, yes, there is. Janine."

"Mmm. Is she recent?"

"Not really. She's been around at least since he came here. A couple of months. She's always on the phone to him, and once she turned up in a flashy red BMW and swanned straight up to his office without as much as a by-your-leave. Not the sort to demean herself by speaking to a pleb like me."

"Sounds just his type."

"That's not true, Fizz." A touch of frost entered Donna's tone. "Tam's not the snooty type. I can't imagine how he could fall for a bitch like Janine but, I have to admit it, she really is fantastic-looking. Like a fashion model, with one of those faces that looks like it has never been used and legs up to her armpits. And you should see her hair, it's silver-blonde and sort of . . ." The utter hopelessness of her position seemed to strike her all at once and her voice stuttered into silence.

"Looks don't matter," Fizz told her firmly, and then felt that was going too far. "Well, up to a point they do, of course. I mean, a pig with lipstick isn't going to have to carry Mace, but anybody who's anything like half-decent can get any man she wants."

"You really believe that?"

"Sure I do."

Now, that was a lie, and Fizz knew it. Buchanan wasn't ever going to fall for Donna, not even if Fizz worked on him for years, which she had no intention of even starting to do. The very fact that Donna thought she had a hope in hell of attracting him was proof enough that she didn't have two brain cells to rub together. In fact, apart from her hair, which was quite

24

nice, she didn't have a lot going for her at all. Her face was, at best, ordinary, and she would have been the correct weight for her height only if she had been eight foot ten.

Perhaps it was unfair to string her along, but her help was absolutely necessary to Fizz and there was no way Donna would give that help without some sort of a quid pro quo. Fizz herself was unhappy with the bargain, not only because she preferred, on the whole, to deal honestly with people but also because she had a feeling she'd have trouble with Donna when her patience ran out. However, she told herself, she'd deal with that problem if and when it arose.

"Since he already has a girlfriend," she temporised, "things may take a little longer than I had calculated, but —"

The door behind Donna opened to admit a stench of tobacco, closely followed by McGuigan. Fizz quickly swung open the cupboard door to hide the computer.

"What's this, then? A little hen party?"

Donna leapt to her feet, hurriedly brushing crumbs from her skirt, but before she could start making excuses Fizz said firmly, "Donna's on her tea break. As it happens, she was just leaving."

McGuigan nodded, his manner suggesting that it was Fizz he'd come to see, which was something of a bummer since the word processor, officially the property of the community drama group, was screened only by the cupboard door.

"Off you go then, Donna. Caroline will be waiting to have her break now." He moved aside just enough to let her squeeze past him, and as she did so, gave her bottom an admonitory pat.

Donna kept going, giving no sign that she had even noticed the contact, but Fizz believed in dealing with things as they came up.

"Try that on me, Mr McGuigan," she said pleasantly, "and you'll be walking funny for a week."

She had the satisfaction of seeing the smile wither on his lips, but he recovered quickly and wafted a careless hand. "Oh, Donna and I are old friends. She knows I don't mean anything. That right, Donna?"

Donna was, by now, out of sight and made no audible reply to this question, but McGuigan switched on his smile again as though he had received absolution. His desire to converse with Fizz had, however, apparently evaporated, at least for the moment.

"Right then, back to work . . ."

Fizz forgot him as soon as the door closed and returned to experimenting with the word processor. The few letters that Buchanan had entrusted to her the day before were typed and ready to be edited by Donna, but she still had a long way to go before she could attempt to type anything while actually under observation. Two fingers and an occasional third were simply not enough. Finding the word processor in the drama group's offices, where it would be unused for the summer, had been a godsend. There would be a row about its redeployment sooner or later, but by then, with any luck, Buchanan would have discovered that she was indispensable.

26

She had only eight weeks to make an impression on him. Once term started, any free time she had would have to be spent in earning her keep, and by then she would hope to be in a position to talk Buchanan into giving her a part-time job with his own firm. It was just a pity that he had got up her nose yesterday. She had intended to be all efficiency and co-operation but he was so damn stuffy for a man scarcely out of his twenties that she couldn't help deflating his ego just a little. Next time she saw him she'd keep her mouth shut and play the perfect employee.

She had saved enough to support herself till she got her grant, but thereafter it would be all lentils and carrots unless she got a job. With so many law students in the city, part-time jobs in law offices were like gold, but getting into Buchanan's good books this early gave her a chance of stealing a march on the others. It was a gamble, but if it postponed stacking shelves in a supermarket it would be well worth the effort.

Just as she was beginning to think about packing up she heard a footstep in the corridor, which threw her into a panic. Switching off the word processor without thinking about what you were doing was liable, as she had already found out, to make an entire morning's work disappear into oblivion, but although the cupboard door hid the hardwear it didn't cover the noise it made. Luckily it was only Murray Kingston, who leaned round the doorway and raised a diffident eyebrow.

He looked marginally calmer than he had yesterday, but his eyes were still cagey and his clothes still had the

27

look of being borrowed from someone else. The grey linen slacks he wore were well cut but, like his polo shirt and bomber jacket, they seemed not only two or three sizes too big for him but dated as well.

"Well, hello," she said, smiling at him because he was clearly half expecting a rebuff. "If you're looking for the boss fella he's not here on a Tuesday. Just Monday mornings."

"Yes, I know. He told me that yesterday."

He edged into the office, looking round at everything as though he hadn't noticed his surroundings on his first visit. Since he was evidently in no hurry to state his business and depart, Fizz indicated the chair recently vacated by Donna, but he declined it with the faintest twitch of his head.

"I was just passing and thought I'd . . . well, I wanted to thank you for yesterday."

Fizz smiled absently, concentrating on saving her morning's work. "There's nothing to thank me for . . ."

"Oh, but there is. You were great." His fingers drummed nervously on the back of the chair. "I can't begin to tell you how much you helped by just listening to me. You're the only person I've spoken to who doesn't think I'm a paedophile."

"Except Buchanan, surely?" Fizz had missed a good deal of what had transpired in Buchanan's office yesterday, since the door was pretty thick and she was afraid of being caught with her ear against it. Even when they stopped speaking in such subdued tones — i.e. after she had knocked on the door to tell them she was leaving — she had barely managed to keep track of the conversation.

Murray's hands tightened on the chair back. "Tam doesn't believe me. Not really. Oh sure, he said he'd review the evidence — you were right, by the way, his conscience wouldn't let him refuse — but that doesn't mean he believes me right now. An open mind. That's all I can expect from Tam till he turns up some concrete evidence."

"Well, he will, Murray," Fizz told him with more confidence than she had a right to feel. "I know he'll do his very best for you and, like you said, the evidence has got to be there somewhere. It's only a matter of time."

"Just keep saying that, Fizz." He tipped his head on one side and beamed at her like a fond father, a look she was familiar with but which never ceased to irritate her. He was, after all, no more than thirty-one or two, and he knew damn well what age she was because she had put him right on that yesterday when he'd made the usual mistake of taking her for a teenager. She began, rather pointedly, putting the cover on the VDU, which prompted him to say:

"Time for your lunch break?"

"Yes . . . well, that's me finished for the day. I only work mornings, Monday and Tuesday."

"Maybe we could have lunch together. There's a nice place in the Grassmarket."

Fizz considered this momentarily. He was definitely not somebody she wanted to get involved with. Losers were not her type, and Murray Kingston was a loser, it was written all over him. Besides, she might be convinced that he was innocent of all the charges against him, but she had been known to be wrong in the past, and, looking at it logically, an adult woman with the looks of an immature seventeen-year-old might appeal strongly to somebody with Murray's alleged tastes. On the other hand, the Grassmarket was on her way home, and a free lunch was a free lunch.

It was only much later that she remembered there ain't no such thing.

They went to the White Hart, which was really just a glorified pub but which was still basking in the distinction of having been home to Robert Burns in 1791. Undeterred by Murray's lack of appetite, Fizz stoked up very satisfyingly on French onion soup, vegetarian lasagne and home-baked apple tart with ice cream. It was a lot more than she usually ate at that time of day but it meant she wouldn't have to cook an evening meal.

"So, what are you doing with your time?" she asked when she could spare a moment for conversation. "I suppose you'll have to start looking for a job?"

"Soon. Yes." He stared moodily at his coffee, splashing it about with his teaspoon like a spoiled child. It was hard to believe he was the same age as Buchanan. In appearance he was much older but, of course, that could be accounted for by his spell in Saughton prison. There was something unhealthy about his face. It managed to be both thin and puffy, and the skin was dulled with a wash of grey that was almost black under his eyes and in the creases of his brow. Probably he hadn't spent much time out of doors over the last few years and, well, they said that sex offenders were given a pretty hard time by their fellow inmates.

He drew a long breath. "I've only been back in circulation for three days. Maybe next week I'll feel like getting myself organised. Right now all I want to think about is clearing my name and getting Debbie back."

"Debbie's your daughter?"

"Yes."

The word was bitten off short, as though he didn't want to talk about her, which Fizz found not altogether surprising given the circumstances. Whether he was, in fact, guilty of abusing the child or not, the separation from her was clearly causing him a lot of pain.

He lifted his head and looked around at the occupants of the nearby tables, none of whom were close enough to overhear him. "Somebody set me up, Fizz. Somebody put it into Debbie's head to say those things about me." His voice shook. "A four-year-old kid, for Christ's sake! I'll kill the bastard if I get my hands on him!"

He looked half mad as he said it, showing a lot of white round the iris, the veins sticking out a bit in his thin neck. Quite suddenly, Fizz found herself absolutely certain that he was speaking the truth. She had been sure of it before but now there was something in his eyes which, she felt, could not be counterfeited and which communicated an agony that she could well understand. The thought of some evil person tampering with a child's mind, putting horrendous images in her wee head, revolting words in her mouth, made Fizz feel sick to her stomach. It was almost as foul as physical abuse and it made her furious to think that Buchanan, in the absence of hard evidence, would probably do nothing about it.

"I wish I knew the whole story," she said. "Like you said yesterday, nobody who is, basically, convinced you did it can really be a hundred per cent effective in examining the evidence. But I'm certain that if you and I really put our minds to it we would be able to turn up something that would, at least, merit further investigation."

"I wouldn't even know where to make a start," he said, spreading his hands. "Buchanan's my only hope."

Fizz frowned at him, striving for patience. "That's all very well, Murray, but he may take forever to get through all the paperwork, and there's a fair chance he'll find nothing that can help you. But meanwhile, surely, you and I could be attacking the problem on other fronts, couldn't we? A little active searching for clues wouldn't go amiss."

The look he gave her might have been directed at an overimaginative child. "Well, that's not as easy as you make it sound, Fizz."

There were some people, Fizz firmly believed — and most of them were graduates of some kind or another — who wouldn't believe anyone capable of tying their own shoelaces unless they held a fully authenticated certificate of competence. It was clear that Murray was one of those people, so there was nothing else for it but to embroider her CV.

"No, it's not easy," she said, "but fortunately for you, I have some experience in that line. I worked for two years with a private detective in Toronto, and although I never handled the serious crime cases I have plenty of expertise in questioning suspects."

This was virtually impossible to check up on and, quite coincidentally, had the added advantage of being partly true. She *had* worked for a private detective in Toronto, but the reason she had never handled any serious crime cases was that she had been employed in an au pair capacity. Such questioning of suspects as she had carried out had been on the rare occasions when she had been required to phone and ask them if her employer could call on them.

Murray was regarding her with amazement. "Well, that's the first bit of good luck I've had in years," he said, reaching across the table to touch her wrist. "And you'll help me, Fizz? I don't know where the money's going to come from but I reckon I can at least cover your expenses."

"Don't worry about that. We'll keep expenses to a minimum. There's just one thing I'd ask of you, Murray." She leaned towards him and held his eyes for a moment. "Don't say anything to Buchanan about my involvement just yet. He's an old-fashioned fuddy-duddy, as you probably know, and he might just possibly decide to put the kibosh on the idea on the grounds of client confidentiality or some such rubbish."

Buchanan might not want her to get involved in the case but he couldn't fail to be impressed if she managed to prove that Murray had been framed. Impressed enough to give her a job, perhaps.

Murray shrugged happily. "If I'm not worried about that I don't see why he should be but — sure, if that's what you'd prefer. It doesn't affect Tam's operation, after all. So, where do we start?"

"The first thing I need to know," Fizz told him, already half believing in her credentials, "is the background. The name of everybody who had access to Debbie, the identity of anyone who might have had it in for you, and anybody else you suspect. But not here."

The one-thirty influx of diners was now starting to fill up the dining area, the tables next to them were occupied and the noise was climbing to a level that made *sotto voce* conversation difficult.

She reached for the jacket she'd slung over the back of her chair. "Let's take a walk round the Meadows. It's the only way we'll get some privacy."

He followed her without argument, indeed with a visible eagerness that surprised even Fizz. It was always a source of amazement to her when people believed her lies, but if a trace of guilt bothered her it was only for a second, and she had no trouble absolving herself, on the grounds that she was merely giving him the confidence to help himself.

They walked fast (i.e. at Fizz's normal speed) up Lady Lawson Street and down Chalmers Street till they reached the Meadows, and then, because Murray was obviously feeling the pace, slowed to a geriatric amble. The usual traffic of joggers, students and dog-walkers was thin enough, at this hour, to give them all the privacy they needed.

34

Fizz wished she'd thought to bring her notebook and yellow pencil. "Okay," she told Murray, "I think the best thing would be for you to tell me the whole story from the beginning."

"Yes, right," he said without hesitation. Evidently he had been getting his thoughts in order on the way over. "The first thing I knew about it was when the police turned up at my house —"

"Just a minute. That's not the beginning, Murray. Give me a bit of background first. How were you and Debbie living? What about your wife?"

"Oh. Okay. Well, Anne died . . . my wife died five years ago when Debbie was just two." He drew a long breath, thought about it, then added, "Committed suicide, in fact."

"Jeez. That's tough, Murray." She would have liked to know the details, how she'd done it, who'd found her, etc., but decided now was not the time. "Do you know why she did it?"

"Depression. It started after Debbie was born and never really cleared up. It had been getting worse for months and she wouldn't hear of taking pills for it." He looked away into the distance where the Salisbury crags rose above the trees. "We were living down in Berwick when Anne died. I was teaching English at Tweedside High School, and was careers officer too, so I was kept pretty busy, but our house was only a few streets away so I could pop home at lunchtime and sometimes between periods. I hired a childminder, of course, and Debbie went to playgroup in the mornings, but I made a point of being with her as much as I could."

"She missed her mum, I suppose."

He thought about that for a minute. "Not as much as I'd have expected, I don't think. At least, she didn't show it much. She'd always been used to being left with other people for short periods. Anne had often parked her with her sister, Phillis, when she was feeling down and needed to escape for a while, and our neighbour, Mrs McCaulay, had also helped out that way as things got worse. So, no, I don't think Debbie was very deeply traumatised — not enough to account for . . . for the stories she came out with later."

He walked on a bit in silence, his mouth clamped shut in a straight line. Fizz held her tongue, and presently he started talking again without having to be prompted.

"Sometimes she woke up in the night and called out for her mummy but I'd . . . I'd take her into bed with me and she soon settled down. I don't think that happened for more than a few months, though. She became very fond of her childminder and she still saw Mrs McCaulay, who sat with her in the evening if I had to go out, and I'd have said she was as happy as any other four-year-old. There just wasn't any reason for her to . . ."

He shook his head angrily, glaring at the path in front of his feet, and the silence lengthened while they both thought about what he'd said. Fizz led the way to a bench facing down Middle Meadow Walk to the whale-jaw arch. A small group of students was having a lunchtime t'ai chi session under the trees, spelling out tranquillity with slow movements.

"So it came as a shock to you when the police turned up on your doorstep."

"To put it mildly, yes. Half past ten at night. Two boot-faced zombies, plus a policewoman who sat with Debbie while they took me to the police station for questioning. Even now I can't believe it happened."

"What evidence did they have against you?"

He rubbed a hand across his brow. "Oh God, I can't remember what they came up with at that stage and what came later. It was a nightmare, Fizz — all these hate-filled faces, the accusations, the pseudo-politeness. 'And on these occasions, sir, when your daughter shared your bed, sir, did anything improper occur, you bastard?'"

A squirrel appeared a yard from Fizz's feet and eyed her hopefully. She found a packet of sunflower seeds in her pocket, chucked it some, and ate some herself. Murray declined a share with a look of distaste.

She said, "I suppose it's not always easy to keep an open mind."

"Fact is, they knew me, knew who I was. Some of them had even been in my house. But you'd never have known it, the way they treated me."

"How come they knew you?" Fizz wondered.

"Oh, I'd had a camera nicked a few weeks before, that's all. All very pally about *that*, of course."

"Still, I bet you weren't too polite yourself when they hauled you in."

He said, "I reckon I more or less went to pieces. It doesn't matter how often you see that sort of thing on TV, you know, it doesn't prepare you for it. There's none of this 'I'm saying nothing till I've spoken to my lawyer' or 'Couldn't this wait till the morning, Officer?' You're so shocked you just start yelling and swearing and demanding to be driven home. I was panicking in case Debbie woke up with a complete stranger, and I was blazing mad because I thought the whole scene was some sort of mistake and somebody would be hauled over the coals for it in the morning — either the copper who was questioning me or one of the people who had laid the allegations in the first place."

"What people?" Fizz said. "Who had laid the allegations?"

"The playgroup, primarily. Primrose Hill Day Centre, it's called, and it's run by a woman called Pam Torkington. She claimed that Debbie had been saying things and also doing bizarre drawings that had made her wonder if something suspicious was going on. She contacted the social work department and they started making enquiries: Mrs McCaulay, the childminder, Anne's sister, the staff at Tweedside High." His lips twisted in a curve that was not a smile. "It's surprising how few of them felt able to put me in the clear."

Fizz shook her head. "You can't blame them, Murray. It's such a deeply emotive subject and, you know, anybody would be inclined to err on the side of safety. Kids can't defend themselves — parents can. You'd have to be awfully sure about a person before you could say with absolute certainty, 'No, I'd swear that he simply could not do a thing like that!' I mean, what if you were wrong?"

"It went further than that, Fizz," he said. "Once you start suspecting somebody there's always some tiny incident you can call to mind and then blow up into something significant. If parents knew how easily their actions can be misinterpreted they'd never hug or kiss their kids in public, never take someone else's kid on their knee, never offer to have one of their kid's friends stay over."

A jogger in a new grey cotton tracksuit and pristine white trainers toiled past them, heels thudding on the path. He'd have buggered his Achilles tendons in a fortnight, Fizz reflected, supposing he hadn't packed in by then. She waited for Murray to go on speaking. Obviously there had to be more evidence against him. What he had related so far was much too circumstantial to base a prosecution on. Finally, when he didn't speak, she said:

"So they had no real reason for holding you at that point?"

"No. They let me go home." He stared at his clasped hands for a moment. "I didn't go to work the next morning, I was too . . . I hadn't slept and . . . Well, when I phoned the deputy principal to tell him I wouldn't be there, he said the police were already going over the careers office with a fine-tooth comb and it would be better if I stayed away."

"Nasty." Fizz was beginning to appreciate the nightmare quality of the story: the inexorable progress of evil, the feeling of sheer defencelessness, the realisation that neither truth nor logic would make the slightest difference to the outcome. She said, "So what happened then?"

"So then the same two zombies reappeared with a warrant to search my house, and the next thing that happened was that I was taken down to the station and charged."

Fizz became aware that they had missed a bit. "Charged?" she said. "So they'd found something? Real evidence?"

"So they claimed," he said, darkly, and chewed on his lip a while. "They produced a pile of pornographic magazines — really appalling stuff: hard core — claiming they'd found it hidden in my office. Then they produced a pair of Debbie's pyjama trousers which, they told me, appeared to show traces of semen."

Fizz's heart gave a horrible little flutter like a budgie in a sock. If semen had been produced in evidence it had to have been subjected to a DNA test, therefore it had been proved to be Murray's.

That was a toughie. Not one that could be brushed aside as inconclusive. In fact, Fizz told herself, one might have to consider the possibility that one had made an error of judgement *vis-à-vis* Murray Kingston. In which case, what had one got into here, and how could one get the hell out of it?

CHAPTER
THREE

The only problem with the legal firm of Buchanan and Stewart, as far as Tam was concerned, was that there was one Buchanan too many. The senior partner, Tam's father, who was now sixty-seven, had been promising to retire for years but couldn't quite stay out of the office.

His machinations to make it appear that there was too much work for Tam and Alan Stewart to manage on their own were becoming laughable, but Tam was not laughing. He had his father to thank for landing him with the free legal advice clinic at the community centre (but only for another four months, thank God!), and he kept finding his diary full of legal aid cases while the old boy creamed off all the interesting work for himself.

It was a worrying situation. He could understand the old boy's unwillingness to hang up his wig and gown but, for the moment, his son's career was on hold and the practice was beginning to stagnate. One of these days they would have to come to an understanding.

While not exactly rushed, he certainly had enough on his plate without wasting almost an entire morning on Murray Kingston's case. He'd known before he started on Murray's account of the evidence that he'd have a fat chance of turning up any anomalies that he could take to the Procurator Fiscal, and he found himself deeply reluctant to pry into what he knew would be a real can of worms. It was a depressing and distasteful business, he wasn't getting paid for it and, frankly, he didn't feel like putting himself out for Murray Kingston.

Sure, they went back a long way: they'd gone through senior school together and, later, shared a flat in Greyfriars for a spell during the time they were at university. From the beginning, Murray had regarded Tam as a soul mate. He referred to him as his "buddy" and managed invariably to give mutual acquaintances the impression that the two of them were like brothers. But underneath the pallyness was an intensity that Tam recoiled from. All along, he had the suspicion that Kingston could turn spiteful if he were too firmly rebuffed.

Gradually, over the years, they saw less and less of each other. Kingston scraped through his English degree and took a job with Scottish TV and, two years later, Tam got a respectable upper second in law and joined the family firm. After he married Anne, straight from university, Kingston seemed to lose much of his dependence on Tam and made fewer claims on his time, but there were still occasions, like birthdays and Christmas, when he made it obvious that Tam's absence would blight the entire proceedings.

As far as possible Tam went along with this: not because he had any real affection for Kingston, and certainly not because he feared the outcome of telling him to get lost, but because the alternative would have caused friction and he preferred a quiet life. Besides, he was rather fond of Anne, who was sweet and pretty and a fantastic cook, and who was patently dotty about her husband.

After a couple of years Murray left STV and went into teaching. He and Anne moved to Berwick and, inevitably, Buchanan saw them only now and then. They seemed happy enough and Anne was thrilled when she found herself pregnant. Her depression, as far as Buchanan could tell, started shortly after Debbie's birth the following year. At the christening Tam had been shocked by her appearance and had spoken to Kingston about it, but Kingston had made light of it.

"Just a bit tired, Tam, that's all. The baby's been keeping us awake at night, I'm afraid. No rose without a thorn!"

This didn't seem to Buchanan an adequate explanation for Anne's lack of sparkle, and he said so. "It's so unlike her. I've seen her tired before but I've never seen her look so downright melancholic."

"They get like that sometimes, you know Tam, after the baby arrives. Post-natal depression, it's called." Murray nodded ponderously, as one privy to the arcane secrets of obstetrics. "Perfectly natural, if you ask me. After all, you spend nine months waiting for this little bundle of joy to arrive and brighten up your life, and suddenly you find yourself enslaved to a screaming monster who doesn't give a damn whether you just got to sleep or not. You spend your days ministering to it, rocking the pram with one hand and mixing formula with the other, patting up windy-pops, disposing of shitty nappies, creeping around when it sleeps, stimulating its sodding intellect when it's awake, never a single minute of the day to yourself. No bloody wonder she's depressed."

Tam tried to take this on board but he could see Anne on the other side of the room, taking no notice of her guests but staring morosely out into the garden, and he remained unconvinced. "I know what you're saying, Murray, but I've got a feeling it's more than that. I think I'll have a word with her, if you don't mind. I'm sure she'll open up to me if there's anything worrying her."

"No, I don't want you to do that," Murray said, with a shortness that surprised Buchanan. "It won't do any good. In fact, it may do a lot of harm to let her see that her mood swings are causing comment. No point in embarrassing her. She'll be over it in a week or two, you'll see."

But she wasn't over it in a week or two, though Buchanan wasn't around to know that. The invitations to dinner at the Kingstons' stopped coming, and they were no longer around the places where Buchanan had been wont to run into them. If he thought about this at all he put it down to the arrival of the baby and assumed things would get back to normal soon. Months passed before he saw Murray again, and when he did, Anne wasn't with him. She had taken Debbie to her parents' home in the Dordogne for a short break but was, Murray assured him, much brighter.

After that Buchanan had thought very little about either of them till late one November evening when he got caught in a fiendish blizzard on the way back from Perth. The motorway was a death trap and he didn't fancy crawling along in the half-dark with idiots sliding all over the road in front of him, so he pulled off at the next intersection and booked into a small inn in the middle of nowhere. And there they were, Kingston and this red-haired girl, who he half-recognised, gazing into each other's eyes in a corner of the bar.

Buchanan reacted with instinctive speed. He got out, hopefully before they noticed him, and tried to forget what he'd seen. But although he told himself that it was none of his business, he now knew the cause of Anne's depression and it saddened him to see her being hurt. He had never had any particular desire to maintain his connection with Murray, and he now felt uncomfortable at being a helpless witness to a painful situation which had, plainly, been going on for a while. Soon Buchanan realised that the affair was common knowledge but, as friends predicted a divorce and Anne retreated into alcoholism, Murray seemed incapable of bringing matters to a conclusion. Buchanan saw very little of either of them for a long time and the news of Anne's suicide, when it reached him, put an end to all pretence of friendship for good.

Even before the news of Murray's arrest reached the papers there had been no communication between them for almost two years. He had not approached Buchanan for legal help, and Buchanan, thoroughly sickened by the whole business, had resisted learning any more of the gory details than he could avoid.

He would have avoided learning them now if the sight of Murray's tears had not shamed him into at least listening to the bloke, and if Murray had not pled his innocence so passionately, in spite of all the evidence against him. Whatever else he had been, Murray had always been a lousy liar. He'd never had a hope of concealing his infidelity from Anne or of persuading Buchanan that her depression was merely hormonal. Yet his determined denial of the charges against him was so convincing that Tam's firmly held belief that he had received a fair trial was shaken. Not severely shaken, perhaps, but shaken enough to make him spend valuable time going over the notes he'd taken during his talk with Murray for any sign that he could, as he claimed, have been set up.

But as yet, after two hours of patient perusal, there was no such sign. Quite the opposite. Apart from the damning forensic evidence, which Murray had been unable to explain, the testimony from various outsiders who had patently nothing to gain from lying would have impressed any jury. More than one claimed to have heard Debbie make worrying remarks about her father, heard her calling out in the night, or noted unnaturally explicit details in her drawings. It was difficult to imagine how anyone could have persuaded Debbie to exhibit these phenomena without an unlikely degree of time and patience. She was not quite five at the time of the trial, so she could give little direct testimony, but the expert who had spoken with her at some length was convinced that she had been abused.

Child abuse, particularly of an infant, was notoriously difficult to prove, but there appeared to be sufficient evidence in this case to establish Murray's guilt beyond all reasonable doubt.

By lunchtime Buchanan felt he needed something to take his mind off his reading matter and decided to invite Janine out to lunch. This was not something he made a habit of doing but, as it happened, Janine was currently somewhat piqued at him for reneging on a promise to go to a gallery opening with her a couple of evenings back, so a face-straightening operation wouldn't go amiss. Janine was a special lady, he thought as he dialled her number, and a little gesture was definitely called for.

"Pzazz Fashions. Can I help you?"

"Hi," Buchanan said, grinning the way he always did at the bossy voice she affected at work.

"Hi yourself," she said, relaxing into her usual intimate purr. "You just caught me. I was about to dash out for a quick bite."

"How about I treat you to something nice at Poseidon?"

"Mmm," she said, on a three-note scale that indicated interest tempered with doubt. She made a big deal of being in the shop to keep an eye on her staff but she was a sucker for seafood. "I shouldn't really. The window-dresser's coming at two and I like to be around to make sure she displays what I want to push."

"You could leave a message for her with Marie," Buchanan said, dutifully pointing out what she knew as well as he did.

"Well . . . Actually, I do have to drop off a wedding outfit at the Scandic Crown. I could save time by doing that on the way back, couldn't I?"

"Sure you could."

"Okay. We'll take my car then; I don't want to squash the box in with your golf clubs and your smelly petrol cans. I'll pick you up in about ten minutes."

"Right. See you then."

He spent the time making a couple of phone calls while watching for her from the window so that she wouldn't have to bother finding a parking place. Right on the stroke of one, just as he was reaching for his jacket, his eye was caught by a figure on the other side of the road. If it hadn't been taller and slimmer than she was, he would have thought it was Fizz.

She was dressed in a neat black skirt and grey boxy jacket, and her hair was twisted severely into a bun, with only a few determined tendrils escaping above her ears. She was working her way carefully down the other side of the street, looking at the name plates and brass plaques of the neighbouring business premises.

The similarity was striking, but the dissimilarity was even more so. Fizz was immature, gauche and a sloppy dresser: this elegant young lady looked about five years older than Fizz, eight pounds lighter, infinitely more attractive and had quite sensational legs. Practically simultaneously with this reflection came the realisation that, notwithstanding all the above, it actually was Fizz, and that, furthermore, she appeared to be looking for his office.

Some sort of self-preservation made him grab his jacket and rush outside to waylay her. Just what disaster he feared might occur if she once penetrated even the outer defences of his sanctum, he did not pause to think through. The possible results of a meeting between Fizz and his father, who would adore her sweet, innocent exterior, or even with the wonderful Beatrice, who would regard her as an abomination, were too awful to contemplate.

The look she turned on him as he came up behind her and spoke her name was so plainly of the "what-the-hell-do-*you*-want?" variety that he could have bitten off his tongue. It was quite obvious that he was the last person she had expected to see, and that if he had only had the sense to leave her be she would have gone on her way without realising that she had been practically on his doorstep.

"Oh . . . it's you! Sorry, I wasn't thinking . . ."

"No, it was my fault . . . barging up behind you like that."

She was looking at him with a sort of bemused expression, probably wondering why he had bothered to run to catch up with her. Now that he *had* caught up with her it was impossible to escape: he had to say something, but what did one say to this svelte, grown-up version of Fizz?

"I wasn't sure it was you. You looked quite different and . . . and I hadn't expected to run into you round this neck of the woods."

She looked around the square of old Georgian town houses, most of them now the premises of financial consultants, insurance companies and lawyers. "Yes, I don't know the area too well. In fact I'm a bit lost. I don't suppose you know an estate agent called Waring MacKay Properties, do you?"

"Sure. You just passed it back there at the corner. It's a basement office, that's probably why you missed it."

She looked relieved. "It's a good job I left myself plenty of time. I've got an appointment in ten minutes about a flat they have to rent."

"You're moving house?" He looked beyond her to the corner that Janine would be turning any second now, giving him the excuse to make his escape, but there was no sign of her yet.

"I don't know. Thinking about it. And what brings you here . . . Oh, I expect your office is around here."

"Yes," he said, and avoided giving her a more precise location by rushing on, "I'm just nipping out for lunch. Well, mustn't keep you . . ."

"I met Murray Kingston the other day," she said, overlapping his last words. "In the Meadows. He was looking a bit brighter."

He turned back to her with a faint sense of foreboding. "You were speaking to him?"

"Uh-huh." She gave a tiny shrug. "We were both going in the same direction so we walked together. He seemed fairly confident that you'd take him under your wing. Will you?"

"Take him under —" Buchanan choked with exasperation. "Listen, Fizz, you really shouldn't be talking to him about his case. It's a breach of client confidentiality, and if —"

"Oh, pooh!" she said, laughing in his face in a rather refreshing, Shirley Temple-ish sort of way. "Murray doesn't give a shit about client confidentiality. He wanted to get the whole thing off his chest to anybody who'd listen. He told me all the gory details about the pornographic magazines and the semen stains and all the rest of that stuff."

Buchanan stared at her. "He did?"

"Sure. And I have to tell you, the prosecution came up with some real heavy-duty evidence. They made him look like the Creature from the Black Lagoon."

"But you're not convinced?" He had to say it even though he knew he shouldn't be discussing the case with her.

"Are you?"

"I haven't had time to think about it properly yet."

"But you're beginning to wonder . . .?"

He turned his face away to avoid her amused stare and suddenly noticed that Janine's car was parked directly across the road and that she was watching them with close attention. Giving her a quick wave he said, "Sorry, must dash, there's someone waiting for me."

"Right," she said, glancing across at Janine. "I'll see you Monday morning then . . . Oh, hang on a minute."

Before he quite knew what she was about he felt the touch of her hand on his cheek: just the briefest contact, then it was gone.

"Bit of soot," she said, smiling. "You're respectable now. Have a nice lunch."

She turned quickly and walked away, her high heels clicking on the pavement. Just for a moment he was mesmerised by the sexy swish of her slim legs, and as he watched, she turned as though aware of his eyes on her and gave him a cheeky and almost coquettish wave. He was too surprised to respond.

Janine's profile was rigid and unsmiling as he climbed into the passenger seat. "I do hope I didn't arrive at an inopportune moment," she said crisply, pulling away with a sudden acceleration that pressed him back in his seat.

He grinned at her, rather touched by her jealousy. "Quite the reverse, darling. I was looking for an opportunity to escape."

"Exactly the interpretation I'd have put on your body language." She gave a tight smile, her knuckles white on the wheel. "And clearly the young lady was of the same mind. One could tell she was simply aching to be elsewhere."

Buchanan had to laugh. "I don't know what it looked like to an outsider, but I can assure you, there was nothing sinister about it. I hardly know her, she's just a —"

"Really, Tam." Her laugh was cool and musical, like ice rattling in a gin and tonic. "Let's not make a big scene of something so ridiculous. If it gives you a kick to have young ladies patting your cheek and making goo-goo eyes at you, who am I to say you nay? Now, let's talk about something more congenial. Did you book a table?"

Her ability to make things out to be his fault was always a source of amazement. It appeared, suddenly, that it was he who was making a big scene, not her. Clearly he was expected to feel guilty for encouraging a person of the female sex to pass the time of day with him on the public thoroughfare — not only for encouraging it but for having the audacity to deny it in the face of clear evidence to the contrary.

Knowing he could, with a few words, relieve her mind completely, he ground his teeth and confined himself to returning expressionless answers to her remarks, while deep in his guts, the acid started its slow, agonising drip.

CHAPTER
FOUR

Even dead elephants were scary. Okay, they weren't going to start trumpeting and waving their ears about, but the sheer bulk of them, seen close up, was severely off-putting. This one in particular had clearly met its maker many years ago and didn't look to be in particularly good nick. All it needed, Fizz reflected, was for one of those megalithic forelegs to cave in and they would be scraping her off the linoleum like a blob of strawberry jam. She moved prudently round to look at the Indian elephant, which was a whole lot less overpowering than the African variety.

She felt a bit more confident about playing detective since checking on Buchanan's feelings about the case, but she was still a long way from being one hundred per cent sure of Murray Kingston. She wasn't, for instance, going to be alone with him at his house, as he had suggested, nor was she keen on letting him know precisely where she lived, let alone inviting him to come there for a project meeting. Public places like the Chambers Street museum had their distractions but they also had a lot of people around, which was hugely reassuring.

She had envisaged having a longer talk with Buchanan — perhaps even in his office, if her plan of "running into" him had not come to fruition — which was why she had got herself all tarted up in her sole formal outfit and heels. However, she felt that her long vigil, wandering up and down the ghetto of estate agents and legal firms while she waited for him to emerge, had not been entirely in vain. Like all lawyers, he unmistakably believed that a blank face hid his thoughts like a brick wall, whereas it did just the opposite — especially when it was assumed only in response to a leading question.

He had told her nothing that she could have quoted in a court of law — nothing at all, in fact, not in words — but she was fairly certain that, even knowing all the facts of the case and knowing Murray as well as he did, he half believed his one-time buddy was telling the truth. It wasn't much but it was, combined with her own convictions, at least enough to be going on with.

Such further research as she had been able to do — much of it through an Irishman she had known for years and who was now working with the *Scotsman* newspaper — had persuaded her that the possibility of a frame-up could not be entirely ruled out.

"So, what have you been doing since I saw you?" she said to Murray as they headed upstairs to the geology exhibit, which was usually a lot quieter than the natural history hall.

"Not a great deal."

She was pleased with the way he looked this morning, since it was, arguably, an indication of the new confidence she had begun to build in him. He was standing taller, she rather thought, and had lost much of the hangdog look he had worn when he had turned up at the community centre. He had also got rid of the droopy bomber jacket in favour of a black polo-necked sweater and a donkey-brown sports jacket in which he was almost passable.

"I made out the list you suggested, but that's about all I got around to, really." He produced a sheet of yellow paper and handed it to her.

She ran her eye down the column of names. It didn't take very long. "This is all? There weren't very many, were there?"

"That's the ones who gave evidence in court, but there may have been others, for all I know, who put in their tenpence worth but weren't called as witnesses." He regarded a piece of metamorphic chloride-schist with zero interest while she gave the list a closer look. "Thought about starting on some of them but I wasn't sure what questions to ask."

Fizz nailed him with a firm look. "I'm glad you didn't do that, Murray. It wouldn't be a good idea. Much better to leave it to me. People are bound to react more emotionally to you, whereas a stranger — an ostensibly neutral stranger — can get a lot more out of them." She held the paper out to him. "I should have had you write down opposite the names exactly what evidence each of them gave. Just briefly. Like, I know what the police forensic chappie had to say, but what about the others?"

56

She could see he hated even looking at the list. "Okay," he said, in the flat tone he had used a couple of days ago when he had told her the story of his arrest. "Mrs McCaulay, she was our next-door neighbour. She sat with Debbie sometimes. She claimed that Debbie said suspicious things. So did the childminder, Sue Young, and also Mrs Torkington from the playgroup. Mrs Torkington also said that Debbie's drawings were 'worrying' and produced some horrendous examples. Phillis, she's my sister-in-law — Anne's sister, that is — she said that Debbie always wanted to stay with her and didn't want to come home with me after a visit and that she gave some strange reasons. This John Herriot is the — *was* the deputy headmaster, and Zoe Paton was a fellow teacher. They gave evidence about the porno magazines being found in my locker. And Roberta Hogg, from the social work department — Hogg by name and hog by nature, that woman — some of the stuff she claimed Debbie told her — Jesus!"

He turned and walked away to the end of the gallery, leaving the paper lying on top of the display case they had been leaning on. Fizz picked it up and made some notations on it in case she forgot who had said what, and then followed him.

"What about a coffee?" she said. "They do a rather nice currant scone downstairs."

"Sure."

There were rarely more than one or two people in the café at this hour of the morning. Fizz knew it well from her time as an art student, way back in the dear dead days beyond recall. The lecturers had always found it easier to send a class round to the Chambers Street museum to sketch than to actually teach them anything. Or so she had thought at the time. Given the chance again, she wouldn't be such an anarchist. Maybe.

"So, what's your feeling about this lot?" she said, when she'd disposed of two currant scones and poured herself a second cup of coffee. "Do you get the feeling that any of them were deliberately trying to drop you in it? I mean, they can't all be lying, so it looks like Debbie probably *was* saying some strange things about that time, and the people who reported these remarks didn't necessarily have it in for you. They might only have been trying to protect Debbie."

He put his elbows on the table and gripped his hands together, pressing the laced fingers against his lips. She could see that he was trying to keep calm.

"That's what gets to me, Fizz. The thought that somebody has been mucking about with Debbie's memory — putting these thoughts into her head, poisoning her mind against me."

The muscles in his cheeks moved as he clenched his teeth on what he wanted to say. Fizz could have said it for him and would have enjoyed meeting the perpetrator and personally kicking him a new arsehole.

"I don't give a damn about clearing my name. That's not going to happen, is it? Whatever we — or Tam — finds out, I'm not going to come out of this smelling of violets. The newspapers aren't going to publish a retraction of all the lies they printed about me. There

58

isn't going to be an item on the national news to tell the world that Murray Kingston was totally innocent of any crime. Oh sure, maybe the verdict would eventually get around my friends by word of mouth; some of them might believe I was wrongly accused, some of them would say the verdict was overturned because of a legal technicality. Besides, who gives a damn about me any more?"

Fizz tried to say something that was both comforting and not too obviously rubbish, but couldn't make the match.

After staring out the window for a minute with eyes that were full of hate and hopelessness he turned and said, "But even if I don't clear my name, even if I never get Debbie back . . . if I could just get my hands on the animal who did that to her . . . Killing's too good for the bastard. I want to get him in a cellar somewhere . . ."

He saw Fizz's face and stopped, forcing a wry smile. "Don't worry, Fizz. These things prey on your mind over the years, you know. I was in solitary for a long time and I guess I had too long to brood about my problems."

This casual revelation caused Fizz a small flutter of alarm. As far as she was aware only violent prisoners were kept in solitary confinement. She said:

"Why were you in solitary?"

"For my own protection." She could see his cheek muscles working while he remembered something, but he evidently decided not to share it with her. "Sex offenders are fair game for everybody. The other cons make a sport of attacking them every time the guards turn their heads away. I took as much as I could but finally I asked to be transferred to Saughton so that my mother could visit me. All the sex offenders worked in wood assembly there, so because we were segregated, working time wasn't too bad. But in the route move, that's when we were moved from place to place, they'd step out of doorways and slash us or get the boot in and then disappear. And when we were locked in at night —"

He gulped at his coffee. You could see he was trying to stop talking about it but couldn't resist sharing it with somebody.

"You had to share a cell?"

"Only people with long sentences get a cell to themselves. I was twoed-up for the first six months with a Tarzan — that's what they call rapists. He used to — well, I won't go into his little habits. Anyway, he wasn't the worst of them."

"But you had the option of solitary confinement?"

"Protection. It's called protection, but solitary is what it amounts to, by and large, so you don't ask for it lightly. I stood the bullying for eight months, lost a few teeth, had a few ribs broken, but by then —"

He broke off, staring over her shoulder with his face suddenly frozen and his lips apart. Fizz turned and followed his eyes but saw nothing more alarming than a tall woman in pink culottes who must have entered by the street door and was just pulling back a chair to sit at a distant table.

"Know her?" she said, but Murray gave no sign of having heard her and his eyes didn't even blink. Curious, she returned her attention to the woman and was therefore aware of the moment when she finished unloading her tray and lifted her eyes to meet Murray's stare.

For a split second it looked as though she had been jabbed with a cattle prod. Her whole body gave one galvanised jerk then became unnaturally still. Her eyes fluttered away and then, as though she realised the impossibility of pretending she hadn't seen him, returned to Murray.

Fizz found this quite riveting, and her one worry was that — as seemed likely — they would agree to ignore each other and she would never find out the truth of their relationship. Accordingly she lost no time in pushing back her chair slightly and sending the woman a look of firm encouragement.

It was enough, but only just. The woman stood up in a series of small jerks like time-lapse photography but then hesitated, visibly unsure of her reception, and only moved towards them when Murray, in turn, rose from his place to receive her.

"Murray . . ." Her voice was low-pitched and husky, a little breathless with uncertainty. "I can't tell you how good it is to see you."

"It's good to see you too, Zoe."

Fizz's interest rose another notch at the name. Zoe Somebody was one of the people on the list of witnesses but she couldn't remember which. She stole a glance at the yellow paper beside her plate. Zoe Paton, fellow teacher.

Murray leaned towards Zoe and brushed her cheek with his lips, and as he did so, she coloured up a little and broke into a smile.

"No hard feelings, then?"

He smiled back. "No hard feelings. Never were. Why don't you join us? This is Fizz, she'll be interested to meet you."

"Are you sure?" Zoe said, giving Fizz an enquiring smile, but sitting down at the same time. "I don't want to intrude."

They messed around for a minute or two while she slipped off her coat and Murray collected her snack and bought more coffee, then she said:

"You're looking well, Murray. How long have you been . . . back in town?"

"A week today." He smiled and indicated Fizz with a dip of his head. "And you don't have to worry about Fizz, she knows just about all there is to know."

Zoe gave Fizz a fleeting glance, more embarrassed than dismissive. It looked to Fizz as though she hadn't quite recovered from the shock of running into Murray, which was understandable since her evidence had played a part in getting him put away. Above table level she appeared quite cool, even placid, but Fizz could hear her shoes grating and tapping on the marble floor in a nervous gavotte.

"Still at Tweedside High?" Murray was asking.

She made a face. "Stuck it till a year ago, but by then I'd had as much as I could take. You know Carson got your job? Yes, and a right layabout he turned into, I can tell you. Then, the year before last, old Hetherington retired and Gallacher got head of department."

"Gallacher?" Murray looked appalled at this piece of news. "Whose brainless idea was that? If anyone got Hetherington's job it should have been you, Zoe."

"Yes, well, I must admit I thought . . . Anyway, I got out. Moved up to the Big E. I'm at Leith Academy now and quite enjoying it."

"Zoe teaches English," Murray said to Fizz. "She's also a bit of a writer."

"Really?" Fizz tried to look impressed, in the belief that anybody who got up on their hind legs and exposed themselves to criticism needed all the support they could get. Lack of positive feedback had been what had done her head in as an art student. "What do you write?"

"Short stories, mostly," Zoe said, fiddling with her cup. "There's a novel simmering away on the back boiler but I'm not one of those people who can rise at dawn and dash off five thousand words before going to work in the morning. One of these days I'll take a year off and get it out of my system."

"What about your TV scripts?" Murray prompted. "I thought your career would have taken off in that direction by now?"

She lifted her eyes uncertainly to his face. "You haven't seen Dianne?"

The quick glance he threw at Fizz alerted her to the fact that she had heard something significant.

"She's not in town at the moment. I think she's gone off to New York for a couple of weeks."

"But, surely she visited you?"

"No," he said, looking down at his coffee and shaking his head. "I couldn't let her do that, Zoe. Think what it would have done to her career if it had come out that she was involved with a convicted paedophile."

They both looked at their coffees for a minute, then Zoe said tentatively, "But you've been in touch? You know . . . her news?"

"That she's married? Oh, yes." He didn't like it, Fizz saw, but he was putting a good face on it, and with a reasonable degree of success. "She wrote to me regularly up till this spring, but after her wedding it didn't seem such a good idea. Sherry is a nice guy and I'm sure he still expects us to be friends, but only to the extent of a card at Christmas, not a regular correspondence."

Judging by his bland expression, he was taking this rather well, but Zoe apparently found this remarkable, since she kept sending him tiny puzzled glances when he wasn't looking. She said, "So, she must have told you we decided to go our separate ways?"

Murray levitated his eyebrows. "That happened before I was put away, Zoe."

She thought about that. "It did. You're quite right. Well, Dianne stuck to TV and I concentrated on the printed word. *Not*," she added with a wry smile, "the wisest decision I ever made, as things have turned out, but there you go."

It suddenly occurred to her — you could see it happening, she had that sort of face — that Fizz had been on the sidelines of this conversation for too long. She switched on an interested look.

"And what do *you* do to earn a crust, Fizz?"

Fizz didn't mind telling her. "Nothing at the moment. Living off my fat. I've been abroad for a long time and just got back to Edinburgh a few weeks ago. Next session I'll be doing law at the Uni."

"Law, wow! You don't believe in the easy options, do you?" She and Murray exchanged pseudo-fascinated glances. "What made you choose law?"

Fizz wasn't entirely sure about that herself. Certainly, it was in the blood. Her father, who she scarcely remembered, had been a lawyer and, according to Grampa, had hoped she'd follow in his footsteps, but up till a few months back she had been set against the idea. Her abortive attempt to get an art degree, straight after leaving school, had given her a distaste for programmed learning that she had expected to last all her life. But suddenly — maybe she was simply a late developer — came the need to give up the nomad existence she had been leading and settle down to doing something positive with her life.

She shrugged. "Oh, I don't know. Partly because, in a law exam, there's only one correct answer to a question. It's not a matter of somebody's opinion. Or, at least, that's more the case than in an arts degree."

Zoe straightened and looked at her watch. "I'd like to hear about your travels too, Fizz, but right now I have to get moving — I've a hair appointment at twelve.

How about you and Murray coming round for a bite to eat some day soon?" She looked anxiously at Murray to see if this was some kind of social gaffe, or if his relationship with Fizz was compatible with a joint invitation.

He looked quite keen on the idea. "That would be nice, Zoe. Actually, we'd both like to talk to you about . . . about the case. Fizz is helping me to look for some evidence that would clear my name and help me to get Debbie back."

She looked at Fizz, then Murray, then back to Fizz again while she took this in. "But, that's wonderful. I'm so glad you haven't given up hope, Murray. I don't know if I can be of any help at all but you can be sure I'll do everything I can." She reached across the table to lay a hand on his sleeve. "I hope you realise, Murray, that I never doubted your innocence. Anyone who knew you . . . I had no choice but to tell them . . ."

"I know that, Zoe," he said, nodding at her reassuringly. "It was the same for most of the witnesses for the prosecution. No hard feelings."

She pulled on her gloves and rested her hands for a second against the table edge, as though getting her words in order. "I want to make up for it, Murray. It's been on my conscience all these years, so, please, if there's any help I can give you — anything at all . . ."

"Sure."

They walked to the door together, sorting out what evening they could meet for dinner, and settled on Monday, her place, seven o'clock. She lived at the top of Leith Walk, which was within walking distance (as was most of the city) of Fizz's flat in the Royal Mile.

Fizz found herself rather looking forward to the nosh-up, not merely because it was a free meal but because she quite liked what she'd seen of Zoe. She came across as an intelligent, well-bred person. Maybe her apparent warmth and interest was nothing more than received politeness, a store-bought charm that was merely a façade, but even that was something to be appreciated these days.

They watched her pacing away in her high-heeled boots, and Fizz's toes twinged sympathetically, still not recovered from their unaccustomed interface with heels the day before. She stomped her Docs therapeutically on the pavement as she turned to Murray.

"Nice lady," she said. "Pal of your ex-girlfriend's, I take it. You didn't mention Dianne."

He grinned, looking decidedly shifty. "There was no point in bringing her into it, Fizz. As you no doubt gathered, it's all over between us, and besides, she never had anything to do with the case, wasn't involved at all, didn't even give evidence at the trial."

"I see. Right." However, that didn't mean that Fizz was about to forget all about her. She might now be a thing of the past but, though there was no point in saying so at this juncture, around the time it mattered she had presumably played a significant part in Murray's life. Fizz headed down towards Chalmers Street and Murray moved round her to take the outside edge of the pavement like a true gent. "They were co-writers, were they?" she asked.

"Well, in a way. They'd been collaborating for a while, without success, when Zoe joined the staff at Tweedside High. Zoe showed me some of their stuff because I'd worked for a spell in STV and had some good contacts. It wasn't wonderful material — they were still learning their trade — but I managed to get them started and they sold one or two things."

"How come they split up?"

"Oh, I don't know exactly. It was on the cards. Not many partnerships last in that business, you know, not for more than a year or two, and, to be honest, Zoe was never in the same class as Dianne. On her own, as you saw, she's still dependent on teaching for her bread and butter. But, for all that," he added, as though not wishing to appear disloyal, "I used to think they made a good team. Zoe had a lot of imagination but her writing lacked that special something. Dianne, on the other hand, was a born storyteller but wasn't quite Zoe's equal when it came to creativity."

"But whereas Zoe is still teaching, Dianne is, presumably, managing to survive without a day job, right?"

"When last I heard from her, yes." He gripped her arm as they dodged through the traffic and turned down the Bridges. "Not that she'll have any money worries now that she's married, of course. Sherry isn't short of a bob or two."

"You don't feel too badly about her finding somebody else while you were inside?" Fizz asked as they waited to cross the High Street. It was time to give Murray the elbow. Not only was her flat just down the hill, but the high court was round the corner, and she didn't want to run into Buchanan in case he objected to her involvement.

He lifted a shoulder negligently, watching for the green man. "I hadn't seen her for so long. It doesn't matter how good a letter-writer somebody is, it just isn't the same as being with them in the flesh. Your memory of them becomes a bit blurred round the edges. I'm not saying we couldn't have rebuilt our relationship when I got out, just that it all seemed pretty inevitable. Maybe it wasn't that deep a relationship in the first place, I don't know. Maybe I was more concerned with getting Debbie back. Maybe she'd gradually become more of a friend than a lover over the years and I hadn't realised it."

"Right." Fizz nodded at this as though she was taking it on board, but a little red fault-light was flashing at the back of her skull. Okay, he didn't give the impression of being cut to ribbons about it, but you didn't need a Ph.D. in applied psychology to smell a rat somewhere. Common sense would suggest that someone in prison with few — if any — visitors and no female companionship would become more deeply dependent on his girlfriend than the reverse.

She took a long look at him as they crossed the road, but he didn't meet her eye. She was sure he was bending the truth somewhere along the line, but was he also lying to himself? That was the question. It could be that this was the way he was dealing with his hurt.

"I go this way," she said, with a wave that encompassed everything from the traffic lights where

69

they stood to the blue waters of the Firth of Forth a couple of miles away. In fact, her flat was only a stone's throw away, but he didn't have to know that. "You're seeing Buchanan on Monday morning, aren't you? Right, I'll see you then."

He looked seriously dischuffed. "Monday? I was kind of hoping we could get something moving this weekend."

"No way." Fizz waved the list at him. "I want time to study this first. I have to select which of them would be best to talk to. I have to work out what questions to ask. I have to choose who to interview first. Somebody who's doing this sort of thing all the time might be able to dive straight in, but I don't want to make any mistakes at this stage. You question the wrong person first and they're liable to warn somebody else on your list so's they're ready for you by the time you call."

"Sure." Murray nodded, which proved what a mug he was.

She could have told him the truth, which was that she was going home to Am Bealach for the weekend to check up on Grampa, but that would have been giving away more than she wanted to. Till she felt more certain of his bona fides, the less he knew about her the better.

CHAPTER
FIVE

"Aberdeen?" Buchanan echoed, trying to keep his voice level but becoming increasingly rattled. "What's taking you to Aberdeen so suddenly?"

"I told you, darling. It's perfect for me if I'm to open another branch outside the capital. Heaven knows, I've been going on about it for months, so you needn't pretend you never knew it was in the offing." Janine's telephone manner turned suddenly silky. "I met Elliot Ross last night and we went for a meal. It turns out he's giving up his antique shop in the Kirkgate and he wants to take me up to Aberdeen to have a look at it. It could be just what I'm looking for."

It suddenly dawned on Buchanan what Janine was playing at. Really, she was so transparent. He caught sight of his reflection in the mirror, grinning wolfishly, and checked his teeth while he thought about how to respond.

There was no question of Janine opening another branch in Aberdeen, or anyplace else, for that matter. This bit of sabre-rattling was just her way of reminding him that she was an independent, together, modern woman and that he was only a small part of her very full and successful life. None of which had any actual basis in fact. The truth was that her small, chic dress shop, financed originally by her daddy, was only just in the black and had long since ceased to be the fun she'd thought it would be.

Her current plans for the future included marriage to Buchanan, a smart flat in the New Town, preferably around Heriot Row, and a life of sybaritic ease; therefore, the message he was supposed to be receiving right now was that the time was fast approaching when he'd have to state unequivocally how he viewed this scenario.

There were quite long periods when Buchanan could see little wrong with marriage to Janine. This, as it happened, was not one of those periods, but that didn't mean he was going to give her the old heave-ho. It needed thinking about. He was knocking thirty, for God's sake, and he was going to have to settle down sooner or later. Furthermore, he had invested quite a lot of time and effort in Janine: teaching her to play golf, weaning her off Spielberg films, inuring her to his chronic untidiness. She was not only beautiful but intelligent, witty, easy-going (most of the time), and fitted in very well with his lifestyle. She also had a very jealous nature, but — hey! — there were worse faults.

It was plain that jealousy was behind this latest fit of pique — jealousy of Fizz, which was a laugh! He gave himself another Jack Nicholson grin in the mirror, imagining Fizz's reaction if he told her the result of her innocent gesture.

"I may stay over," Janine was saying lightly. "Elliot says he has plenty of room at his place, and it would save travelling back down tonight. I don't know. I'll see how I feel."

"Oh, stay over if you get the chance." Buchanan decided he would be damned if he let her suspect she was beginning to get to him. Elliot Ross was six foot four, weighed, at best, maybe ten stone and had the sort of face you'd see reflected in the back of a soup spoon. Definitely not Janine's type, but handy to have around when she wanted to needle Tam. "It's too far to drive there and back in one go. You don't want Elliot falling asleep at the wheel."

He could hear her breathing at the end of the line as she thought of a suitably cutting reply to this, but finally she said only, "Right then. I'll give you a ring when I get back."

"Not tonight," he murmured, unable to resist a tiny twist of the knife. "I won't be home myself till pretty late. Hear from you tomorrow. Take care."

She hung up on a gritty, "Bye, then," having got the message, and Buchanan felt immediately swinish. He reached for the phone to call her back, but at that second the door opened and Fizz stuck her head round the edge. She was wearing the huge sweater again and had returned to looking plump and childish. It was uncanny, the way she could change her persona from day to day.

"Murray's here, if you're ready for him now."

Buchanan winced. "Just a minute, Fizz, I'd like a word with you first. Come in and shut the door, please."

"Oh-oh," she muttered, doing as she was told, with exaggerated trepidation. "Don't like the sound of this."

He gave her a small smile. "I just want to suggest that you call clients by their surnames, that's all. I know you'll say that Mr Armitage didn't appear to object to being referred to as 'Mr A.' and that Mr Kingston might be classed as a special case, but it's not very businesslike, is it? And calling Mr McGuigan 'Mac' really puts his back up. I'm sure even you can see that."

"Well, I'm not going to be losing any sleep over McGuigan, for a start," she said frankly. "I wouldn't call a piss-artist like him 'Mr' if I was getting paid to do it, which I'm not. And as for the other two: I was calling Armitage 'Mr A.' before I was officially employed here, and Mr Kingston suggested I call him 'Murray' while he was waiting to see you last week."

"Okay," Buchanan temporised. Knowing Fizz, even as little as he did, he'd suspected she'd talk her way out of it. "However, if you could bring yourself to extend the courtesy of a title when referring to me I'd be much obliged. I've heard you, once or twice this morning, referring to me as 'Buchanan', and I happen to think it sounds discourteous. I prefer my employees to call me 'Mr Buchanan'."

"Yes, but I'm not your employee, am I?" she said, reasonably, smiling at him as though he was a little slow on the uptake. "The way I look at it, we're both working for the public, so it's not quite the same. However," she added quickly, perhaps noting the flush of annoyance he could feel warming his brow, "I don't

74

mind calling you 'Mr' in front of clients, if that keeps you happy."

"Thank you. And while we're on the subject," he added, halting her in the act of escaping, "a nickname like 'Fizz' isn't exactly businesslike either, is it? I presume you don't want me to call you 'Miss Fitzpatrick', do you? So what's your Christian name?"

"I don't use it," she said lightly, pausing on the threshold. "And, you're right, I'd hate the 'Miss' so I'm afraid we're stuck with 'Fizz'. Tough."

This was not satisfactory to Buchanan, but before he could point it out she had turned her head and said, "Come on in, Murray. Buchanan's free now."

The omission was so deliberate that Buchanan was within an inch of telling her to pack her spider plant and go. Only the realisation that it would cause an embarrassing scene prevented him from doing so, and even then, he told himself, it was only a postponement, not a reprieve. Her help this morning had made his work considerably easier and he had begun to relax into the luxury of having an assistant at last, but he wasn't going to put up with having his authority undermined at every turn.

He stood up to greet Murray, noting the sudden change in the other man's expression as he offered him his hand. It had been an unconscious gesture but he supposed it was an indication that sometime over the weekend his steadfast belief in Murray's guilt had weakened a little. Fizz, snooping in the doorway, had also recognised the significance and was smiling as he frowned at her.

75

The smile vanished. "Coffee?" she said, which in itself was an admission of guilt since she had never before offered to make it.

He kept the conversation on innocuous subjects till she arrived back with the tray, but before she had finished unloading it, Murray cut in impatiently:

"You've studied the case then, Tam? What do you think?"

Buchanan indicated Fizz with a glance, but Murray, following his eyes, merely brushed the warning aside. "You can speak in front of Fizz, Tam. I've been talking things over with her so there's nothing she doesn't know already."

"It's very irregular," Buchanan said, suppressing a desire to choke the life out of the idiot. "You could just conceivably get me into trouble with the Law Commission, you know. Fizz is not officially my employee. But still, there *is* the matter of client confidentiality, and it might be wise to remember that. It's a ruling that's there for a purpose, you know."

"Yes, I know all that, Tam, but I'd still like Fizz to sit in if you don't have any serious objections."

Buchanan did have serious objections and was under the impression that he had just pointed them out, but there seemed to be little point in digging in his heels. After all, as soon as this interview was over, Fizz was for the high jump, so her presence at the discussion as a friend of the client couldn't be said to matter unduly.

"It's your choice, Murray. Want to bring through a chair, Fizz?"

"Okay," she said, as though he was twisting her arm. "I'll just get myself a coffee too. Won't be a sec."

"Murray," Buchanan said, as the door shut behind her, "I'd like you to be circumspect in anything you say to Fizz. You don't know her well and neither do I — she only started work here last week, for God's sake! I know she looks very sweet and innocent, but, believe me, she's one tough lady under the skin. Please try to have a little sense."

Murray pretended to think about this for a moment, but Buchanan was not surprised when he said, "Really, Tam, I can't see what harm it does to involve her. She's almost the only person who believes in my innocence and — to be frank — I need people like that right now. Besides, I think she's a whole lot brainier than she looks. Two heads are better than one, Tam."

"Please yourself," Buchanan told him, having wasted enough time and breath. "Just remember when it's told-you-so time that it was your idea, not mine. I would have thought, however, that some of the evidence would prove embarrassing when shared with a girl you barely know."

"She's not a bit squeamish," Murray assured him blithely.

This information, while new to Buchanan, did not, he discovered, surprise him greatly. Fizz returned while he was organising his papers and commandeered a disproportionate amount of his desk for her coffee cup, notebook and yellow pencil.

"Right," he said, when she'd settled down, "I have to tell you straight off, Murray, that the prosecution didn't put a foot wrong. Their case is pretty well unassailable, as it stands, and given the nature of the charge it would have been a brave jury that acquitted you. They submitted solid forensic evidence and a telling amount of corroborative — if circumstantial — testimony, all of which points the finger at you and nobody else."

He let that sink in while they looked at him with identical expressions of frustration, then he said, "Okay, where does that leave us?"

It was a rhetorical question and he didn't need Fizz to answer it, but she did.

"Somebody set him up."

He tipped his head sideways: not a nod but a polite acknowledgement.

"Well, you must have considered that possibility, Murray. What are your thoughts on it? Anybody got it in for you?"

Murray's shoulders moved beneath his jacket. "Not to that extent. I can't believe that. I've done nothing in my life to merit so much hatred."

Buchanan looked him in the eye. "You can be sure of that, can you? When you say 'nothing', do you mean 'nothing' or 'nothing that could be found out'?"

"Nothing!" Murray's face reddened but his eyes never left Buchanan's. "You know I'm not a malicious person, Tam."

Buchanan kept his face blank, but he was seeing again that cosy scene in the remote inn, and the way Murray had looked at the red-haired girl who had turned out to be Dianne. If Anne had still been alive — and if she had been a vindictive person, which she never had been — she would have had a perfectly comprehensible motive. Murray, however, had either no qualms of conscience about that business or was concealing them well.

"If we are to accept that someone deliberately plotted to have you put away — and for a crime that would wreck your personal life fairly comprehensively — there has to be a reason. If revenge isn't the motive, what other reason could there be?"

"Maybe someone wanted him out of circulation for a year or two," Fizz offered, once again pre-empting Buchanan, who had been about to present this possibility for Murray's consideration.

Murray looked blank. "Why would somebody want that?"

"You tell us," said Fizz, with a stare that said, "I'm just giving you the ideas, it's up to you to make them work."

Seeing that Murray was unable to respond to this remark with anything helpful, Buchanan raked through the papers till he found the forensic report. "Okay. Let's assume, for the moment, that somebody did set you up. How did they go about it? Well, first of —"

But Fizz was already telling them.

"Easy. They got next to Debbie — regularly over a period of weeks or even months — and started to put thoughts into her mind. I bet it wouldn't be hard to do with a four-year-old. You'd just keep saying things like, 'You told me Daddy does nasty things to you in bed, didn't you? He makes you cry, doesn't he?' I bet if you kept that up over a period of time the kid wouldn't know what to say when she was questioned by the social workers."

Buchanan said, "Yes, but —"

"And the magazines," Fizz kept on without drawing breath. "Anybody could have got into Murray's room to hide them there. He never locked it and people were popping in and out all day."

"And the forensic evidence?" Buchanan tapped the pile of papers and looked from Murray to Fizz and back again, seeing bafflement on both faces. "How about that, Murray? Any ideas how that could have been faked?"

No one hazarded a guess about that.

Buchanan checked his notes. "Debbie's pyjama trousers were found in your rubbish bin. They were torn at the waist and there were traces of semen in two places."

"It has to be a mistake," Murray said. "Somebody told me that some doubt has been cast recently about the validity of DNA testing. They're saying it's not one hundred per cent reliable."

"You heard that, did you?" Buchanan rubbed a hand down his face wearily. If that was the best they could come up with they were really up against it. "Trouble is, Murray, that even if you got some expert to throw doubt on the result of the tests, you'd be left with the question, 'If it wasn't your semen, whose was it?' And I'm afraid that, given all the corroborative evidence, you'd still be the most likely suspect."

Murray stood up as though he wanted to walk up and down, but since there was no room for that, he contented himself with sticking his hands in his pockets and staring out of the window. Fizz, Buchanan noted, was doodling on her notebook. She had drawn a parrot's perch with a smiling vulture chained to it by one leg. Sticking out of the feeding dish was a human foot.

She looked up at Murray's back. "Somebody could have saved it and put it on the pyjamas and hidden them among your rubbish, knowing they'd be found."

This had not occurred to Buchanan. It implied not only that the projected "somebody" was willing to go to a lot of trouble — well, if someone *had* framed Murray, that went without saying — but that that person had been close enough to the case to know when the police were likely to search the rubbish.

Murray's only response was a curt shake of the head, but Fizz was unwilling to leave it at that. "Not to be indelicate, Murray, but it would be easy for your girlfriend to save a condom. How sure are you that Dianne —"

Murray turned on her fast, irritation writ large on his clamped lips, and flicked a split-second glance at Buchanan before he snapped, "That's out of the question. Take my word for it, Fizz. She wasn't even in this country at the time. She'd been in New York for three weeks for the International TV Festival."

"And there was no one else?" Fizz persisted.

He looked for a second as though he wanted to hit her, then he let out his breath noisily and said, "No, Fizz. There was no one else. I'm sorry, but you'll have to take my word for it; your theory won't stand. I wish to God it did."

He turned back to the window and Buchanan could see the tension in his shoulders and neck. One leg was jittering slightly at the knee and he seemed unable to stop it.

"The only other explanation is that the police fixed it." Fizz put her elbows on the table and supported her chin on two clenched fists. She raised her eyebrows at Buchanan. "How likely is that? I mean, you could see how it might be a temptation, couldn't you? There they were with a mass of circumstantial evidence and a wee girl who was liable to be in severe jeopardy if they couldn't nail the culprit. All they needed was something that would stand up in court."

Buchanan shrugged. "Similar cases have come to light."

Murray turned from the window. "That's what happened this time," he said with finality, and sank back down into his chair as though he were exhausted. "I'm damn sure they lied about the forensic report, there's no other explanation that rings true. And if they did, there's no way we're going to prove otherwise."

"Well now, I'm not sure you're right about that," Buchanan said. "If we can throw doubt on some of the other witnesses, I think we could have the forensic evidence re-examined."

He was immediately aware that he had, with these words, put the interview on a different footing. The atmosphere changed instantly. There was an almost audible shifting of gears. Fizz relaxed in her chair and Murray sat up in his, all evidence of exhaustion erased.

"You'll take on the case then, Tam?" Murray said in a voice that croaked a bit on the last word.

Buchanan felt miserably depressed. He knew for a fact that he was going to waste weeks of precious time trying to prove something that had no hope of being proved, and not because he believed with any certainty that his client might be innocent, not because he envisaged the slightest possibility that he could pull some previously unsuspected evidence out of thin air, but solely as a sop to his conscience.

"I'll do what I can, Murray, which isn't much. Ideally you should be employing someone who makes a speciality of investigative work. It's not my line of business, as you know, and I have too much on my plate already to give it the time it's going to take."

"But I can help," Murray put in. "I have plenty of time, Tam. I can —"

"You can't do all the re-questioning of prosecution witnesses, Murray, it simply wouldn't work. They would probably refuse to speak to you at all, and even if you got them to agree to an interview, you'd get nothing out of them. You won't get legal aid so there'll be no money to employ an investigator. I'll have to do all that myself, and it'll take weeks to fit it all into my schedule."

"I can do that," said Fizz, fixing him with a look like a laser beam. "There's no earthly reason why I shouldn't, and you know I'd be good at it."

That was the trouble: he did know she'd be good at it. She wouldn't necessarily know the questions to ask

— he'd have to prime her beforehand about that — but, whatever her other faults, she had a decided talent for getting people to talk. Both Murray and Mr Armitage had told her much more than wisdom dictated.

Murray was leaning across the desk. "I can't take another six months of this, Tam, I want to get something moving right away. If Fizz can save you some of the legwork, I don't see why she shouldn't, otherwise it's going to drag on for ever."

Every way Buchanan looked at it, allowing Fizz a hand in the game seemed the sensible thing to do. He was doing this as a favour for a friend, after all, not acting as his legal adviser. It would certainly speed things up, he himself would still be in control of the investigation, and it would greatly limit his own involvement in what was, unarguably, a wild-goose chase. It was, in short, the perfect solution.

Why then did he have this haunting suspicion that he was about to do something he might come to regret?

CHAPTER
SIX

Zoe was renting a flat on the tenth floor of a new development at the head of Leith Walk. From her windows you could look out across the shoulder of Calton Hill straight down the length of Princes Street to the Georgian town houses where Buchanan lived, worked and had his being.

It consisted of two rooms, both of them smaller than Fizz's, and was probably costing Zoe at least fifty per cent more in rent, but then, unlike Fizz, she had the use of a lift and so didn't have to climb seven flights of stairs to reach it.

The living room was vinyl-silked in dark cornflower blue, which made a nice background for several unremarkable prints and a small collection of cross-stitched platitudes of the genus: *Today is the tomorrow you worried about yesterday and all is well*. One or two might have been Victorian, but it was difficult to envisage the others ever being worth wall space.

Zoe had gone to the trouble of setting a pretty table with a bowl of sweet peas in the middle, and she was all dolled up in an emerald-green cheongsam, gold choker and impasto eye make-up. She was one of those people you sort of assume are good-looking till you actually look at them one day and discover they are quite aesthetically challenged. She had a big mouth and her nose was too small for the width of her face and her eyes weren't worth writing home about, but somehow you didn't notice that. She had spent a lot of time and money on her hair and her skin and her nails, and although it didn't make her a stunner, she deserved an A+ for trying.

Fizz had arrived deliberately early so that she could have a private chat before Murray arrived, but the plan wasn't all that successful. Zoe was one of those compulsive hostesses who had to have every napkin folded and every candle lit before she could relax, and even when she eventually settled down, Fizz could see she was still checking off a mental list of things she'd meant to have done before her guests arrived. This made interviewing her awkward, but at least (maybe?) she wasn't concentrating too much on her answers, which made them that much more revealing.

"I feel really bad about Murray," she said as she refilled Fizz's sherry glass. "I should have made a point of visiting him in Saughton but . . . well, I assumed he'd have plenty of visitors and . . . Oh, I don't know, you're never sure whether it would just be an embarrassment to him . . . whether it would be better just to pretend it never happened and maybe look him up again after his release."

"You were more than just colleagues, then, before his arrest?" Fizz wondered.

"Oh yes. Murray and I go back a long way. It was thanks to him that Dianne and I got a start in writing.

He was the sort who'd really put himself out for a mate. He used to read over our work and make suggestions. I owe him a lot."

"Yes. He told me he'd had a spell in TV before going into teaching. I suppose he had a lot of contacts that would be useful to you." Fizz helped herself to some cheese nibbly bits. "And to Dianne, of course."

Zoe's eyes drifted back from the table, which she had been checking over, and came to rest on Fizz's face in a look of surprise and speculation which was quickly veiled over. She smiled faintly. "Quite."

Fizz tried not to look too smug. After all, it had been glaringly obvious to her from the first mention of Dianne, that her only interest in Murray had been in his TV contacts. She had done well out of her relationship with him and then dumped him when he could be of no further use to her. The real question was: why was he taking it so well?

"How long were they an item?" she asked baldly. Normally she would have pretended to be deep in Murray's confidence and allowed her interviewee to assume that he or she was merely confirming what she already knew, but with Zoe there was no need. She was recognisably a gossiper and needed no encouragement.

Zoe pursed her lips and looked at the ceiling. "Oh, gosh . . . Let's see. Must be about eight years ago that they got together. It was around Christmas time, I remember, and there was this party at a place in . . ."

Fizz tuned her out while she did a spot of mental arithmetic. Eight years ago was just before his wife's suicide. The two might not, of course, be directly related, but if Anne knew what her husband was up to it certainly wasn't going to boost her *joie de vivre*, was it? Some sort of clinical depression might have had something to do with her topping herself, but it apparently wasn't the whole story. *Cherchez le merde*.

"Eight years is a long time," she said when Zoe had finished her reminiscences of that fateful Christmas party. "You'd have thought Murray would have been pretty choked when she suddenly married someone else. He doesn't strike me as at all the sort of person who can take these things with a hey-nonny-nonny, but if he's cut up about it he's certainly hiding it well."

Zoe made a baffled face. "You're right, it's not like him, but . . . well, it's been five months now, I dare say he's over it. He's changed so much in the last three years, I'm not sure I know him any more. He's a different person. Maybe he's a person who has so much angst in his life right now that the loss of a lover is just a drop in the ocean."

"Yeah. Right." Fizz was willing to take her word about that. She herself had never been all that immersed in any relationship, never relinquished her own individuality for the dubious luxury of being half of a pair, and had no desire to do so. She said, "What's Dianne's attitude to Murray these days?"

Zoe stood up to take a look in the oven, the split in her cheongsam falling open to display a rather chubby thigh. "I hardly see Dianne at all these days. To be honest with you, Fizz, since she moved into the big time she doesn't seem to have a lot of time for us proles. She still lives in Scotland, but she's down in

London half the time for TV interviews and script conferences and God knows what else."

Fizz sat up. "You mean she's a personality? It didn't occur to me that we were talking about somebody famous."

Zoe was poking something in the oven with a long fork and took her time before answering. "Sure. I thought Murray would have told you that. She's Dianne Frazer Ballantyne."

This meant nothing to Fizz, since she had been in Canada for the last year and in Israel for the two years before that. "I remember you — or was it Murray? — saying she'd had some success, but no one told me she was famous. What does she write?"

"TV drama. She's one of the top five in the UK. Even when we were working together she was hot stuff. Just after we split up, one of her plays was nominated for a TV award at the New York International Festival. And, of course, she's headed straight for superstardom now that she's married to Sherry . . ." She saw Fizz's blank look and added, "Sheridan Reid — don't tell me you haven't heard of *him*?"

"You're kidding!" Fizz was suitably impressed. She had co-habited throughout a Torontonian winter with an Australian girl who was not only the most boring humanoid on the planet but utterly besotted with Sheridan Reid. There was scarcely a room in the flat where you could be sure he would not be leering at you from a poster, popping his oily muscles like something that had been inflated with a bicycle pump. It seemed unlikely that someone who looked like that could also act, but he had already netted an Oscar and several other less prestigious awards, and was probably in line for a knighthood one of these days. You had to hand it to Dianne: she sure knew how to pick useful lovers.

Zoe went rabbiting on about Sherry's latest film, and Dianne's chances of getting work in Hollywood, in the middle of which Murray arrived with a litre bottle of Chardonnay and a long story about taking the wrong turning at Tollcross. Zoe cut short his excuses with slightly transparent good humour and one eye on the oven, and made them come to the table right away.

It was a meal that must have taken all day to prepare. It began with an exotic salad incorporating microscopic pastries with spicy fillings, ham and cream cheese spirals, stuffed tomatoes and mushrooms, sculptured radishes, frilly cucumber, and a lot of other stuff that looked, to Fizz, more like floral art than starters. This was followed by salmon en croute with scalloped potatoes, broccoli, matchstick carrots, and petit pois. Then there came a frothy confection of fresh raspberries, meringue, whipped cream and some sort of liqueur.

By the time they'd reached the coffee and mints stage Fizz was ready for a nap, but she felt she had to lend a hand with the clearing away, since Zoe wouldn't leave it be and Murray insisted on helping her. Fizz had had a tiring weekend, much of it spent meandering through the Perthshire hills on whimsical public transport *en route* to her grandfather's farm, and she was already beginning to think affectionately of her bed. Not so, however, the other two.

Zoe settled cosily in the corner of the couch, kicking off her shoes and curling up her legs. In the light from the low table lamp at her elbow she looked almost seductive, a fact that was not lost on Murray, whose face glowed with susceptibility and Chardonnay, he and Fizz having demolished the latter between them, thanks to Zoe being TT.

"You used to drink, surely?" Murray said to her. "I remember plenty of Saturday nights we used to meet up at the Beau Brummel or Bennets. You weren't on tonic water in those days, were you?"

She made a rueful face. "It got totally out of hand, Murray. I was buzzing around trying to sell my work, trying to make contacts, and alcohol was so much a part of that scene. I was always meeting people for drinks or getting myself invited to launch parties or hanging around the pubs where the right people drank." She smiled at him mistily and extracted a mint from its paper envelope as though she were undressing it. "It's not easy for me to be moderate. I can't paddle: I have to either dive straight in or stay out of the water. So I gave up alcohol altogether."

"Smart girl," Murray said.

"Well, I'd seen the grief you'd gone through —"

She stopped suddenly and reached for her coffee cup, stirring it unnecessarily, but Fizz was on to her and had already grasped the significance. Keeping her voice drowsy, she said:

"Anne had a drink problem, did she?"

Zoe glanced at Murray and said nothing.

"Yes. For a while," Murray said shortly.

"This was after Debbie was born, was it? When she was suffering from depression?"

He nodded, turning his face away.

"What caused it, Murray? It wasn't just post-natal depression, was it? Not for that length of time?"

"Oh, I don't know. We were going through a bad patch around that time. Her drinking made it worse. It was a vicious circle."

"When you say 'a bad patch', what you're telling me is that you'd met Dianne. Or am I jumping to conclusions?"

He moved reflexively in his chair, sitting up and uncrossing his legs. Fizz thought for a moment that he was going to stand up, perhaps even walk out of the room, but he kept his seat.

"You're right, of course, Fizz. I should have been more frank with you but I was hoping I'd be able to keep Dianne out of it."

"Oh God, I should have realised . . . but, I thought . . ." Zoe exclaimed.

"It's not your fault, Zoe. I did say Fizz knew everything, and she does — everything relevant to the case, that is." He made an effort to smile at Fizz and gave a weary shake of his head. "It's not an episode I'm particularly proud of, Fizz, but I suppose you should know about it, if only to put you in the picture."

He leaned forward to help himself to another mint and toyed with it for a moment the way people do when they are sorting out things in their mind. Probably he was wondering how truthful he had to be, bearing in mind that Zoe had been witness to the relationship and its repercussions from day one. This thought had clearly struck Zoe also, because she drifted away into the kitchen and took her time refilling the percolator.

"I didn't know what hit me when I met Dianne," he said, not looking at Fizz. "Zoe wanted us to meet because she and I had been discussing their work, so she brought her along to some Christmas party or other and . . . and it was like stepping out of the darkness into a brightly lit room. I'd never met anyone like Dianne before: she was so beautiful and so . . . Well, I suppose I lost my head." He looked round with a slow smile. It was a tad bitter, Fizz thought, but any smile at all under the circumstances had to be a plus.

"'He lost his head.' That's how they phrase it, and really, that's what it feels like. I could tell myself that I was acting despicably, that I couldn't get away with it, but the message never really reached my brain. I tried to keep it from Anne, but of course, she suspected from pretty early on that something was amiss and she didn't take long to confirm it. That's when she started to drink."

He had folded the mint packet into a tiny wad and now set it carefully in the ashtray, investing the action with such concentrated deliberation that Fizz half expected him to point at it and say "Stay!" There was a longish pause but Fizz made no move to break it, and in the end, he went on in a gravelly tone:

"It was hell. Anne kept parking Debbie with whoever would take her and going off on a binge. Sometimes she didn't show up for two or three days and I'd have to take time off work to look for her and to be with

Debbie. She used to have her regular hideaways — ghastly cheap boarding houses — where nobody gave a damn what she did as long as she paid her tab."

Perceiving that she was supposed to feel sorry for his having to put up with this peevish behaviour, Fizz said coldly, "But it didn't occur to you to stop seeing Dianne?"

He looked at her briefly and then rubbed a hand over his face. "I did. Several times, but it never lasted. Once, after we ran into Buchanan in a Perthshire inn, I didn't see her for six weeks. But it never lasted. I just wasn't able to make it last."

That seemed to be it. He just sat there, looking at his clasped hands, his lips pressed tight together like a dressmaker holding a row of pins. Fizz let the silence drag on but it didn't prompt him to continue, and in a minute Zoe came back and started refilling their coffee cups.

"It's easy to make snap judgements, you know, Fizz," she said softly, as if she'd managed to follow the gist of the conversation from the kitchen, which, given the thinness of the walls, she probably had. "But nobody outside a relationship can ever know all the facts, and until something like that happens in your own life, you can't know how hard it is to do the right thing. Dianne was — still is — a very special person, and personally, I don't find it hard to imagine her having that sort of effect on a man. It's just very tragic the way things worked out."

Fizz considered this statement to be a load of codswallop. It seemed to her much more likely that

Kingston had seen the opportunity to have a bit on the side and had gone for it. Whatever you thought about the morals of that action, you couldn't ignore the fact that he now considered himself the injured party. All his protestations of heart-searching and attempted self-denial were a complete whitewash and he couldn't hide the fact that he felt Anne's reaction to his affair was over the top and deserved no sympathy whatsoever.

It was one thing to be a bastard, she thought, but it was quite another to be a bastard pretending to be the one deserving sympathy. Lilies that fester smell worse than weeds.

She didn't make any comment, since she liked Zoe too much to tell her she was defending a spoiled brat. She had been well on the way to liking Murray as well, but that had gone by the board entirely, and had she not been enjoying the prospect of being a detective she would have told him he could go back to jail without either passing "Go" or collecting two hundred pounds.

Suddenly she wanted out. She didn't feel capable of making polite conversation with Murray, not for the moment, and she felt like demonstrating her disapproval in actions if not in words.

"I have to go," she said, but when she looked behind her at the clock she was amazed to see it was only nine fifty.

Zoe blinked at her. "Surely not already, Fizz? There's some Cointreau left from the dessert. I was going to —"

"No, honestly, Zoe, thanks all the same. I've things to do before I go to bed tonight. I have a date tomorrow with Buchanan the Magnificent, from whom all blessings flow. He's coming into the office to drop off the details of the guys he wants me to start interviewing, and I'll want to be ready to start on it in the afternoon."

"Who's first on the list? Did he say?"

"Phillis, Anne's sister, who lives in Aberdour," Murray said. He was only half looking at Fizz, as though he wasn't sure what he'd see in her face. "She has custody of Debbie now. It's quite a train journey for you, Fizz."

"Don't either of you have a car?" Zoe said. Seeing that Fizz was on her feet and determined to leave, she went and got her coat from the bedroom, talking all the way there and back. "It would be far better if I drove you there. No, listen Murray, you can't do this by public transport. Your witnesses are scattered all over the place and you may have to go back to talk to them again and again, so, please, let's not argue about it. When I said I wanted to help, I really meant it."

The wicked shall flourish like the green bay tree, Fizz told herself as she walked home in the turquoise and gold twilight. Here was Murray Kingston, a selfish bastard who didn't deserve to be peed on if he was on fire, and yet all sorts of people — herself included — were falling over each other to help him. Sometimes there seemed to be very little justice in the world.

She was inclined to be angry with Buchanan for not putting her properly in the picture. Both he and Murray were willing to let her do all the dogsbodying but they were obviously going to keep her in the dark as far as background information was concerned, which was simply not on. Operating on a need-to-know basis would severely impair her ability to process any information she might turn up, and there was no fun in that. The whole point in being involved in the first place was to have a go at uncovering some worthwhile evidence to show that Murray was innocent, not just to be the support team for those doing the real brainwork.

By the time she reached the High Street she had worked herself into a mood of righteous indignation. Her lion's share of the Chardonnay was still fizzing and popping in her bloodstream and she was in a mood for action. She stood at the corner of North Bridge and looked across it at the lights of Princes Street.

Buchanan lived just down there, in the warren of pricey eighteenth-century mews properties that sloped down to Dean Village. She knew this because she had seen his home address on the mail he brought into the office to open, and she had already done a quick recce when she passed that way *en route* to waylaying him at his office.

If they were going to work together on this project he'd have to be put straight regarding the ground rules, and there was no time like the present. Of course, given his "me boss, you menial" attitude, he might be pretty brassed off to find her on his doorstep.

Tough.

CHAPTER
SEVEN

The work that Buchanan had brought home from the office was still spread all over his dining table. If somebody had made a still-life painting of it you would have taken it for a scene of productivity only momentarily deserted by the instigator, the dynamic flow of work suspended, the pen hastily cast down. In fact Buchanan had been sitting staring at the same few pages, reading the same meaningless words, for two hours and had progressed not at all. It wasn't as if he didn't have time to do all the work in the office, but he found it easier to concentrate here than being constantly interrupted.

As soon as it was too late to do so he had realised that he should have gone for a round of golf instead of wasting a perfect evening staring out of the window. He could see a stretch of the Water of Leith, no great distance away, slow and turgid, and edged with willows, and he envied the people who ambled along its banks soaking up the last of the sun.

When he could no longer delude himself that he was achieving anything by just sitting there, he decided to go for a pint at the Pear Tree, where he could be sure of meeting someone he knew. There were tables outside in the courtyard there, and although it was already almost as dark as it was likely to get at this time of year, he was desperate for some fresh air.

He was just zipping the last document into his briefcase when the doorbell rang. His mind flew immediately to Janine — who else could it be at this hour? She must have just arrived back from Aberdeen — suitably repentant for being so childish — and decided to come straight over. He made a dive for the door.

"Hi," said Fizz, smiling up at him through her lashes, as friendly as a muddy dog.

"Good God!" he said, feeling the expression on his face change with a rapidity that was almost injurious. "What the hell are you doing here?"

"You weren't in bed, were you?"

"Do you . . . have you any idea what *time* this is?"

She blinked at him, and two minute vertical lines appeared between her brows, half puzzled, half hurt. "It can't be much after ten. I need to talk to you. There are things I've found out."

His heart sank. It was extremely unlikely she could have found out anything of value, but it was just as unlikely that she was going to disappear off his doormat. He stood aside and let her walk past him across the lobby and into the lounge. She was dressed in her customary jeans and Docs, plus a blue silk shirt open over a cream vest. No jacket, no handbag, no make-up. As if she'd stood up and walked out of the house just as she was.

"Crumbs," she said, standing in the middle of the room and spinning slowly to take it all in. "You're really a 'thing' person, aren't you?"

"I'm sorry?"

"Such a lot of *things*: books, pictures, tapes, photographs, little souvenirs of this and that." Her eyes ticked off every item as she paced around. "Television set, VCR, music centre, cordless phone, computer . . . Fascinating."

Buchanan looked about him with a baffled scowl. "It looks perfectly ordinary to me. Sit down, won't you?"

"It probably is pretty ordinary — in certain socio-economic groups. It's just that I haven't been moving in those circles for so long. When you're travelling about a lot you tend to forget how 'ordinary' people live."

She zeroed in on his bookshelves and did a rapid survey of the titles, then turned to him with one of her bright looks. "God, I could use a cuppa. I don't suppose you'd have any herbal teas in the larder?"

Buchanan sighed, all hope that she would tell him her news and take herself off dying a painful death. "Herbal, no: Earl Grey, yes."

"You talked me into it."

Following him into the kitchen she checked out the microwave, the food processor and the cafetière, and restrained herself only with manifest difficulty from opening the cupboards. Buchanan watched her covertly while he filled the kettle. She was as nosy as a bloodhound, and he had a strong suspicion she'd contrive to see the rest of the apartment before she left.

100

There were condoms — and God knew what else! — in the bathroom cabinet, he suddenly remembered, and made a mental note to get there before she could. Ridiculous to mind about something like that, but he couldn't stop thinking of her as childlike and shockable.

"I've run out of milk, I'm afraid," he said. "I hope you can drink it without."

"That's okay. I don't take it. I'll add it to your shopping list, shall I?" She scribbled on the ceramic shopping list over the refrigerator and then leaned back against the work surface with her arms folded. "You like cooking, I see."

"What?"

She indicated the appliances, the row of copper-based saucepans, the spice rack. "Cooking. I had you down as more of the carry-out type. Maybe the occasional Welsh rarebit."

Buchanan looked at the kitchen. Perhaps it had been his intention, when he had moved in three months ago, to do more of his own cooking. He had simply bought everything on a list made out by Janine but it had turned out much easier and quicker to eat out at lunchtime and grab a takeaway on the way home at night. Sometimes Janine rustled up supper for them, and now and then his mother took it into her head that he wasn't eating properly and filled his freezer with flans and cooked chickens, which didn't last long. Otherwise Fizz couldn't have been more right in her original assumptions.

"I boil a mean egg." He smiled, giving nothing away, and carried the tray back to the living room.

Fizz sat on the floor and took off her Docs. Tiny feet in surprisingly expensive-looking black silk socks. "I'll be Mummy, shall I?" she said, her face making some kind of feminist — he supposed — comment which he pretended to apprehend.

"So what's this evidence you've come across?"

She emptied her cup by two-thirds. "Not evidence. I said I'd found out something."

"Okay. What have you found out?"

"I found out that you and Murray are not giving me all the background information I ought to have if I'm to play an effective part in this investigation."

He was inclined to smile at this, since as far as he was concerned, he was innocent as charged, but he could see by her expression that he was supposed to understand that she was angry.

"What information are you talking about?" he said carefully.

"The information about Murray's affair with Dianne Frazer Ballantyne and the part it played in his wife's suicide."

"Christ!" he said, unguardedly, the word punched out of him by surprise. "Who told you about *that*? Not Murray, that's for sure. How did you find out?"

"No thanks to either of you. That's the point I'm trying to make. I shouldn't have to waste time scrabbling around for data that you and Murray are already aware of. It's not good enough. Either I'm an equal member of the team, or I'm out."

She didn't have the right kind of face for transmitting malevolent rage, but she was doing her best. Buchanan watched her with a dawning respect. Somebody who could uncover information of this quality in the space of time she had been on the case was somebody well worth humouring. The realisation that she was extremely bright had been growing in him for some time, and he was now ready to accept the fact. He said:

"But how did you find out, Fizz?"

"I should tell you?" Her chin gave a sharp upward jerk, expressively dismissive. "You and Murray tell me nothing but I'm supposed to share all my sources with you? Not on. If you want a free and full exchange of information I want your promise that I get to know everything you know as soon as you know it. Is that agreed?"

"Agreed," he heard himself say, without a moment's hesitation. "From now on you're on equal terms with Murray and me, I promise you, but I want to know how you found out about Murray's affair."

"From Zoe Paton. You know who she is?"

"Zoe . . . yes." Tall, black-haired, attractive in a curvy sort of way and, as he eventually discovered, Dianne's one-time writing partner. Yes. She'd know about the relationship if anyone did. "How did you get on to her?"

"She's living in Edinburgh. We met her, Murray and I, in the Chambers Street museum last week. I made an opportunity to talk to her alone so that I could fill in some of Murray's background."

"It's years since I saw her last. What's she doing now? Still writing?"

Fizz helped herself to a fourth biscuit. "Yes, but not as successfully as Dianne, not selling enough to support herself. She's still teaching English."

Buchanan's fairly hazy recollection of Zoe began to take shape like a wraith in the shadows of his brain, images flicking through his mind like photographs in an album; images from the days when he had known her only as a colleague of Murray's and not as the friend of his mistress. He saw her in a brocade jacket at a Festival performance, in a fake fur coat at a Hogmanay party; arguing passionately with Murray and another chap in some pub or other around the same time. She had been part of the new crowd Murray had taken up with after moving to Berwick, a crowd that impinged only occasionally on Buchanan's social scene, but he was sure he'd been introduced to her at some point or other.

"I didn't know her well — or Dianne either, for that matter — but from what I've heard of her she didn't have the drive it takes to get to the top. Dianne did."

"The killer instinct, you mean?"

He looked at her. "Maybe."

"Dianne had an eye on the main chance, didn't she? That's what attracted her to Murray — the fact that he knew people in TV, producers, controllers, people who could be of use to her. I think she got her claws into him and bled him white."

She could have plucked the words straight out of Buchanan's subconscious. "He certainly had the sort of contacts that would have been useful to her in getting her career off the ground, there's no doubt about that, but she'd have got to the top one way or another. And nobody could accuse her of being short of talent. The critics said *Fade to Black* was the best serial the BBC have screened in years."

"But once she'd got all she wanted from him," Fizz insisted, "she might have had trouble shaking him off. He must have been pretty besotted with her, considering what he allowed his wife to suffer. Maybe she decided to frame him with something that would keep him out of her hair for a while."

Buchanan thought this unlikely but didn't like to put her down too forthrightly. "Well, maybe, as you say. It's a solution that might appeal to an imaginative person like Dianne, but I don't see her needing to resort to that. She strikes me as more the sort of person who'd just tell him to get lost or she'd have somebody kick his teeth out one dark night."

Fizz looked pleasantly surprised at this. He rather thought Dianne had gone up in her estimation. "The funny thing is," she confided, "that Murray seems to be taking the whole business of her getting married etcetera remarkably well, wouldn't you say? I mean, if he was as madly in love with her as the facts imply, how come he's not up there putting shit through her letterbox?"

Buchanan recoiled. "For God's sake, Fizz, do you have to be so crude?"

She gave a long gurgle of laughter, tipping back her head so that her neck showed round and tender and inexpressibly childish. "What an old fuddy-duddy you are, Buchanan. If a man had said that, you wouldn't have batted an eye, so why should there be rules against women expressing themselves in the most graphic phrase that occurs to them?"

Buchanan struggled to be a little more post-modernist, and failed. "I don't feel the need to speak like that and I don't see why you should."

"Not even with other men?" She saw him hesitate and laughed again. "You see what I mean? Why pretend that women are a different animal?"

"I don't claim anything of the sort — I just think it's possible to express oneself without being offensive. However, we were talking about Murray's attitude to Dianne's marriage," he said, sticking to a discussion that had some hope of leading somewhere he wanted to go. "It's something that had occurred to me too. I was wondering if he'd met someone else."

Fizz considered that possibility, reaching absently for the last biscuit. "Now you mention it, I wouldn't be at all surprised, but if he has, he's not telling. He's very keen on damage limitation. He was doing his best to keep Dianne out of the picture, not that I blame him considering what a splash their relationship would make in the tabloids." She munched thoughtfully for a minute. "I don't suppose there'd be any point in asking him."

"I imagine not. But I don't think it's something we have to worry about at this stage. Whoever his new lady is — if she exists at all — it's unlikely to be someone involved with the case."

"Dianne was writing to him in jail right up to her marriage, so that relationship was still ticking over up till February of this year. That means we're talking about someone he met in prison . . . a social worker . . . a lawyer . . . a nurse, maybe?" She looked up at him. "A man?"

"Let's not get carried away, Fizz," he said firmly. "It was only a hypothesis and, as I said, it's not important right now. We have to concentrate on looking for inconsistencies in the evidence that was presented in court. If that draws a blank we'll widen our net, but not until then."

"Right," she agreed, delicately removing a crumb from the corner of her mouth with the tip of her tongue. "Though I wouldn't mind a long chat with La Dianne. I get the feeling she must be quite a character. Was she really all that irresistible?"

Buchanan thought he could probably have resisted her without too much trouble, given the chance, but then he had never got that close to her. "She was certainly very dynamic . . . and beautiful too, I suppose."

"Murray says so," Fizz stated. "And so does Zoe. I must try and locate a photograph of her."

"Just a minute," Buchanan said, sorting through a jumble of recent unfiled memories. "I saw a photo of her yesterday . . . or today . . . where was it?"

There was a pile of newspapers, magazines and junk mail on the floor beside the couch. It took him ten seconds to pick out the Festival Fringe programme and find the page.

"There. The 'Meet the Author' advertisement," he said, passing it to Fizz. "She's going to be making public appearances for the first week of the Festival. If, by that time, you're still interested in her you can go and see her at the Assembly Rooms." By the end of a couple of weeks, he sincerely hoped, their enquiry would have been wound up, one way or another, and probably without involving Dianne.

Fizz studied the fuzzy black and white photograph with no noticeable enthusiasm. "Probably doesn't do her justice," she said sweetly and fell to leafing through the pages as though she'd forgotten he was there.

Buchanan looked at the time and was amazed to see it was after eleven. He said, "It's getting late, Fizz, and we've both got work in the morning. How far do you have to go? Did you get fixed up with a new flat the other day?"

She lifted her head from the programme and regarded him with a blank expression. "Sorry?"

"The flat you were going to see about when I ran into you outside my office."

"Oh, yes, I'm with you. The flat." She stuck her hands over her head and stretched. "No, it was too expensive. I decided to stay where I am for the present. It's just up in the Royal Mile."

There was no way out of it; he had to say, "I'll give you a run home."

"No need," she said, lacing her boots. "I'll be home before my coach turns into a pumpkin."

"You shouldn't be walking the streets at this time of night . . ."

She found this mildly amusing. "Don't get your Y's in a knot. There's not a soul in the streets. It's like a flag day in Aberdeen out there. I'll be okay."

Buchanan was much inclined to believe her. If anyone had the mistaken temerity to accost her she would probably have his jugular bitten through before he could cough. At the same time, he was quite sure that if he didn't see her to her door he wouldn't shut an eye.

"I feel like a breath of air anyway," he said, quite truthfully.

"Okay. If you insist." She fluffed up her riotously curly hair with both hands. "I'll just check out the bathroom first."

It was an unfortunate turn of phrase and brought the memory of the condoms crashing back. Too late.

"Right across the hall," he said, grinding his teeth. It was stupid to forget — it was even more stupid to care! — but he was only thankful that he had thrown out the dayglo selection that he had won at his brother's stag party.

CHAPTER
EIGHT

When Fizz emerged from the community centre just after one fifteen the next day she found Zoe sitting in a black Peugeot at the back of the car park, wearing an apple-green mohair top with matching tights, navy-blue shorts and three-inch heels. Pretty much what she might have chosen herself, Fizz thought, had she been a semi-demented fashion victim, which she wasn't. However, since she was intending to pass herself off as some sort of paralegal this afternoon, she had changed into the grey jacket and black skirt which constituted her entire formal wardrobe.

It had been a terrible morning. Buchanan had given her a totally unreasonable amount of typing to do, McGuigan had been in and out of the office like a piston, and she'd had to take a load of snash from Buchanan's girlfriend, who had phoned when he was engaged.

"And just who am I speaking to?" she had snapped when Fizz refused to put her through.

Fizz took instant exception to the tone. "The name is Fitzpatrick, madam, and I am also the person Mr Buchanan asked to hold his calls. If you'd care to call back in about ten minutes I'm sure Mr —"

"Indeed I *will* call back, miss, you can be sure of that, and when I do I will inform Mr Buchanan that the efficiency of his staff leaves much to be desired!"

"I'm not his staff —" Fizz began, but the bitch hung up on her. Choking with fury, she pre-empted the complaint against her by giving Buchanan her own — slightly doctored version as soon as he was free. Luckily for him, he merely shrugged and said just to put Miss Hutcheson straight through in future, but that didn't wipe the incident from Fizz's memory.

Everything went downhill from there on in, and she was heartily glad to shut the office door behind her and see Zoe waiting for her. "Hi," she said, getting into the passenger seat. "Sorry I'm late, I had a bit of trouble with the word processor."

"Doesn't matter. I told Murray we might be late." Zoe folded up the *Scotsman* she had been reading and threw it over her shoulder on to the back seat. "You weren't rushing, I hope? That's not what caused the computer trouble?"

"The girl in reception says she can straighten it out. Apparently there's a limbo facility which allows you to resurrect files you've erased in error. I sure as hell hope so."

They moved out into the lunchtime traffic and crawled down the hill to Dalry Road. Even here, well off the tourist beat, there was evidence that the Festival was looming on the horizon. A couple of the larger lounge bars were carrying posters that identified them as venues for the Jazz Festival, and every school, bingo parlour and church hall was advertising their imminent metamorphosis into bases for stand-up comedians or Fringe theatre companies. Fizz was reminded of the advertisement Buchanan had shown her the night before. She said:

"Buchanan tells me your old sidekick is making a public appearance in the Fringe."

"Dianne, you mean? Is she? I haven't seen a Fringe programme yet."

"She's taking part in the 'Meet the Author' evenings at the Assembly Rooms. Will you go to see her?"

"Oh God, no! I hate those things. Is Tam going?"

The implied familiarity threw Fizz for a second, then she remembered that Zoe had probably known Buchanan in the old days. "I'd forgotten," she said. "You must have known him when you and Dianne and Murray were part of the same crowd."

Zoe slid into a space between a bus and a dilatory VW and turned left. "He was never really part of our crowd, but I used to see him around. Had the hots for him for a while, actually, but he was glued to some frightful female advocate at the time and didn't know I was alive. I spoke to him two or three times but I bet he couldn't have picked me out of a police line-up half an hour later."

"You had a lucky escape," Fizz told her, concluding that Buchanan must have been a lot different in those days to have held Zoe's attention for any length of time. Then again, he still appeared to have women throwing themselves at him from all sides, so, clearly, blue eyes and a cute bum meant more to some people than personality. "If he wasn't one when you knew him, Zoe,

I can tell you he has now turned into the most pompous bore imaginable."

"Is he seeing anyone at the moment?"

Fizz eyed her sideways and smiled a little. "Yes. A silver-blonde stick insect with a red BMW. But I have the feeling it won't last."

Zoe changed lanes deftly at the corner of Melville Drive, and as the traffic lights turned to green, roared away ahead of the pack, skirting Bruntsfield links and heading for Morningside.

"Oh, by the by," she said, "take a look in the glove compartment. I think there's a tape recorder in there. It might be useful to you."

It was one of those mini-tape models, not much more than four inches by two. "I don't know," Fizz swithered, playing with the buttons. "I'm not into technology. If it's anything like that bloody word processor I'd probably get home and find it hadn't recorded. I think I'll just stick to my good old notebook and pencil."

"I wish you'd give it a try, Fizz. You can cover it with a thin scarf — there's one on the back seat — and you'll find people are more at their ease that way than if you're noting down what they say. Besides, you can play the whole interview back to Tam. That way he can't blame you if you fail to report anything. It could happen that something you didn't consider worth mentioning turns out to be significant."

Fizz hummed and hawed for a while but finally stuck it in her shoulder bag without promising to use it.

Murray lived in a square 1930s bungalow that had, till her recent demise, belonged to his mother. It looked bleak and dingy, with peeling paintwork and a garden that showed signs of long neglect. He was waiting for Fizz and Zoe on the pavement in the terminal stages of impatience. The look he turned on them as they drew up was like a hyena spotting a wounded gazelle.

"Relax already," Fizz told him as he climbed in. "We have all afternoon to get there, you know. You look as though you were just about to take off without us."

He was all smiles. "I suppose I'm not the most patient person in the world. It just occurred to me while I was waiting for you that if we were in Aberdour a few minutes early we could park near the house and perhaps catch a glimpse of Debbie playing in the garden."

"Don't see why we shouldn't, d'you, Fizz?" Zoe said. "Actually, I'd love a look at Debbie myself."

Fizz could find nothing to object to in this. She said to Zoe, "Did you know her as a baby?"

Zoe arched an eyebrow over her shoulder at Murray. "I don't remember ever seeing her. Did I, Murray?"

"Probably not. She'd have been with Mrs McCaulay or Sue in the evenings. She's a big girl now; all legs and arms."

"You mean you've seen her since you got out?" Zoe said, and he caught her eye self-consciously in the driving mirror.

"First thing I did. I was on the train to Aberdour thirty-five minutes after the prison gates shut behind me. If you climb the hill behind the house you can look

114

down into the garden. I could have got some good snaps of her with a telephoto lens, but I lost my camera in a break-in years ago and never bought another."

"How did she look?" Fizz asked. "D'you think she's happy with Phillis?"

"She looked great. She was playing with some other kids, running about and yelling, but she was always like that on the surface. The things that troubled her only came boiling out of her in dreams."

And in her drawings, Fizz only just stopped herself from adding. She too was looking forward to meeting Debbie, and not just seeing her but hopefully talking to her as well. The schools were still on holiday so Debbie might be around the house when she called, but she had a feeling that Phillis would keep her well out of her way.

Murray had sussed out the best viewpoint on his last visit: a shaded stretch of railings half hidden by bushes. The hill was laid out as a public park, with a small area for swings and roundabouts and the usual swathes of annual bedding plants.

They waited for ten minutes, in a freezing north-easterly whipping in off the Firth of Forth, and Fizz was just about ready to pack in when a small figure wandered round the side of the house carrying a flat wickerwork trivet. She was nipping buds and seedheads off whatever took her fancy, and one rather hoped she had permission to do so, otherwise she was in big trouble. In a minute or two she was joined by a tall, very bald man with a beard and a pronounced stoop.

115

"Larry!" Fizz heard Murray mutter, under his breath, but it was difficult to tell from his expression whether he was merely surprised or perhaps a little concerned. It must have been hard to reconcile his natural jealousy with the realisation that Debbie had, apparently, formed a close bond with her new father.

It was clear, even from a distance, that they were comfortable together. Larry had brought with him a collection of what looked like old yoghurt cartons, and Debbie took them from him and started filling them with her seedheads while he looked on companionably. Fizz knew that, had she been Murray, she'd have been saying, "That should be me down there."

He was silent as they got back into the car to drive round to the house. Fizz tried to get him to give her some background information about Phillis and Larry, some pointers on how to approach them, but got very little out of him. All he could contribute was that Phillis was a cold bitch and they had both hated him from day one, which wasn't really a whole lot of help.

Standing on the doorstep, waiting for someone to answer her ring, her confidence suddenly drained straight out of her, and she began to wonder if she were actually a victim of her own hype. She hadn't a clue how to go about eliciting honest answers to the questions Buchanan wanted her to ask, and she had a horrible suspicion that these people would see through her at a glance and send her packing. The tape recorder also made her nervous. Both Murray and Zoe had urged her to use it, but she was worried that someone might spot it through the chiffon scarf and take violent umbrage.

The door opened. Phillis. Five foot ten and heavy with it. Late forties. Straight hair tinted honey-blonde. Thatcherite jacket and skirt. Good pearls. Hostile.

"Miss Fitzpatrick? Please come in."

She led the way down a long passage that bisected the modern bungalow and into a hexagonal conservatory built on at the back. The glass doors that gave on to the garden were open, but they faced away from the wind, so it was still uncomfortably warm. Two rattan couches and a matching chair were grouped about a long coffee table, and the rear wall was almost hidden by a magnificent jasmine.

"I'm afraid I have a surgery at four fifteen so I can't spare you any more than about twenty minutes." She waved Fizz to a seat and sat down facing her, crossing her meaty legs.

"Oh, you're a doctor?" Fizz said, surprised out of her nervousness. Phillis was turning out to be quite the opposite of the colourless suburban matron Murray's lack of information had led her to expect.

"I am a GP, yes. My husband and I run the local practice between us." She sat straight in her seat, making no pretence of settling down to a nice cosy chat, and her expression said plainly, "Let's do without the preamble, okay? Just ask your questions and get out."

Fizz took a deep breath, and switching on the tape recorder, she set it openly on the table between them before taking out her notebook. Phillis, miraculously, made no comment, merely raising her faint brows a little.

"I imagine," Fizz began with growing confidence, "that Mr Buchanan explained, when he phoned you this morning, the reason why we wanted to speak to you."

"He did." Phillis stretched her lips in a minimalist's smile. "But I can tell you, as I told him, that it's a waste of his time and mine. I have nothing to add to what I said at the trial and there is nothing to be gained by resurrecting what was a very painful experience for all of us. As far as I'm concerned, Murray Kingston has served his sentence — paltry as it was — and he should now have the grace to disappear and allow the past to bury its dead."

"But if there's a possibility that he was wrongly convicted —" Fizz began, unwisely.

"Rubbish! Utter rubbish! If that's what he's now trying to claim, the man is out of his mind!" A wash of high colour spread across Phillis's forehead and temples. She was trying to keep her voice level and not finding it easy. "There is no question in my mind — nor in the minds of anyone familiar with the situation at the time — that Murray Kingston richly deserved all he got, and a good deal more. Hanging's too good for the beast!"

Fizz nodded wisely at these sentiments, taking her time in the hope that a few seconds of calm reflection would allow Phillis to get a grip.

"I know it must be painful for you to have to bring it all back to mind," she said, in the tone of one doing a distasteful job purely as an economic necessity. "But hopefully this enquiry should end the matter one way or another. I just have one or two points to clarify and then I'll be out of your hair."

Phillis's manner thawed marginally but would still have been an asset to Birds Eye. She glanced pointedly at her watch, prompting Fizz to say:

"I believe you saw quite a bit of Debbie before . . . before the police became involved?"

"You could say so, yes — depending on what you mean by 'quite a bit', of course. My sister was not always able to take care of her, so she would occasionally leave her here for a day or two."

"How often would that be . . . on average?"

Phillis looked out at the garden and drew a slow sigh as though, really, it was too much bother to work out. "Oh . . . once a month, possibly, something like that."

"And she stayed overnight?"

"Sometimes, not always."

"That must have been awkward for you and your husband with a busy practice to run, I mean."

"It was, and it still is." No beating around the bush here. "To be honest, Miss Fitzpatrick, Debbie's continued presence has caused considerable disruption in our family and in our professional life. We chose not to have a family of our own and I can't pretend that I enjoy being saddled with the responsibility of a child at this stage in my career. However, Debbie has no other living relations, so one has to make the best of it."

"I see." The picture of Larry, hand in hand with Debbie in the back garden, floated into Fizz's mind. "And your husband? How does he feel about it?"

"As I do." She lifted her eyebrows in a cool stare as though this were an insolent question. "But we were both extremely fond of my sister, who also suffered very deeply at the hands of Murray Kingston, and we do what we can for Debbie for her sake, as well as for her child's."

Fizz held her eyes. "You blame Murray Kingston for his wife's suicide, then?"

"Of course. He was no kind of a husband to her, never at home, constantly dashing off to PTA meetings, evening classes, writers' circles — anything to get him out of the house. And where was he when Debbie was born — at a time when a woman needs all the support her husband can give her? With another woman, it turns out, this . . . this *writer*!"

She used the term pejoratively, as though nothing better might be expected from one who told lies for a living. Fizz nodded sympathetically. "You didn't know at the time about Dianne Frazer Ballantyne?"

"No. But, of course, other people did, and it filtered back to me in due course. But Anne was gone by that time and Murray's other sins had caught up with him, so . . ." The recollection was perceptibly a painful one. Her gaze became momentarily withdrawn and drifted, with fulminating malevolence, to an unwitting geranium, which, Fizz was amazed to note, did not immediately wither and die.

120

"But I take it you met her around that time, when she and her co-writer were part of Murray's social scene?"

Phillis redirected her bitter look to Fizz. "No, I did not. Murray took good care to keep that side of his life private. All I know about his mistress is that she is an egotistic, self-centred and conniving woman, and an extremely poor writer."

"You don't like her TV dramas?"

Phillis closed her eyes lightly and seemed to shudder. "I missed the first one — *Fade to Black*, wasn't it? — but there was so much talk about it that I felt I had to see the others. Of course, by the time the second one came out I knew of her connection with Murray, so that made me curious as well, but it was such rubbish that I only watched two or three episodes. And the next one was just as bad in my opinion — trite situations, poorly drawn characters, one cliché after another."

This was stated with such belligerent conviction that Fizz, even if she'd held a firm opinion, would have thought twice about disagreeing. But she was not surprised. Given Phillis's animosity towards the woman who had wrecked her sister's marriage, it would have taken a better writer than Dianne Frazer Ballantyne to impress her.

"But presumably, if you were close to your sister, you must have met a number of Murray's friends and colleagues."

Phillis didn't reply, but her left eyebrow said, "So?"

"It would help if we could establish if, in your opinion, Murray had any enemies, if there was anyone, for instance, who might have deliberately framed him?"

"Framed him? Is that what he's claiming?" Phillis's smile was like a razor slash. She mimed a short laugh. "Dear me. If it weren't so frightening it would be comical." She leaned towards Fizz and spoke with chilling conviction. "My dear child, make no mistake about this: Murray Kingston was not framed. He is one of the most evil men I have ever known and it is a reflection on the present legal system that such a monster should be free again to prey upon some other child. Take great care — and tell Tam Buchanan to do likewise — or you may end up returning Debbie to the hell she was suffering before it all came out into the open."

Fizz nodded soberly. "I think we're all very much aware of that danger, but it's also very important to be quite sure, should Murray turn out to be innocent after all, that the person who coached Debbie to say the things she did is caught and punished." Phillis did not deign to dignify this hypothesis with an answer, so Fizz went on impulsively, goaded by a need to know, "I hope you won't mind my asking — I know it's none of my business, really, but I'd like to know — as a doctor, do you think Debbie will be permanently damaged by what she's been through?"

Phillis appeared to debate with herself whether to satisfy such impertinent curiosity or not, then her hard face relaxed a little and she said, "That depends, to

122

some extent, on whether you are right about Murray Kingston being framed, or I am, Miss Fitzpatrick. If what Debbie said at the time had no basis in fact, as you suggest, and if her relationship with her father is restored, then I see no reason why she should not put the experience behind her. But even if I am right and she was abused by her father, I believe that, with the careful counselling she has been receiving from my husband and me . . ."

Fizz heard no more of her remarks, since she was distracted by the sudden appearance of Debbie in the back garden. She was carrying a black cat — wearing it would have been a more accurate description — draped loosely over one forearm like a fox fur, and neither she nor the cat seemed to be aware that it was there.

Phillis was now looking at her watch again, drawing back the cuff of her jacket and raising her wrist in case Fizz was slow on the uptake. She had not noticed Debbie's approach, which was out of her line of vision, so Fizz did her best to distract her by making extravagant preparations to leave.

"Well, thank you for giving me so much of your time. I'll just leave my telephone number with you if I may, in case you remember anything that might be helpful to me. It would be much appreciated." She stood up and made a gesture that turned Phillis's eyes to the back wall. "I couldn't help noticing this wonderful jasmine. How old is it?"

"Oh, it must be . . . Well, it was there before we built the . . ."

"So there you are! Uncle Larry said you were busy. When are you coming to see the shop I've made?"

The childish treble chimed like a bicycle bell and Phillis's reaction was instant. She moved towards the open doors with her hands held down and away from her sides, the palms forward in a gesture that was both prohibitive and shepherding, but Fizz was right beside her.

"Hi!" she said, giving the kid a big smile. "I bet you're Debbie. I'd almost forgotten — I brought a little pressie for you!"

Debbie locked eyes. "What kind of pressie?" she said, eschewing all inessentials like introductions. The cat poured off her arm like an oil slick, stuck its tail in the air and stalked back out to the garden.

"Well, just let me get my bag and I'll show you."

Phillis sat down again while Fizz struggled to extract the package without dragging forth all the rest of the junk she had shoved in on top of it.

"There you go. I hope you like it."

"Really," Phillis said, with a token smile, as Debbie set the package on her aunt's lap and tore off the paper, "you didn't have to do that. What do you say, Debbie?"

Debbie, having discovered a drawing pad and a comprehensive collection of drawing implements, was already engrossed in trying out the colours. "Thank you," she said absently, and placed one of Phillis's hands on the pad to steady it while she drew.

Fizz started to ask her if she liked drawing, but Phillis cut across her opening words as though she hadn't heard them.

124

"I'm afraid Miss Fitzpatrick is going away now, Debbie." She quickly transferred the drawing equipment to the coffee table, and Debbie followed it without lifting her eyes. Standing up, she led the way to the door before Fizz could elicit more than a distant "Bye-bye" from the engrossed child.

As they moved down the hall a door opened just ahead of them, and Larry appeared, frowning, on the threshold. He looked older than he had from a distance. His bushy beard and bald head gave the impression of one of those trick faces that you can turn upside down so that they look bald and sad one way up, bushy-haired and happy the other way. Larry was at present looking bald and sad, and when he looked at Phillis you could tell he knew he was in trouble.

"I thought Debbie was making herself a shop in her room," he said.

"She was with us in the conservatory," Phillis told him. Her voice was calm and honey-sweet but her face, which Fizz couldn't see, was probably like the Eiger seen from Lauterbrunnen. "This is Miss Fitzpatrick. She's just leaving."

The last remark was clearly a reminder to Fizz rather than a matter of any interest to Larry, but Fizz gave him a big smile and shook hands. "Oh my!" she said, looking past his shoulder to the room beyond. "Are those all Debbie's drawings? Would you mind awfully if I took a quick peek?"

Phillis started to point out that she would mind awfully but Larry, at the same time, said, "Certainly," and stood aside, probably earning himself another dose of aversion therapy from his wife.

It was a square, sunny room with a window overlooking the side garden. Debbie's "shop", a collection of jars and yoghurt cartons filled with various unidentifiable substances, bunches of weeds and coloured pebbles, was laid out on a low work table, and a blackboard on an easel gave a list of misspelled prices. All four walls, from ceiling to floor, were covered in Debbie's drawings. There must have been hundreds of them, in a variety of mediums: watercolour, wax crayons, coloured pencils, felt tips and collage.

"What an output!" Fizz couldn't help exclaiming. "How long did it take Debbie to produce all this?"

"Oh, some of it goes back years," Larry said. "She can't bear to throw away a drawing. If she has no room for a new one she just sticks it on top of an old one. Now and then we have to sneak in while she's at school and thin them out a bit."

"Her grandfather, my father, was an artist," Phillis offered, a trace of pride creeping into her tone. "A very respected illustrator. Anne inherited the talent from him to some extent, but she was never brilliant, never showed the promise that Debbie does."

"When did she start?" Fizz asked, wondering if the drawing habit had taken root after her early trauma.

Phillis and Larry exchanged questioning glances. "I think . . . as soon as she could hold a crayon, don't you, Larry? I remember Anne buying her those big fat crayons and encouraging her to scribble. She can't have been a year old at that time."

126

Fizz was fascinated by the collection. She was certain that a child psychologist could trace Debbie's development from the dusty portraits consisting of a large round head with arms and legs protruding from it to the latest, somewhat stiff-legged but otherwise quite lifelike, depictions of horses and ballerinas. All aspects of her life were grist to her mill. If the pictures had been dated you could have told when she joined the Brownies, when she acquired her black cat, the point when she lost interest in dressing up and discovered Narnia.

"Are there any from three years ago?" she said, knowing it was highly unlikely but asking anyway.

"I don't think so," Phillis said, but Larry did a quick scan of the upper walls.

"The ones with the holes down the side. Remember the pile of computer paper you gave her when she used to come to stay, Phillis?" He stood on a chair and tugged down a yellowed sheet. "There's one she made of her friends at school — well, it would be nursery school, I suppose."

It wasn't one of the more descriptive works, most of which dated from a later period. In fact it consisted of nothing but a mass of matchstick figures, but it was probably remarkable work for a pre-school kiddie, and Fizz was loath to give it back.

"I'd like to borrow this for a few days," she said to Larry, since he appeared to be more likely to fall for the I-have-a-perfect-right-to-do-this-anyway approach than his wife did. "I'll give you a receipt for it."

"Oh, don't bother. It's not one of the ones the police were interested in, but you're welcome to take it if it's of any use to you." He started to smile, then appeared to catch sight of Phillis's face behind Fizz's shoulder and sobered up again quickly.

"Well, Miss Fitzpatrick," Phillis said crisply, "if you've seen all you need to see I'm afraid I must chase you away. I have patients waiting."

The interview was unarguably over, and Fizz was firmly ejected almost before she could murmur a polite word of thanks. Outside she discovered that she was exhausted, and the walk back to the car where Zoe and Murray were waiting for her seemed interminable.

CHAPTER
NINE

Buchanan was in the shower when the telephone rang. He had finished early at the office, for once, and was planning on nipping over to the Braid Hills for a quick nine holes before the light started to go. He was pretty sure Janine would be calling some time this evening but felt it wouldn't do her any harm to find that he wasn't sitting here with his hand on the receiver waiting for the phone to ring.

At the same time, however, he was pleased enough by the thought that she had wasted no time in contacting him that he ran across to the living room before the answering machine could cut in and snatched up the receiver.

Of course, it wasn't Janine, it was Fizz.

"Hi. Thought you'd want to know how I got on at Aberdour."

He pushed a fringe of wet hair out of his eyes. "Fizz? Oh, hello. Look, you caught me at a bad moment . . ."

"You've got company?"

"No, actually, I was in the shower."

"Oh, well, I'll just give you the main points, will I?"

"I'd rather you called me back later, I . . ."

"Can't. I'm going to a free preview at the Lyceum. Anyway there's not much to tell. Phillis wasn't giving much away except that she thought Murray dunnit and should be put down."

"I could have told you that," Buchanan sighed, resigning himself to listening to her. He flicked drops off his legs and torso and wished he'd taken a minute to pick up a towel. "I don't suppose you saw anything of Debbie?"

"Just a glimpse. Phillis wasn't going to let me ask her any questions — not that I'd have said anything to remind her of what happened, but she was taking no chances. But I did see her drawings. Hundreds of them."

"Hundreds?"

"Well, maybe not hundreds, but lots. That kid churns them out like a production line."

"Yes, well . . ."

"I've got one. It's a picture of the kids in her nursery school class."

Buchanan considered this but failed to see the significance. "Her chums. Uh-huh. Are you saying there's something to be learned from it?"

"Maybe," she said, sounding a little huffy, as though she had expected a more enthusiastic response. "We'll have to study it. I'm going to stick it up on the wall in Zoe's lounge — did I mention that that's where we're going to make our headquarters? Oh, yes, the phone number. You'd better make a note of it in case you need to contact me."

He found a pen and noted down the number, wondering if Zoe had changed much since he last saw her. "Okay, so . . . You'll have to give me a full report later — tomorrow maybe. Let's see . . ."

"Yes, there's lots more but — listen, I got it all on tape. Zoe gave me a tape recorder and I taped the whole thing — well, most of it. I could bring it over to your office tomorrow if you —"

"No, don't bother," Buchanan said quickly. Fizz's willingness to pop in at a moment's notice or none at all fell short of being endearing. He could well imagine the effect that her informal attire and egalitarian manner would have on his father — or, for that matter, on Beatrice. "Why don't the three of you meet me for lunch at the High Court, about one o'clock, say."

"If that is your desire, oh Star of the Universe. Oh, but Murray has a meeting with his parole officer or social worker or somebody — he told me who but I've forgotten. Zoe and I will be there, though. What time did you say?"

"One o'clock. At the reception desk. And don't expect the Ritz, it's only a snack bar."

"Mingy bastard," he heard her mutter. Then, "Roger. Over and out."

He stood looking at the phone for a minute after he had hung up. There were advantages in having Fizz do all the legwork, but he was clearly going to have to spend time on keeping her on a tight rein. Already she had enlisted another member to the team without as much as a by-your-leave, and if he didn't take care she'd be getting the idea that she was in charge of the entire investigation, which clearly would not do.

He had given her a list of questions to put to Phillis but it sounded very much as though she had gone off on some tack of her own. The tape recording would prove that, one way or the other, but if it turned out she hadn't followed his instructions, he'd have to sort her out.

Zoe was another matter. His recollection of her was too hazy for him to be sure she was the right sort of person to be helping with the case. Admittedly she was only peripherally involved, but such matters had a habit of escalating — particularly if Fizz had anything to do with it — and it behoved him to suss her out before she became too much of a fixture. Having her place as a headquarters, however, was a bit of a bonus and would save him having to fork out for debriefing sessions in public places. He didn't mind buying them lunch tomorrow, as he was likely to be in court much of the day and it would save him time in the long run. Besides, Fizz (and probably Zoe too) was likely to be putting in a lot of work, and a snack lunch, viewed as a one-off *ex gratia* payment, wasn't exactly spoiling her and gave him a chance to renew his acquaintance with Zoe.

The shower was still running. Hearing it, he realised he was chilled to the bone and dashed back under the spray to thaw out, but almost immediately, the doorbell rang. This time it was Janine.

"Oh darling, you were in the shower!" She stood on tiptoe to kiss him and then bustled past him, her arms laden with groceries, exuding amiability, determination and Anaïs Anaïs in roughly equal proportions.

"Don't stand there looking like thunder, sweetie. Get back into your shower, for goodness' sake, before you freeze. I'm going to make us a glorious bolognese and tell you all about my trip. Did you miss me?"

From the bathroom he could hear the clatter of cutlery and the slam of the refrigerator door, and after a minute or two the thought came to him that perhaps he should have looked more thrilled to see her. One didn't want to appear to be grovelling, but a welcoming word or two would not, perhaps, have gone amiss. Then again, she was evidently feeling remorseful about the way she'd treated him, so why not keep the advantage while he held it? She was the guilty party, not he, so it wasn't necessary to be too conciliatory right away. She'd have to learn that she couldn't tread all over him with impunity.

All sounds of culinary activity had ceased by the time he got out of the shower, and as he dressed he began to sense something odd about the silence. Normally Janine would put on one of her favourite tapes and sometimes even hum along as she set the table. Tonight — nothing. No music, no singing, no more appetising noises from the kitchen. He went into the lounge to investigate.

Janine was standing with her back to the window, watching the door, and as soon as he pushed it open she straightened her shoulders and said, in a voice that trembled with anger, "I think it's time we had a talk, Tam, don't you?"

Buchanan blinked at her. "What do you want to talk about?"

"Our relationship." He could tell that she already had the whole conversation scripted out in her head. "I don't think you are being totally honest with me and I'd like to know just where I stand."

Oh God, Buchanan thought. Is this it? Is she actually going to make me decide, here and now, whether my intentions are honourable or not? "I think you'd better clarify that," he said carefully.

"Don't pretend you don't know what I'm talking about, you bastard!" Janine's face suddenly went bright red and she took two paces towards him. "Do you think I'm so stupid or naïve that I don't know what you're up to? How many women do you need at one time?"

Buchanan was thunderstruck. He almost laughed aloud, then decided that he wouldn't. "What on earth are you talking about?"

"You know damn well what I'm talking about. You're seeing someone else!"

The memory of Fizz brushing his cheek darted into his mind and was instantly dismissed. This was something much more serious. Janine looked so ugly, with her face all dark and blotchy and her mouth twisted with rage, that he felt he was dealing with a total stranger and didn't know how to communicate with her. He stared at her in amazement. "What on earth makes you think that?"

"For one thing — this!" she said, waving the object she'd been clutching in one hand and which he now recognised as the ceramic shopping list from over the fridge.

He took it from her and read, in Fizz's flowery script, "Milk. Herb teas, pref. Rosehip or Lemon Verbena. Not Camomile. Ta."

It didn't seem to warrant Janine's blazing temper. Certainly it was a very feminine hand, but for heaven's sake, it was scarcely evidence of infidelity. Was he going to have to put up with this kind of scene every time she caught him in the same room with another member of the female sex, regardless of age or availability?

She started marching up and down, making jerky gestures and glaring at him and talking rubbish.

"I don't have to put up with this, you know. One would think after all this time that you'd have the decency to at least let me know where I stand. I don't think that's asking too much, do you, Tam? A mere schoolgirl, for God's sake!"

"Janine, this is all —"

"A teenager! What on earth you can possibly see in an empty-headed dolly bird not much more than half your age . . . Your friends are laughing at you, did you know that? I didn't believe Daddy when he said he'd seen you with her late last night — I couldn't imagine you making such a fool of yourself! Well, that's your privilege, Tam, but you're not damn well making a fool of me! I'm not going to have it!"

This was a new Janine: a loud, scarlet-faced, out-of-control and rather repellent Janine. He began to be quite glad he'd made her acquaintance now rather than at a later stage in their relationship. For the moment he couldn't bring himself to be placatory.

"I really don't see what you have to complain about," he said coldly. "It's not as if you don't go out with other men."

"*One* man!" she shrilled. "And you know damn well it was business! And you weren't sitting at home all alone while I did it, were you?"

"As it happens, no, I wasn't. But . . ."

"And I actually believed you all those times when you said you'd brought work home to finish." Her voice rose to a squeak. "How long have I been falling for that one, I wonder? Clearly long enough for another woman to settle in here to the extent of writing out the shopping list! I must be sick in the head! Oh . . ."

Words suddenly failed her at a point when she had just reached meltdown. Tears of rage and frustration spurted from her eyes and with a wordless cry she snatched up an avocado, which she'd probably had in her hand when the apparent truth of his infidelity had struck her. Before he could believe she was actually going to do it, she straightened and, with a wide and easy swing which she had never once exhibited on the golf course, fired it straight at his head. It missed him by a hair's-breadth, exploded against the wall behind him and splattered everything in the room with a fine green spray.

Buchanan couldn't believe that one medium-sized avocado could cover such an area. It was like the miracle of the loaves and fishes. The keyboard of his computer looked like a dog's breakfast, and the

136

wallpaper sported a nine-inch blotch that reminded him forcibly of a skull with a knife in the eye socket. He wondered briefly what Rorschach would have made of that one.

He didn't notice Janine slamming out of the flat like a tearful bulldozer and wouldn't, at that point in time, have cared much if he had.

CHAPTER
TEN

Real-life murder, Fizz quickly discovered, was nothing like the fictional variety. Everything was a great deal more prosaic.

She looked at the knife for a long time, bemused by its innocuous appearance. In the average kitchen drawer it would have passed without comment: a well-used carving knife with a bone handle and a steel blade that was honed away to a four-inch stump. If she'd been planning to inflict a massive amount of internal damage she'd have chosen something at least a couple of inches longer and with a stronger blade. It was just bad luck that this apology for a murder weapon had succeeded in hitting a vulnerable spot.

In fact, the whole morning's proceedings had been depressing rather than dramatic: just a summary of predictably tragic events which involved endless repetition, painful nitpicking and basically very boring people. Even the members of the defence team looked as though they were having trouble staying awake while the Advocate Depute bored on and on.

There had been a brief spark of interest early on when one of the prosecution witnesses had tried to get away with a pack of quite transparent lies and the defence advocate had turned on him like a chain saw. His subsequent humiliation and disintegration had provided the sadists in the courtroom (Fizz included) with a few delicious minutes, but after that things had gone rapidly downhill.

It was the same story over and over again, from witness after witness. Group A, consisting of some half-dozen unarmed youths, had spotted Group B infringing their territorial rights and had decided to see them off. Since Group B consisted of only two youths and a girl, the aggressors had expected no resistance, but one of the lads in Group B had a knife and (probably terrified out of his skin) had used it, with fatal effects.

As Zoe said, more than once, no amount of questioning was going to change the facts and they might as well go round to court six where Buchanan was assisting a client in some even less exciting case. However, Fizz was beginning to discern a subtle undertone in the questioning of the defence advocate and suspected that, in the end, the jury would be wondering if, perhaps, the deceased had brought along the knife himself and had fallen on it in the struggle. The leader of Group B was probably as guilty as hell but he might still get off with a "not proven" verdict which wouldn't, she thought, be entirely a bad thing. He was, after all, nothing but a daft laddie who'd probably only carried a weapon because he was scared, and a period of detention in the company of hardened criminals wouldn't necessarily make him a better citizen.

Zoe also pointed out that the accused looked like a nice lad, which was true. His counsel had him all tarted up in a lounge suit and a short back and sides, neither of which he would have been found dead in outside the courtroom, but which may have fooled the jury. Unfortunately, no one had thought to extend the window-dressing to his supporters, who filled the back row of the public benches looking like a cross between the Addams Family and a random selection of serial killers. Fizz made a mental note to ban several of her more bizarre friends from the courtroom if she should ever find herself in the dock.

There was a mention of calling forensic experts, at which Zoe woke up a little, but His Lordship, in the best Hitchcockian tradition, decided to break for lunch before he heard their evidence, and the court was cleared. It wasn't yet one o'clock but as they walked back towards the reception desk they paused to admire the Signet Library and spotted Buchanan walking up and down chatting to a colleague. Eventually they managed to attract his attention, and after a few quick words to his companion, he met them in the doorway.

"Hello. You're early."

"We've been watching a murder trial in court eleven but it's stopped for lunch," Fizz said, and tipped her head at Zoe. "You two know each other, I believe?"

They said all the usual things to each other, neither of them listening to a word of it. Zoe had switched on that inexplicable charm of hers at full blast. Her voice was soft and breathless and she managed to look as though she were photographed through gauze like

Greta Garbo. Buchanan, who had started off looking like the Ghost of Christmas Past, suddenly got quite Tiny Tim-ish and escorted them downstairs with the air of one who was rather looking forward to his lunch.

The food itself was better than Fizz had steeled herself to expect, but not hugely. The soup was oxtail, so she confined herself to a veggie risotto with fresh fruit to follow. Buchanan, she couldn't help but notice, ordered a very oleaginous casserole of lamb which would have had any normal person writhing with heartburn within the hour.

She and Zoe conversed quietly as they ate so that Buchanan could scan through the tape of Fizz's conversation with Phillis.

"If you had leaned on her a bit," he said finally, "you might have got her to come up with the names of other people who had it in for Murray. You seemed to let her off the hook too easily on that one."

"Yes, well, if you want that woman leaned on you can lean on her yourself, coz I won't be doing it for you. Not unless I'm getting some pretty serious danger money, okay? She's like something out of *Jurassic Park*."

Buchanan nodded, sipping his coffee. "Mmm. You're probably right, Fizz. It would be better if I did the interviewing myself."

This was not at all what Fizz had in mind and she suspected that he knew it. "What I'm saying is that leaning on Phillis is not the way to get information out of her. All you have to do is get her riled up and let her run — only I didn't have time to do that yesterday so

I'll have to go back again in a day or two. Believe me, she really has it in for Murray. She blames him for Anne's suicide as well as for the Debbie business. Ten minutes alone with him and she'd be wearing his balls as earrings."

Buchanan and Zoe studied their plates.

After a minute Zoe said, "She's clearly very embittered as far as both Murray and Dianne are concerned, but I felt she was presenting a very unbalanced view, didn't you? No outsider can really judge who's to blame when a marriage fails, and as for the way she slated Dianne, both personally and professionally, it was almost entirely undeserved. I'd hate you to think otherwise."

Buchanan hooked an eyebrow at her. "I haven't seen any of her plays, so I can't venture an opinion, but you have to admit that the last two have taken a real mauling from the critics."

Zoe shook her head impatiently. "It's so unfair. The original Scottish production team was almost totally replaced, for the later productions, by blue-eyed boys from London who had all the slick tricks but didn't really appreciate the cultural subtext. The hero of *A Cure for all Diseases*, for example, was the skipper of an Aberdeenshire fishing boat, but he was played by an English actor whose attempt at an Aberdeenshire accent sounded — as the *Herald* critic put it — 'like a middle-European Jew with strong Pakistani connections and a cleft palate, speaking from a command module on the far side of the moon'." She outstared their smiles. "I don't understand the thinking behind that sort of casting. Maybe they think the English audience won't know the difference and there are so few Scots that they don't matter, but the fact is, it deprives the dialogue of all credibility and it demoralises the rest of the actors."

"But Dianne could have objected, surely?" Buchanan put in. "She must have known the effect it would have on her work."

Zoe turned her hand over: a small gesture but eloquent of impotence. "She was a raw beginner with only one success behind her and no clout. Believe me, in that line of work you don't make waves, and besides, she probably felt that the producer had a lot more experience than she did and that she should take his advice."

Fizz waited to hear if Zoe had any excuses pertaining to the third production, but she appeared to have run out of honeyed words. Compared with the more realistic view of Dianne she had presented when she and Fizz were alone last Monday, her assessment of Dianne's work now smacked of sycophancy, and it was quite obvious that she wanted to appear all sweetness and light in Buchanan's eyes. You had to laugh.

"I know what you're thinking, Fizz," she said, looking a little sorrowful. "And you too, Tam, I suppose. You're thinking that a lot of the success of *Fade to Black* was due to Murray — more, perhaps, than Dianne realised — and that once she had used him to get a start in TV she framed him to get him out of the way, only to find she was no good without him."

Neither Buchanan nor Fizz tried to deny that this scenario had occurred to them.

"It's not true. Honestly. Listen to somebody who knows them both." Zoe laid a hand lightly on Buchanan's sleeve and leaned towards him. "I won't deny that she made use of Murray in the beginning, but only because he knew the people who mattered, never for help with her writing. Oh sure, he would read what we produced, maybe make an occasional very minor suggestion, but never more than that. To be honest, Murray doesn't have an original idea in his head. He's an excellent teacher, he can read something and tell you what's wrong with it, but don't ask him to produce anything of his own. He hasn't got it, he never had it, and he could never have produced *Fade to Black*. Not in a month of Sundays."

Fizz was much inclined to believe this assessment. She already felt she knew Murray well enough to tell that he was of a more practical, matter-of-fact turn of mind, and she had never been truly comfortable with the suspicion that he had played any part in the creation of a TV masterpiece.

"I'm sorry now that I didn't see any of the plays," Buchanan said, stealing a sideways glance at his watch. "It would have been interesting to compare them."

Zoe nodded, and seemed to hesitate for a second before she said, "I videoed them at the time. I think I still have them at home if you'd like to see them."

"Really?" His sudden thirst for knowledge looked entirely spurious to Fizz. She started to comment but was interrupted by a loudspeaker above her head announcing that the hearing in court one was about to reconvene, and by the time it was finished Buchanan was already saying, "Yes indeed, I'd welcome an opportunity to view the first production with the other two, just to see if I could perhaps detect any difference in writing style. Not that I'd expect to, of course, but it would be an interesting exercise."

"Why not pop round tomorrow evening, then?" Zoe preened her hair in a disinterested manner. "I'll cook us something we can have on a tray while we watch them."

"I'd enjoy that very much. Thank you."

"Sounds great." Fizz nodded cheerily. "I've been curious to see them myself."

Zoe's eyes travelled slowly across the tablecloth and climbed Fizz's blouse button by button till they reached her face. They were not smiling.

"Right," Fizz said, hastily reaching for her jacket. "In that case I think we ought to get a move on, don't you, Zoe? If we're going to see this woman Torkington at the playgroup, we can't afford to hang around."

Buchanan said, "I thought Beatrice had made you an appointment?"

"Any time before three thirty — that's when they close. We'd planned to see Mrs McCaulay, Murray's ex-neighbour, before going to the playgroup, but Beatrice is getting no reply to her phone calls. Maybe we could call round afterwards, on spec. Want me to phone you afterwards, or can the debriefing wait till tomorrow night?"

"Better give me a ring at the office if you can make it before five." Buchanan helped Zoe on with her coat and picked up his briefcase. "Try to find out if anyone other than Murray ever collected Debbie from playgroup, Fizz. If you're planning on recording the interview I can pick up the tape from you tomorrow."

Fizz gave him a nod. "Roger and out."

Zoe was uncharacteristically silent on the way to the playgroup. At first Fizz assumed that she was just peeved at the way her planned dinner *à deux* with Buchanan had been undermined, but as time passed it became apparent that Zoe had more on her mind.

"There's something I have to talk to you about, Fizz," she said finally. "I'm not sure it's fair to involve you, but . . . I don't know what to do."

"Shoot," Fizz told her tersely.

Zoe glanced at her briefly and looked away again. "Okay, but I want you to promise . . ." Her voice faded, as if she felt that was too much to ask, and then she said in a mumble, "I'd really appreciate it if you'd treat it as confidential, okay?"

"That heavy, huh?" Fizz asked, noncommittally.

Zoe swallowed. "I think . . . I *know* that Murray is still seeing Dianne."

Fizz hadn't expected anything of that magnitude. She watched the fields whizzing by outside her window and let the implications sink in. What the hell was Murray up to?

Zoe was taking it seriously. "I saw them together last night, going into the Hamilton House Hotel — that's where Dianne always stays when she comes back to Edinburgh. He had his arm round her."

"Why didn't you say anything about this to Buchanan just now?" Fizz couldn't get her head round this new development. She couldn't see why Zoe was taking it so hard, or why she was being so secretive about it.

Zoe looked in her mirror, pulled over on to the grass verge and stopped. Resting her forearms on the steering wheel she turned to look at Fizz. "I'll tell you why I didn't want to say anything, Fizz," she said wearily. "Because I know exactly what Buchanan's going to do when he finds out."

"He'll bodybag him!" Fizz felt she was stating the obvious.

"Fizz . . . If I tell Buchanan . . . if *we* tell Buchanan he'll drop Murray's case right away. He'll be so angry to find that Murray has been holding out on him about something so important that he'll tell him to go to hell."

Fizz found herself in complete sympathy with this projected course of action, and said so. It was a pity that her career as a private detective should be so swiftly curtailed, but it was clear to her that if she couldn't trust Murray to tell the truth about Dianne, she couldn't believe him when he denied abusing Debbie. She said that too.

"Of course you feel like that." Zoe massaged her temples and stared anxiously out through the windscreen. "But you see, Fizz, I know . . . I just *know* Murray is innocent. Don't ask me for proof — I haven't got proof — but I'm utterly convinced in my own heart that he could never have done the things he was accused of."

This testimonial didn't carry much weight with Fizz, but since she could see Zoe was waxing tearful, she refrained from mentioning it and let her ramble on.

"I wish I'd never seen them. If there hadn't been such a traffic hold-up in Princes Street I'd never have gone round that way and would never have known about it. And now I have to decide what to do. If I tell Tam he'll drop the case, and if I don't tell him I'll be deceiving him about something that could be important." She drew in a breath that made her buttons creak. "It's a cleft-stick situation, isn't it, Fizz?"

"Not for me it isn't," Fizz told her. "But then, I'm not so convinced of Murray's innocence as you are."

"It's not just that I believe in him," Zoe said. "It's that I gave evidence that weighed against him at his trial. I can't let him down again, I just can't."

"You should have challenged him on the spot," Fizz said, knowing perfectly well that Zoe didn't have that sort of bottle. "You should have let him know that you'd seen him and told him he'd better come clean with Buchanan."

"Maybe he has a good reason for not being frank about it," Zoe offered hesitantly.

"Okay, let him tell you what it is. You can tell him you saw him with Dianne and give him an ultimatum: either he admits it to Buchanan himself, or you spill the beans. He doesn't have the right to ask you to lie for him or to keep your mouth shut about it either."

148

Zoe gnawed on that for a minute and then nodded. "That's what I'll have to do. He may drop round tonight, but if he doesn't, he'll be in touch by tomorrow night and I'll invite him round to watch the videos of Dianne's plays." The thought of having to face up to Murray was evidently not one she enjoyed. "But please, Fizz, I'm asking you, as a friend — don't mention it to Buchanan till I've had time to talk to Murray about it and find out what he's playing at."

Fizz had a fair idea what Buchanan would say if he found out he was the last to know. "Twenty-four hours," she told Zoe firmly. "I'll keep my mouth shut for twenty-four hours on one condition. Do not tell Buchanan you told me, okay?"

"I would never do that," Zoe returned, looking hurt. "I'll take care to keep you well out of it. I just hope I get the chance to talk to Murray alone."

"Just *do* it, Zoe. If he doesn't call round tonight you can get him alone before Buchanan and I arrive tomorrow night, or after we've left, but make sure you talk to him tomorrow at the latest, you hear? This thing's a hot potato and I want rid of it."

Zoe was awash with gratitude and promises. She appeared a little more cheerful as she drove the rest of the way to Berwick, but the fact that she was worried about her coming confrontation with Murray was written all over her. Fizz let her stew, merely shouldering the burden of the conversation till they pulled up in front of the compact Edwardian villa that housed the playgroup.

"I suppose," she said then, in a spirit of generosity, "this is one you could sit in on, if you wanted to. I mean, it's a public place, sort of. It's not as though I were insinuating you into someone's home."

Zoe cheered up momentarily and then shook her head. "Not a good idea, Fizz. You know Tam would be furious if he found out."

"Why should he find out? I'm not going to mention it and neither are you, and it's unlikely he'll be having any direct contact with the staff here. Just let me do all the talking so that your voice won't be on the tape."

Zoe looked for a minute as though she were getting ready to tag along, but then she made a face and decided against it. "No. It's not worth it. If I can't even speak I won't be able to make suggestions. It's simply not worth the risk of getting you into trouble. I might as well wait till I hear the tape."

Fizz didn't bother to sell her on the idea, but treated her to a long, amused stare just to let her know that she wasn't taken in by all this sudden concern for her well-being. It was quite obvious that Zoe was unhappy about risking Buchanan's disapproval for her own sake, not Fizz's. Well, if she had set her sights on the boss-fella, she was due for a disappointment. Fizz might not want him for herself but she was damn sure her plans for his future did not include Zoe, any more than they did Donna.

The gate was locked, evidently to prevent the escape of any of the inmates, of which some dozen or so could be seen messing about with sand and water in the garden. Candy-striped overalls seemed to be *de rigueur*, green for the boys and lilac for the girls, and a somewhat less than adequate police presence was being maintained by two youngish women in aprons, one of whom waved and headed, smiling, towards the gate.

She was beaten into second place by a bullet-headed three-year-old with several missing teeth and a smart-arse face that was a strong argument in favour of family planning.

"*You* can't come in here," it stated with odious assurance. "*You're* not one of our helping ladies."

Fizz leaned across the gate and brought her face down to the level of the poison dwarf. "Push off, tortoise-face," she growled, and straightened in time to flash a smile at the approaching helper.

"Miss Fitzpatrick, is it? Mrs Torkington said to keep an eye open for you." The helper unlocked the gate with one hand, restraining an opportunistic mass break-out with the other. "Come on in. Mrs Torkington's — *stop* it, Andrew! — Mrs Torkington's inside with the wee ones. You'll get a bit of peace to talk in there . . . if you're lucky! Andrew, don't start, okay? Just don't start!"

She led the way though a terrazzo-floored hallway from which a magnificent oak staircase climbed to the upper storey, and opened a door to the rear of the house. A faint but evocative smell of babies emerged, warm and milky, reminding Fizz of a period when she'd worked as a mother's help in Malaga. There was music playing quite softly — "Venus", from *The Planet Suite*.

"The young lady from the lawyer's office has arrived, Mrs Torkington. D'you want to speak to her in here?"

The reply was inaudible but was evidently "yes", because Fizz was ushered in with a smiling gesture.

It was a smallish room: once, perhaps, a bedroom in the days when the house had been solely a home. Orangey-pink curtains had been partly drawn, giving the room a sunset glow, evidently for the benefit of the two babies and three toddlers who were disposed here and there in various attitudes of deep repose.

Mrs Torkington stood up from behind the desk, where she had been working on something that looked like account books, and advanced on Fizz with outstretched hand. She was a small, fat lady with eyes like a blackbird, close together over a beaky nose, and a mass of frizzy hair in what must have started off that morning as a French roll.

"How d'you do, Miss . . . ah . . . Fitzsimmons."

"Fitzpatrick, actually. How d'you do?"

"Oh, dearie me, if there's a wrong way of picking up a name I'll find it! Don't bother about these sleeping beauties. They're used to a bit of background noise. Now, let's see if we can clear you a space to sit down." She began throwing toys off couches, neither dropping her voice nor making any other concession to the dormant infants, who slumbered on regardless. The background music segued seamlessly into Debussy's "Clair de Lune".

"So." She dropped into an overstuffed armchair, removed an unexpected wooden building block from under one hip and settled back against the cushions. "I believe you want to talk to me about poor wee Debbie Kingston."

"That's right." Fizz brought out the tape recorder. "I hope you won't mind if I use this? My shorthand's not all that wonderful."

"By all means. It doesn't bother me at all, but to be honest, my dear, I doubt if I can tell you anything worth recording. I've rather pushed that incident to the back of my mind, you understand, and I'm not sure how reliable my memory is after such a long time."

"But you remember Debbie?" Fizz suggested, just to get her started.

"Oh yes, of course I remember Debbie." The blackbird eyes flashed briefly with pain and rancour. "I'm not likely to forget her, dear, not after what happened. A quiet wee thing, but not shy. Not at all shy."

"How long was she with you?"

"Ah . . . now, that's where my memory lets me down, you see." She tucked a free-floating wing of hair back into her French roll and frowned with concentration. "Not very long, I think. Maybe a couple of years."

"And did she seem quite happy while she was here?"

"Certainly. She wasn't one of our most extrovert kiddies — not what you'd call chatty, no, but she joined in perfectly well with the others and was always quite cheerful, as far as one could judge. She was as happy as any normal child. I remember we all agreed about that at the time — my helpers and I. There was never a hint that she was distressed about anything."

"But it was you, wasn't it, or one of your helpers, who first realised that there was something sinister going on?"

"Yes, that's true. I feel it's my responsibility to keep an eye open for suspicious signs. You hear so many worrying stories nowadays, don't you?"

"Do you recall what initially made you uneasy?"

Mrs Torkington thought about that for a minute, her eyes following the movement of her hand as it stroked the arm of her chair. "It seems to me now that I had sensed a difference in her — a withdrawal, a lack of spontaneity — I don't quite know how to describe it. And then, of course, she did come out with some very ambiguous remarks about 'Daddy's little piggy', etcetera. They became less ambiguous later, you understand, but the *first* inkling I had that something was seriously wrong was when I saw the picture she drew of her daddy."

"Which was . . .?

"Well, let's say, rather detailed."

"You mean, unclothed?" Fizz prompted. "But surely plenty of kids have seen their dads like that? Lots of parents try not to make nakedness a big deal."

Mrs Torkington looked pointedly out of the window. "Perhaps 'detailed' is not the correct word. 'Explicit' might be a better choice."

They exchanged a meaningful look.

"You mean . . .?"

"Exactly. It's not normal for a child to see her father like that."

"Right."

Typical of Buchanan not to make that clear. Both he and Murray, she now realised, had rather glossed over the details, allowing her to assume that the drawing was rather less specific. No doubt Buchanan would expect to be struck by a divine thunderbolt if he ever uttered the phrase "hard-on" to a lady.

Some ballet music by Chopin that Fizz couldn't put a name to swelled into the silence, making one of the toddlers mumble in his sleep.

"I don't suppose there could be any mistake, could there? I mean, I've seen some of the drawings Debbie produced about that time, and they're — well, they're amazing for a pre-school kiddie, okay, but they're not exactly faithful representations of her subjects. You could easily get the wrong impression from an accidental scribble."

"Of course." Mrs Torkington's eyes closed momentarily as she nodded. "That's exactly what I thought the first time it happened."

"There were more?"

"Yes. I told the helper who brought the picture to me that it would be a mistake to jump to conclusions, so she gently encouraged Debbie to draw more pictures of her daddy to see if it happened again. And, of course, it did."

A faint wail from behind her brought her quickly to her feet. She lifted a perfect little Asian doll from a pile of cushions on the floor and returned to her chair with him cradled against her ample breast. Showing no interest in Fizz, he stuck a thumb in his mouth and slipped back into a semi-doze.

"Naturally, we informed the authorities straight away." Mrs Torkington carried on as though there had been no interruption. "I had thought to try questioning

Debbie a little before going so far, but the general feeling among my helpers was that the social work department had specially trained people for that sort of questioning and we might do more harm than good if we rushed matters."

There didn't seem anywhere Fizz could go from there. She couldn't help coming to the conclusion that all her questioning thus far — taking both interviews into consideration — had done more to prove Murray's guilt than disprove it. It was unlikely that Mrs Torkington could have misconstrued the message of the drawings, and it was even less likely that the social work department and the Lothian and Borders police force could have been similarly mistaken.

"I suppose," she said wistfully, "you did see Debbie herself drawing the pictures?"

Mrs Torkington's eyes closed again, either in weariness or in an effort to marshal her recollections. "I feel sure I must have, my dear, but if I didn't, my helper certainly did."

"Uh-huh. And who was the helper? Is she still here?"

"Oh, dearie me. I'll have to think about that. Who was it, now?" She heaved the soporific toddler across to the curve of her other arm, which disturbed him not at all, and pressed a hand to her forehead, dislodging the independent wing of hair. "Yes . . . yes, I remember who it was. Nice lassie. I can see her face as clear as I can see yours, but her name . . . no, it's gone clean out of my head. Wait a minute . . . Collingwood? No, she came later. Um . . . I get the feeling it began with a J."

Fizz glanced at the ledgers on the desk. "You wouldn't have a note of it somewhere?"

"No. She wasn't one of my regular helpers, I'm sure of that." A thought struck her, and for a moment she appeared to follow a hopeful line of mental reconnaissance, but then shook her head. "No — I was thinking of someone else. What was I saying? Oh yes . . . staff. I only employ one or two full-time helpers. The others are really only casual employees who help out for an hour or two a week, and they rarely stay with me for long, so I don't keep records. Even the full-time helpers come and go all the time. I think Shona, who showed you in, is the only one who's been here more than a year or two."

"Was Shona here at the time all this happened? Maybe she would remember this other helper."

"We could ask her. I'm sure she was with me at the time." Mrs Torkington stood up and walked to the window. As she did so the boy woke up again, and she lifted him against her shoulder, making comforting noises in his ear. "No, I don't see her. She must be round at the sandpit. Do you want to take a walk round?"

Fizz thought she might as well, since there wasn't another thing she could think of to ask Mrs Torkington, so she thanked her and made her own way out through the shadowy hallway. On the way, since there seemed to be nobody around, she took the opportunity to peep into the other ground-floor rooms. There was a toilet, a kitchen, a cloakroom and a large playroom with a Wendy house, an area for water play and the usual gallery of finger-paintings and "useful-box" artwork. The whole set-up looked well organised and generously equipped, and Debbie's period as inmate had probably cost Murray an arm and a leg.

Outside, after the muted indoor light, the sunshine was almost painful. There was no breeze at all and the afternoon seemed weighted with the heat. The sounds of the children and the occasional passing car had a muffled quality, and even the still air felt thick with dust motes. It should have been siesta time in Equador, not two forty-five of a Berwick afternoon.

Shona was sitting on the wall of the sandpit in an attitude of non-interference, while a committee of four-year-olds debated the construction of a tunnel. She appeared to view Fizz's approach as a welcome diversion.

"Hi. Are you looking for the way out?"

"No. Actually I'm looking for you," Fizz said, sitting down beside her. "It's about Debbie Kingston."

"Yes, I know. Mrs T. told me."

"You remember her?"

Shona made a bleak face. "I'll never forget her as long as I live. Even when you're only peripherally involved in something like that, you don't get over it in a hurry. I still wake up in the night in a frenzy to get my hands on that guy and tear him into small pieces."

"Yeah." Fizz suddenly remembered the tape recorder and got it out of her bag. "You don't mind this, I hope? It saves me taking notes."

Shona moved a hand negligently. "Sure. But look . . . I have to say that if you want me to help you get that animal released from prison, you're not on. If it was up to me I'd throw away the key."

"Is that the way you heard it?" Fizz shook her head. "Well, the facts are slightly different. Murray Kingston has already served his time. Three years of being systematically bullied and reviled by the other prisoners. He's had ribs broken, teeth punched out and his nerves shot to ribbons."

"It's too good for him," Shona stated bluntly.

"I agree," Fizz said, "if he was guilty. Unfortunately, there's now a possibility that he was the wrong guy. What I'm . . . what my boss is trying to do is to make sure that the real culprit is brought to justice. I take it you wouldn't mind having a hand in that?"

Shona didn't answer. She appeared to be digesting the unwelcome thought that the child molester was still walking the streets.

"What I wanted to ask you," Fizz pressed on, "was if you remember the helper who brought the first drawing to Mrs Torkington's notice. I believe she was the one who encouraged Debbie to make more pictures of her daddy."

Surprisingly, Shona nodded brightly. "Yes, I do remember her. Quite well, actually. A tallish girl with a round face. She wasn't here long."

Fizz had to resist grabbing her arm. "Do you remember her name?"

"As a matter of fact, I do. It was Kate. I remember that because she was reading a Catherine Cookson paperback called *Our Kate*, and every time I see that book I remember her."

"And her surname?"

"No. I don't suppose I ever knew it." She leaned over the wall to restrain a small tunneller who was wielding a spade too energetically. "Careful, Simon, you nearly hit Alison just then. No, we don't usually bother with surnames. Casual staff come and go so regularly that it's all I can do to remember their Christian names."

"It would be a help if I could contact her," Fizz said, handling her disappointment well. "If there's anything you remember about her that might give me a start, it would be tremendously helpful."

Shona pursed her lips and thought for a minute. "It's funny, but when I have to come up with something specific I realise that I don't really remember her that well at all. Unless it's a memory that's being constantly reinforced it just sinks into the morass, all mixed up with snippets about a dozen other helpers. I have a vague recollection that she lived round about the town centre, but I couldn't even swear to that."

There didn't seem much point in pressing her any further. "Well, there's always the chance that something will come back to you. If so, could you get in touch? Mrs Torkington has a note of the office number."

"Sure. I'm sorry I couldn't be more of a help to you, but I'll keep thinking about it."

Fizz was conscious of an unfamiliar sinking of spirits as she walked back to the car. Self-confidence had never been her short suit but she was now having to face the fact that there was more to this detective business than met the eye, and maybe she was simply not up to it. In two — no, three — interviews she had

160

been unable to come up with one single piece of useful information, and she was not one step closer to her goal than she had been when she offered her services.

"How'd it go?" Zoe demanded.

"Great." Positive thinking.

Any hope of saving the day by getting some juicy gossip from Murray's neighbours died an early death. There was no reply to Fizz's prolonged lean on the bell, and no sign of life visible through the letterbox.

It was a long drive home.

CHAPTER
ELEVEN

Buchanan got home about five thirty and opened all the windows, in the hope of getting a through draught. It didn't make a lot of difference to the temperature but a peppery smell of nasturtiums and geraniums came drifting in from his neighbour's window box, and there was such a Mediterranean feel about it that he opened a can of McEwans and sat sipping it in a civilised manner while he decided what to do with his evening.

Janine didn't even come into the picture. He was still traumatised to the core by the way she had bawled him out the night before, and he had no intention of simply letting bygones be bygones. She could damn well apologise for her shrewishness or she could get lost. There was no way he was going to put up with that sort of slanging match every time he fell short of her idea of the perfect mate. Nor was he going to spend his life studiously avoiding any woman who might give Janine cause for concern. Not that she'd had cause this time. If it had been anyone else but Fizz, for God's sake, he might have understood.

One thing to be grateful for: at least it had happened in private. She could just as easily have walked in on him at lunchtime today and taken exception to the

162

presence of both Fizz and the exotic Zoe. There had been moments during that meeting when it would have been difficult not to draw the wrong conclusion.

Zoe, he seemed to remember, had always been a bit of a hot number, but it wasn't easy to be sure whether she gave the come-on to every man or whether she was more specific in her predilections. On the whole, he rather hoped she didn't have designs on him. It always made him nervous when a woman backed him into a corner, and besides, there was still the chance that Janine would see the error of her ways. He decided to play nine holes and have a bite to eat in the clubhouse, where the food was sometimes quite reasonable, but while he was showering his thoughts kept drifting back to Janine. Maybe it wasn't entirely her fault that she had put two and two together and made five. After all, Fizz had looked very different — possibly quite elegant, even, at a distance — that day outside his office, and looking at it in retrospect, her actions might easily have been misread to imply an entirely spurious intimacy.

One had to bear in mind that Janine had never met Fizz and therefore was quite unaware how far she was from being Buchanan's type. In point of fact — it suddenly occurred to him — he couldn't remember ever telling Janine that he had acquired an assistant for his free legal clinic at the community centre.

By the time he had changed into his golfing clothes his self-righteous hostility had been replaced by the suspicion that he had been at least in part to blame for the misunderstanding. It wasn't fair to blame Janine for getting her sums wrong when she had been short of a couple of digits. The least he could do was give her a ring and clarify matters.

The conversation had already played itself out in his head before he had tapped out her number: the usual "In that case, I'm sorry I lost my temper" and "Well, I'm sorry too" scenario culminating in his departure for the golf course with a clear conscience and the prospect of a suitably chastened Janine.

"Janine Hutcheson."

"Hi. It's me."

"Tam? Really." There was muted surprise in her tone, as though she hadn't expected him to have the brazenness to show up again.

"Yes. Really." He forced a short laugh. "You're not going to persist with this silly quarrel, surely?"

"Oh, it's a silly quarrel, is that all? Is that all it means to you?"

"That's all it *is*, Janine. Just a silly misunderstanding. This mystery woman you've got yourself all worked up about is only a girl who's been helping out at the community centre."

"Really? And that makes a difference, I suppose? You've been seeing more of her than of me lately, by all accounts, but because you met her at the community centre that's supposed to make it kosher, right?"

"Janine, she's been doing some work for me . . ."

"At nearly midnight? In your own home?"

His eyes were drawn to Janine's photograph on top of the bookcase, where a shaft of sunlight illuminated her smooth skin and silver-gilt hair, making it appear as

164

though she were lit from within. Her nose, he registered for the first time, was her least attractive feature.

"We're working on an important case right now and she's been putting in a lot of work — unpaid work. It's not going to last longer than a week or two, and shortly after that she'll be leaving to go to university."

"University?" There was a thoughtful pause. "She scarcely looks old enough."

He didn't omit to answer that remark deliberately, he was just taking rather a long time to consider whether it needed answering when she pressed on:

"I can't quite see why that should necessitate her being in your kitchen. Not only *being* there, but feeling sufficiently at home to make out a shopping list. I'm sorry, Tam, but this story doesn't really hang together, does it?"

That, Tam, decided later, was where she blew it. Between one speech, where she had appeared to be starting to melt, and another, when she had got right up his nose, the whole scene changed. One thing he was not going to do was crawl.

"I've told you the facts, Janine. Make of them what you will. I'm off for a round of golf before the light goes, but I'll be in later if you want to let me know what conclusions you've come to."

It was some small consolation that she slammed down the phone first. There was no reason why he should be the only one to be rattled. As he stood glaring at the receiver the doorbell rang.

His immediate reaction was a fervent hope that it was merely some flag-seller or meter-reader, but when

165

he opened the door to find Fizz leaning against the jamb he found himself rather pleased to see her. This was the more surprising since he had, only minutes ago, been irritated by the way she kept turning up on his tail like some heat-seeking missile and had been planning on telling her to cut it out. It shouldn't have been necessary to point out that it wasn't polite to pester her boss at his home, but then, she would probably never learn to regard him as her boss, and the mores of polite society meant nothing to her. If she wanted to do a thing she did it, and you could like it or lump it.

Tonight he was in a mood to like it. In fact Fizz was just what he needed to make him feel that Janine and not he was causing the friction between them. He couldn't imagine Fizz ever getting into a neurotic tizzy over some imaginary offence. She might banjo a wayward partner with a frying pan in his sleep, but she wouldn't regard it as an insurmountable blow to her psyche. Self-sufficiency was her middle name. Or possibly her first, as far as he knew.

She held out her hand and opened it to show a tape. "I thought I might as well drop this off."

"The playgroup stuff?" he said, taking it from her. "Anything special?"

"Nothing mind-blowing. Nothing that gives us any leads to follow up, anyway."

She straightened from the doorpost as though she were about to go, and he heard himself saying, "Want a coffee since you're here?"

166

"You sure know how to sweet-talk a girl. I could murder one."

Only when he led the way back into the lounge did he realise what a mess the place was in. Hurriedly kicking a pair of boxer shorts under the bookcase, he cleared a space for her to sit by sweeping his bathrobe and a pile of newspapers off the couch on to the floor.

"If there's nothing on this that needs to be followed up, I'll listen to it later," he said, putting the tape on the mantelpiece. "To be honest, I hadn't expected a great deal from Mrs Torkington anyway. She did confirm that it was actually Debbie who drew the pictures, I suppose?"

"Well, not exactly." She threw off her jacket and fell on to the couch in a manner guaranteed to do incalculable damage to the springs. The skimpy garment she was wearing looked more like an undergarment than a dress. Made of some thin material, it had shoestring shoulder straps and stopped well short of her knees. On someone like Zoe it would have been almost indecently sexy, but Fizz merely looked more schoolgirly than ever.

"She's not willing to swear to actually witnessing the act — it's been more than three years, after all — but there's another woman who could back her up: somebody who used to help out on a part-time basis. Trouble is, nobody can remember her name."

"No way of tracking her down?"

"Nope. Not unless some forgotten fact occurs to them. I said to let us know."

167

Buchanan shrugged, padding around in his bare feet, looking for his slippers. "I don't suppose it's worth bothering about. It was a long shot anyway. What about . . . No, never mind. I'll get it all from the tape. How do you want your coffee?"

"I don't suppose you've any herb teas?"

He was reminded, rather painfully, of the shopping list and felt a prickle of annoyance, swiftly censored as being nothing to do with Fizz. "Sorry, no. In fact I've run out of tea bags also, so it's coffee or nothing. A soft drink, maybe?"

"No. Coffee's fine. Could I have it white?"

This, quite fortuitously, he could manage, since Janine's rapid exit the evening before had left him with a pint of milk he'd probably have forgotten to buy for himself. Fizz followed him into the kitchen and surveyed the littered work surface and sinkful of dishes without comment while he heated the milk in the microwave.

"I don't know why it is," she said, picking some dead leaves off a parsley plant he'd forgotten he possessed, "but I'm getting a funny feeling about Murray after talking to him on the way to Phillis's place yesterday. I'm kind of suspicious that he's not being a hundred per cent frank with us. Do you ever feel that?"

"I'm not sure," he said, thinking about it. "I don't take everything he says as gospel, but then I never do that with any client. Murray . . . I imagine he could have the odd skeleton in the cupboard that he doesn't want us to see. I don't think we have to worry about it.

There wasn't anything specific that made you uneasy, was there?"

"I don't know." She ran her fingers contemplatively along the edge of the hob, picking up something sticky which she dislodged with the dish mop. "I got the impression he was lying when he said he was seeing his social worker today — nothing definite, just a sort of shiftiness. Also, there are areas he doesn't even want to discuss. Dianne, for instance."

Remembering the milk, he snatched it out of the microwave just as it started to bubble over. He could never be bothered with the timer but set it for ten minutes on full whatever he was cooking. "He doesn't want her involved. You can see why. Her career isn't going too well at the moment, and if it emerged that she'd been romantically linked with a convicted child molester, it would just about finish her."

"Yes, sure, I can accept that." She poured the milk on to the instant coffee and carried it through to the lounge, while he followed with the tray. "But let's face it, she belongs to somebody else now. The way it looks to me, she stiff-armed him from the day he was convicted and grabbed the next career-booster that happened to be passing. Why is he still protecting her?"

"He loves her?" Buchanan suggested.

"All the more reason to hate her. Frankly — okay, you know him better than I do, but as I was saying the other day, he doesn't strike me as the type to turn the other cheek, and if he wants Debbie back as much as he says he does, you'd think he'd be willing to drop Dianne in the clag without too much soul-searching.

Don't you get the feeling there's something more to this than meets the eye?"

"Possibly. But it doesn't have to be something sinister. If it has nothing to do with the case there's no reason he should make us privy to his private business."

That was not what she wanted to hear. Her bottom lip stuck out and she commandeered another biscuit as though to make the point. "It's not just that he's holding something back, it's the way he's doing it. He's definitely shifty."

"You could be right," Buchanan said, more to humour her than because he shared her suspicions. "I'll do a little gentle probing next time I'm talking to him and see how he reacts. I think a lot of the trouble is that he has tunnel vision when he's looking for a suspect. He is still concentrating on the people who gave evidence against him at his trial, but maybe we should be looking further afield."

Fizz sat up and drained her mug. "Who benefited by his being in jail? That's the crux of the matter." She held up her fingers. "One: Dianne. She got him out of the way while she married Sherry."

"Not much of a motive."

"Well, but she also effectively silenced him while she grabbed all the kudos for the script they'd produced already."

"Mmm. Maybe."

"Okay. Two: Phillis. She got revenge for what he did to her kid sister."

"She also got custody of Debbie."

Fizz erased this possibility with a sideways sweep of her hand. "That's the last thing she wanted. She admitted quite frankly that Debbie was nothing but a nuisance to her."

"Yes, I heard that on the tape, but we don't have to take her word for it. What age is she — forty-something? And childless. So maybe she doesn't have space in her life for a family, but the opposite is just as likely, isn't it?"

This seemed to strike Fizz as an interesting concept. She got up and wandered over to the window, staring out and nodding to herself at some unshared thought.

The band of sunshine that threw her shadow on the opposite wall was now so low that Buchanan's game of golf was effectively cancelled. He wasn't sure whether he cared much. He said, "Want some more coffee?"

"Love some."

He could see her through the half-opened door while he moved around the kitchen and knew that she was looking curiously at the avocado stain on the wallpaper. He should have done something about it before now, of course, but it took some time to psych himself up for that sort of thing, and besides, he rather liked the idea of leaving it there for a week or two to remind Janine of her intemperance.

Next time he looked she had switched her attention to his towelling bathrobe.

"Gosh, what a weight's in this thing," she said, pulling it on on top of her dress and knotting the belt around her waist. It came down almost to her bare feet and the sleeves hung well over her hands.

Buchanan had to smile. He came to the kitchen door to look at her. "You know what you look like? One of the seven dwarfs. Dopey, I think —"

Suddenly the smell of boiling milk hit his nostrils, and just as he made a leap for the microwave the doorbell rang.

"I'll get it," sang Fizz and disappeared.

"Dammit to hell!" In his haste his hand slipped on the wet handle and the jug went flying across the work surface, spraying super-heated milk on to the floor and catching his bare feet with a few tiny but agonising droplets. He let out a shout of pain and hopped sideways, stepping into the pool of milk which, on contact with the linoleum, had, mercifully, cooled slightly. He couldn't hear what was happening at the front door and he couldn't follow Fizz without tramping a trail of milky footprints across the living room carpet, so he had to wipe off the residue with the nearest thing to hand, which happened to be the dish towel. By the time he reached the lobby she had closed the door and was returning to the living room.

"Who was it?" he panted.

"Nobody," she said, throwing the bathrobe on a chair. "Just a woman looking for people called . . . Starling, I think she said. Something like that."

He frowned. "Can't think of anybody of that name around here."

"I'd have come to ask you but she seemed in rather a hurry."

"What did she look like?"

"Oh . . . grey-haired. Quite skinny."

He could hear a car outside pulling away with screeching tyres but by the time he reached the window it had gone. "Well, she *was* in a hurry, wasn't she?" he muttered. "Damn woman. Come and see the havoc she caused."

Together they cleared up the mess, Fizz wielding a mop and bucket as though she'd served her time at it, which, knowing Fizz, she probably had.

"You're wasting your time with that," she told him, watching him trying to ease the pain of his scalded foot by holding it under the cold tap. "You want some antihistamine ointment."

"Haven't got any."

"Try mind over matter."

He looked at her over his bent-up knee. "You don't believe in that rubbish, do you?"

"I've seen it work." She perched herself comfortably on the counter top and helped herself to a plum from the fruit bowl. "I worked with a girl in Sydney once. Agnes. She was a stripper."

Buchanan forbore to ask what position Fizz had held at that point.

"She was insanely proud of her hands and did everything she could to draw attention to them: scarlet nail varnish, huge sparkly rings, you know? Flashed them around a lot when she talked." She demonstrated with balletic movements. "Well, one day she said to me, 'You know, when I was a child I had the most ugly hands you ever saw. My fingers were so short and thick they looked like chipolata sausages. Then one day a friend of my father's told me about mind over matter.

He told me to look at my fingers every morning and say — *every day, in every way, my fingers are getting longer and longer*. And every morning since then I've done that — and just look at them now!'"

"And they were beautiful," Buchanan supplied obediently, curling his lip.

"Nope. They were like chipolata sausages."

Buchanan looked at her. He started to say, "I thought you said you saw it work?" then he realised that, from one point of view, it had worked, since Agnes was happy. Then he realised his foot had stopped hurting.

By the time they eventually sat down with their coffees Fizz seemed somewhat withdrawn.

"I really ought to be going," she said, glancing at the clock across the rim of her mug. "I hadn't realised it was that late. What about tomorrow? Do you still want me to see what's-her-name . . . the neighbour?"

"Mrs McCaulay. Yes, I think it's probably worthwhile," Buchanan said. "She looked after Debbie quite a bit at times, outside the playgroup hours, and you never know, you may be able to pick up a bit of useful gossip. Neighbours often know more of what's really going on than one would suspect. I'll get Beatrice to phone and make an appointment for you. What's your best time?"

"Any time suits me, but better make it after eleven if you can. Zoe likes a long lie."

He thought about saying something to her about Zoe's involvement in the case but then decided there was no point in putting her back up as she'd do what she liked anyway. Then he thought, the hell with it, and

174

said, "Speaking of Zoe . . . I think we have to be careful about involving too many people in this business, you know. As long as Zoe is confining herself to taxiing you and Murray around that's okay, but —"

"Oh, sure." She finished her coffee and stood up, looking round her for her jacket. "Zoe has no intention of muscling in. She wouldn't take the chance of putting a foot wrong where you're concerned." A small smile turned up one corner of her mouth. "She fancies you something rotten, you know."

"Rubbish," he returned unhesitatingly, keeping embarrassment at bay with the knowledge that her sole aim was to put him off balance. The fact that she was possibly speaking the truth mattered not at all: he was gradually learning how to handle her.

"And I'd be a lot happier, Fizz, if you'd resist making it your business. Frankly, I'd just as soon you and Murray hadn't recruited Zoe without clearing it with me, but since there's nothing to be done about it now, it would make things a lot simpler all round if you'd at least try not to make waves, okay?"

She raised her eyebrows. "Oooh. Touchy!"

"So, I'll see you tomorrow, then," he said, ignoring her. "If you record the McCaulay interview I can get the tape from you at Zoe's."

"Okay. Ta-ra then."

It was too late by the time she'd gone to start anything: too dark for golf, well past closing time at the paint and wallpaper shop. Blaming Fizz for his dissolution, he put on his shoes and socks and walked up to the Pear Tree for a pint.

CHAPTER
TWELVE

After a night of thunder, lightning and torrential rain a cool breeze swept in off the firth and the morning dawned like a day in spring. Fizz went for a walk through Holyrood Park, climbed Arthur's Seat and Salisbury Crags, came home, had a shower, did some washing and walked over to Zoe's place before ten thirty.

Zoe looked pretty rough. She said she hadn't slept well and spent much of the drive to the McCaulays' place in Berwick trying to justify to Fizz her belief that they weren't wasting time and energy on Murray Kingston. It was evident that she was still dreading having to talk to Murray that evening about his relationship with Dianne, but Fizz wasn't in a particularly sympathetic mood right then. She had her own daemons to deal with this morning.

She had never been a martyr to conscience; had never been able to afford the luxury. For the past nine years she had been on her own, making a life for herself in various parts of the globe, and she had learned the hard way that nobody gives a sucker an even break. She had her own moral limits, which she truly believed were no wider than the next guy's, but within these limits she did what she had to do to survive. If she had to lie, she lied. As long as it did no lasting harm. If she had to manipulate people, that was okay too, but only if it was necessary.

Unfortunately, her behaviour yesterday evening had been way outside the limits. By no stretch of the imagination had it been necessary, and the lasting harm it had caused was still to be evaluated but, in terms of the Janine/Buchanan relationship, was probably considerable.

She was still unable to justify it in her own mind except for the fact that it had started out as an admittedly childish bit of leg-pulling and had simply got out of control: a defence mechanism, in fact, which had gone off half cocked.

As soon as she'd spotted the silver-blonde head emerging from the BMW below her she'd known that a confrontation was imminent: a confrontation in which Janine held the high ground. Superiority was Janine's weapon, and she'd use it: the faintly amused appraisal, the condescending handshake, the hint of raised eyebrow at Fizz's skimpy chain-store dress and the subsequent thinly veiled insolence in every word till Fizz took the hint and buggered off.

The idea of answering the door dressed in Buchanan's bathrobe had popped into her mind, and she had responded to it impulsively, in the hope of wrong-footing Janine before she got into her stride.

It shouldn't have happened the way it did. Buchanan should have followed her to the door immediately and put Janine's mind at rest — or nearly at rest — by saying, "This is Fizz, my assistant at the community centre. She's just trying on my dressing gown," or words to that effect. Janine, having been just about to throw a wobbly, would then be totally off balance, not knowing whether to believe him or not and too demoralised to act the duchess to Fizz.

Close up, however, she was even more obnoxious than the picture Fizz had formed of her from (a) her one telephone conversation with her in the legal advice office, and (b) the comprehensive character reference Donna had given her, based on her frequent phone calls to Tam which Donna had eavesdropped on as a matter of course.

Overtopping Fizz by about six inches, she weighed in at no more than eight and a half stone: boobs like bee stings, hips like elbows, and arms like ET's. Her abundant silver-blonde hair was cut in a smooth, jaw-length bob that would have cost enough to keep Fizz for a month, and her face had the eggshell purity that only expensive make-up can achieve. She was wearing black: skin-tight pants and a loose silk blouse, topped with a short ermine bolero.

It was the real fur that did it. If it had needed anything further to tip Fizz's mental scales in favour of deliberate devilry, that was it. Deep in her guts she believed that a woman who could kill several beautiful animals just to decorate her own body — and on a day like this, who needed a bolero? — deserved everything that was coming to her. Her hand froze in the action of opening the robe and the words of explanation died on her lips.

"Darling —" Janine had started to say as the door opened, then her immaculately tinted lips fell apart in disbelief and her eyes narrowed to malign slits. For perhaps three heartbeats she stood there, radiating outrage, and then, without a word, she whirled and ran down the stairs, slamming the lower door with a crash.

Fizz knew she had gone too far. She knew she should have run after her, uttering loud cries of reassurance and apology, or at least she should have alerted Buchanan to the imminent end of a beautiful friendship. But for some reason, she did neither. And it was this anomaly, rather than the trick she had pulled on Janine, that was the main cause of her uneasiness.

There was a huge gulf between administering a tiny, well-deserved pinprick and letting things go so far as to cause what might be a serious rift between Buchanan and his girlfriend. Had that been her hidden agenda from the beginning, and if so, why? Not for Donna's sake, because she had never had any intention of talking up Donna to Buchanan and would have been wasting her time if she'd tried.

Okay then, did she think she was doing Buchanan a favour? What favours had he ever done her? And if he got himself hooked to a selfish, jealous and ill-tempered virago, what business was it of hers?

Even the episode of the shopping list had not been totally innocent, as she had tried to tell herself, otherwise why had she written in such exaggeratedly baroque handwriting, full of loops and twirls and with a tiny circle instead of a dot above the "i"? She'd hoped

Janine would see it and wonder a little, that's why. And subsequent events seemed to indicate that she had.

What, Fizz wondered, had got into her to make her lose all sense of proportion, all control over her impulsive actions? And why, for that matter, had she been so inordinately pleased to discover that there were still the same number of condoms in the bathroom cabinet as there had been on her first visit?

No acceptable explanation occurring to her in the interim, she was glad to get out of the car at the McCaulays' house and turn her mind to other things.

A dog's barking started in the distance and rapidly increased in volume as it raced to the door.

"Quiet, you! Oh, get over, Bracken!" said a man's voice which continued without a break as the door opened. "Hello, you're right on time. It's just struck eleven. Come away in and don't bother about him; he's just a big softie. Get down, Bracken, you pest! He didn't rip your tights, did he?"

Fizz had already dealt with Bracken in her own sweet way by giving him a sharp and unexpected knee in the chest as he leapt upon her, unnoticed by his owner but jarring enough to let him see that boisterousness was not going to be tolerated. In fact, he was a magnificent golden retriever with a good head and intelligent, well-spaced eyes, and his only problem was immaturity. He was almost fully grown but still had the loose-jointed hocks of a puppy, and would probably be a useful dog in another six months or so.

He rushed ahead of them into the lounge, plumed tail waving importantly, as though he wanted to be the

180

first to announce the arrival of a visitor to the woman who was just emerging from the open kitchen doorway beyond.

"Here's your lady from the lawyer's office," said Mr McCaulay, adding as Fizz shook hands, "I'll take this brute out for a run and leave you to it."

"Don't let me chase you away," Fizz said quickly. "I'm just looking for some background information about Debbie, but I expect you knew her fairly well yourself. If you'd care to stay and give us the benefit of your opinion I'm sure it would be all to the good."

"Oh, I don't know." He sat down uncertainly and looked at his wife. "I don't think there's much I could contribute."

Mrs McCaulay returned his look blank-faced. It was impossible to determine whether they were trying to communicate some unspoken thought or not. They were so alike that if Fizz hadn't known they were man and wife she'd have taken them for not just brother and sister, but twins. He was the taller, though not by much, and they were both dark-eyed, dark-haired and grossly overweight. Neither of them could sit upright in their armchairs but had to lean backwards at an angle of forty-five degrees to make room for their bellies to fit in between their ribcages and their thighs.

"You might as well stay," Mrs McCaulay said. "But put him in the kitchen first or we'll get no peace. And you can bring through the tray. You'll take a cup of coffee, Miss Fitzpatrick? Bracken, go to your basket. That's better."

Fizz removed several golden hairs from her skirt, okayed the use of the tape recorder, and was ready to start before Mr McCaulay returned with the coffee things.

Mrs McCaulay forestalled her. "I must say I'm surprised at them sending a wee lassie like yourself to talk about a nasty business like this. When they said 'Miss Fitzpatrick' I thought it would be an older woman."

Fizz gave a little sigh. "If you knew some of the cases I've had to deal with, Mrs McCaulay! This one's not so bad."

"The lady who phoned from your office said that there was some question as to whether Murray was really guilty or not."

"That's right." Fizz nodded. "Does that surprise you?"

The McCaulays exchanged glances. "Well, I don't know, really," said she. "It's not easy to believe that a father would do that to his own wee girl — what they said he did. Oh, I know it happens, but it was hard to credit that Murray would be a man like that."

"Mind you," her husband qualified, "when the police tell you they can prove a thing, you start doubting your own judgement a bit. You can't help it. Doesn't matter if you've known a person for years, you start to wonder. Things that you wouldn't have thought twice about before — well, you look at them a different way. Know what I mean?"

A little trill of hope fluttered at the back of Fizz's skull. Mrs McCaulay pushed a plate of shortbread towards her, and she took a bit, carefully not looking at either of them. "What was it that made you unsure about Murray?"

Their eyes met again across the coffee table. Clearly, anything necessitating the voicing of an opinion had to be a committee decision. This time the unvoiced proposal was rejected.

"I don't think it would be very neighbourly to say, really," said he, earning an approving nod from she. "Even if he's not a neighbour any more."

Fizz put down her coffee cup and gave him a gentle smile. "I know how you feel, Mr McCaulay. But it's Murray who's instigating this enquiry and, let's face it, the truth can't do him any further harm, it can only help him. So, please don't worry about telling me anything that might look to you as though it were libellous. I'm sure that's not your intention, and anything you tell me will go no further than my boss, Mr Buchanan, who's in charge of the enquiry."

"It was all very problematic anyway," Mrs McCaulay muttered, flashing a sideways glare at her husband for proffering this information without clearing it with her.

McCaulay looked embarrassed. "You can't help jumping to conclusions, you see. First he's arrested on this disgusting charge and then there's these people at his door, looking for him."

"What people were these, Mr McCaulay?" Fizz breathed.

"Two young lads. Well, men really. Must have been in their middle twenties at least. Gay, they were. That's what they call it nowadays, though you can't help thinking it's a bit of a misnomer. Life can't be very gay for the poor devils, can it? Wouldn't wish it on my worst enemy."

"When was this?" Fizz didn't bother to debate the issue.

"Just after Murray went into jail, wasn't it?" Mrs McCaulay, now reconciled to having it out in the open, confirmed this with a nod. "Before the house was sold. They came knocking at his door once or twice and then they rang our bell to ask if we knew where he was."

"We didn't tell them, of course," said she. "None of our business. I told them he was away for a while but his mail was being forwarded so they could drop him a letter."

"Probably nothing to do with Murray's . . . um . . . habits," said he, "but you can't help putting two and two together."

"Absolutely not," Fizz reassured him, firmly resisting the impulse to mention that this kind of thinking started the Holocaust. "Did they say why they were looking for Murray?"

A quick committee meeting produced nothing.

"Is there anything else you could tell me about them, I wonder? Anything that might help me to trace them?"

Synchronised head-shaking.

"Well, never mind," Fizz said, generously. "I'm glad you told me anyway, it might repay looking into. Now then, how about Debbie? I expect you saw quite a bit of her?"

Mrs McCaulay's face softened. "Every day of her life, till they took her away. Anne used to park her pram out in the garden, down there at the fence in the shade of our apple tree, and when she wasn't napping she was waving her wee fists around trying to reach the leaves and squealing away blue murder."

"And when she got older, Anne and Murray used to leave her with you sometimes?"

"Now and then, just. They started sending her to that playgroup place down by the park when she was not much more than a toddler." There was a hint of disapproval, smugly repressed, in her tone. She had her own standards of child-rearing, Fizz was to understand, and these had not necessarily been shared by the Kingstons.

"Anne had a drink problem, I believe?"

The McCaulays clashed eyes, and he said, "You know about that? Yes, they had their share of problems, those two, and no mistake."

"And that's when Debbie started being left with you?"

"Yes." Mrs McCaulay hauled herself up in her chair to pour more coffee. She had to splay her legs to make way for her belly, and this exposed a panoramic view of (thankfully long) white knickers and wall-to-wall cellulite. "A cheery wee thing she was, and no trouble. I'd have had her every day if her parents had wanted it. They didn't have to go spending all that money on playgroups and baby-sitters, but you can't tell young parents anything these days. If a thing costs money it's got to be good."

"I expect they didn't want to impose on you," Fizz lied, knowing that the playgroup would have had her

185

money if she could have afforded it. A bright child like Debbie needed stimulation, not cotton wool.

Mrs McCaulay confirmed this. "They said they wanted her to be with other children, and I suppose it did her good. She was a bit of a little madam before she started there. A bit precocious, the way they get when they're with grown-ups all the time."

"So she was still coming to you occasionally, even after she started at playgroup?"

Mr McCaulay took that one. "Right up to the time of the trial, yes, but only at weekends, when Anne's sister out at Aberdour couldn't take her."

"Or," put in his wife, "when Sue wasn't available to let him get out to his evening class."

This was news to Fizz. "What was he studying at evening class?"

Mr McCaulay looked amused. "Not studying, my dear. Teaching."

"Of a sort," Mrs McCaulay expanded. "He used to run some sort of writers' circle. Wednesday nights. Most times he had Sue in to babysit, but now and then she couldn't come, so one of us would sit with her. Just two or three hours, it was. He was always back by nine thirty or so."

"Did she ever wake up?" Fizz asked. "Ever have any nightmares or anything?"

They checked with each other and agreed on a negative.

"So, what drew your attention to the fact that she might have been subjected to abuse?"

This question needed no referral. They had been expecting it. "She kept complaining of a sore bottom," Mrs McCaulay stated, her face, in spite of the time lapse, slackening with distress. "I didn't twig at first — well, you don't immediately leap to a conclusion like that — but she mentioned it again when I was taking her to the toilet, so I had a look and found quite a bit of inflammation. As soon as Murray got home I told him about it and offered to take her to the doctor, but he said no, he'd see to it himself, and that was the last I heard of it. Debbie didn't mention it again and I never gave it another thought till the social worker came round asking me if I'd seen anything suspicious, and then, of course, it came back to me." Her voice wavered and she gave herself a couple of sips of coffee. "If I had only been a wee bit more suspicious at the time, I might have prevented . . ."

Mr McCaulay leaned a little towards her but resisted patting her hand. "Don't start all that again, Joan. You know you couldn't possibly have known what was going on."

"Maybe nothing was going on," Fizz pointed out. "If it turns out that Murray spent three years in jail for something he didn't do, you'll be very glad that it wasn't you who started the process that put him there."

"There," said he, leaping upon this premise like a legionnaire upon a favourite camel. "That's something you never thought of."

It took her a minute to digest it. "So, if it wasn't Murray, who could it have been?"

187

Fizz gave her head a baffled little shake, munching shortbread and waiting to see where that train of thought led her.

"They had some funny friends, mind," she said to her husband, eyeing him as though she could plug into his memory as well as her own. "All those TV people, remember? Noisy bunch they were, with their coats over their shoulders and their scarves all wound round and round their necks as if they just wanted to be different. In and out at all times of the night. Drunk as monkeys most of the time, and the women — they were the worst!"

Mr McCaulay raised his eyebrows at Fizz and nodded knowingly. "That's where you should be looking, my dear. You know what they're like, those London folk: into all sorts of things. Drugs. Adultery. Anything for kicks. You only have to watch the plays on the telly. You can tell they think everybody's at it."

Joan was still rummaging through her recollections. "That actor, Alan. What was his name? Barry Something. Used to be in the soup advert."

"Barry Coben."

"Barry Coben. Yes, and his wife. She was an actress too. The one who played . . . ? You know. In the Dickens thing."

"Margot Something . . ."

"Margot Cole, that's right. And there was that woman with the red hair. That writer. Dianne Frazer Ballantyne. We spoke to her several times, didn't we, Alan? A right one for the drink she was, I don't mind telling you. She was never out the place."

"What was she like?" Fizz asked, with a smile that admitted to nothing other than a normal curiosity about one of the Other Half.

"Seemed very nice," Mr McCaulay admitted. "Not that she ever said very much: just handed Debbie over and went on her way, really. We saw her fall down the steps one night, didn't we, love? Must have been well pickled."

"Handed Debbie over." Fizz nodded gently. "So she looked after her too sometimes."

"Oh, yes, quite often."

Glances were exchanged, then Mrs McCaulay murmured, "I don't know if you're aware . . . but . . . I think there was something going on between them."

"Her and Murray," Mr McCaulay clarified. "She stayed overnight plenty of times — after Anne's death, that was, of course. We used to see her leaving in a taxi in the mornings."

Fizz eyed the last piece of shortbread, decided against it, then thought, why not? and reached for it. After all, a small celebration was surely in order. What the McCaulays had told her proved that Murray had been lying when he said Dianne had nothing to do with the case. If she'd had access to Debbie for any length of time she was as suspect as anybody else, and Murray knew it.

Next question: was Murray Kingston merely trying to protect his girlfriend, or was he up to his scrawny neck in a whole new ballgame?

Nice one, that. She couldn't wait to phone Buchanan.

CHAPTER
THIRTEEN

There was a lift up to Zoe's tenth-floor flat, but Buchanan cut it dead and took the stairs, since he had been stuck behind his desk all day. He was, therefore, just a smidgeon out of breath as he rang the bell, and the sight of Zoe didn't help. She was wearing a dress of some shiny material which fitted her like a surgeon's glove, and her hair was all piled up and falling down again in a style that was definitely seductive.

"Hi. C'mon in, Tam. You're first to arrive."

He hadn't expected that. It was already twenty to eight and he had assumed, given Fizz's penchant for free food, that she, at least, would have been there before now. He gave Zoe the box of chocolates he'd brought her and allowed her to hang up his leather bomber jacket in the hall, and then followed her into the sitting room. A smell of cooking drifted in from the kitchen, something garlicky that reminded him of holidays in the south of France.

The late sun was slanting in at the window, giving the room a cosy glow. There was a crocheted throw over the back of the sofa, and the covers on the scatter cushions were hand-done patchwork — or so he deduced from the unfinished one that lay on a sewing table by the window, as if thrown down at the sound of the doorbell. All this was another surprise, establishing Zoe as an old-fashioned girl, a home-maker, which only went to show that one shouldn't be taken in by appearances.

He watched her tidying away her sewing things, the material of her dress stretched tightly across her round bottom.

"Nice dress," he said innocently when she turned and caught him looking.

"It's new." She smiled, and did a twirl with her hands held above her shoulders. "Jenners' sale. I had a super time this afternoon after we got back from Berwick. They had Charnos lingerie at half price, three shower gels for the price of two, *wonderful* swimwear at a fraction of what you'd normally pay, and hats to *die* for at a third off! Couldn't believe it!"

The doorbell rang and she hurried out to the hall to answer it, wobbling interestingly in her three-inch heels.

It was Murray. Their voices drifted in from the hall while she, presumably, relieved him of his jacket. He heard Murray say, "Sure, I can get a taxi home, but what's it about?" Then Zoe mumbled something inaudible and Murray answered, "Why can't you tell me now?" Zoe replied in another cryptic whisper, but it was perfectly clear to Buchanan that they were involved in something he was to know nothing about, and he didn't like it. This impression was confirmed when they both came in seeming somewhat distracted.

Murray appeared altogether much healthier than he had that first day in the legal advice office, but Tam still found him infinitely depressing. Every time he saw him he was reminded that he was looking at a man who had been only two classes above him at school; a man with thinning hair and baggy eyes, a man whose shoulders were bowed and whose skin was blotchy, and who gave the appearance of being headed irreversibly downhill to the grave. It wasn't nice. No matter how often Buchanan drew to mind the example of his other close friends, most of them within a year or two of his own age and in their prime, Murray always managed to loom larger in his vision.

It was plain, however, that Buchanan had the opposite effect on Murray.

"Tam! Good to see you." He set a bottle of Spanish plonk on the table and sank on to the couch with what appeared to be his last ounce of energy. "My God, Zoe, what's that wonderful smell? I hope it's for us."

"It's nothing exciting," she protested, busying herself by setting out napkins and cutlery. "Just chicken goujons with ratatouille and some garlic bread. I thought it would be easy to have on our knees."

Buchanan thought he could detect a certain tenseness in her manner since Murray's arrival. No doubt she was thinking about the information Fizz had uncovered from the McCaulays regarding Dianne's access to Debbie, and waiting for the inevitable altercation. Well, the matter was bound to come up at some time during the course of the evening, but in deference to one's hostess, one could at least postpone it till after they'd eaten.

192

He kept the conversation on safe subjects, stalling Murray's demands to be brought up to date, till Fizz arrived, just on eight o'clock, dressed in her usual baggy sweater and jeans. She removed her Docs and curled up in a corner of the couch opposite Murray. "When do we eat?" she asked Zoe, brightly.

"Now. We've only been waiting for you, and I'm sure we're all starving. Murray, would you be a sweetie and open the wine? Tam, I'm putting you in charge of the videos. We're going to have to view as we eat, otherwise we'll be here all night." Zoe wiggled into the kitchen, followed by Fizz, and they both returned, after a short conversation, with trays of food.

When everyone was settled Tam started the video, and the conversation died as the opening credits of *Fade to Black* started to roll.

They sat through the entire hour and a half virtually without exchanging a word. Zoe was the only one of them to have seen it before, but even she was drawn into it so deeply that she forgot the food on her lap. The story of a young homosexual man's search for happiness, his loving relationship with an older man and his subsequent death from AIDS, it never for a second descended to the purely sentimental, and when it ended, both the girls had wet eyes and Murray looked as moved as Buchanan felt.

After a brief post-mortem Tam started the second video, *A Cure for all Diseases*. It took about ten minutes for the fidgeting to start, and by halfway through, Fizz was sighing audibly and trying to catch everyone else's eye, her finger clearly itching for the fast forward button. Neither Zoe nor Murray made any comment, although at one rather unfortunate piece of dialogue Tam did hear himself mutter a faint, involuntary, "Oh dear!"

It was after eleven when *A Cure for all Diseases* reached its all too timely end, and there seemed to be a general consensus of opinion that the less said about it, the better. Number three was entitled *Throw Away the Scabbard*. The characters were reasonably well drawn but the situations were unlikely, and there didn't seem to be any discernible plot. Buchanan felt himself totally in sympathy with Fizz and Murray, who both expressed themselves as bewildered, and he voted unhesitatingly in favour of Fizz's motion to skip to the end. Zoe was the only one who didn't appear relieved when the picture faded from the screen, but it must have been solely a feeling of loyalty to her ex-partner that kept her looking so enthralled.

"Well," said Fizz, who didn't give a damn what anyone thought of her, "I'm sorry about this, folks, but in my opinion the nicest thing one can say about Dianne is that she failed to live up to her early promise."

There was no way anyone could deny it, not even Zoe, who busied herself in tidying away the plates and coffee cups while Murray made excusing noises and, quite patently, cudgelled his brains for some extenuating circumstances to cite.

"You can see she was trying for something different in the last two. Going more for atmosphere and character. Okay, maybe it didn't quite come off, but the blame for that has to be shared by a fair bunch of people: the director, the lighting director, the camera-man, the casting . . . I think, personally, that with more sensitive treatment both productions could have achieved what she hoped for."

"Yes, and I'm Margaret Thatcher," said Fizz rudely. "Come off it, Murray. You know crap when you see it, or what were you doing teaching English?"

Murray immediately reddened up and started to bluster, but Tam broke in calmly, putting a firm brake on the escalating asperity.

"The difference between the first play and the other two is very marked, whatever the cause. Even given the premise that Dianne was trying for something different — and why would she do that when her strengths were quite clearly well displayed in the original format? — I think we'd all agree that the latter two could almost have been written by a different person."

"No, that's not necessarily the . . ." Murray began, but then caught Tam's eye and decided to shut up.

"I'm not saying they were, Murray. Even in the first one there were jarring notes, similar to those we saw in the other two, but the strength of the plot was enough to mitigate them. What the subsequent work lacks is any real depth of feeling." He paused, letting this sink in. Fizz started to open her mouth but he frowned her down. "So, you see where this leads us, Murray? I'm sorry, but it's pointing quite unequivocally back to the old question of whether you had a hand in number one."

"I swear to you, Tam," Murray said, raising his eyes from his clasped hands to fix them fully on Buchanan's, "as God's my judge, I never wrote a word of that play. I never even saw it in typescript. Tonight was the first time I ever saw it."

Tam studied him, his suspicions irresistibly hamstrung by Murray's convincing sincerity. Dammit, he told himself, Murray has to be lying, so why do I believe him? "All right," he said, "if it wasn't you who helped her, who was it?"

Murray's eyes clicked open another f-stop. "I don't know. Nobody. If there had been someone helping her I'd have known about it. There wasn't anybody."

"Then why were the other two so . . . different?"

"I've no idea, Tam. I haven't spoken to her since my arrest."

Fizz made a sudden movement as though she was about to say something, but Zoe spoke first, gently but with an undertone of urgency that struck an odd note.

"Listen, Murray, it's important that you tell us everything you know. If you're holding something back — even something that seems unimportant — don't do it. Please. It might be something that Tam can use to clear you — to help you get Debbie back."

He spread his hands in an attitude of helplessness. "If there's the least chance I might get Debbie back, you can bet I won't be leaving any stone unturned till I get her. I spend my days trying to think of anything I could have missed."

"Like the fact," Tam said in a low voice that blanketed his anger and frustration, "that Dianne frequently had access to Debbie just before your arrest?"

Murray's face twitched. He kept his eyes on Buchanan's, but warily, as though watching for an early warning of wrath to come. "Not frequently, Tam. And not for about two years."

"Dammit to hell, Murray, what are you playing at?" Buchanan tried to keep his voice level but he heard it grate. "You swore to me she had nothing to do with the case, never came within a mile of Debbie, couldn't possibly have anything to do with it."

"Tam, listen to me, it's God's truth I'm telling you." Murray leaned forward, stretching out a hand to Buchanan but not touching him. "Dianne is a side issue. She was nowhere near that business. She may have looked after Debbie once or twice but she had no reason in the world to bear me a grudge. I'd have told you she looked after Debbie sometimes but you'd only have wasted time checking her out." He looked round at Fizz and Zoe and then back at Buchanan, clearly searching for the right words.

"We . . . we were very deeply in love, Tam. She was completely devastated when I was accused but she never doubted my innocence — not for a second. She was the only person who stood by me, and she would have gone public about our relationship, if I'd let her, in the hope that it might have swung the jury. Dammit, I told you — she wasn't even in the country when it all blew up."

"That's true, Tam," Zoe put in gently, her face pinched by her anxiety to calm down the situation. "I remember that. Dianne was in New York for the International TV Festival. We were all excited about it. She couldn't have been in Edinburgh at the time, and that's a simple fact."

"It's not about facts, it's about *knowing* Dianne." Murray shook his head in apparent irritation at being unable to convey the certainty he felt, and added, without much confidence, "If you could understand the sort of relationship we had . . . if you'd seen how distraught Dianne was, you'd know that . . ."

"That's not the point," Fizz put in, sticking out her chin aggressively. "The point is that you don't trust us enough to tell us the truth."

"No, that's *not* the point," Murray returned sharply, showing a spark of aggression of his own. "The point is that *you* wouldn't have trusted *me*! If I'd admitted that Dianne had access to Debbie you'd have insisted on quizzing her about it."

"Well, that's what's going to happen now," Tam told him. "If you want Fizz and me — and Zoe too — to spend any more of our time on this business, Dianne will have to be questioned whether you like it or not."

"She's married now, Tam," Murray pleaded, kneading his hands. "You must see what an embarrassment — how dangerous, professionally and personally — it is for her to be connected to me in this way. I wouldn't be surprised if even Sherry knows nothing about our relationship."

"We'll be discreet," Fizz reassured him, but not with any visible effect on his spirits. No doubt he was thinking, as was Buchanan, that the two concepts, discretion and Fizz, didn't even belong in the same sentence. He was probably much relieved when Buchanan said tiredly:

"It won't be necessary for us both to see her. I'll talk to her myself, Murray, and you can be assured I won't cause her any embarrassment."

Fizz wasn't at all pleased about that and didn't mind showing it, though she stopped short of actually voicing a complaint. Bouncing to her feet, she strode across the room and stood glaring at Debbie's drawing which was pinned to a cork memory board together with lists of witnesses and sundry notes. Taking it down, she folded it into her pocket. Murray and Buchanan ignored her but Zoe eyed her with a slight frown, as though she was waiting for an outburst.

"Okay," Murray was saying, "but let me arrange it. I don't want you to be phoning her at a time when Sherry is likely to be around. He'd wonder who you were and what you wanted to see her about, and I don't want her to have to start telling lies or covering up anything."

"Sure. Don't worry about it. But make it soon, Murray. Tomorrow or the next day." Buchanan glanced at his watch. "God, look at the time."

Zoe stood up and headed for the door to get Buchanan's jacket, but halted before she got there and said, "Tam, did you tell Murray that there were people looking for him?"

Murray sat up. "Who? When was this?"

"You'll hear the tape," Buchanan said. "The McCaulays mentioned a couple of young men who'd been trying to reach you shortly after you started your sentence. They told them to write to you, so I suppose it's no news to you. Was it something we should know about?"

Murray furrowed his brow. "Young men? Were they . . . Oh, right! Yes, I know who they were, they contacted me eventually. No, it was nothing to do with the case."

"They were pretty anxious to see you, apparently," Fizz said, coming back to her seat and leaning forward so that she could see his face.

"It wasn't anything important."

"Mr McCaulay seemed to think they were homosexuals." Fizz clearly felt that she had uncovered a clue and was not going to abandon it without a fight. "It made them wonder about you, rather. Can't blame them."

Murray flushed, and his hand twitched in the sort of reflex gesture people make when they see a fly but know that it'll move before they can swat it.

Zoe had, by now, returned with Buchanan's jacket and was able to put Murray out of his misery. "I bet I know who they were." She gave him an impish smile. "They were just lads from your evening class, weren't they?"

He returned her smile gratefully. "Yes, they were. What with all the worry and hassle, I'd forgotten to cancel the classes and they didn't know what was happening."

"I thought so." Zoe gave him a smile and then extended it to include the others. "What about another cup of coffee? You don't have to rush, do you, Tam?"

"Not for me, thanks, Zoe," Buchanan said, just as Fizz was transferring the last chocolate to one cheek to say yes. "I'm going to have to drag myself away."

Fizz made a swift, and quite visible, choice between another coffee and a possible lift home, and rejected the former. Murray settled back in the couch and accepted.

"Okay," Buchanan said, while Zoe poured, "so tomorrow, Fizz, you're seeing the baby-sitter, right?"

"Tomorrow?" Zoe looked from one to the other, furrowing her brow. "I thought we were interviewing her on Monday?"

"We were," Fizz said, pausing in the lacing-up of her Docs to tap her forehead. "I forgot to tell you. She phoned Beatrice to say she'd be in Edinburgh tomorrow, so we don't have to drive down to Berwick. I'm meeting her at lunchtime."

"Great." Zoe stretched like a cat, testing the seams of her red dress almost to destruction. "That means I get a long lie."

"What time's your appointment?" Buchanan asked Fizz.

"Twelve thirty. The baby-sitter — what's her name? Sue? — she's got shopping to do in some boutique in Princes Street, so we're meeting for a sandwich lunch in the Gardens."

"Right. Are you clear on what you're going to ask her?"

"Just the usual, I guess. What made her suspect Debbie was being abused, and if she ever said or did anything else that might either confirm or contradict that idea."

"You could also find out if she knew of anyone else who might have had access to Debbie. It's not unknown for baby-sitters to take friends along to keep them company." He stood up, digging in his pockets for his car keys. "Can I give anyone a lift?"

He wasn't surprised when Fizz accepted, nor was he surprised when Murray didn't. It only confirmed his suspicion that Zoe had asked Murray to stay on after the other two left, and it made him very curious indeed to know why.

CHAPTER
FOURTEEN

It was now three days since he had seen or heard from Janine, and Buchanan's thoughts on the matter had changed almost hourly. He had fully expected her, on hearing his explanation for the misunderstanding, to pop round fairly soon with the makings of a cosy dinner and an attitude of conciliation and atonement. When this had not transpired, his own sentiments had cooled sharply and a "stuff *her*" reaction had set in, accompanied by the conviction that she would come crawling to him rather than vice versa.

He found it particularly hard to swallow that, after knowing him for more than seven months, she could so misread his character as to suppose him capable of running two women at the same time. It made a farce of their partnership and made him wonder if his own estimation of Janine was based on anything but the most superficial evidence. This led to a period of considerable soul-searching, during which he began to realise that he had come uncomfortably close to making a misguided Life Decision, and resolved to get to know Janine a lot better before taking any hasty steps towards regularising their relationship.

Three days after the avocado incident, however, it was getting to look too much as if Janine were taking the initiative to break off friendly relations, and that was another matter entirely. It should be a mutual decision, at the very least.

On the one hand, he had made a firm resolution that *he* would not be the first to contact *her*, but on the other, why should she have the last word? Finding himself with twenty minutes clear before lunchtime, he grabbed the phone and dialled the number of Pzazz.

"Pzazz Fashions. Can I help you?"

Familiar response. Unfamiliar voice.

"Can I speak to Miss Hutcheson, please?"

"I'm sorry, *Ms* Hutcheson is not here at the moment. This is Ms Brodie, the manageress, perhaps I can be of assistance?"

Manageress? He recognised the name as someone who had worked in the shop for a couple of years, but since when had she been the manageress? Buchanan said, "Thank you, no. It's a personal matter. When will Ms Hutcheson be available?"

There was a short pause. Buchanan could hear papers being shuffled. "It's Mr Buchanan, isn't it?"

Buchanan grunted corroboration.

"In that case, Ms Hutcheson left a message to let you know she has decided to open the shop in Aberdeen and will be away for some weeks."

It felt like a punch in the throat. "I see. Is there a phone number where she can be contacted?"

"Not at the moment, Mr Buchanan, I'm afraid. She said she'd be in touch when she got settled."

"I see. Well, when she phones in, ask her to give me a ring, would you?"

The realisation that it was as final as that came as a complete surprise. He sat for several minutes trying to work out how he felt about it — *really* felt, underneath the surface reaction of anger and exasperation — then Beatrice came in with some letters to be signed and made him shelve the matter by saying:

"Miss Fitzpatrick called and wanted a word with you, but I told her you were engaged and might not be in the office this afternoon." Her thin face registered mild indulgence. "I noticed that your diary is clear, and since you have your golf tournament on Saturday . . ."

Buchanan had begun, only half an hour ago, to consider the possibility of a couple of practice rounds, but he was well used to Beatrice's habit of being a step ahead of him. He nodded. "Thank you, Beatrice. What did Miss Fitzpatrick want? Did she say?"

Beatrice dipped her rigorously permed head to refer to her notebook. "She couldn't say it in front of Murray, but she thinks there's more in the two gays than meets the eye, and do you want her to follow up that line of enquiry? She's phoning back after her lunchtime appointment."

"No," Buchanan said. He didn't want Fizz dashing at what she perceived to be clues like a bull at a gate. If he decided to point her in that direction he wanted to prime her carefully beforehand. "Tell her 'no', Beatrice. Not before we discuss it. Tell her I'll be home by six thirty. She can phone me then."

In point of fact, the matter of the two mystery callers had been at the back of his mind all morning, and now that he brought the matter under closer scrutiny he was rather inclined to believe that there might be more in Murray's patent embarrassment than having his sexual predilection thrown into question. One couldn't help but connect the two visitors with the hero of *Fade to Black*, which led to the question: was one of the two young men Dianne's collaborator on the screenplay, and if so, was it Murray who introduced them?

The significance of the fact that Murray had been jailed just before the screening of Dianne's first drama was not lost on Buchanan, and it was easy to see that if he were the only one, apart from her secret collaborator, to know that she had cribbed the entire story, it would be very much in her interest to have him out of the way and his word discredited. The further one looked into the facts of the case, the harder it was to discount the evidence against Murray's ex-lover.

Clearly, she should have been interviewed before now, and if Murray didn't set something up within the next couple of days, the matter would have to be taken out of his hands. But before he talked to Dianne, it might be productive to have a word with the two young men. If they had any connection with the TV play it would be as well to know it before confronting its putative author.

He would, he thought, be interested to know how Fizz proposed to track them down. There had been some mention of an evening class, but with Murray's old school closed for the summer recess, any details about that would be hard to come by. One could, of course, go straight to Murray for the information, but if he had anything to hide, or suspected that Dianne had, it would be too easy for him to deflect the investigation down time-consuming dead ends. And besides, if there were some real evidence against Dianne it would be so much more satisfactory to slap Murray in the face with it out of the blue, just to teach him a lesson for being so bloody dog-in-the-mangerish.

Remembering that Zoe seemed to have some knowledge of the class, Buchanan reached, on an impulse, for the phone and dialled her number.

"Zoe? Tam."

"Oh . . . Tam . . . hello." She sounded breathless, as though she had run for the phone.

"Zoe, listen. You remember the evening class you mentioned last night — the one those young men were in? Can you tell me anything about it?"

"Well, actually it wasn't an evening class, as such," she said. "I seem to remember it was more of a writers' circle. It was run in connection with a clinic or a hospice . . . something like that . . . a place for AIDS victims. They had a day centre — I went to a jumble sale there one time with Murray and Dianne. It was run by a voluntary organisation but I can't remember the name."

"How come Murray was involved?"

"I don't know, really. I think the guy who ran the place . . . he was a social worker of some sort . . . I think he thought it would be good for the patients to

207

get their thoughts down on paper. Murray helped out for quite a while. Couple of years maybe."

Buchanan reached for his pen. "Whereabouts was this place?"

"Quite near Tweedside High, where we taught," she said. "I can't remember the name of the street, offhand, but it was just off the main avenue. Something House, it was called, I think."

"You don't know anyone who might know the name of the street?"

There was a second or two of silence, during which he could hear her tapping her teeth. "Haven't a clue, Tam. Sorry. Do you want to trace the two guys who were trying to reach Murray?"

"Yes. I think I ought to check them out." Frowning at his blank notebook, he drummed his pen and said, "Any ideas how I could locate the place?"

More tooth-tapping. Then, "I bet I could find it without too much trouble. I think I remember the route okay. Want me to try?"

"Zoe, that would be terrific. You're sure it's not —"

"No trouble," she said, and he could hear her smile. "Fizz doesn't need my services today and I'm at a bit of a loose end. Besides, it's in a good cause."

"Right. I'll drive and you can navigate."

So much for the golf practice this afternoon. Still, there would be compensations. Zoe might not be someone he was particularly drawn to, but as a balm to hurt pride she was just what he needed. She might or might not fancy him "something rotten", as Fizz phrased it, but she certainly knew how to massage a guy's ego.

The only negative factor was that they weren't likely to run into Janine.

Fizz had been sitting on a bench just below the floral clock for about ten minutes before Sue Young came along, and it was a surprise to see that she was Chinese. Her face was not the small, faun-like triangle so common in Asiatic girls, but broad and flat and the colour of a soda scone, and her eyes were tiny, with pronounced epicanthic folds. When she smiled, however, the sun came out.

"Sorry I'm late," she said, in a distinctly Edinburgh accent. "It takes you all morning to find what you're looking for in department stores these days."

"I know," Fizz said amiably, although she hadn't been in a department store in Edinburgh since her return.

Sue nodded with a "bet-your-ass" expression. "Who's crazy idea started the fashion of arranging everything by colour instead of by the type of garment? I've spent hours looking for something to wear with a black skirt, but instead of scanning the blouse section I had to work my way through the entire stock of separates."

"I suppose they hope that you'll see a pair of trousers you fancy while you're looking," Fizz offered.

"Maybe, but in fact I didn't have time to finish looking, so they lost a sale. And it's so hot in those places! That's why I like to take my lunch break in the Gardens. Get some fresh air."

"Right," Fizz agreed. She didn't usually eat much lunch, unless someone else was paying for it, but she had brought along some fruit so that Sue wouldn't have to eat alone.

"What's happening," she said, getting out her trusty tape recorder, "is that Murray Kingston is trying to get together some evidence to prove he was innocent of the charges against him, we — my boss, that is — are handling it for him. So, at the moment I'm talking to the people who gave evidence at his trial in case they can come up with any information that might help us."

Sue opened her eyes to their fullest extent, which wasn't much. "But he was guilty, wasn't he?"

"Well, maybe not. He says he wasn't, and my boss, who's known him for yonks, believes him. Actually, I have to say that, in spite of everything, I believe him myself. I think he might have been framed."

Sue chewed thoughtfully. "Who by?"

Fizz shrugged and gave her a sly smile. "To tell you the truth, I have my suspicions but I'm not naming any names, and anyway, I'm just the dogsbody. What about you? Know anybody who'd have liked to get the knife in?"

"Plenty," she said with conviction, giving Fizz a sharp but short-lived surge of optimism. "But only since the trial. I'd have castrated him myself if I'd got my hands on him." Her wonderful smile flickered briefly. "Just as well I didn't, if he turns out to be innocent after all."

"But you were pretty certain, at the time, that Debbie had been abused; if not by Murray then by someone else?"

Thick, stubby fingers broke a piece off her roll and threw it to a hopeful squirrel. "No. Actually, I never thought about abuse till afterwards. It was only after Mr Kingston had been arrested that I remembered Debbie complaining that her bottom hurt her."

"How often did she complain? More than once?"

"More than once, certainly. For a week or so, I think. Can't remember really. I told her dad but he said he knew about it and it was just a rash she'd got from wetting the bed."

"You didn't examine her yourself?"

"No way." She gave Fizz a quizzical look and shook her head. "I was, like, seventeen or something, and I was being paid to baby-sit, not to be a paramedic. Besides, if there had been signs that she'd been abused I wouldn't have recognised them ... Wouldn't recognise them even now, I don't suppose."

"No, nor would I," Fizz said. She could see that Sue had been blaming herself, like most of the other people involved, for not being more on the ball at the time. "I wouldn't like to be in the position of suspecting somebody, I'll tell you that. It must take guts to drop somebody in the clag. You'd have to be awfully sure."

Sue raised her eyebrows and looked away across the grass. "Not for me. Not any more," she said quietly. "If ever I suspect some kid's being got at I'll scream blue murder. Don't care if it's a false alarm."

Fizz looked at her with some sympathy. The whole business was a moral nightmare, no matter which way you looked at it. "Did you think of telling anyone else about Debbie's complaints?"

"Just Mrs McCaulay, but she said she'd already mentioned it to Mr Kingston and he'd said he'd consult the doctor."

"You were in contact with Mrs McCaulay, were you? Did you see much of her?"

"She lived next door. Also, I was going out with her son, Billy."

Somehow Fizz had not imagined the McCaulays with a family. Their almost telepathic closeness didn't seem to permit of any third party or parties. "So, it was through the McCaulays that you got the baby-sitting job?"

Sue didn't look any too sure. "Well, I suppose it was. Mr Kingston knew me from school, of course."

Fizz finished her apple and donated the core to the squirrel which was still hanging around in a belligerent sort of manner, chittering menacingly. She rather liked its style. "Were you in his class?"

"No. Billy was, but I got Miss Paton for English."

Fizz found herself smiling at the thought of Zoe as a schoolteacher. She couldn't resist saying, "How did you get on with her?"

"Miss Paton?" Sue looked surprised at the question. "She was okay. The boys thought she was the bee's knees. Used to draw schematic drawings of her on the toilet walls."

Looking forward to apprising Zoe of this fact and watching her reaction, Fizz smiled and said, "What about Murray Kingston? Was he liked?"

"He got you through exams," Sue said with an emphatic nod. "Better than Miss Paton did, that is. But he was pretty tough; wouldn't take any messing about. Billy and he were like cat and dog, but that was Billy's fault. He was always a bit of an anarchist, Billy was."

"You don't see him any more?"

Sue's eyes flickered. "Billy's been dead for nearly five years."

"I didn't know," Fizz said. "The McCaulays didn't mention him. What did he . . . was it an accident, or . . ."

"A bomb. He was in the Gloucesters, manning a road-block in Crossmaglen. He'd only been in the army for six months."

"Jeez."

A couple of American football graduates cruised by and paused to enquire if they might share the bench, ignoring the fact that there were several empty ones nearby. Fizz dismissed them with something short and pithy, erased the remark from the tape in case it gave Buchanan palpitations, and got back to business.

"About Debbie. Did she ever speak about her daddy: ever seem scared of him?"

Sue had still not recovered from the shock of Fizz's syntax. She looked at her roll as though she'd forgotten what she was about to do with it, and laid it back in the box. "I don't think so. I mean, I don't think she was scared of him. She was just like any other kid. She used to want me to give her her bath and put her to bed rather than have her dad do it, but I don't suppose that proves anything. It's one of those things you remember afterwards, though."

"When you were baby-sitting, did you ever take anyone along to keep you company?"

"Sometimes Billy came along later in the evening and waited to walk me home." She tipped her head defensively. "Mr Kingston knew about it. He didn't mind."

"Nobody other than Billy?"

"No. I didn't mind being on my own. I could watch a video or something, and Mr Kingston was never very late." She clipped the lid on her sandwich box and put it back into her shoulder bag. "Must go. I've still got to find a couple of tops for my holidays. Was that all you wanted to ask me?"

Fizz felt she could have used another ten minutes or so quite effectively, but she shook her head. "No, that's fine. Maybe, if I think of anything else, we could have lunch again?"

"Sure. Any time. I just wish I could have come up with something worthwhile for you. Mr Kingston was okay to me, always bunged me a bit extra at Christmas and that sort of thing. I'd like to think he didn't do what they said he did."

"Yeah. Well, you've given me some things to think about anyway," Fizz told her. "Maybe they'll lead us somewhere."

"Really? I hope so." With a final hundred-watt smile Sue walked away, hurrying up the steps to Princes

Street, and within seconds was lost in the lunchtime throng. Fizz sat on for a while, enjoying the sun and the passing scene, debating with herself whether to drop the tape off at Tam's office right now or to catch him at home later.

There was a danger, if she chose the second option, that she would run into Janine — assuming that the said Janine was still on speaking terms with Buchanan. If that happened, the encounter would not be a happy one, since Janine would know that she had staged the bathrobe incident deliberately to dismay her, and if she had, by now, discussed the matter with Buchanan, there would be hell to pay.

Oh, what a tangled web we weave, she told herself, not for the first time, and decided to phone the office first. Buchanan might be there after all, in spite of Beatrice's vague prognostications, in which case she'd be able to judge how much of Janine's side of the story was known to him. Failing that, he might have left a message for her to follow up the identification of Murray's two mystery callers, in which case she could hang on to the tape for a while.

She found a telephone booth outside the post office and dialled the office number. Buchanan, said the switchboard operator, was not in the office. Fizz asked to speak to Beatrice.

"Good afternoon, Miss Fitzpatrick. Yes, I gave Mr Buchanan your message, and he said he would prefer it if you didn't pursue the matter, and that he and Miss Paton will be following it up this afternoon. He'll be home by six thirty if you'd care to phone him then."

215

Fizz was too stunned to speak. She set down the phone and stood staring out through the glass, barely registering the skinhead beyond who started to motion her to hurry up, then, suddenly seeing her expression, walked hurriedly away.

Zoe and Buchanan! Off together following up *her* clue. Hadn't even the nous to see the significance of the two gays for themselves, but fast as shit off a shovel when it came to dashing in and grabbing the credit. Bastards!

Zoe, it was perfectly clear, had been able to throw light on the whereabouts of the evening class she had referred to last night, and the pair of them had gone trawling off to trace the ex-pupils without so much as a "thanks a bunch" to Fizz for all her groundwork.

What was even more galling was that Zoe probably didn't give a monkey's chunky for the promising line of enquiry. All she cared about was getting into Buchanan's Ys. And that, Fizz decided, was definitely out of order.

CHAPTER
FIFTEEN

Zoe filled the car with a flowery scent that was inviting without being aggressively so. Her husky voice, commenting on this and that, held a veiled encouragement that acted like verbal Elastoplast to Buchanan's wounded pride.

He took his time traversing the A1 out to Musselburgh — not that he could do anything else, given the traffic situation — and rather enjoyed the drive south through East Lothian. The rolling Borders countryside and the beaches of Gullane, Aberlady Bay and Port Seton all held memories of school holiday day trips with his parents and his brother, Stephen. The islands were hazy with the afternoon heat, the Bass rock sticking up out of the water, grey and white, like a rotting molar in the mouth of the Forth.

Berwick was another matter. The centre of the town had been designed before the days of the motor car, and it was now too late to do anything about it. Lorries and tour buses surged unexpectedly out of alleyways, and sudden bends in the road disclosed hordes of jaywalking tourists photographing each other against historical backdrops.

Zoe navigated the way through the old town to an area of terraced houses close to the ramparts of the ancient walls.

"It's around here somewhere," she stated, but in a manner that suggested to Buchanan that she was trying to convince herself rather than her listener, and the expression on her face was none too confident. It occurred to him that if Zoe *had* set her sights on him, which was beginning to appear probable, she could have set up this expedition as a way of throwing the two of them together, whether or not she actually remembered the site of the rehab centre, or whatever it was.

He wasn't sure how he would feel about that scenario if it turned out to be the case. Admittedly, Zoe wasn't the type he'd necessarily be making a play for, all things being equal, but she had three things going for her: she was attractive, in a cuddly sort of way, she was sweet-natured, and she was *there*.

They wound their way through a maze of streets, each of them lined with identical terraced villas with hanging baskets and well-stocked front gardens. Zoe gave every sign of trying hard, her head turning from side to side, peering out through the windscreen and leaning forward to see past Buchanan to the right-hand side of the road.

"Oh dear. It's not as simple as I'd thought," she admitted as Buchanan stopped to check their progress on their street map. "I had a picture of the area in my head, but now I'm here, I don't know, it's all so similar."

"Well, don't worry about it," he told her. "It's not all that vitally important. If the worst comes to the worst we can always ask Murray the address. I'd just hoped to turn up the evidence without his assistance, that's all."

Zoe looked uncomfortable. "I know. It's very irritating, the way he keeps things to himself, but you can tell it's just because he's still so much in love with Dianne. It's hard to blame him, really."

Buchanan found it not at all hard, but said only, "If he's still in love with her, you've got to hand it to him, he's taking the loss of her pretty well. Don't you think?"

She seemed to be interested in something to be seen out of her side window, then he saw that she was chewing the side of her lip as though in the throes of a decision.

"Tam . . ." she started to say, and then changed her mind and tried to cover up by rummaging in her bag for a hanky and blowing her nose.

"Yes?" he prompted.

"Sorry?" She opened her eyes at him as though she hadn't a clue what he meant.

"I thought you were about to tell me something?"

"No . . . at least, if I was, I've forgotten what it was."

Her eyes were still wide and innocent, but a wave of colour swept over her face from brow to throat. She was nowhere as good a liar as Fizz was, Buchanan reflected, trying not to smile. He couldn't imagine what she had been about to say. They'd been talking about . . . what? Murray and Dianne.

He said, "Zoe, is there something you know about Murray and Dianne that you're not telling me?"

She whipped her head away and stared out of her window again, but a second later, she turned back to him, her big hazel eyes barely meeting his. "Murray's going to talk to you about it himself when he sees you on Monday. Maybe we should leave it to him."

"No, Zoe," Buchanan said tersely. "Let's not. Monday's two days away, and if there's something everybody knows except me, I'd like to hear it now."

She dragged in a long breath that made her blue angora bosom swell. "Please don't be angry, Tam. I should have told you before now, I know I should, but I was afraid it would be the last straw to make you drop the case. The fact is, I'm pretty sure Murray and Dianne are still . . . an item. I saw them together the night before last, and they looked . . . well, close."

Buchanan felt utterly crushed. "You're sure about this, Zoe? No, of course you are." The thought had been at the back of his mind all along, he supposed, but had seemed simply too unlikely to be given credence. He dealt the steering wheel an exasperated slap. "Good God, what are they playing at, those two? She's only been married a matter of months, and to Sheridan Reid, for pity's sake!"

Zoe knotted her hands together, little bits of white lace hanky sticking out between her fingers. "I wanted to tell you right away, but I thought . . . that is, I wasn't sure . . . I don't mean this in a nasty way, Tam, but I wasn't sure whether you'd lose patience with Murray altogether and refuse to help him any more. Please, Tam, don't do that." He heard her swallow noisily and realised she was more upset even than she appeared.

"You're the only straw Murray's got to hang on to right now, and if you turn your back on him he'll . . . I think it would just about finish him. Oh, he knows I'd go on doing what I can, and maybe Fizz would too, but you're the one he's relying on."

"Exactly," Buchanan retorted, now thoroughly angry. "He can rely on me but can I rely on him? Like hell I can! I'm given half the facts — and most of those are shaky! — and expected to work miracles. If somebody had thought to put me in the picture a week or more ago, we might be getting somewhere by now!"

"You're mad at me." Zoe sniffed.

"No, not at you, Zoe." Buchanan sighed, defeated by the vagaries of the female mind. "I'm very grateful to you for telling me, Zoe. It certainly explains Murray's attitude, and also makes his implicit trust in Dianne a little easier to understand. Both Fizz and I wondered why he wasn't mad at her for ditching him but I don't think this explanation occurred to either of us. Not seriously."

"I'm absolutely certain he hated having to deceive you, Tam," Zoe said, eyeing him anxiously. "You know he thinks the world of you, don't you? He's always telling me what a friend you've been to him since you were boys together, and he trusts you absolutely. I think he feels you're the only person who didn't kick him when he was down."

Something in her tone made Buchanan turn and look at her, and, catching his eye, she shrugged and gave a little forced smile.

"We all let him down, you know: all of his old friends except you. Even though we'd known him for years and couldn't really bring ourselves to believe him guilty, we all gave our evidence when we were asked to. I suppose the others felt just as I did — that we had to speak up to protect Debbie, but it weighs on my conscience just the same."

Buchanan wondered for a moment if she were giving him a sly dig. It might easily appear to her that Murray's old pal should have been in there like a shot, offering to act as his legal representative, or, at least, standing as a character witness. The fact that Murray had asked him to do neither was proof that he knew how low he had fallen in Buchanan's esteem after his wife's suicide, and was loath to approach him for any favours while he still had other options open to him. Nonetheless, there had been moments since then when Buchanan's conscience had given him a bad time on the grounds that he'd had no proof that Anne's suicide was due solely to Murray's betrayal. He could never be certain that he had judged him fairly on that score, but it was something of a comfort now to have his original assessment of Murray's morals so unambiguously confirmed by his association with another man's wife.

"You didn't have any other choice, at the time, but to do what you did," he told her. "Murray doesn't hold it against you, I'm sure, and you've surely cleared your account by being such an enormous help with our enquiry this last week or two. Besides, I don't think the evidence you gave was crucial to the verdict, was it?"

"No, I suppose not, but one can't tell what goes on in the minds of jurymen. Maybe the discovery of the pornography was just enough to swing someone who was undecided." She shook her head slightly as though dislodging an uncomfortable memory. "They were quite horrendous magazines, you know, but it was the boy who found them that I reported to the headmaster, not Murray."

"But they turned up in Murray's filing cabinet, didn't they?"

"Yes, they did. Murray wasn't in that day — we found out later, of course, that he was being questioned by the police, but at the time, we thought he was just off sick. I'd sent the lad in to get the register, and when I went to see why he was taking so long I found him reading the magazines. I'm afraid I really blew my top! Just at that moment the headmaster stuck his head round the door to see what the noise was about, so I turned the whole distasteful business over to him as fast as I could. The idea that they might have been Murray's magazines — or that anyone could even allege that they were — just didn't occur to me. I naturally assumed that they belonged to the boy, and . . . well, I suppose I was so furious I never gave him the chance to say he'd found them there."

"I see." Buchanan drummed his fingers thoughtfully on the steering wheel. "I wasn't clear on how that had happened, but it's fairly obvious that if someone were trying to frame Murray, it would be easy enough to plant the magazines where they'd be found as soon as someone went for the register."

"No problem." She nodded. "The office was never locked, even at night, and there was an entrance leading to the football pitch only a few steps away, so anyone could have nipped in from outside. It didn't even have to be someone in the school."

"But someone knew where he kept the register," Buchanan pointed out.

"No, I'm afraid not. They weren't in the same drawer as the register, they were tucked down the side of the filing cabinet as though they'd been hidden there but had slid forward so that they were visible to anyone using any of the drawers."

"Great. That means that if it wasn't Murray who hid them, the field's wide open. Back to square one." Buchanan leaned forward and started the engine. "So, the only remaining ray of light at the end of the tunnel seems to be coming from the rehab centre. I've got a feeling that if we can find out what the score is there — and preferably before Murray has a chance to muddy the waters — we'll at least be a step closer to knowing what he's been trying to keep us from finding out. Let's give it a few more minutes."

The projected few minutes went nowhere, but they carried on doggedly from block to block, peering hopefully down side streets and pausing at those crossroads that Zoe seemed to find familiar. Half an hour went by without any progress, and they had begun to go over ground they had already recced when she spun round to look over her shoulder.

"Wait a minute, Tam! Can you back up? There, beyond the pillar box."

It was an entrance between two tall buildings, a narrow lane that led into what had once been spacious rear gardens. At the end of the lane was a single-storey building made of concrete blocks, an architectural cross between an outsize public toilet and a World War Two gun emplacement. Around the outside walls someone had made an attempt to create a border of pansies and alyssum, but lack of direct sunlight wasn't helping any. The only indication as to what went on within the unprepossessing walls was a metal plaque bearing the words "Arundel House".

Inside it smelled of coffee. There was the sound of two guitars playing in unison, and beyond that, a hubbub of several voices and sporadic bursts of laughter. Zoe pointed to a pair of swing doors.

"That's where the jumble sale was held."

She swayed over to squint through the glass panels, teetering rather cutely on her high-heeled sandals, and, there being no signs to assist the casual visitor, he followed her.

There were four or five young men with guitars practising in the hall beyond. One of them, a short, bearded guy in an Aran sweater, stood up and walked over to open the door.

"Looking for somebody?"

"Yes. We're looking for whoever is in charge," Buchanan said. "The administrator or whatever."

"You found him. Colin McCaig. What can I do for you?"

Buchanan fished out a business card. "I'm Tam Buchanan and this is Miss Paton. We're conducting an enquiry on behalf of Murray Kingston, who, I believe, used to have some connection with your work here."

McCaig's speculative look flicked between them for an instant, then he said, "Hang on a sec then."

He went back to his group of guitarists and gave them some project to be getting on with, and then came back and led the way across the entrance lobby, down a windowless corridor, through a common room full of tables and chairs where a few people were sitting chatting over coffees, and finally into a minuscule office with an uninterrupted view of a dirty stone wall.

By the time they had brought in an extra chair from the common room there was practically no free space at all. They were sitting virtually knee to knee, which made for a weird kind of pseudo-intimacy.

"What sort of enquiry?" McCaig asked as they got settled.

Buchanan said, "There's a possibility that Mr Kingston's conviction may have been unsound. We're looking for any evidence that might support that theory."

McCaig frowned. "And what has that to do with the centre? Murray Kingston ran a writers' workshop for us for a couple of years, but there were no children involved . . ."

"We're trying," Buchanan said, "to establish if there's any possibility that Mr Kingston could have been framed."

"Framed?" McCaig glared refutation at both of them and spluttered a short laugh. "Mr Buchanan, if that's the line of enquiry you're following, I can assure you,

you are looking in the wrong place. What I'm running here is a support centre for people with full-blown AIDS. People who are not buying five-year diaries, if you follow me. They are concerned with getting through one day at a time, not with interfering with the life of a casual acquaintance, which is all Kingston was to most of them."

"I appreciate that," Buchanan said soothingly. "This is just one link in a long chain, Mr McCaig. It may lead nowhere, but unfortunately it's my boring job to check it out. I'm sure you understand."

McCaig relaxed a bit and shouted through the doorway for someone called Victor to rustle up three coffees.

Buchanan invested a few minutes in explaining the background of the case. "What I'm particularly after," he wound up, "is the names of the people who were in Kingston's writers' workshop."

"Oh God, now you're asking." McCaig shook his head. "I don't keep records of that sort of thing. I've got enough paperwork already without that. There's a pile of it in that cupboard the size of — well, if it falls on me it'll kill me, right?"

"Couldn't you remember any of them?" Zoe asked softly.

McCaig blinked hopefully at the light fixture. "They were a bit of a mixed bunch, I remember that. There was Flora. We used to have a poem of hers on the common room wall for a while."

"Can we talk to her?" Buchanan asked, and McCaig shook his head with a depressing finality.

"We're talking about — what? — three or four years ago? That's a long time in this set-up." He squeezed aside to let a young man in slashed jeans sidle in with a tray of mugs. "Thanks, Victor. Listen, while you're here, you remember the writers' workshop?"

Victor swept the visitors with a swift, assessing glance that took in Buchanan's business suit and Zoe's legs. "Sure. What about it?"

"Remember any of the people who were in it?"

"Mmm . . . Flora . . ."

"Yes. I remembered her. Who else?"

"Um . . . Wasn't Kirsten's brother in it? And that guy he buddied. Remember? What was his name?"

"Adrian Ballard." McCaig's eyes saw something outside the room. "Right," he said, stretching the word out into two thoughtful syllables. "Thanks, Victor. Give us a shout if you remember anyone else."

He waited till Victor had gone, and then passed round the coffee, still visibly involved with his own memories. Buchanan waited.

"I seem to remember one of the lads was keen to contact Murray after we abandoned the writers' workshop."

"Kirsten's brother?" Zoe breathed. She had clearly intended to allow Buchanan to do the talking, but found his habit of asking as few questions as necessary a little hard to take.

"Yes. Donald Fergusson." McCaig nodded, smiling at her but still seeing something else. "We had to drop the writers' workshop rather suddenly, of course, when Murray was arrested, and there was no one else to run

228

it so there were inevitably a few administrative cock-ups. Some people didn't get their manuscripts returned, that sort of thing."

"And Donald was one of them?" Buchanan asked. "Is he still . . . around?"

"He's still alive, if that's what you mean." McCaig smiled. "Donald wasn't a sufferer. He and Kirsten were voluntary helpers. We don't see much of him these days, since he got a job, but Kirsten's still with us. She you can talk to. She's here at the moment."

Buchanan indicated that this would make his day, and when McCaig left the room to locate Kirsten he met Zoe's optimistic stare with a restrained nod. "Yes, it looks hopeful, doesn't it? I liked the bit about manuscripts not being returned, didn't you?"

"Absolutely," Zoe breathed, one eye on the door. "And also the bit about this Donald 'buddying' some guy. It all ties in so beautifully."

"We'll see," Buchanan told her. "Don't get your hopes up. And remember, don't put words into Kirsten's mouth. Let her tell us what she knows in her own way."

"Won't say a word, Tam. Promise."

Footsteps approached across the common room and McCaig stepped through the door, followed by a girl in her early twenties who overtopped him by at least four inches. Her hair was light strawberry blonde, cut short and flicked forwards around a thin, intelligent face.

"Hi," she said, and shook hands confidently with them both in turn. "I'm Kirsten Fergusson. Colin says you want to contact my brother?"

"Actually, we're trying to contact anyone who was in Murray Kingston's writers' circle," Buchanan said. "You weren't a member yourself?"

She chuckled at the back of her throat. "Not me. My talents lie in other directions. But Donald was, yes. Not that he was ever any better than I am at putting words on paper, but he was buddying somebody at that time who was heavily into writing."

"Yes. Adrian Ballard. We're interested in anything you can tell us about Adrian. What sort of thing did he write?"

"Adrian? I don't know, really. He was always pretty shy about it. He used to say he couldn't bear anyone to read what he had written because it felt like taking one's clothes off in public." She glanced at McCaig, who had given her his seat and was standing in the doorway. "The stuff they did in the writers' circle was pretty much directed at helping them develop ideas or portray characters or write descriptions. Sometimes they tried a bit of poetry."

"But Adrian, you said, was really into writing," Buchanan encouraged gently. "Didn't he try anything on his own?"

She raised her eyebrows, wrinkling her forehead. "He was obsessed with writing. He didn't just produce a few lines now and then to look willing: he was at it all the time. Donald said it was an autobiography."

"Do you know what happened to it?"

"Haven't a clue."

McCaig spoke from the doorway. "I'm sure Donald was looking for the manuscript after Adrian died, but it had disappeared." He spread his hands, indicating the overflowing desk and cramped filing cabinets. "I felt bad about it, but God knows what happened to all the writers' circle stuff when it became defunct."

"Donald may have found it, for all I know," Kirsten offered. "He wouldn't necessarily have mentioned it to me if he had. You'll have to speak to him if you want to know."

"Fine," said Buchanan. "How can I contact him?"

"Weekends are difficult," she said, "but you'll get him at home on Monday. I can give you his telephone number, But leave it till the afternoon. He likes to sleep late if he's had a busy weekend."

"He works weekends, does he?" Buchanan passed her his notebook to let her note down the number. "What does he do?"

"He's a disc jockey." She smiled, twitching one eyebrow as though inviting them to be amused. "He does gigs all over the Borders and the Edinburgh area, but if you're in a hurry to reach him, he's always at Werrit Zat in the Grassmarket on Saturday nights."

Buchanan smiled back looking faintly pained. "I'm not in all that much of a hurry, thanks. It'll wait till Monday." He pocketed his notebook and stood up. "You've been very helpful and very generous with your time. I'm grateful."

"What do you think?" McCaig asked as he walked with them to the door. "Is there really any concrete evidence to point to Murray's innocence? I'd like to think that he was innocent after all."

Buchanan pursed his lips. "Concrete evidence, no. A slight suspicion, yes."

But as he walked back to the car he knew that, lack of evidence notwithstanding, he was beginning to suspect that there was a good deal more in this business than had ever come out at Murray's trial.

CHAPTER
SIXTEEN

Buchanan felt as if he had died and gone to hell. He also felt as if he had partaken of a large dose of some mind-numbing drug, or fallen victim to the early onset of Alzheimer's disease, or that his body had become host to an extra-terrestrial entity that had taken over his brain and was making him do things that would never have occurred to him in his normal state.

The fact that he had permitted Fizz to talk him into being part of the demonic orgy at Werrit Zat was proof that either his judgement or his free will was seriously impaired. It couldn't be said that he hadn't had at least a fair idea of what he was getting himself into. He'd had serious doubts about the matter, and although Fizz had, naturally, pooh-poohed his reservations, he had taken her assurances with the pinch of salt they deserved. But she had been so adamant about the necessity of forging ahead, and she had so clearly been willing to nag on about it till she got what she wanted, that it had begun to appear scarcely worth the effort to deny her demands.

The fact that he had been fighting from a defensive position hadn't helped either. He hadn't expected for a minute that she would be so furious about Zoe and him checking out the rehab centre without inviting her to participate. He was still smarting from some of the home truths she had hit him with, and the impact of her graphic vocabulary — particularly her description of him as two pounds of shit in a one-pound bag — still rang in his ears. It had looked, for a minute or two, as if she was about to withdraw her support altogether, and the shock of discovering how much he'd miss her input made him see the wisdom of allowing her this one concession.

But there was more to it than that. Any other Saturday night he'd have been organised with something to do: perhaps a drive down to Gullane in the afternoon for a round of golf with Janine and a few other friends, followed by an early dinner and a couple of good seats at the Usher Hall or the Festival Theatre. It had to be admitted that a large part of his willingness to be dragooned into accompanying Fizz to this hellhole was that he had a horror of spending a Saturday night in the company of the group of unattached bachelors who were his *ad hoc* golfing companions. Another reason was that if he hadn't accompanied her, Fizz would be here on her own, and he had felt, at the time, that if anything happened to her he wouldn't want to have it on his conscience. Which was a laugh, actually, because it was quite clear that she was very much more at home in this environment than he was.

He should have expected that, of course. She hadn't said anything specific about her background, but he had picked up from various snippets of information the idea that, whatever the set-up, she had been there, done that, and bought the T-shirt. Her self-sufficiency was staggering, even in one who had wandered the world on her own, virtually constantly, since the age of eighteen or so, and she seemed to fit neatly into any situation as though it were her natural milieu.

Right now she was making the most of a one-foot-square area of space in the middle of the heaving dance floor, undulating around in her own unique interpretation of what Buchanan identified, he supposed, as body-popping, in total disregard of her partner's style, which was more reminiscent of one of the All Blacks performing a pre-match haka.

He could scarcely see her through the rainbow-tinted half-dark and the haze of tobacco and cannabis smoke, but she seemed to be enjoying the experience of Edinburgh nightlife a great deal more than he was. Which wasn't saying much. She even blended into the garishly dressed throng better than he did, although her cotton top and the all-purpose black skirt that appeared to be her only formal attire scarcely matched up to the bizarre leather, rubber, chain mail, dayglo Lycra, satin and sequinned gear of the other dancers. There were pretty young things in rubber body suits and stockings, gays in glistening leather and near-drag, a sprinkling of boned corsets, an embarrassment of see-through blouses and a profusion of pierced and tattooed flesh.

Buchanan had had no idea that such places existed in Edinburgh, even in the cultural hinterland that was the Grassmarket after dark, and if he had known Werrit Zat for what it was, as Fizz clearly had, he'd have been in better shape to withstand her verbal bludgeoning. As it was, he was now trapped here in this maelstrom of noise and humanity, waiting for her to return to him so that he could tell her, to hell with it, they could leave questioning Donald Fergusson till Monday afternoon.

He had fended off the attentions of a snake-hipped youth in cycling shorts, two would-be dancing partners and the offer of a selection of two-tone capsules before Fizz shouldered her way through the crowd in front of him and yelled something laughingly in his face.

"What?" he yelled back, bending down to bring his mouth to within an inch of her ear.

She shook her head despairingly, filling his mouth with hair, and, grabbing his arm, charged towards the exit like a Scottish forward going for a touchdown at Murrayfield.

"Dear God!" she groaned as they emerged into the relative peace of the foyer. "People actually pay to go in there!"

"I thought you were enjoying yourself."

She looked at him sideways. "When in Rome, you know. I always believe in melting into the natural cover."

"Hm-mmm. We're leaving then, are we?"

"Leaving? Why would we be leaving? We haven't spoken to Donald What's-his-face yet."

"Fizz, it really isn't a matter of life or death. We can reach him on Monday."

She fixed him with a look. "Don't let's go through all that again, Buchanan. We're within an inch of making a real breakthrough. Let's do it while we're still young, for God's sake! Besides, Donald gave me the nod while I was dancing. He'll be taking his ciggie break any time now."

Buchanan sighed and allowed himself to be jostled closer to the wall by a group of Goths. Fizz had earlier managed, by dint of sheer determination and some boldly innovative lying, to get a brief word with the disc jockey and had arranged to see him in the foyer when he could spare a minute, but that had been a long two hours ago, and enough was enough.

"It's ten to two," he said wearily, "and, frankly, I've spent a more enjoyable two hours in the dentist's chair. I vote we call it a day."

"Please yourself," she said with a touch of impatience. "If it's all too much for you, why don't you just toddle off home to your wee bed and I'll talk to Donald on my own."

Buchanan ground his teeth. He was becoming seriously allergic to this woman. Every time he spent any length of time in her company, his stomach started giving him gyp. She knew damn well that, even knowing her to be well able to take care of herself, he wouldn't dream of abandoning her here. He had brought her and he would be taking her home, but, please God, let it be soon.

They waited a further twenty minutes before Donald showed. Fizz spotted him at the far side of the foyer, waving them towards the exit, and they fought their way through the jam of bodies to meet up with him outside on the pavement. He had donned a thick cardigan over the acid yellow of his satin jumpsuit and he looked quite unremarkable till you noticed the sheen of eyeshadow and the pink lipstick. His floppy brown hair was streaked with gold and his skin glowed with a pseudo-Bahamian tan.

He lit up a cigarette and inhaled deeply. "Lord, it's *dead* in there tonight. Like a wet Sunday in Stirling. Gerry was to have taken over for me half an hour ago but he got held up with some zombie OD-ing in the loo."

"What did he OD on?" Fizz wanted to know.

"Who knows? Gerry dumped him at the ER and scarpered." He looked closely at her and his eyes narrowed. "Is that natural or permed?"

"Natural," Fizz answered without blinking. "You think I'd do this to myself deliberately?"

"Don't put yourself down, sweetie. It's very 'you'. Try running a little mousse through it and letting it dry naturally."

Buchanan closed his ears to this conversation and led them a few steps away from the crowd around the club doorway. They were in a poorly lit side alley that showed the traffic in the Grassmarket at one end and a flight of steps leading up to the Castle at the other. The few shops that edged the pavement were robustly shuttered, and black polythene refuse bags were piled in the doorways. A chill wind sent litter scampering along the gutters and cut through Buchanan's silk shirt like a knife.

"I don't want to be long, my dears," Donald said, drawing his cardigan tightly around him. "Gerry's a poppet but he'd make two short planks look like tissue

238

paper and I don't like to leave him for more than about ten minutes at a time, particularly tonight. I think he'd been at the dog's hayfever pills before he even got here. You said it was about Murray Kingston?"

"Yes." Buchanan had had enough of hanging around and was quite happy to dispense with the social chitchat and cut to the chase. "Your sister told us that you were in his writers' workshop together with Adrian Ballard and that there was some mix-up over a manuscript of Adrian's. Can you tell us anything about that?"

Donald drew smoke into his lungs and regarded them both through squinted eyes. "What's this about, exactly?"

Buchanan sighed and prepared to go back to square one, but Fizz leapt in with her usual lack of patience.

"There's a chance that somebody got their hands on that manuscript and sold it as their own work. We think it's possible that Kingston was framed to get him out of the way, so that he wouldn't be around to blow the gaff."

Donald stared at her, then turned his gaze on Buchanan. The pupils of his eyes, which should have been enlarged in the poor light, were like pinpoints.

"Well, dear me, no. I can't say I know anything about that," he said finally. "I do know there *was* a manuscript at one time, but what happened to it after Adrian died is the mystery of the decade. Disappeared off the face of the earth, playmates, I tell you no lie."

It seemed to Buchanan that his camp act was rather overdone. That might have been because it was his trademark as a disc jockey — something to set him apart from the herd — or it might have been deliberately assumed in order to distract his inquisitors. His voice was light and not particularly low in pitch, and it seemed to Buchanan that with careful make-up he could appear a tall but not unattractive woman.

"You did make an attempt to locate it, then?" he prompted him.

"One *was* a teensy bit curious, to be honest, never having been allowed to see a word of it." He parked his cigarette in the corner of his mouth and used both arms as a chest protector. "It was weeks afterwards that I asked about it at Arundel House, but no one knew a thing about it. The writers' workshop had simply withered away by then because Murray was in trouble with the police, and any bits of writing that were lying around had been stuffed into a few cardboard boxes in the basement. No sign of Adrian's papers. Not a page. But then somebody, I forget who, told me there was a rumour that Adrian had given the manuscript to Murray just before he died. Gerry and I went to his house a couple of times to ask him about it, but he'd been locked up by then. In the end, we wrote to him in prison, but answer came there none." He flashed Buchanan a chirpy smile. "Now read on."

"But you must have seen something of what Adrian was writing. Just a glimpse over his shoulder, even?" Buchanan suggested. "Wouldn't there be any passages you might recognise?"

"Oh, I shouldn't think so, dear." Donald took a final drag, dropped the stub of his cigarette to the pavement

240

and ground it out with his toe. "Adrian never let anyone read his stuff. The rest of them used to read out what they'd written and discuss it, but Adrian wouldn't go along with that. He didn't want anybody to know him that well, not when he was alive."

"You think he waited till the end before giving Murray his autobiography?" Buchanan asked.

Donald shrugged. "*If* he gave it to Murray."

"If he didn't give it to Murray, who did he give it to?"

"He could have given it to the Dalai Lama for all I know, sweetie!" Donald exclaimed, waving delicate hands whose nails, Buchanan suddenly discovered, were painted bottle green. "This guy was a non-communicator. I mean, we're talking *mega* here, folks. Half the time he was too busy writing to want anything to do with me, and the other half he was stoned. I had to climb out on to the window-sill and slash my wrists to get two minutes of his attention. We never really had a relationship."

"So you wouldn't be able to recognise any of his life story, even if you were to read it now?"

"Not a word. *Desperately* sorry, love. He had a sister called Rosemary who got married and went to Canada. That's the sum total of all he ever told me. No help to you, huh?"

"Wasn't there anyone else at Arundel House that he might have talked to?" Fizz put in.

Donald hugged his cardigan tighter around his chest, indicating with a shiver and a bleary look not only that he was frozen stiff but that the subject had ceased to be of interest to him. "Look, poppet, we're talking about a guy who'd make a clam look like a Kentucky auctioneer. If you said 'Good morning' to him he'd be lost for a reply." He shook back his floppy hair and straightened from his slouch. "Sorry, people, Daddy gotta go make pennies now."

Buchanan forced himself to look grateful. "Thanks for your time, Donald. You've been very helpful. If I need to get back to you I'll give you a ring at home, if that's all right? Your sister gave me the number."

"Well now, that *would* be nice," Donald said, politely. "But don't phone in the morning, will you, sweetie, because I must get my beauty sleep." He twiddled his green fingertips as he walked away. "Miss you already."

They negotiated the throng at the club doorway and walked back to where Buchanan had parked his car, Fizz plainly fighting a compulsion to giggle and Buchanan ready to annihilate her if she said one word, but by the time they reached Leith Walk she had sobered up.

"Had it occurred to you," she said thoughtfully, "that we could be way off track in thinking Dianne's at the bottom of this? I know it's starting to look as if she nicked Adrian's story, possibly with Murray's connivance, and then framed him to get him out of the way while she cashed in on it, but there's at least one other possibility. It occurs to me that if it was an *autobiography* that Adrian was writing, it could be a real hot potato, couldn't it? Who knows what ghosts are locked up in *that* cupboard? What if he'd spilled the beans on somebody who was worth blackmailing?"

242

Buchanan thought about that for a while. "I find that rather hard to swallow."

"Okay, it's a bit of a rat sandwich, I agree, but it's possible. Just because *Fade to Black* was about gays, we can't assume it was based on the same story. It would be quite natural for Murray, working with AIDS victims, to be telling Dianne all about the stories he was hearing from them, and if Dianne put them all together and knitted a sort of composite drama out of them, well, there's nothing criminal about that, is there?" She glared at him through a curtain of windswept tendrils. "I'm not saying there necessarily *is* more to this business than meets the eye, I'm just saying it's a possibility we shouldn't lose sight of."

"I hear what you're saying," he said neutrally. Actually, he was rather impressed by her lateral thinking and thought that her approach showed a degree of open-mindedness that would stand her in good stead as a lawyer, but he felt totally unable to say so without being slammed for being patronising. He was still smarting somewhat from the slagging she had given him yesterday, and he was trying to tread warily.

There had been a time, and not so long ago, when he had considered himself something of a smoothie where women were concerned, but he had managed to rub both Janine and Fizz up the wrong way within the past week, and had had it pointed out to him in quite unambiguous terms by both of them, and his self-assurance was, in consequence, pretty much at an all-time low. Thank God Zoe at least was still being sweet to him.

CHAPTER
SEVENTEEN

Fizz had now just about got her Monday mornings arranged to her satisfaction. It took her about twelve minutes to walk down to the community centre from the High Street, so that if she left home around ten past nine she had time for a quick coffee and news round-up in reception before Buchanan showed. Any typing she couldn't find an excuse for postponing was bundled, any old how, on to a computer disk, which Donna edited and printed out while they had their tea break around eleven. And between times all she had to do was hand out standard advice, most of it in pamphlets, answer the telephone and chat to waiting clients.

It wasn't, on the face of it, the most challenging job she'd ever had, but it wasn't the worst either. It certainly beat melon harvesting, cooking for sheep-shearers and waitressing.

She had already amassed a wealth of stationery, which was a source of deep contentment to her every time she looked in the drawers and cubbyholes of her desk. Apart from the typing paper and notebooks she had a right to requisition, she had also acquired ballpoint and fibre-tipped pens in a variety of colours, adhesive labels, plastic folders, bulldog and paper clips, ring binders, staplers and a selection of rubber fingerstalls in various sizes.

She did not ask herself what she was going to do with these. It wasn't about doing anything with them. It wasn't symptomatic of a nest-building instinct such as she descried in Zoe's flat, nor did it confirm or glorify some facet of her own character, as she suspected was the case with Buchanan's nicknacks. No part of her collection would ever leave the office: anything unused when she left in October — which meant virtually everything — would be returned to the stationery cupboard, but in the meantime they really made her day. Part of their charm was that each of them represented a minor victory over the parsimonious McGuigan, who guarded the stationery cupboard with a jealous zeal and would have had a massive coronary if he'd discovered the extent of her hoard.

Murray arrived, as he usually did, just before twelve. He looked a lot healthier than he had appeared on his first visit, but he still had trouble relaxing and had to be pacing up and down all the time.

"How're things going?" he wanted to know right away. "Has there been any progress at all since I saw you? How did you get on with the baby-sitter?"

"Well, it depends what you'd call progress," Fizz flannelled, not wanting to spoil the impact of the revelations which she knew Buchanan was about to deliver. "Sue told me a thing or two I didn't know already, but whether they have any bearing on the case I don't yet know."

"What did she tell you? Did you tape it?"

"Yes, I taped it, but we were in Princes Street Gardens and the background noise makes it very hard to listen to. Buchanan will let you hear it if you want to bother."

"Never mind. Just tell me what she said."

Fizz rummaged for her notebook, taking her time because she wanted to string out this part of the conversation till Buchanan had finished dealing with his last client. "She mentioned Billy McCaulay. I hadn't heard about him before."

Murray's eyes cranked open a notch. "Billy McCaulay? You're not telling me he had something to do with this business?"

"No. I just wondered why nobody had mentioned him. Sue said he used to keep her company sometimes when she was looking after Debbie, so I'd have thought he might have made the list of possible suspects."

Murray shook his head. "He'd been dead for a while when I was arrested, and before that he'd been away in the army for . . . must have been six months or so."

"Yes, Sue told me that. Did he join up straight from school?"

"Within a few months, I think. But the army wasn't his first choice. When he left school he had a fancy for a career in nursing, but I talked him out of it. He didn't have the temperament for that sort of work. Much too volatile." Murray shook his head. "Sue used to keep him in order. Nice girl, Sue."

"Yes, I thought so. She —"

The door to Buchanan's office opened and he emerged, ushering his last client of the morning to the door. He spared Murray barely a nod as he went past, but on the way back he bade him good morning, looking no more austere than he usually did. Both men went into the inner office, and Fizz followed them, carrying her notebook and yellow pencil as though they were an entry permit.

"So, are we any further forward, Tam?" Murray asked as soon as they'd got themselves settled.

Buchanan was clearing his desk, packing his papers into his briefcase, and took his time about answering. His face rarely if ever showed what he was thinking, but Fizz rather thought he was ready to bite Murray's head off if he gave him any trouble.

"Oh, yes. I think you could say we're a little further forward," he said finally, swinging his chair round sideways so that he had room to cross his legs. "And I suspect that by the time I've heard the answers to the questions I have for you this morning, we'll be further forward still."

Murray nodded. "Zoe told you, then? I'd hoped she would let me do that myself."

"Was that what you arranged on Thursday night after I left?" Buchanan asked.

Murray shrugged. "That's what I understood the arrangement to be. Not that it matters."

"She didn't intend to tell me, as a matter of fact, but I suspected she knew something she was keeping to herself, and I had to know what it was."

Murray twisted a dry smile. "Yes, you could make her talk, Tam; I've seen you in court. How many people know about it?"

"More people than would have known about it if you'd trusted me with the information in the first place," Buchanan told him sharply, anger clenching the muscles around his mouth. "You never were much good at leading a double life, Murray, and evidently you don't find it easy to learn from past mistakes. I don't suppose it will do any good to point out that you are playing with fire?"

Murray rocked forwards and backwards, studying his locked hands and flicking quick glances up at Buchanan's face. "I know how it looks to you, Tam, but it's not as simple as all that. I wouldn't dream of coming between Dianne and Sherry or doing anything to endanger their marriage."

"Oh, that's a relief, then," Fizz put in brightly. "Sherry doesn't mind you poking his wife?"

"Fizz —" said Buchanan in a gravelly voice, and turned back to Murray with manifestly strained patience.

Murray recrossed his legs and clasped his hands tightly over one knee. "I'm going to have to trust you both with information that simply can't be allowed to go any further. Is that understood?"

Buchanan merely looked impatient, as though such assurances were implicit in their relationship.

"What about Zoe?" Fizz temporised. Whatever you thought about Zoe, at least she could be trusted to keep her mouth shut, and either she was part of the team or she wasn't.

"Okay, but no one else. You'll see how important it is." He kept them hanging on while he, apparently,

248

psyched himself up to say it. "Dianne and Sherry's marriage . . . well, it's a marriage of convenience, you might say. They've been very close for years but . . . but, it was never sexual. In fact, Sheridan is a closet homosexual."

Fizz was utterly thunderstruck and could do nothing but gape wordlessly. Buchanan gasped out, "Dear God!" which, admittedly, wasn't much, but compared with his usual taciturnity was comparable to a primal scream.

"It's not possible," Fizz got out at last. "He's the most macho thing on the screen! That guy is sex on a *stick*! Take away the macho image and there's nothing left."

"Exactly." Murray nodded. "That's why it's so important to him to appear straight. That's why he needed a wife. It suited Dianne perfectly as well, because it gave her career the boost it needed after her second play was slammed by the critics." He spread his hands helplessly. "Marrying me was out of the question after my arrest, and she couldn't envisage ever wanting to marry anyone else, so it seemed a worthwhile arrangement on both sides. Sherry continues to have very discreet liaisons and doesn't enquire too closely into what Dianne is doing much of the time, but you can see how devastating it would be to them both if the media got hold of the story."

Buchanan set his elbows on the desk and clasped his head. Fizz would have liked to make use of the opportunity to establish if there had been a long history of insanity in Murray's family, but she was forestalled by the ringing of the telephone in the outer office.

It was Zoe. "Just touching base," she said. "Has Buchanan spoken to Murray yet?"

"Just getting around to it," Fizz told her, aware that Buchanan and Murray could hear every word.

Zoe got the message. "They can hear what you're saying? Okay, I'm with you. Just answer yes or no. How is Tam taking it? Is he furious?"

"I think you could say that, yes."

"Crumbs!"

Fizz couldn't believe there was anyone left alive who still said that. "My thoughts exactly," she murmured.

"What do you think, Fizz? Tam's not going to drop the case, is he?"

"Well, it's a little too soon to be sure," Fizz said. "But I'd give about ten to one against."

"Thank God! I haven't stopped thinking about it all weekend. Think they'd care to come over for supper?"

"I'll ask." Fizz raised her voice half a decibel. "But I suspect Buchanan will be playing golf this evening. He has a match on Saturday. Hang on, I'll see what he says."

She could see by their faces that they had followed the last part of the conversation without difficulty and hardly needed the recap. Murray accepted right away, and Buchanan hesitated only a second before grimacing, yes, Fizz was quite right, he had better take the chance of a couple of hours' practice while he had the opportunity.

By the time Fizz had relayed this message and returned to the inner office, Buchanan was back on the attack. "Okay," he was saying, "you don't need me to tell you that you're walking a tightrope. You've been doing that since the day you met that woman. I don't know what sort of hold she has on you, but it looks to me as though when she says 'Jump!' you don't even ask how high."

"I love her, if that's what you mean," Murray said grimly. "I'm going to do what I can to make her happy. What's wrong with that?"

"Sure. You loved her enough to break Anne's heart," Buchanan said, looking as tough as Fizz had ever seen him. "You loved her enough to park Debbie with whoever would take her just so's you could be together. I think you also loved her enough to steal a dead man's work for her. The work that formed the storyline of *Fade to Black*."

Murray didn't move a muscle. His eyes were fixed, unbelievingly, on Buchanan's face and didn't flinch as he stopped speaking. He seemed to be afraid to move in case he shattered into pieces and fell to the floor with a sound like breaking glass. A small muscle started twitching at the side of his eye.

Buchanan took his silence as an admission of guilt. "I'd have thought you might have had trouble squaring that with your conscience."

Murray stirred himself and drew a long breath, as though waking from a deep sleep. "How did you find out?"

Buchanan moved a hand impatiently. "Via the two gays who called at your house. You were taking a big chance, Murray."

"Not really. I mean, I didn't plan for it to happen." He slid his chair closer to the desk and set his hands on it, leaning closer to Buchanan. "I never intended to let Dianne use the story, Tam. I let her read it, yes, but that was because I thought it was publishable and wanted her opinion. It was only when Adrian died — just as she finished reading it — that she realised we were the only people to have read it. Adrian had no relations, it wasn't as if we were depriving anyone of the royalties, and it was so important to Dianne."

Tears came into his eyes. He pulled out a handkerchief and blew his nose. "I didn't like it. Of course I didn't like it, but she didn't want to hear about my qualms of conscience. As far as she was concerned, this was a gift from the gods and she was keeping it."

"So, you had a fight about it?" Fizz demanded.

He gave her a weary smile. "Not really. I didn't put up much of a fight. Tam's right. Whatever Dianne wanted was okay with me, basically."

"Okay. So let's just get our chronology right," Buchanan said, reaching for a scrap of paper. "How did this fit in with your arrest? You were already in jail by the time it was televised, I think you said?"

Murray drew a hand roughly down across his face, making a little colour rise to the surface. "I was arrested at the beginning of June, so it must have been about six months previously — maybe December of the previous year — that I gave Dianne the manuscript to read. Yes,

December, because Adrian died just before New Year. I'm not too sure when it was televised. I had no access to TV while I was getting protection so I wouldn't have seen it anyway."

"But you did know that she intended to plagiarise it?"

"She gave me the manuscript back, but I knew she had photocopied it," Murray admitted with a shrug, "so I suppose I knew she meant to make some use of it. Only . . ."

"But you didn't realise how much?" Buchanan prompted, and, as Murray looked away, insisted, "It came as a bit of a shock to you the other night when you saw it for the first time?"

"Not really a shock, no." He made an irritable gesture and got up to stare out of the window. "I know what you're thinking, Tam, but you're not going to make me start wondering about Dianne. There was no way she'd have had any trouble from me, even if she'd used that manuscript word for word. As far as I was concerned, it didn't belong to anybody, and the only harm we were doing was in not putting Adrian's name up there under the title alongside Dianne's. Okay, I've said I didn't like it, and I didn't, but Dianne knew that I'd never have given her away. She didn't have to get me out of circulation to protect herself. No way."

Fizz could scarcely contain her exasperation. As far as she was concerned, it was a complete waste of time looking any further than Dianne for their culprit, and the fact that Murray still insisted on refuting any possibility of her guilt was simply proof that his mind was deranged. She tried to catch Buchanan's eye, but he was having none of it.

"You're saying that Dianne didn't have a motive for framing you," he said to Murray. "But what you really mean is that she *may* have had a motive but you don't know what it was."

"No, that's not what I mean!" Murray spun round from the window and came back to lean over the table. "I'm telling you, Tam, I'd trust that woman with my life. I'm not blind to her faults. I've known her for eight years and I know what she's like. She's quick-tempered, she's opinionated, and as far as her work's concerned she's the most selfish person I've ever known, but she loves me. I'm as sure of that as I am of anything in this world, and I know she'd never do anything to hurt me. In any case, she was out of the country when I was arrested, and had been for a few weeks. Whoever planted evidence in my office and in my home, it wasn't Dianne."

"Sit down, Murray," Buchanan said wearily, and Murray slid back into his chair, silently simmering.

"Okay. You've got your opinion, I've got mine. I'm sorry if it annoys you, but the facts do point in Dianne's direction. She has the motive, the means and the opportunity. I'll want to talk to her alone, then I'll want to talk to you both together, and I'll want some straight answers from you both, otherwise please stop asking me to waste my time on this case. Do you understand that, Murray?"

Murray nodded miserably. "She'll see you. She wants to see you, Tam. She's always said she'll do anything she can to help get things cleared up, but I . . . Anyway, she'll see you tomorrow morning. She'll be at her hotel all morning. Sherry won't be there because he has a meeting in London today and won't be back till tomorrow afternoon."

"Right. I'll try to get away about eleven thirty." Buchanan seemed to become aware of Fizz's pointed look without actually turning his eyes towards her. "Don't even think about it, Fizz."

Snubbed, she made a dignified exit, more hurt than angry, and started putting the cover on her computer. She wasn't really surprised that Buchanan chose to keep the good interviews for himself, but he might have let her tag along as an observer. He offered her a lift home as he passed through on his way out with Murray, but she declined with just enough coolness to let him see he was not, at present, her favourite person. Murray she would see later at Zoe's, but Buchanan had his mind on other things and made no arrangements to see her again before next Monday. It was as though she had suddenly been relegated to the level of office staff, without so much as a "thanks a lot".

Just as she was locking up, the phone rang, and Donna's voice, sounding clipped, informed her that Buchanan had just walked right past her desk without even looking at her.

"I said, 'Hi, Mr Buchanan. Another day, another dollar, huh?' and he never even heard me. You'd think, if you'd been sort of bringing me to his attention like you said, he'd at least hear me talking to him!"

Fizz had known this would happen sooner or later. "Gimme a break, Donna, it's only been a fortnight."

"Yes, but you said —"

"I thought we agreed we weren't going to rush things? Come *on*, is he worth waiting for or do you want to ruin the whole thing by being too heavy-handed? Just tell me, Donna. We'll do it your way if you like."

"It's not that I want to rush things, it's just — well, I'm keeping my side of the bargain. I'm just about working around the clock doing all this editing for you in my spare time, and I don't see any progress with your side of things."

"You may not see it, Donna, but believe me, it's happening. You haven't seen Janine around lately, have you?"

That made her pause.

"Janine's . . . out of the picture?"

"A thing of the past," Fizz assured her, her vestigial conscience dealing her a sharp, but passing, pang. "We're getting there, one step at a time."

"Yes, but he doesn't seem to be any more *aware* of me. As a woman. Even when he gives me a wave you can tell he doesn't really *see* me. I've seen people waving at *taxis* with more affection."

"You'll see a big difference any day now, Donna," Fizz assured her robustly. "Besides, I won't have to lean on you much longer; my typing speed's getting better every day."

"Well, I just wanted you to know how I feel about this arrangement of ours. You've got to admit it's been a bit one-sided up till now."

256

Fizz mollified her as best she could, but she had a feeling Donna was a bit of a loose cannon. It was never a good idea to promise something that was impossible to achieve. Fizz appreciated that, but when you had nothing to bargain with, all you could do was bluff and pray for time. In time, after all, anything could happen: Donna could drop dead, Buchanan could drop dead, Donna could meet someone else, Buchanan could go bald, Donna could turn frigid, or Buchanan could lose his mind and fall for her off his own bat.

However, in this instance, time appeared to be running out, and Donna could cause a fair bit of trouble if she so chose. What to do about it? One could, of course, try to improve one's secretarial skills, and, in the meanwhile, try to impress Buchanan with one's general usefulness around the place; but that wasn't going to happen overnight, and it was severely off-putting to have Donna ticking away like a time bomb in the background. Now, Fizz could see, was the time to be earning a few Brownie points from Buchanan, just to have something to fall back on when the shit hit the fan.

She sat for a while rearranging her stationery and tidying her desk, and her mind kept going back to the crayoned picture she had requisitioned from Phillis's house. She had been thinking about it on and off since she'd taken it from Zoe's flat on Thursday night. There was something about it that she found intriguing.

There were nine figures in the composition, all of them roughly the same size and with the same big round heads, smiley mouths and stick-like arms and legs. Three of them were dressed in green, which at Sunnyside Playgroup identified them as boys, and five of them wore the lilac smocks that were issued to the girls. There was, however, a ninth figure that wore neither green nor lilac but a shade of turquoise that, although not vastly different from the green of the boys' overalls, had been quite clearly chosen deliberately to indicate a different person.

Admittedly, it was just a kiddy's scrawl, and you couldn't regard it as a faithful representation of what she was looking at when she drew it, but you could see that she'd been really trying. The nine figures were similar in outline, but you could tell that they were based on actual people. One wore Wellington boots, one had an unmistakable sticking plaster on his knee, one little girl had plaits, and there was a variety of hair colouring that showed Debbie's intention to get it right. Of course, it was always possible that the ninth figure had been coloured in a different shade because she had run out of green, but Fizz was beginning to doubt that.

That single dissimilar figure had to be an adult, had to be wearing an apron, not a smock, had to be the helper who was working at the playgroup during the time Debbie was allegedly being abused. Therefore, it had to be a representation of the person who had altered the particular drawings that had put Murray in jail. Okay, it wasn't going to provide a photofit picture, but if it proved to be who Fizz thought it was, Buchanan was bound to be impressed by her deductive powers.

The trouble was, the only people who could identify the figure were Mrs Torkington and Shona, and that meant leaning on Zoe to give her a lift to Berwick, which was not on, particularly after Zoe had appropriated her hospice lead. She wanted all the credit for this one to be her own.

She had things to do in the afternoon: tickets to be picked up for a half-price performance at the Lyceum, books to go back to the library before they incurred a substantial fine; but both of these could be postponed till the evening. She could hop on a train and make it to Berwick well before the playgroup closed for the day. The fare would make a hole in her week's spending money, but she hadn't travelled the world for seven years without learning how to avoid ticket collectors, and even if she had to cough up, it would be worth it. Buchanan couldn't fail to be impressed if she managed to pinpoint the culprit, especially with no more to go on than he'd had himself.

The trains, unfortunately, weren't all that frequent, which meant she had to jog all the way from the station, and the last of the kids were just checking out as she arrived. Shona was on gate duty.

"Come on in and have a cup of coffee with us. Mrs Torkington and I usually put our feet up for half an hour before we start heading for home. By this time in the afternoon we're in dire need of a little peace and quiet, and it gives us a chance to talk over the events of the day and compare notes."

Mrs Torkington had already got the coffee going and was setting out mugs and biscuits on her desk. While

Shona went to get another mug, she kicked off her shoes and sank into an armchair, propping her small fat feet on a handy pushalong pony.

"Oh, dearie me, I'm getting too old for this job, I really am." Her blackbird eyes invited Fizz to refute that imputation, but, getting no response, she went on, "The children are much more difficult to handle these days than they were when I started in the business, you know. Much more confident. Much more articulate. I put it down to the amount of television they watch."

Shona arrived back with the extra mug and passed round the coffee and biscuits. "I had a feeling we'd see you again," she said. "Didn't I, Mrs Torkington? We've been trying to remember some more details about Kate, but we haven't been able to come up with anything worthwhile, I'm afraid."

"Actually, I have something here that I was rather hoping might jog your memory." Fizz drew out Debbie's picture and passed it across. "This is a picture she did at her aunt's house round about the same time she was drawing the strange pictures here."

Shona held the paper sideways to share it with Mrs Torkington, and they both nodded appreciatively.

"Yes, I could almost have recognised it as one of Debbie's," Mrs Torkington said, looking at Shona for confirmation. "She used to love drawing her chums."

"You can tell it's a picture of playgroup," Shona pointed out. "The smocks. Green for boys and lilac for girls."

260

"Yes, that's what drew my attention to this figure." Fizz leaned across and tapped the half-formed splotch of turquoise. "It's neither a boy nor a girl, is it?"

"No, it's probably a helper," said Mrs Torkington, and then held the picture closer with sudden interest. For a moment both she and Shona studied it closely, then Shona said:

"It's Kate, isn't it? That red hair."

"That's who it is, dear. We never had another helper with hair that colour."

They both lifted their eyes in unison to look at Fizz, and Shona said, "Does that help you at all?"

"It could turn out to be significant. I'm not sure yet." Fizz tried to look noncommittal, but it wasn't easy. She had tried not to let her suspicions outrun the facts, but she couldn't help remembering what Mrs McCaulay had said when she'd been talking about the visitors to Murray's house before his arrest. It had been something like: "And there was that woman with the red hair. The writer. Dianne Frazer Ballantyne."

No matter what Murray had to say on the subject, it was beginning to look as though his girlfriend had a lot of explaining to do.

Fizz was so flushed with success that the forty-five-minute train journey back to Edinburgh passed in a blur. Her mind, forced into an unaccustomed period of contemplation, went into overdrive, and she emerged at Waverley Street full of ways to prove Dianne's guilt. First stop had to be her friend in the *Scotsman* reference library.

CHAPTER
EIGHTEEN

It had to be the hottest day of the year. A day for lounging around in the Meadows, or sipping iced tea in a pavement café in the High Street, or paddling on the shore at Portobello. Not a day for haring around the city like a mad thing in the sweater and jeans one had donned in the cool of the morning.

Fizz had spent an hour in the *Scotsman* offices on North Bridge while her friend, Keiran, tracked down the organising committee for the relevant International TV Festival. It wasn't easy, in fact he told Fizz every ten minutes that it was impossible, but in the end he came up with a phone number that he claimed would put her in touch with the office of the organisers. Unfortunately, it was a New York telephone number, and there was no way he was going to dial it. Not even for an old friend.

A call like that could cost plenty, Fizz realised. She might have to hold on for several minutes while somebody looked up three-year-old lists of nominees, and she didn't have that kind of cash to spare. That meant she'd have to use a free phone, and the only free phone she could access was in the legal advice office at the community centre. She still had the keys in her pocket, and if she got a move on, she could just about make it before it closed for the night.

Donna gaped at her in amazement as she skidded past reception and thumbed the lift button.

"Forgot something!" Fizz made circling motions beside her temple with a forefinger and rolled her eyes up in mock exasperation. Luckily, the lift door opened before she had to go into details, but she knew that Donna would be lying in wait for her when she came back down.

The rest of the operation went surprisingly smoothly. She got a line that sounded as if it was connected to the next-door office, and the secretary who answered the call was smoothly efficient. It took her four minutes to find the information and to inform Fizz that no, there had been no Dianne Frazer Ballantyne among the nominees the year in question. Fizz thanked her effusively and hung up fast before McGuigan should catch her red-handed.

She shoved some blank typing paper in an envelope and scribbled an address on the outside, then dashed back downstairs, waving it at Donna.

"Buchanan would have killed me if I'd forgotten to post this!"

"Leave it with me." Donna held out a hand for it. "It can go with my mail."

"Thanks, but I'm going to dash up to the main post office with it. It may catch an earlier collection." Fizz made for the door, but Donna wasn't finished with her yet.

"You seemed to take a long time up there."

Fizz smiled into her hard eyes. "Had to go to the loo."

Outside, she kicked herself for not thinking of a better excuse. She'd have to spend a little time on Donna in the near future, but right now her mind was too busy with the implications of what she had just turned up. She phoned Buchanan from a call box in the High Street, but there was no reply. He had probably already left for the golf course, which was a nuisance because she didn't dare tell Murray and Zoe about Dianne's false alibi without clearing it with Buchanan first.

By the time she'd had a shower and changed, it was twenty past seven, so she had to take a bus round to Zoe's. It was hotter than ever, and although Zoe had every window wide open, her flat was stuffy and the smell of fondue hung in the still air like damp washing.

Zoe and Murray had evidently been discussing what had transpired in the legal advice office that morning, and returned to that topic as they sat down to eat.

"I know that you're worried about dragging Dianne's name in the mud, Murray," Zoe said, pouring wine with a delicately arched wrist. "But I think you made a serious mistake when you chose not to tell Tam you were still seeing her."

"So do I," Fizz told him. "You might have known it would all come out anyway, and you weren't exactly discreet, were you?"

"Normally we were totally discreet," Murray insisted. "I usually only visited her at her hotel in the evenings. The time that Zoe saw us, I'd just met her as she got out of her taxi. We weren't on the street for more than a couple of minutes."

"Yes, it was bad luck I happened along, Murray, but in another way, perhaps it was just as well. It brought out something that Tam needed to know."

"Why, for God's sake? What the hell difference does it make whether I'm still seeing Dianne or not?" Murray gulped wine and set down his glass. "There was no need for her name to be connected with this business at all. It could be disastrous for her if it got into the tabloids, as Buchanan must realise, so I don't know why he has to take this dogmatic attitude."

That got right up Fizz's nose. "I don't think you have anything to complain about in Buchanan's attitude," she told him. "In fact it's my opinion that he has been too damn lenient with you all the way along the line."

Murray was obviously taken aback by this attack. "What do you mean, lenient with me?"

"I mean," said Fizz, "that if it had been up to me I'd have lost patience with you as soon as I discovered how much you were keeping to yourself. You've got a brass neck expecting to waste his time on your case when you can't even trust him with the facts."

"That's ridiculous!" Murray snapped. "I never held back anything that would have been of use to him."

"I just don't understand how your mind works," Fizz declared nastily. "My God, if you can't trust Buchanan to keep his mouth shut about your girlfriend, who can you trust?"

Murray glared back at her, swallowing a mouthful of bread as though he had tonsillitis, but before he could voice a retort, Zoe interrupted smoothly, asking if anyone would like fruit to follow. She had a way of speaking softly that was an unspoken rebuke and a reminder that this was a social occasion, and both Murray and Fizz took the hint and changed the subject. But later, when they were sitting with their second cups of coffee beside the open window, things flared up again.

It was Fizz's fault, she accepted that, and she knew that the unshared information she held about Dianne and the TV award was behind her irritation. Murray so manifestly thought the sun shone out of Dianne's ears and he would hear no word against her. His final mistake was to claim that Dianne would sacrifice her career in a minute if it would clear his name.

"Where are you coming from, Murray?" Fizz sighed. "You keep on telling us that Dianne's the second Christ, but the facts simply don't support that hypothesis. Every single thing I hear about her points to the fact that she's a self-seeking, conniving, manipulative opportunist."

Murray reared back as though he'd been punched, and gripped the arm of his chair. "Just shut up, Fizz, would you? You haven't a clue what you're talking about. You've never even met Dianne, but you think you can sit there and —"

"I don't have to meet her! Anyone with half an eye can see she's got you utterly pixillated! All that bosh about her marriage being one of convenience! If you'll believe that you'll believe anything!"

266

"It happens to be true," Murray said, with cold dignity. He uncrossed his legs and stood up. "I'm sorry about this, Zoe, but I think it would be better if I just left. There doesn't appear to be anything I can say to convince Fizz that she's got the wrong end of the stick, and I don't want to cause any more contention."

"Don't take it so seriously, Murray," Zoe said, catching at his sleeve and trying to pull him back down. "I'm sure Fizz didn't mean to upset you!"

"Oh, stop it!" Fizz interrupted. "I'm sick of being treated like an idiot child. If it upsets you, Murray, that's too bad! But don't ask me to accept that Dianne and Sheridan are just good friends. Even if Sheridan *were* a homosexual — which I find hard to believe — I just don't —"

"*What?*" Zoe's arm jerked spasmodically, knocking over a glass figurine on the table beside her. She stared at it uncomprehendingly, and then turned back to Fizz. "Are you trying to say Sherry's a homosexual? Is that what you're saying?"

"So Murray told us this morning," Fizz said. "But —"

"But that's ridiculous!" Zoe turned to Murray, her face almost a caricature of incredulity. "Why should you say a silly thing like that?"

"There's no point in this discussion. I'm leaving."

"No, Murray, wait a minute, please." Zoe stood up and put a hand on the back of her armchair, as though to have something to hang on to. Fizz could see at a glance that she had something unpleasant to say and was gearing herself up to it. "You're saying that Dianne

267

and Sherry's marriage is a sham — that it's a cover-up for Sherry's homosexuality. Is that what you believe, Murray?"

Murray didn't answer. He walked over to the couch where he'd left his jacket, and slung it over one shoulder.

Fizz watched him with simmering exasperation, and answered for him. "That's what he believes, Zoe, and that's what he expects us to believe, and I for one have had enough of being strung along like a fool. Anyone but a besotted lunatic could see at a glance that it's a load of codswallop!"

"It's certainly very far from the truth," Zoe said, halting Murray in the doorway. She shook her head. "Sherry's not a homosexual, Murray. I don't care who says it, it's simply not true. I know that for a fact."

Murray's jaw worked but he said nothing. Fizz could almost see his brain churning in an effort to find an out. She said, "How can you be so sure, Zoe?"

Zoe looked at Murray as if she were asking his permission to go on, but he just stared back at her like some dumb animal awaiting the stun gun.

"I've known Sherry as long as I've known Dianne. Longer. I saw a lot of him when he was just starting to get himself noticed. He was doing rep at the Lyceum, and he and I . . . It wasn't all that serious, but, well, once or twice we ended up together after a party." Zoe's voice faltered uncertainly. "I'm sorry, Murray, he's definitely not gay. There were other girls before me — and after me as well."

Murray's face was drawn, but he wasn't going to go down without a fight. "He may not always have been gay — he may even have been bi at that point — but —"

"Murray," Fizz said, hanging on to her temper with both hands, "you can't keep on turning your back on the facts. Dianne doesn't even have a nodding acquaintance with the truth. She just tells you what suits her at the time."

Murray's face flushed. "Damn you, Fizz! Why don't you just mind your own bloody business, huh? I never asked you to push your —"

"Okay!" Fizz shouted at him, losing the place altogether. "Okay, already! But just let me say one thing, Murray. You don't know everything about Dianne Frazer sodding Ballantyne, and maybe if you did you wouldn't be such a pain in the butt!"

She knew she had said too much as soon as the words were out. Both Murray and Zoe were looking at her with expressions in which doubt did not play a part. They knew she had information which she was not sharing, and they wanted to hear it.

"You've found out something else about Dianne," Zoe said.

Fizz shrugged. "I haven't even told Buchanan yet, but . . . Oh hell, what difference does it make? Well, for one thing, I have to tell you, Murray, that the way things are looking, it may have been Dianne who doctored Debbie's drawings."

Murray threw up a hand like a man fending off a blow. "That's insane! It's . . . it's . . ."

Fizz went to her shoulder bag, which she had thrown on the floor beside the TV set, and pulled out Debbie's drawing. It was beginning to look a bit dog-eared but she smoothed it out and stuck it back up on Zoe's memory board. "Debbie drew this at Phillis's house just before you were arrested. That figure with the red hair," she jabbed at it with a forefinger, "isn't a kiddy, it's a helper who called herself 'Kate'. She was the one who attracted Mrs Torkington's attention to the strange drawings that supposedly originated with Debbie. Then she disappeared without trace." She left Murray examining the paper and walked away to the window.

Nobody said anything. After a minute Murray turned his back on the other two and sat down on the arm of the couch. His jacket slipped from his shoulder and slithered to the floor. Moving quietly, Zoe poured the last of the coffee into his cup and took it to him, laying a hand on his shoulder.

She said, "You know, just because this helper had red hair —"

"Exactly," said Murray, straightening and looking at her with pathetic gratitude. "It proves nothing! You can't even know for sure, Fizz, whether this red-haired person is a helper or not! A head and four stick-like limbs — Christ, it might not even be a woman! And how do you know he or she was the one to alter Debbie's drawings? You're making bricks without straw. It's only a kiddy's drawing — red could have been the first crayon to come to her hand!"

Zoe saw Fizz's anger at this negative reaction and sent her a warning glance. "Fizz, I think you've said

270

enough, okay? Whatever else you've found out about Dianne, I think you should let it lie for the present. Murray's had enough to cope with for —"

"No!" Murray said, roughly, glaring in Fizz's direction. "If you have something to say, spit it out. You're determined to poison my mind against Dianne one way or another, so let's get it over with."

Fizz had intended to keep quiet about the second piece of information till she had cleared it with Buchanan, but she was now beyond thinking about discretion. "Okay, Murray, since you want the facts: I did some research this afternoon on the International TV Festival where Dianne got an award — the one you told us she was attending for the three weeks prior to your arrest. She wasn't there, not as a nominee, she wasn't."

Murray had lost his bluster. His voice sounded shaky and uncertain. "You can't possibly know that."

"I can. I phoned New York this afternoon. You can check up yourself, Murray, I'll give you the number. But you can take my word for it; when Dianne told you she was picking up an award in New York, she was lying to you. That's one we can prove."

The sound that escaped from Murray was neither a howl nor a groan but a shocking combination of the two. He spun away sideways, clamping both hands tightly around his skull, and only then did Fizz realise how the pain had been building up inside him with every allegation. He seemed to be sobbing, only the sobs were words, punched out of him by the force of some emotion Fizz could only guess at. She couldn't make out what he was saying, but the effect was frightening. She caught him by the shoulders and pulled him round to face her. There was so much violence in him that she could feel it buzzing through her fingertips. "Stop it, Murray," she said, shaking him firmly. "For God's sake cut that out!"

He pulled away from her, twisting to send an anguished look at Zoe, as though he hoped she could come up with some sort of explanation. Zoe, however, looked so shocked by his reaction that she was unlikely to be any good to anybody.

"There could be an explanation . . ." Murray whispered.

Fizz stared at him, amazed by his tenacity. "Accept it, Murray," she said, gently for her. "Somebody framed you to get you out of circulation. I think you know who it was and I think you know why."

"Yes," he said so softly that the word seemed to fall from his lips like a feather.

"The manuscript?" Fizz asked.

He didn't answer. His face was grey with pain and his eyes seemed sunk back in his head. "How could she do this to me?" he moaned, suddenly clawing furiously at his scalp as if he thought he could dig some agonising thought out of his brain with his fingernails. "She strung me along all those years to keep my mouth shut, and all the time she . . . Jesus! How could she do that to Debbie? I'll throttle the bitch!"

"Murray, there's no proof against Dianne!" Zoe stepped in front of him as he grabbed his jacket and lunged for the door. "You're jumping to conclusions —"

He barged past her as though she weren't there, and slammed out before she could grab at him. Zoe whirled on Fizz, ashen-faced. She said, "Do something, Fizz!"

Even Fizz was a little shaken, but she didn't move from the window. "Do what? He's got the edge on me for both weight and reach, and I don't think he's in the mood to do me any favours. If he wants to have it out with Dianne, he's got my blessing. It's about time they got their differences straightened out, don't you think?"

"I don't know what to think," Zoe muttered, stepping away from the door as though she had no clear idea of where she was headed or what she was going to do when she got there. "I'm just scared he'll do something silly."

"Like what? You don't think he'll really throttle her, do you? Murray? Are you kidding?"

"I think we should go after him," Zoe said, big-eyed with worry. "I just can't sit here and let him run amok like that. He might hurt Dianne — he might throw himself under a bus! We can't simply shrug our shoulders and let him get on with it! Come on, Fizz, you'll have to help me stop him!"

"You're crazy," Fizz said. "You'll never catch him up now, and you don't even know where Dianne's staying."

"Yes I do. She's at the Hamilton House Hotel. She always stays there when she's in Edinburgh." Zoe ran for her coat and car keys.

Fizz was inclined to think Zoe was over-reacting, but she had to admit that, if Murray were to do something silly, she herself wasn't going to come out of it smelling of violets, since she had been the one to light the blue touchpaper and retire. Buchanan wouldn't like that.

"Listen," she said, determined to stay calm, "at the rate Murray was moving just then, he'll be there before you can get the car started. The Hamilton House Hotel is only ten minutes away if you cut across Calton Hill. Why don't you just phone Dianne and tell her he's on his way?"

Zoe stopped in her tracks and stared at the telephone. She shook her head. "Can't do it. We haven't seen each other for years — way before this Debbie business — and she'd think I was mad if I suddenly popped up out of nowhere screaming that Murray was on his way to beat her up. Maybe I *am* mad! He'll probably have cooled off by the time he gets there."

"*If* he gets there," Fizz pointed out. "He may not be headed for Dianne after all."

Zoe made for the door. "I think he is. And it's our fault, Fizz. We should never have sprung it on him like we did, and you know as well as I do that Tam is going to be furious with us when he finds out. Now's the time to attempt a little damage limitation, don't you think?"

Fizz followed her unwillingly, scooping up her bag *en route*. "I think it's a bit late to be thinking about it," she said, but with considerably less truculence.

The streets were busy with pedestrians, parties of Japanese tourists, young people setting out for late dinners or early discos, fly-posters pasting up advertisements for Festival Fringe productions, but there was very little traffic on the roads. It was just sheer bad luck that every traffic light was against them.

CHAPTER
NINETEEN

Even on a normal morning Buchanan was not among those who leapt from between the sheets with a glad cry to welcome the new day. It took, on average, some ten minutes and the top half of a mug of coffee before his eyes opened more than a slit, and he liked to spend those minutes gently piecing himself together, functioning on auto-pilot and with all cerebral activity reduced to a minimum.

To be wrenched, at six twenty a.m., from a state verging on catalepsy wounded his psyche deeply and plunged him into a state of depression which only intensified as the day advanced. Bad enough to be woken at that unchristian hour, but to be plunged, courtesy of BT, into a scenario that included a client being held on suspicion of murder and two close associates helping the police with their enquiries threw him seriously off-balance.

He got into the shower and turned both the temperature and the flow to maximum while he tried to get his thoughts in order.

Dianne was dead. That appeared to be the crux of the matter. According to Detective Inspector Fleming of B Division, she had fallen, or been pushed, from the window of her hotel room. Murray was involved in the incident — and quite closely too, otherwise he wouldn't currently be languishing in the incident room at St Leonard's police station. But what were Fizz and Zoe doing there? How the hell had they become embroiled in the affair?

Of the three pieces of news, it was the last one that was the least palatable. Dianne was, after all, practically a stranger to him, and Murray could, frankly, jump off the Scott Monument any time he chose, and the sooner the better. Fizz and Zoe were, however, in a different category, being in effect voluntary helpers, and as such he could be said to have a duty of care towards them.

He swung the heat control as far to cold as it would go and administered a thirty-second blast of iced water, howling agonisedly throughout. This satisfactorily jump-started the waking-up procedure to such an extent that he was shaved, dressed and in the car within ten minutes, and thanks to the empty streets, made it to St Leonards by just after ten to seven.

He spotted Fizz as he stepped through the door.

She was standing in a waiting room area off the main lobby, being fussed over by a young constable and a middle-aged sergeant. She was doing her "motherless child" act and, typically, getting as much mileage as she could out of the situation. Buchanan was struck anew by her ability to shed ten years at the drop of a hat. He would not have been in the least surprised, as she crossed the hall towards him, escorted by the sergeant, to see her take his hand and skip.

"Good morning, Mr Buchanan," said the sergeant, giving Fizz a final smile and a fatherly pat on the shoulder as he transferred her to Buchanan's protection. "I'll just let DI Fleming know you're here."

"Hi," Fizz greeted him, and opened her eyes in an expression of wild surmise. "What about all this, then?"

It was quite clear that she was having the time of her life. "Well, what about it?" Buchanan countered. "You appear to know more about it than I do. All I was told was that Dianne had been found dead and that Murray was being questioned."

"It's not one for the squeamish," she said with relish. "Evidently Dianne took a header out of her bedroom window and was kebabed by the railings beneath. Zoe is taking it real bad."

Buchanan followed her glance and saw Zoe through the open door of an interview room. She looked as though she were in a state of shock. She was sitting on a hard chair with both hands wrapped around a polystyrene cup of coffee, and her blank eyes were huge in a face the colour of cream cheese. He knew he ought to go over and say something comforting and supportive, but he wanted to find out what Fizz had to tell before Fleming arrived.

"Just tell me you weren't with him when it happened."

"You're damn tootin' I wasn't there!" Fizz gave vent to a tiny explosion that was half laugh, half snort. "And I'm quite certain that Murray wasn't there either."

"How did you and Zoe get involved, then?"

"Bloody Murray had left a note for Dianne, earlier in the day, leaving Zoe's number in case she wanted to contact him in the evening. The receptionist had seen him going in, maybe an hour or two before Dianne's body was found, so since she had forgotten to give the note to Dianne, she gave it to the police."

Wonderful, Buchanan thought briefly. If Murray had intended to immerse himself in as much trouble as possible, he could hardly have done it better. "Yes, but why did the police want to question you both?"

She shrugged and looked away. "We were with him earlier at Zoe's place. He started to put two and two together and decided that, after all, Dianne had to have been the one to frame him. Then he worked himself into a real tizzy and took off to have it out with her. I wasn't —"

"Just a minute." She had that offhand look about her that he now recognised as a danger signal. There was something he had missed. Something she had intended that he should miss. He said, "What d'you mean, 'worked himself into a real tizzy'? The last time I talked to him he'd have staked his last breath on Dianne's innocence."

Fizz drew a long breath. She looked over at Zoe, as though willing her to come to her aid. "Okay. Well, I'd found out a couple of things, yesterday afternoon, that made us wonder about Dianne."

"Such as? And be as brief as you can, Fizz, I need to know this before I see Murray."

She knew how to cram a fair amount of information into a few words, he had to give her that, but her

279

delivery was so fast he wasn't sure he had grasped all the facts.

"Okay," he said, holding up a finger to stop her. "We're to suspect that the red-haired helper at the playgroup was Dianne because she wasn't out of the country when she said she was. How do you know she wasn't out of the country? You confirmed that? How?"

"Through a friend of mine who works in the *Scotsman* reference library. She wasn't even nominated for an award, as she claimed at the time."

There was no time to delve deeper into the details of how Fizz had corroborated this evidence — if indeed she had. "Okay. So what happened when Murray stormed out?"

"Well, I wasn't too bothered myself, but Zoe got it into her head that he might do Dianne an injury, so in the end, we got her car out and trundled after him. I knew we hadn't a hope of catching him, but —"

"You knew where he was headed?"

"Sure. Zoe knew the hotel where Dianne always stayed when she was in Edinburgh — the one she'd seen them going into together about a week ago."

"Right. And were you in time to stop him?"

"No chance. It must have taken us twenty minutes or more to get there. Then we spent ages arguing about whether to go in after him and finally just hung around for a while in the hope he might come out. It wasn't all that long before he showed up."

"And how did he look? Would you have thought —"

"No!" Fizz interrupted, shaking her head so vigorously that two wispy ringlets sprang loose and dangled into her eyes. "He looked fine. He'd had it out with Dianne and he was now even more convinced that she was so pure in spirit she'd make Mother Theresa look like the Boston Strangler."

"So what did you do then?"

"Went home. Zoe dropped me off at the North Bridge and then drove Murray home to Morningside. End of story."

"You're sure that's all, Fizz? I don't want any nasty surprises when I'm in there with Murray."

"That's it. Honest." She gave him the Brownie salute: two fingers to the right shoulder. "And Zoe must have said basically the same thing . . . although . . . she may not have seen it in exactly the same light as I did."

"Meaning?" he said tersely, willing her to get a move on.

She glanced over at Zoe and pursed her lips. "I don't know. She's not saying much but I get the impression that she's . . . that she's not quite sure what happened."

The door behind her opened and Fleming came out, accompanied by another officer.

"Are you saying she thinks Murray did it?" Buchanan said in a whisper.

Fizz regarded the approach of the two policemen, and turned back to him calmly. "That's the impression I get."

"Great," he muttered, and held out his hand to Fleming, whom he'd met several times before.

"Good to see you, Tam," said the DI, gripping it with one hand as he indicated his companion with the other. "This is DCI Melville, who's in charge of the case."

They looked like a comedy duo: Fleming, surely the minimum height for a policeman, balding and boot-faced; Melville, built like a grizzly bear, with a shock of grey hair and a Santa Claus smile. "Sorry to drag you out at this hour," the DCI said, "but we've had Murray here since two a.m. and there doesn't seem to be much point in hanging around."

Buchanan nodded grimly. Under Scottish law, they could only hold Murray for six hours, after which they had to either charge him or let him go. And what Melville was saying was, in effect, that he felt they had enough evidence to charge him.

"I'd better see him, then."

"Of course." Melville swung round and almost trod on Fizz, who had been hovering just within earshot. "And this little lady," he beamed, "and her friend can run along home as soon as they've signed their statements. I think we have them ready now."

"You'll see them safely home, I hope," Buchanan murmured. "They're both still pretty shocked."

Fleming, at a nod from the DCI, beckoned the young constable and gave him orders to get a car out and take the girls home. Buchanan tried to catch Zoe's eye before he left, but she gave no sign of being aware of him.

"Better give me a ring at the office this afternoon," he said to Fizz. "I'll have to talk to both of you about this in more detail."

"Roger."

They had Murray in a downstairs interview room next to the cells, sitting alone with his thoughts and clearly not enjoying the experience. He was looking as ghastly as Buchanan had ever seen him, and had obviously been crying a good deal. Guilty or not guilty, it was beyond Buchanan to feel anything but pity for him.

"Tam! Thank God!"

He would have jumped up had Buchanan not put a hand on his shoulder to prevent him.

"Okay, Murray. Just take it easy. We're not going to get anywhere unless you pull yourself together. Let's see if we can rustle up a coffee and get ourselves organised."

"I've had a coffee."

"Have another."

The sergeant who had shown Buchanan in now caught his eye and sent him a quick nod before leaving them alone. Buchanan put his case on the table and took out his pad and pen.

"You know what's happened, Tam?" Murray burst out, tears brimming in his eyes. "She's dead! Some murdering bastard pushed her out a window, and . . . Oh God! Did they tell you what happened to her, Tam . . ." He started to snort and slobber, beating a fist on the table and rocking violently back and forth in his chair.

Buchanan forced himself to look at him. "That's enough, Murray," he said, gripping him firmly by the arm. The biceps muscle felt soft and stringy beneath the flesh. "You have to stop thinking about it now. There'll be a time for grieving later, but right now you have to put it out of your mind and think of other things."

None of this had any visible effect on Murray, but Buchanan kept talking, in the belief that if he went on long enough, sooner or later he'd say the right thing.

"Things are bad, Murray, but they could be worse. If you don't start talking your way out of this you're going to end up back in jail."

That appeared to have some sort of effect. Murray drank some of the coffee when it was put in front of him, and used Buchanan's hanky to wipe his face.

"Okay, Murray. Just tell me what happened last night from the time you left Zoe's."

"It doesn't feel real. It's like I was watching it on TV."

"Yes, sure, but just get on with it, will you? We don't have a lot of time." Buchanan looked at his watch. It was five past seven and he was starving. "What time did you leave Zoe's place?"

"I don't know exactly. Must have been somewhere around nine."

"And how long did it take you to reach the hotel? Ten minutes?"

"Five minutes or so. I was running."

Buchanan could picture him. In the state he was in he wouldn't have gone round by the road, as Zoe and

Fizz would have had to do in the car, but would have taken the pedestrian short cut over Calton Hill. Not the most salubrious spot in the city during the hours of darkness, but that wouldn't have bothered Murray at that point in time. "You went over Calton Hill?"

"Yes."

"When you reached the hotel did you speak to anyone?"

"Only to the receptionist. I asked if Dianne was in her room."

"Can you remember the words you used?"

"I think . . . I think I just said, 'Is she in?' "

"And the receptionist knew to whom you were referring?"

"Yes. She knew me from several previous visits."

"Then you went straight up to Dianne's room?"

"Yes."

"Right. So just tell me what happened, Murray, and try not to leave anything out in case it turns out to be important."

"We talked." Murray spread his hands. "I told her that we'd turned up several facts that made it look as if she had been the person who framed me. And I mentioned all the . . . the points Fizz and Zoe had made earlier."

Buchanan lifted a finger. "When you say you talked, Murray, d'you mean you discussed the matter quietly?"

This question seemed to upset him. He did a lot of sniffing, knuckled his eyes like a schoolboy and said, "We rowed. I said a lot of things . . ."

"Okay. You yelled at her. What was her reaction?"

"Well, she yelled back for a while, then she denied everything."

"Did she offer any explanations? After all, she must have realised that you had grounds for your suspicions."

"When you looked at it, it was all circumstantial." Murray leaned earnestly across the table. "What had been worrying me most was the fact that she hadn't been out of the country during the three weeks prior to my arrest like she'd told me at the time. But she was able to explain that, so I felt —"

"Just a minute." Buchanan stopped him. "What are you trying to rush past me, Murray? Don't try to be smart. You won't get away with that in court."

Murray rolled his red eyes. "She wasn't at the TV Festival. She was in a clinic . . . drying out. She phoned them up, there and then. She let me listen in while she asked the manager to tell her what dates she had stayed there, and then she gave me the phone and made me talk to them. Made me confirm for myself that patients are not allowed out during the three-week treatment. Their outdoor clothes are taken away and they're locked in at night. So, you see, there's no way she could have been in Edinburgh." He leaned across the table and grabbed Buchanan's wrist, stopping him from making notes. "I don't want that to come out in court, Tam. You can see why not. Please don't use it unless you have to."

Buchanan took a moment to get his voice under control. "Murray," he said bitterly, "you have the mental age of a six-week foetus. If you had given the

286

police this information they might not at this moment be getting ready to charge you. They think you had a motive to kill Dianne, but you can prove that you hadn't. You can show them that you knew she couldn't have framed you. I hope you know the name of the clinic? The police will want to confirm the facts, and also establish the time of your call."

Murray locked eyes with him. "Can you get them to let me out of here?"

"I'll try, Murray, I'll try. Just let's tidy up a few things first. What did she say to your other bits of evidence? The red-haired nursery assistant, for instance?"

"Just that it wasn't her. And as far as Sherry's heterosexuality is concerned, she denied that too."

"So, what happened after you had established that?"

"I got out. I never stayed with her at night."

"Did you speak to anyone on the way out?"

Murray thought back. "No. I don't remember seeing anyone at the reception desk — they'd probably gone off duty by then, and the night porter was probably in his cubbyhole watching telly as usual — but Zoe and Fizz were waiting outside for me."

"Had you made an arrangement to meet them there?"

"No. They just . . . I think they were worried about me."

"And they ran you home?"

"Yes. Zoe dropped Fizz off at the end of North Bridge and then drove me out to Morningside."

"And what did you do when you arrived home?"

"I made myself some tea and then went to bed."

"Okay, I think that's all I need to know at the moment."

"Can you get me released?"

"I'll do my best. But listen, Murray, if they insist on charging you, just sit tight and say nothing you don't have to say, and I'll see you in court in the morning."

He left Murray sitting at the table and went outside to tell the sergeant on the door that he needed to speak to DI Fleming. Melville might be in charge of the case, but Buchanan knew Fleming and, more importantly, Fleming knew him.

The interview lasted some fifteen minutes, since Fleming had to corroborate Murray's claims about the clinic. He was extremely reluctant to let Murray go, but Buchanan kept insisting that he had no motive and that the two witnesses could testify to his calm demeanour immediately after emerging from the hotel. In the end it was Melville who sanctioned his release, but it was clear that both he and Fleming expected it was only a matter of time before they had enough evidence to press charges.

Buchanan waited while Murray was warned not to leave the country etc., and then trundled him speedily out to the car.

"I hope you realise what a narrow escape you just had," he told him as they pulled out of the car park. "If you hadn't had me there to advise you you'd have talked your way back into Saughton."

Murray lay in the passenger seat as though he hadn't the strength to sit upright. "Where are you taking me?"

"Where do you think I'm taking you? I'm taking you home."

"Not to Morningside, Tam. Please don't leave me there on my own. Can't I go home with you? Just for one night."

Buchanan was so horrified by this suggestion that he braked momentarily, causing the old lady in the Fiesta behind him to utter a word she had forgotten she even knew.

"I don't have a spare bed, sorry," he muttered.

"I'll sleep on the couch. On the floor. I don't care, Tam, but just don't leave me alone tonight."

Tam couldn't bring himself to reply. But nor, in the end, could he bring himself to take the turn-off for Morningside.

CHAPTER
TWENTY

After all the excitement of Dianne's death and Murray's, albeit brief, incarceration, Fizz found the subsequent twenty-four-hour stand-off unbearably frustrating.

Murray, she quite understood, had every reason to want a bit of peace and quiet after the trauma of the night before, but Buchanan's insistence on keeping him company seemed quite unnecessary. She offered to come over and spread a little sunshine but was repulsed with a firmness which she would have found, had she been a sensitive sort of person, less than flattering. They'd talk tomorrow night, Buchanan promised when she phoned him after he got home from the police station. By that time Murray might feel like seeing his friends, and if not, he'd at least be more amenable to being left on his own for an hour or two.

Zoe was just as bad. She seemed to be the sort of person who, when faced with an unforeseen mishap, such as the crucifixion of a once-close friend, simply crawled under the duvet and refused to answer the phone. It was five p.m. before Fizz managed to raise her, and even then it was only for a couple of minutes.

"Honestly, Fizz, I don't think I could face talking about last night. I'm having to try very hard not to think about it, and I really feel in need of a night off. I'm going to have a long soak in a hot bath and watch the Pinter play on TV."

"I could come over and watch it with you . . ."

"No, thanks, Fizz, but . . ."

"We wouldn't have to talk about . . ."

"Fizz . . . no, okay?"

Thwarted, Fizz had no option but to drop in on a couple of ex-art-school friends who shared a studio nearby and convince them that they wanted to see the Pinter play and that they'd enjoy having her watch it with them. Having no TV, she found, was seldom a problem, since on the very rare occasions when she wanted to see a programme, she could usually gatecrash.

That took care of Tuesday evening, but the whole of Wednesday stretched ahead like an Arkansas highway. Bored and frustrated, she hopped on a bus out to Hillend and spent four hours walking off her excess energy: over Capelaw Hill by way of the ski slope, round Glencorse Reservoir, over the shoulder of Carnethy Hill to the main road and back to Flotterstone Inn for a McEwans Export before the bus arrived. The Pentland Hills weren't on a par with the Tarmachan Ridge, on which she had worn out her first pair of boots as a child in Perthshire, but they were better than nothing. The wind was crisp and cool and the silence, after the noise of the city centre, was a pleasure in itself.

Her head, as she walked, was buzzing with thoughts of Dianne's grisly death which she had managed till now to keep at bay. Until midway through the afternoon she felt quite detached from the events, almost as though the whole business had happened a long time ago. Even the description of the crucifixion, which she had heard from the young police constable (Dougie: a bit soft but might be handy to know), had not, at the time, conjured up too graphic a picture. But while she was sitting on top of Carnethy eating a banana and admiring the view, it came back to her with a new and almost emetic clarity. The thought that the perpetrator of that horrific crime might be someone she knew gave her pause for serious consideration. She had thought Zoe's reaction yesterday to be somewhat over the top, but maybe she had just seen things more clearly than Fizz had.

She was starving by the time she got home, but since she didn't hold out much hope of Zoe providing any famine relief, she had to rustle up a stir fry before setting forth for the evening's parley.

Zoe opened the door looking not much chirpier than she had done at the police station. She had done what she could with blusher and mascara, but the result was no advert for Max Factor, and she could barely achieve a smile.

"Heard from Buchanan?" Fizz asked, unlacing her Docs.

Zoe wedged herself into the corner of the couch and hugged a cushion. "Yes, he phoned. He's coming over about half seven." She glanced up at the clock. "Shouldn't be long."

"You know he's got Murray lodging with him?"

"Yes. Poor Murray. He's totally destroyed, Tam says." Her voice shook. "God, what a terrible thing to happen. We have a sin to answer for, Fizz. You know that?"

Fizz looked at her, frowning. "What?"

"It was all our fault. If we hadn't got Murray so fired up, Dianne would still be alive."

"Balls," said Fizz, with a spurt of real irritation. "What you're saying is that *I'm* responsible, aren't you? Let's face it, it wasn't you who dropped Dianne in the shit, was it?"

"No, but I didn't stop you. If I had thought —"

If there was one thing Fizz could not abide it was a wimp. "Listen, Murray is a big boy. It's not up to you and me to hold his hand, and anyway, what are you saying? That Murray had something to do with Dianne's death?"

"You think he hadn't?" A forlorn hope glimmered behind Zoe's eyes.

Fizz drew back and gave her a hard look. "Of course I bloody think he hadn't! You saw him when he came out of Dianne's hotel — he was dancing on his tippytoes, dammit. Did it look like an act to you?"

"I don't know," Zoe mumbled, kneading her cushion. "How could anyone tell for sure? To be truthful, I don't feel I know Murray any more. It's like talking to a stranger. The old Murray couldn't have fooled me for a minute, but he's changed totally since he went into jail — not surprisingly, considering what he went through — and now . . . well, I don't think I'd know whether he were lying or not."

Fizz tried to ignore the sense of uneasiness that was lapping at the edges of her consciousness. "He's not crazy enough to announce himself to the receptionist on his way up to murder Dianne, now is he?" she returned. "Nor is he actor enough to swan out of that hotel the way he did if he'd just shoved Dianne out of the window to a horrible death."

Zoe looked as though she would have given much to believe that. "Some people get really turned on by killing — especially if they are killing for revenge as Murray . . . as Murray . . ." She left that uncomfortable train of thought in mid-flow and went off on a tangent. "The experiences he had in jail, the beatings and the years of loneliness, they must leave deep psychological scars, don't you think? And the raping."

"Raping?" Fizz said, sitting up. "You're telling me Murray was raped in jail? He never said anything to me about that."

"Nor to me," Zoe said quickly, "but I don't think there's any doubt but that it must have happened. He says that homosexuality is rife in Saughton — probably in every prison — and it would be a miracle if an alleged sex offender like Murray managed to defend himself. I don't think a man would ever get over that."

Fizz heartily wished that Zoe had never started on that tack. From being totally convinced of Murray's innocence she was now doubting her own judgement and quickly becoming as depressed as Zoe about the part she had played in triggering his rage. When you

294

boiled it right down to the nitty-gritty, what did any of them know about Murray's thought processes? Wrongly convicted or not, he had spent long years among men with warped and evil minds and had probably been forced to fight evil with evil in order to survive. Buchanan and Zoe had both believed they were dealing with the man they'd known three or four years ago, but in fact, Murray was now as much a stranger to them both as he was to Fizz.

Buchanan, when he arrived, was not as much of a comfort as she might have wished. If he had said that he believed in Murray, that would have set her mind at rest. He was, after all, a lawyer and ought to be able to suss people out if anybody could, but being a lawyer, he wasn't going to commit himself to a definite yea or nay.

"I think we have to confine ourselves to dealing with the facts," he said, in his irritatingly pedantic manner, as Zoe helped him off with his leather bomber and eased him into an armchair, probably wishing, the while, that she could bring him his slippers in her mouth. "As far as I'm concerned, it's no longer a matter of proving Murray innocent so much as finding out the truth for my own satisfaction, but you may well see the matter differently. If you decide it's in your best interests to disassociate yourselves from the investigation at this stage, you have my blessing. In fact, I'd strongly urge you both to do so. Murder isn't something to become involved with unnecessarily."

"There's no chance, then, that it could have been suicide?" Zoe passed round coffee and home-made buns with nuts and bits of orange peel in them. Quite the little mother.

"Apparently not. There were signs of a struggle." Buchanan smiled a thank you, and his eyes lingered a moment as though just registering how rough she looked. "You must be feeling pretty bad about Dianne, Zoe. It's a nasty way to lose a friend."

"It's not that we were that close, really, it's just that I can't seem to get it out of my mind. I keep picturing those railings . . ."

"We should talk about something else," Fizz suggested, as much for her own sake as for Zoe's.

"Trouble is, I have to know a little more about what went on before Murray went on the rampage," Buchanan said apologetically. "It was a miracle that the police let him go this morning without charging him, but they could haul him in again at any minute, and I have to be in the picture so that I know what they're likely to throw at him. He's still totally knocked out by whatever medication the doctor gave him, so he's not much good to me right now."

"It's all right," Zoe said, with a brave smile. "I might as well get it out of my system."

"Okay. We'll start with you, Fizz. Suppose you tell me exactly what you found out on Monday that proved so explosive?"

"I told you," Fizz said, uneasily. She had been congratulating herself on managing to impart the necessary information without being forced to admit to making transatlantic phone calls from the community centre, but now the chasm was yawning at her feet. She spoke fast, hoping to rush him past the details. "Just the matter of the red-haired playgroup assistant and the fact that Dianne was not in New York at the time of Murray's arrest."

"Uh-huh. You actually took Debbie's drawing down to Berwick to have Mrs Torkington identify the figure as the mystery assistant?"

Fizz nodded, and then decided that it would be a smarter move to expand on her answers in the hope that, before she had finished with this particular topic, something might crop up to deflect him from quizzing her about her second discovery.

"Yes," she said. "I was certain the figure in the drawing wasn't a child, because the boys wear green smocks and the girls wear lilac, and this figure was wearing a turquoise apron. Mrs Torkington, and also Shona, her full-time helper, both knew who it was right away because of the red hair. So naturally —"

"Yes — sorry to interrupt you, Fizz, but did Mrs Torkington actually identify this figure as the assistant who first noticed the explicit drawings Debbie was producing?"

"Oh, yes. Not a shadow of doubt. She —"

"Right, so because Dianne has — *had* — red hair you made the obvious connection."

"Well, yes. I thought —"

"So you wondered how, if she were the one who had framed Murray, she had managed to be in New York at the same time?"

"Yes. There were the magazines, you see, and —"

But he was not going to be deflected. He stopped her with an upheld hand, looking at her with a half-grim, half-amused look that she definitely did not like.

"Okay, so you got on to your friend, I think you said, in the *Scotsman* reference library."

"Well, that's where he's working at the moment. I met him in Ireland where he used to be a pig-smuggler."

Zoe gave a snort of laughter, quickly suppressed when she saw Buchanan's face.

He said, "Let's not fool around, Fizz —"

"It's true. You used to get some sort of EU grant for pigs in the north that you didn't get in the south, so there was money to be made smuggling them across the border. He used to —"

"Never mind that, for God's sake!" Buchanan took a deep breath and visibly held his temper. "This guy got the information for you regarding the nominees for awards at the appropriate TV Festival, is that right? I'll want to confirm that. How could he be quite certain that Dianne wasn't there?"

"Well, of course, she *could* have been there," Fizz floundered, glancing at Zoe for help. Some friend! She must have known that Fizz's back was against the wall. "Nobody could prove that she wasn't part of the crowd — just that she wasn't *invited* — that the play she said had won a nomination was never actually in the running."

"I think that was the point," Zoe said, coming to the rescue at the eleventh hour. "It wasn't a matter of actually proving that she wasn't in New York. What got to Murray was that she had been lying to him about the award. Coming on top of the news about the red-haired nursery assistant, it really demolished his trust in her."

"Yes!" Fizz exclaimed, having suddenly thought of another diversion. "And coming on top *also* of the news about Sheridan."

"Sheridan?" Buchanan waited for elucidation. Fizz left it to Zoe.

"Dianne had apparently told him that her marriage to Sherry was in name only. She said that Sherry was homosexual, but I knew for a fact that that wasn't true. I . . . I'm afraid I blurted out that I knew several girls who'd had affairs with Sherry."

Fizz found it rather quaint that although Zoe had not thought at the time to conceal her own involvement with Sherry, she was coy about admitting it to Buchanan. She said, "So, you see, it was a culmination of several bits of information that finally convinced him Dianne was a four-pound-note. I suppose we should have realised how he would take it, but, I tell you, I never expected him to blow his fuse the way he did."

Buchanan stood up and stretched and walked over to the window. Beyond the glass the sky was sunset-pink and the fake Parthenon on Calton Hill was a dark-blue silhouette. In the silence Fizz could hear blackbirds singing and, in the distance, a piper practising a strathspey, doubtless in preparation for the Festival Parade on Sunday.

"I know it could all be termed circumstantial," Buchanan mused, still staring out, "but there is such a body of evidence against Dianne that I'm reluctant to write her off as an innocent victim. I wouldn't be too surprised to discover that she was at least an accessory. But an accessory to *what*? That's the question."

Fizz and Zoe exchanged bemused looks.

"To what," Zoe repeated thoughtfully, but not as if she knew what she meant.

Buchanan turned from his contemplation of the view. "To the fabrication of evidence against Murray, possibly. But if his claim of being framed is not true, we have to ask ourselves if Dianne was involved in some other devilment."

"Let's face it," Fizz stated flatly. "If Murray is lying to us, we don't know our arse from our elbow. If he wasn't framed then we're wasting our time trying to trace the nursery helper who spotted what Debbie was drawing. We only have his word for it that Dianne lied about Sherry's sexual polarity, or about being in New York."

"Not about New York, you have my word for that also. She certainly told me that she had been nominated and was going to go to the States for the full three weeks of the TV festival." Zoe leaned forward to set her empty cup on the coffee table, and then re-curled herself about her cushion. "And if she lied about that, I'm inclined to believe that she lied about Sherry as well, just to keep Murray sweet. You have to accept that she had a strong motive for wanting Murray out of the way. There's no way she could have felt safe if he had been around to see what she was doing with his student's manuscript. She's the only one with a motive."

300

"Well, I don't know about that," Buchanan said, coming back to his seat and taking his foolscap pad out of his briefcase. He riffled through the pages. "I saw some interesting possibilities in some of the remarks you taped, Fizz. Both Phillis and the McCaulays might merit another visit."

"But not the playgroup?" Fizz said, feeling slighted by his obvious lack of interest in what she considered her prime clue. "If Murray really was framed, and I happen to think he was, this woman — who was almost certainly Dianne — is at the crux of the whole matter. If Debbie *wasn't* abused, somebody coached her, over a long period, to say she was, or at least to imply it, and that same somebody also altered her drawings to corroborate what she was saying. Neither Phillis nor the McCaulays had access to her playgroup drawings, so why waste time with them?"

"Anyone could have coached Debbie," Zoe objected. "Mrs McCaulay had her for hours at a time, and so did Phillis. I wouldn't mind betting that both of them picked Debbie up from playgroup plenty of times, so why couldn't either of them bring along a prepared drawing and stick it up on the wall, or into a pile of other drawings, while they were waiting around? The fact is that there is no evidence against the assistant who actually spotted the drawings except the fact that her hair was the same colour as Dianne's."

While Fizz was marshalling her thoughts to refute these assumptions, Buchanan took off up a side street. "The fact that Dianne has been murdered is the only concrete piece of information we possess," he said. "All the rest hinges on whether Murray has been stringing us along or not. Knowing that somebody hated or feared her enough to kill her indicates either that Murray did it out of revenge or whatever, or that she had to be got out of the way for some other reason."

"Maybe to keep her from talking," Zoe suggested. You could tell, Fizz thought, that she'd been watching too many episodes of *The Bill*. "Perhaps she knew something that would incriminate someone."

The hair on the back of Fizz's neck gave a horrible little shiver. She sat up and pointed a finger at Buchanan. "Murray had arranged for you to question Dianne this morning, hadn't he? Someone could have wanted to make sure she didn't speak to you."

It went very quiet. The blackbird had stopped singing and the distant piper had switched to a melancholy pibroch.

"That's true," Buchanan said after a while. The thought had evidently not occurred to him before now, at least in the context of Dianne's murder, and Fizz could see immediately that he wasn't pleased. "You didn't mention that arrangement to anyone, did you, Fizz?"

"I did not," Fizz said, almost crossing her heart in case he didn't believe her. "I didn't even tell Zoe — did I, Zoe?"

"No. This is the first I've heard about it, Tam." She looked from one of them to the other. "Only the three of you were aware of the arrangement?"

Buchanan nodded, and Fizz said hotly, "Well, it sure as hell wasn't me who topped Dianne, so it must have been Murray who didn't want her to talk to you!"

Buchanan drooped his eyelids at her in an expression of weary rebuke. "Don't let's get ahead of ourselves, Fizz. The idea of Dianne being killed to keep her from talking was only one of several possible motives. Let's see if we can establish anything in the way of admissible evidence before we start pinning everything on Murray."

Zoe swung her feet to the floor and set her cushion aside. There was a little more colour in her face, but she still looked pretty fragile. "I just thought of something. Maybe Dianne wasn't exactly framing him: maybe she was deliberately bringing him to the notice of the authorities because she knew he *was* abusing Debbie."

Buchanan considered this. "I think that's a possibility we can't ignore, Zoe. It's perfectly feasible that she could have chosen that way of exposing him to avoid becoming directly involved. It's a good illustration of what I've been saying to you both: it's too early to be latching on to one theory and ignoring all others. New possibilities are presenting themselves all the time."

He looked at his watch and started putting things back in his briefcase. "Murray will be waking up shortly. I left him a note to tell him where I'd gone, but I'd rather be there when he surfaces, if I can."

"You're a good friend to him, Tam," Zoe said, with a sycophancy that made Fizz gag.

Buchanan at least had the grace to look discomfited. "It's only for a couple of nights," he grunted, and turned immediately to Fizz. "I'd like to have a short chat to the McCaulays, maybe today or tomorrow. If you want to come along, give Beatrice a ring tomorrow lunchtime and she'll let you know what she's managed to fix up."

"Sure." Fizz nodded casually, wondering what he wanted to see the McCaulays for. She could have asked, but that would have been an admission that she wasn't ahead of him, and she preferred to see if she could catch up on his thinking before she did that.

She said, "I don't suppose you have the tapes with you? I'd like to listen to them again, just to refresh my memory."

He scrabbled around in his briefcase and brought out a manila envelope. "Take care of these, Fizz, and let me have them back when you're finished with them. Monday, if you can."

"And if Murray is still in need of company tomorrow, Tam, just drop him off here," Zoe said. "Either that or I'll pop over to your place and sit with him till you get home."

You really had to hand it to her: she never missed a trick as far as Buchanan was concerned.

"Thanks, Zoe, but I don't think it should be necessary. If Murray gets a good night's rest he should, I think, be able to go back to Morningside tomorrow. We don't want him to start thinking of himself as an invalid."

"Well, you know, if there's anything I can do . . ."

Buchanan nodded. "You're very sweet, Zoe. I'll tell Murray you offered."

304

That remark lit Zoe like a nightlight. Fizz had a feeling she was planning on doing it in cross-stitch for the living room wall.

CHAPTER
TWENTY-ONE

Buchanan was wakened about half past seven by Murray crashing about in the kitchen. He felt pretty good considering he'd spent the night on the couch in the living room, but that didn't mean he felt like making conversation. He hid in the shower for quarter of an hour and then (since it was that or starve) he wrapped a towel round his waist and headed for the coffee percolator.

Murray was standing in front of the hob, wearing Buchanan's cherished Calvin Klein dressing gown (probably his last birthday present from Janine) and throwing tomatoes into a frying pan with gay abandon. Buchanan snarled a response to his "Good morning" and handed him the butcher's apron.

"Ta. Want any fried eggs and tomatoes?"

Buchanan shook his head, refusing even to think about it. The fact that Murray was feeling like eating today had to be a plus, but the smell of hot fat first thing in the morning was something he could live without. Besides, he had no idea when he'd bought those eggs. He turned his back, breathed shallowly, spooned coffee into the percolator.

"Just like old times, eh?" Murray said over his shoulder, with a not too listless smile. "You never did like taking your turn at the cooking."

"You were always better at it than I was."

"*I*, you see, was brought up to look after myself, whereas *you* always had somebody dancing attendance on you. Your mummy tied your shoelaces for you till you were twenty-five!"

Buchanan forced a grin, only because Murray was making an attempt to be cheerful and deserved encouragement. "She still would if I let her."

Murray swept a pile of newspapers off the table, threw them in the rubbish bin and sat down with his plateful of cholesterol and a packet of bridge rolls that was at least as old as the eggs. "Don't you ever get lonely living here on your own?"

"Lonely?" Buchanan considered this. "Can't say I do, really. There's always somebody I can call on for company if I feel like it. Sharing my space would come hard after all these years."

"Never thought about getting married?"

"Thought about it. Never seriously." Had he been serious about Janine? He couldn't be sure. Already his memory of her was beginning to lose definition, and his angst at her departure seemed at times a tad lacking in conviction. He leaned against the work surface and sipped his coffee, wondering if she would contact him when she got back from Aberdeen. Wondering if he really wanted her to.

Murray lanced the swollen yolk of a fried egg and expelled the yellow contents with his fork. Buchanan looked away.

"What I was thinking," Murray confided, "was that it might be a good idea if I were to stay on here for a day or two."

"No, Murray, that would be a terrible idea." Buchanan lurched away from the counter with such vehemence that he lost his towel and had to set down his mug and retrieve his dignity. "No, no. You don't want to stay here any longer than necessary. What you want is to get back to your own place as soon as possible and start picking up the pieces."

"Just till the weekend, maybe. And, of course, I'd take the couch, Tam, I wouldn't expect —"

"Listen. It wouldn't be doing you any favours. The longer you put it off, the harder it's going to get." Buchanan quickly refilled his mug and made for the door, talking fast. "I'll drop by regularly, and so, I'm sure, will Fizz and Zoe. You won't be on your own —"

"I'm scared, Tam. What if I'm next on the hit list?"

Buchanan braked himself with a hand on the door jamb. "What hit list?"

Murray showed the whites of his eyes. "The guy who killed Dianne."

"You know who killed Dianne?"

"No, of course I don't, but —"

"Then why did you say 'the guy' like that?"

"Oh, for God's sake, Tam, don't be so bloody . . . so bloody *jurisprudent*! I'm just saying, somebody wanted her dead — maybe the same somebody wants me dead

308

too, and it's giving me the shakes. I don't want to be stuck in that damn house on my own, listening to my heartbeats. Gimme a break, Tam!"

Buchanan scowled at him from the doorway. He rather thought Murray's fears were groundless, but he could understand his need for company at this point in his life.

"Okay. Just till the weekend."

"Thanks, Tam. I'll make myself useful around the house, get this place cleared up —"

"You don't have to do that; the cleaning lady comes today." Buchanan sighed, glancing at the wall clock. It was already twenty to nine and he hadn't even shaved yet. He said, "We have things to talk about, Murray. I have to hear your version of what happened at the hotel. Just let me get shaved and dressed and phone the office to let them know I'll be late."

He took his time getting organised, since Murray seemed set on sterilising the kitchen before settling to do anything else, so it was well after nine before he got through to the office. Beatrice received the news of his rescheduled ETA with her usual stoicism, merely reminding him of the few matters which would require his attention at some point during the day. Typically, she left the interesting news till the last.

"There was a phone call, just a few minutes ago, from Mr Sheridan Reid. He's the husband of Dianne Frazer Ballantyne."

"Yes, I know who he is," Buchanan said with saintly patience, not even adding, "Who doesn't?" "Did he say what he wanted?"

"Just that he'd appreciate it if you could spare him some time, hopefully this afternoon, or if not, at your earliest convenience. Something to do with his wife's death, I don't doubt."

"Could be," said Buchanan, grateful for this insight. "Well, you'd better give him a ring back and arrange something, Beatrice, but it will have to be tomorrow morning. I'll have too much to catch up with today and I want to have a talk with the McCaulays some time tomorrow afternoon. I told Fizz to phone around lunchtime today to find out what's happening, so if you can set something up for just after lunchtime tomorrow, that would be ideal. You could tell Fizz I'll pick her up at home."

"The McCaulays — say two-thirty tomorrow if possible. And Mr Reid — tomorrow morning. As late as possible, I suppose?"

"Preferably, yes, Beatrice, thank you." And that, he thought as he replaced the receiver, should prove to be an interesting conversation. Was Sherry coming to ask questions or to answer them? Either way, he couldn't fail to supply a few missing pieces in the jigsaw.

When Buchanan got back to the kitchen, Murray was watering the parsley plant that was breathing its last on the windowsill. The work surfaces and appliances were aggressively clean and the stainless-steel hob glittered as it had not done since the day it was installed.

"I wasn't planning on doing a liver transplant in here," Buchanan growled, noting that his third cup of coffee, which he had left in the percolator, had been swilled down the sink. "For God's sake, leave something for the cleaning lady to do."

Murray looked a bit piqued. "If she's only here for the one day, she'll have enough to worry about in the living room alone." He stripped off his rubber gloves and hung up the butcher's apron in martyred silence while Buchanan started another pot of coffee.

"Apparently Sherry has been trying to contact me," Buchanan said. "Beatrice is setting up a meeting tomorrow morning."

This information effectively focused Murray's attention. "What does he want to talk to you for?"

"Well, I wouldn't be surprised if your name came up."

Murray looked sick. "Neither would I. You'll be careful what you say, won't you, Tam?"

"I'm not going to be telling him anything he doesn't know, that's for sure. Hopefully, it's *he* who will be clarifying matters for *me*."

"What sort of matters?" Murray asked, masking a certain uneasiness by putting mugs on a tray and looking in the fridge for milk.

"He may be able to cast some light on Dianne's involvement in all this. For all we know there's a whole subplot that you're unaware of. We may find that your problems are only a side issue."

Murray thought about that for a few minutes. "You're probably wondering, also, if Sherry killed Dianne?"

"Why would he do that? What motive would he have had?"

Murray shook his head. "I don't believe she was blackmailing him. I can't believe that. But I suppose he could have been jealous about her relationship with me."

"You have to admit it, Murray. It's got to be at least a possibility."

"Not unless everything Dianne told me about their relationship was a lie, and I can't accept that. I can't. Sherry had no reason to resent our relationship. The only complaint he'd have had against us would have been if we'd been less than totally discreet, and we never were. You know yourself how desperately I tried to keep even you from knowing about Dianne and me."

"You were seen going into her hotel," Buchanan pointed out.

"But not regularly, and never at night. The hotel staff accepted that I was her research assistant, and besides, she saw several business associates, journalists, all sorts of people, in her room. Always had done."

Buchanan watched Murray watching the percolator. "Okay, but get this into your head, Murray, if I'm not completely in the picture I won't know what I should say and what I should keep to myself. Is that understood? Because I still get the feeling that you aren't telling me everything you know. Tell me I'm wrong."

"You're wrong," Murray said without hesitation. "I swear to you, Tam, if there's anything I've omitted to tell you, it's not intentional. It's just that I've forgotten. I know I lied to you about Dianne — and now I'm wondering if she'd still be alive if I *had* told you — but

I can't see how she could have been involved. I can't see how her death could have anything to do with me being framed. It just doesn't tie in."

Buchanan carried his coffee through to the living room, and Murray followed. The place was a bit of a mess, with bedding all over the couch, so they had to waste more time while Murray cleared a space for them to sit. Finally Buchanan said, "Leave it at that, Murray, for God's sake, and let's get on. I want you to tell me exactly what happened between you and Dianne at her hotel, and please, try not to leave anything out. What time was it when you got there?"

"Oh, I don't know. Half nine, maybe. We'd probably finished our meal about half eight or thereabouts, then we had a bit of a barney, Fizz and I, about what she'd found out, so it must have been after nine at least when I left Zoe's. I wasn't looking at my watch."

"So you went straight to Dianne's hotel and confronted her with Fizz's findings. Which were, let's see." He checked his notes. "One: that the mystery helper at the playgroup answered her description; two: that there was evidence that Sherry was heterosexual; three: that she wasn't out of the country at the time of your arrest, as she had claimed. Nothing more?"

"No, that more or less sums it up," Murray said morosely. "It was more than enough."

Buchanan was inclined to agree, but had only himself to blame. He had known that Fizz was trouble from the beginning, and he should have kept a closer eye on her instead of allowing her to dash around pursuing lines of enquiry which she had not even mentioned beforehand. He was beginning to doubt his ability — *anyone*'s ability, for that matter — to control Fizz, and rather suspected that their association would not last much longer. Not if he had anything to do with it. He said:

"Okay, so what was Dianne's reaction to your accusations?"

"She was really upset." Murray sat stiffly upright with a hand gripping each knee as though he had to hold on to something. "I went at it like a bull at a gate, of course. I should have just said, 'Here's what's being said, tell me what you think about it.' Instead of which, I went in there like a madman. Yelled at her."

"Not altogether surprising," Buchanan said quickly, seeing Murray's eyes begin to redden again. "She flew off the handle, did she?"

"No, she wasn't angry, just . . . you know . . . hurt. By my lack of trust."

"Did she deny the allegations?"

"Of course. She said it must be purely coincidental that the helper had red hair, and she said that Sherry had once been bisexual but had been homosexual for years, and anyway, it didn't matter to her as long as he didn't expect her to sleep with him or to be celibate."

"And, of course, her lying to you about the TV Festival was understandable under the circumstances."

"I did feel that she could have told me the truth about her stay at the clinic, but . . . yes, I can see how she would prefer me not to know how serious her drink problem was. Particularly with all the hassle I'd gone through with Anne. She knew it would devastate me."

"And how was she when you left her? Still upset?"

"No. She was happy. We'd cleared up any misunderstandings and she had forgiven me for mistrusting her. She was as she always was . . . very loving and . . ."

He turned his head aside, blinking fast and staring blindly out of the window.

"What's going on here, Tam?" he demanded after a minute, glaring at Buchanan as if it were all his fault. "Somebody out there had it in for Dianne and me, and I haven't a clue who it could be. I simply can't believe that Sherry knew we were lovers — or, if he did know, that he would care. He's had lovers too — probably still has — so he has no reason to play the jealous husband."

"So it would seem, but who knows for sure? We may know more this afternoon when Sherry and I have had our little chat." Buchanan rather hoped he was right about that, because right now he hadn't a clue who were the baddies and who were the goodies in this scenario. It was very hard indeed to believe that Murray was putting on an act, but if he hadn't killed Dianne, who the hell had? More than one of the people involved had a motive to have him put away for a spell, either as revenge for past wrongs or because he stood in the way of something they wanted, but the reasons for Dianne's involvement were still not clear.

He stood up and stretched. "Right, I'm off. You won't see me before six o'clock, but you'll have Dolores, the cleaning lady, to keep you company."

"Dolores?" Murray breathed, evidently spotting a glimmer of light in his darkness.

"She's Spanish."

Buchanan let himself out while Murray was hurriedly shaving, and if he felt a bit of a heel for not mentioning that Dolores was well into her fifties and had only four words of English, he comforted himself with the thought that it's better to have anticipated and been disappointed than never to have known hope.

Fizz and Zoe spent much of the afternoon listening to the tapes of the interviews. Zoe was still squeamish about discussing the murder in too much detail, but the effort of sifting every recorded word for useful material helped to focus her thoughts on the practical. Clearly, her natural inclination was to pretend the whole thing hadn't happened, but she knew, because Fizz told her several times, that Murray was bound to be the main suspect and would be back in chokey in no time unless they turned up some evidence in his favour.

In point of fact, there were still moments when Fizz herself wasn't all that sure of Murray. Maybe he had talked himself out of it for the time being, but the fact that he had set off to see Dianne in such a passion of rage, and had been with her in her room around the time of her death, had to weigh heavily against him. Admittedly, his demeanour as he left the hotel was not that of a man who had just killed his lover, but it might be that of a man on drugs, or even of a man whose mind was unbalanced by his recent experiences.

316

Even Zoe, who had never before allowed Fizz to voice any such suspicions, was patently uneasy. "Dianne may have been able to prove that she was in a clinic just before Murray's arrest," she said to Fizz, "but it really has to look as if she was involved up to her neck. The other evidence against her is just too iffy. Whatever she said about Sherry, for instance, nobody's going to tell me he's ever been anything but hetero. If he's gay, so's Popeye."

Fizz was lying flat on her back on the floor with her eyes closed, listening to a drone of voices against a background of children's twittering.

"I'm certain she was the mystery helper at the playgroup," she said doggedly. "I just feel it in my water, know what I mean, Zoe? Not only that, but I'm certain it was that helper who faked up Debbie's drawings to look suspicious. Had to be."

The tape said, ". . . What I wanted to ask you . . ." in Fizz's voice.

Zoe said, "She may have had an alibi for the week or so when everything came to a head, but that's no proof that she didn't have a helper who placed the final clues in position as soon as the police were around to find them. I know it's hard to believe it of her, but all she needed to do —"

Fizz lifted a finger to halt her. "Listen to this bit."

The tape said, "Yes, I do remember her. Quite well, actually. A tallish girl with a round face. She wasn't here long."

Fizz's voice, sounding thin and strained, said, "Do you remember her name?"

317

"As a matter of fact, I do. It was Kate. I remember that because she was reading a Catherine Cookson paperback called *Our Kate*, and every time I see that book I remember her."

"And her surname?"

"No. I don't —"

Fizz pressed the rewind button and ran through the same sequence again, frowning over the tape recorder.

"What does she mean by that, do you think, Zoe: 'Every time I see that book I remember her'? Does she mean, 'every time I see a *copy* of that book', or does she mean, 'every time I see that actual *book*'?"

"The former, almost certainly. You see it everywhere, station bookstalls, the library shelves, it must be into its umpteenth edition."

"Yes, but what if she didn't mean that?" Fizz sat up, staring at Zoe with sudden optimism. "I don't know why, maybe it's just the way she says it on the tape, but I get the feeling she means *that* book. Kate's copy."

Zoe's lips pinched out a small smile. "You're not planning on dashing down to Berwick just to find out, are you? It's a bit of a long shot, surely? I mean, it's nearly four years since this person worked there. What chance is there of her book still being around?"

"It's worth a phone call at least, just to make sure," Fizz said. "Go on, give them a buzz. You can get the number from directory enquiries."

"Oh, all right." It took ages to get the number, because it wasn't listed under Torkington but under Primrose Hill Day Centre, then the number rang and rang before someone finally answered. Fizz claimed the receiver.

"Hello. Mrs Torkington? It's Ms Fitzpatrick." They went through the usual opening gambits regarding the progress of the enquiry, which seemed to go on for ever. Then she got in, "What I'm phoning about, Mrs Torkington, is a book Shona mentioned, *Our Kate*."

"Yes, dear, she told me. That's what reminded her . . ."

"About Kate, yes. But, when she said, 'every time I see that book', did she mean the actual book Kate was reading, or just any copy of *Our Kate*?"

"No, no. She meant the book Kate left here."

"It's still there?" Fizz gasped, exchanging a goggle-eyed look with Zoe. "Really? That's incredible!"

"Well, since you're interested in it, I suppose it *is* lucky that it wasn't thrown out a long time ago, but in fact it's serving a very useful purpose!" She gave a little trill of laughter. "When we got the new storage unit in the playroom, the door crashed into it every time someone opened it. One day, to stop the paintwork being chipped, Shona jammed the paperback into the framework so that the door hit against the book instead of the metal. We've been meaning to do something permanent about it for years, but you know how it is, dear, I suppose we just got used to the book doing the job."

"I can't tell you how pleased I am," Fizz told her. "I'd like to come down to Berwick and pick it up, if I may? Right away, if that's okay with you?"

"Certainly, dear, it will be a pleasure to see you again. I'll go and get it now and have it all ready for you."

"No, don't move it, Mrs Torkington. Just leave it where it is and I'll get it myself. The less we handle it, the better, I think. Thank you so much. See you later."

She turned to Zoe, her face glowing with success. "How about that? It's still there!"

Zoe didn't appear wonderfully excited. "Yes, but what's it going to tell us, Fizz, other than Kate's literary preferences? I don't think you should build up your hopes too much. I mean, it's extremely unlikely that, if she were presenting a false persona, she'd write her real name and address on the flyleaf."

"You never know," Fizz said. "But I think we have to look at it, don't you?"

"Oh, I daresay we should." Zoe looked out at the grey sky. "It's going to rain later, but so what? It's better than sitting around moping."

Fizz's hopes remained high all the way to Berwick.

"You realise," she told Zoe, "that if we can just tie this book to Dianne, we'll know for sure that she was the one who framed Murray."

"Which means that, whether he admits it or not, Murray had a first-class motive for killing her."

Fizz withdrew her gaze from the road ahead to stare at her. "What're you saying? That we should cover up for him?"

"No, of course not," Zoe said stoically, straightening her shoulders as though she were bracing herself for a distasteful task. "If it turns out that Murray murdered

320

Dianne it means that he's unstable. He might kill again. I wouldn't dream of suggesting that we should keep the evidence to ourselves. I'm just saying it would be horrendous if we had to be the ones to put him back inside."

"Yeah," Fizz said, "and what if he gets Debbie back and it turns out he was guilty all along, huh?"

Zoe had no answer to that one.

She waited outside while Fizz went in for the book, which suited Fizz fine because it gave her an excuse not to hang about chatting to Mrs Torkington and Shona. They were both consumed with curiosity as to the significance of the book, and Fizz was unwilling to dash their expectations, so she acted vague and told them they'd hear all about it in due course.

The book was where they said it was, only the spine protruding from the edge of the metal frame. She gave it a quick once-over on the spot, but at first glance, at least, it was disappointingly free of any distinguishing marks.

When she got into the car she put the book in her lap, and while she fastened her safety belt, Zoe reached across and took it.

"No name and address," she said, looking inside the cover. "No interesting doodles, no bookshop price stickers, not even a shopping list."

"Zilch," Fizz said disgustedly, and hurriedly reclaimed it. "Hey, maybe we shouldn't have handled it. There could be fingerprints."

"After four years? I don't think so. Besides, it must be covered with Shona's prints, and probably Mrs Torkington's and half the kids in the playgroup."

"Yes, but the police could eliminate theirs and ours and whoever is left could be the imposter. If Phillis's prints are there, for instance, or Mrs McCaulay's."

"Right," Zoe said. "It's a process of elimination, isn't it, so you may have a clue there after all. You don't think we should take it to the police, do you?"

Fizz found a folded plastic carrier bag in her pocket and put the book in it. "I think they'd laugh us out of the station house, Zoe. It's a very tenuous connection to anyone not involved."

Zoe looked at her curiously. "But you think there might be something to learn from it?"

Fizz made a face and laughed. "No, I suppose not. It's just . . . it's the only clue we've got, see? It's some sort of psychic contact with *her*."

Zoe couldn't restrain a burst of laughter. "You've got to be joking, Fizz!"

"Not entirely. I'm not expecting any thought transmissions or that sort of thing, but, I don't know, I just . . . it sort of concentrates my thoughts. You know, like a religious icon. Same as Debbie's picture."

"Well, if nothing else, it'll be something to read over the weekend!"

Fizz gave an abstracted nod. "Buchanan and I are going back to see the McCaulays tomorrow."

"Yes, I heard him say he wanted to question them again. Did he tell you why?"

"No, I haven't spoken to him since last night."

322

"You think he spotted something on the tape?"

"Looks like it to me," Fizz said, "but I can't think what it could be. I've listened to that interview over and over but I can't see anything worth questioning them about. Could be some minor point."

"Want to come over for a bite to eat afterwards? Save you cooking."

Fizz screwed up her face in an expression of dismay. "Can I take a rain check? I've got a date tomorrow tonight."

"Oh, yes?" Zoe looked unflatteringly surprised to hear this. "With someone I know?"

"Yes," said Fizz, amusing herself by acting reticent.

Zoe's bottom lip stuck out. "Not Tam?"

Fizz choked loudly. "No!"

"For God's sake, not Murray?"

"No, Zoe, not Murray." Fizz was enjoying this.

"Who else do we both know?" Zoe muttered, frowning at her. "You're pulling my leg, right?"

"Nope."

"Then who is it? Come on, Fizz, I give up."

"Dougie Walker."

"I don't know any Dougie Walker."

"Sure you do," Fizz said, grinning at her. "He's one of the cops we were talking to at the police station. The young, good-looking one, naturally."

"I wouldn't have thought he was your type," Zoe said, with a smile that made Fizz wonder what type Zoe would have chosen for her.

She raised a quizzical eyebrow. "Listen to an old hand, Zoe. Listen and learn. Gift horses are an endangered species these days. You don't look them in the mouth — or in any place else for that matter. You never know when you'll need a copper — as my old mother used to say — and this one is going to keep me posted, though he may not know it, as to how the police enquiry is progressing. Besides, he's buying me dinner at Chez Jules."

"Ah," said Zoe as though she understood that the last inducement carried more weight than the first one. Food, and particularly free food, was, of course, high on Fizz's list of priorities, but so was information. And it pleased her frugal Scottish soul to get two birds with one stone.

CHAPTER
TWENTY-TWO

Buchanan's only regret was that he didn't do business more frequently with gentlemen of Sheridan Reid's stamp. It was regrettably seldom that he was invited out to lunch, and even his father, who as senior partner cornered all the perks that were going, had never been treated to a meal, tête-à-tête, in a private suite at the Balmoral Hotel.

Sherry had, understandably, cut short his stay at the Hamilton House after his wife's demise and was now installed in a corner suite of three comfortable rooms on the second floor.

He met Buchanan at the door wearing jeans and a white T-shirt that could have come from Marks and Spencer. He looked like a faded version of his screen image: one with pale eyelashes and a mediocre tan, older than Buchanan had imagined and not quite so tall, but he was still impressive. You didn't get muscles like those without working for them. It made you wonder if a couple of games of squash and a round of golf per week were really enough.

Buchanan followed Sherry into the lounge, which was bigger than his own, with a real-flame gas fire and a dining table in the bay window. He could see the outline of Arthur's Seat and Salisbury Crags through the net curtains of one window, and from the other a soundless stream of traffic crossing the North Bridge.

"I'm most grateful to you for coming, Tam," Sherry said, motioning him to a seat.

First names from the word go, Buchanan noted. No messing about. Did he expect to be addressed as "Sherry"? Why not? Friend of a friend, and all that. "It's my pleasure, Sherry. I think we have a lot to talk about."

Sherry's eyebrows lifted a little. He apparently hadn't thought of this as a two-way exchange of views. "Let's order right away, shall we? Then we can have a quiet drink while we're waiting for it to come up." He handed Buchanan a menu. "What's your tipple?"

"Just a soft drink for me, thanks. I've a fair bit of driving to do this afternoon."

Sherry looked in the drinks cabinet. "There's coke, ginger ale . . . What's this? Soda . . ."

"Ginger ale would be fine." Buchanan studied the menu, swithering between Dover sole and supreme of chicken with asparagus tips, but switched, at the last minute, to a prime grilled fillet of Angus beef with bearnaise sauce.

"What about a starter? The soups are always good here." Sherry leaned over and pointed to the soup section. "Lobster bisque with langoustines. Superb. Trust me."

"No, really, Sherry. I have work to do this afternoon. A house salad with my beef is all I want."

Sherry settled for supreme of salmon and the order was duly phoned down to room service. "Good. Now we can relax."

He settled into an armchair across the fireplace from Buchanan and crossed his legs. At first glance there was little about him of the bereaved husband, but when he stopped talking the animation drained from his face and you saw pain in his eyes and lines of rigid self-control around his mouth. To Buchanan's murmured condolences he merely nodded politely and said:

"It all seems totally unreal in a way. You don't really believe, deep down, that these things actually happen in real life." He took a healthy sip of his whisky and sat for a moment staring into the fake flames on the hearth. Buchanan could think of nothing constructive to say, so he held his tongue.

"DI Fleming spoke to me about you," Sherry finally roused himself to remark. "He said you had been reviewing Murray's case."

"With a view to establishing whether his conviction was unsafe, yes."

"And I'm told you wanted to interview Dianne in connection with that business?"

"Yes." Buchanan nodded, carefully. "But I doubt, in view of subsequent events, that she would have been of much assistance to me. Much of investigative work is like that, as you'll appreciate, but one goes through the motions."

"Of course. They were close friends for a number of years. Long before Murray's conviction. And you, I

327

understand, were a close friend of Murray's for even longer. You must have known Dianne."

"Not well. I ran into her now and then, in Murray's company, but Murray and I lost touch to some extent after he went to live in Berwick."

"But you still believe that he was innocent? You think someone framed him, is that it?"

"I think," said Buchanan, choosing his words with precision, "that there may be an element of doubt. Enough to warrant further investigation. No more than that."

Sherry smiled and nodded. "And have you turned up anything of interest yet?"

"Nothing concrete, no. But it's early days. We've done no more than take a few preliminary statements from people who gave evidence at his trial."

"Dianne wasn't in that category?"

It was a question, and he expected it to be answered. "No. Dianne wasn't around at the time of Murray's arrest, so she had no evidence to give. I merely wanted to talk to her because she was part of Murray's scene at that point in time and might have remembered something of interest. If one assumes Murray to be a victim, he must have had an enemy, but he claims to know nobody who had a motive to ruin him."

"I suppose it might be said that I was a part of that scene myself," Sherry admitted with a faint smile. "On the fringes, so to speak."

This interested Buchanan greatly, but as their lunch arrived at that point he was unable to pursue the subject. He should have thought to ask Murray — or

Murray should have thought to mention — the details of the social life he shared with Dianne. It wasn't surprising, given the parochial nature of Scottish theatre, that Sherry should have crossed orbits with them. He would have been relatively unknown at that point, serving his time at the Lyceum and trying to get known in TV. But how close a relationship had it really been? Sherry was either innocent of all involvement or a fool for mentioning it, but then again, he might have volunteered the information because he was pretty sure Buchanan knew already — or would find out.

Sherry made small talk while they watched the waiter deftly transforming his trolley into a table for two, ready set with silver and crystal, centred with a bowl of carnations. When he had removed the covers and shimmered away, Buchanan got back to the last topic as soon as manners permitted.

"Murray didn't mention that he had known you from way back," he said, ogling Sherry's salmon and wondering if he had chosen wisely. The first morsel of beef reassured him.

"No, he probably wouldn't think it relevant. When I say I was part of their scene, I mean I ran into them fairly regularly. We didn't make arrangements to meet or invite one another to parties, but we'd chat in pubs if we met up. That sort of thing."

"Murray had a lot of friends in theatre and TV at that point."

Sherry nodded, crinkling his eyes in a half-smile that made him look more like his screen persona. "Oh yes, he was a target for all us young hopefuls in those days.

He could introduce you to people with clout. And he did, God bless him. Always willing to do what he could for anybody, Murray was."

"He tells me he was able to be of some assistance to Dianne along those lines."

"He *made* Dianne," Sherry said, with a conviction that surprised Buchanan. "He virtually taught her how to present her work, he got her started in TV, he fixed her up with a good agent, he watched over her like a hen with one chick."

"She was very lucky to know him."

Sherry nodded firmly. "And she never forgot it. All through his trial, all through his time in jail she stood by him. Didn't matter what he'd done, didn't matter what he might do in the future, he was her friend for life."

Buchanan wondered if this explanation for their closeness had actually been Dianne's version, or whether Sherry was its author. It certainly didn't ring true in Buchanan's ears. He suggested:

"It could be said that Dianne had enough talent to get by without Murray's assistance."

"Tam," said Sherry sadly, "we all of us know a dozen talented newcomers who're never going to get anywhere because they don't know the right people or because they don't have the chutzpah to keep on struggling against the system. Before they met up with Murray, Dianne and Zoe had been churning out good stuff for years, but both of them could have papered their walls with rejection slips. Once Murray got them started, however, the same old rejected scripts started to sell. And they deserved to; they were damn good. Better, I sometimes think, than anything either of them produced since. Bloody tragic, the way they split up."

"What about *Fade to Black*?" Buchanan asked casually, spearing a mouthful of beef.

"Ah, well, that was the exception, to my mind. That was Dianne's *magnum opus*, and whether she'd ever have been able to repeat it is something we shall now never know." He concentrated on reducing a leaf of lettuce to thin shreds for a good few seconds, keeping his head well down and breathing somewhat raggedly. "At least it happened for her, which is all any of us can ask." He laid down his knife and fork and took a long sip of his second whisky, then folded his arms on the table and stared out through the net curtains at the hills beyond. "It's all any of us can ask, you know: to make it to the top just once. If it goes on for a year or two, as it has with me, that's a bonus. Dianne would have gone on struggling to get back up there till the bitter end. It was all she lived for."

The words "she'd have done anything" weren't actually spoken, but they were as clear in Buchanan's ears as the ring of silver on china. When somebody wanted something that much, the devil would have a hand in it somehow or other.

Sherry removed Buchanan's empty plate and his own scarcely disturbed salmon and replaced them with the cheeseboard; a thing of beauty replete with grapes and celery and home-made oatcakes. Buchanan's resistance lasted all of fifteen seconds.

"Were you around when the news of Murray's arrest for child abuse hit the papers?" he asked.

"No," Sherry said without hesitation, and then corrected himself. "I was in Edinburgh, actually, so I suppose that constitutes a loose 'yes'. I was playing Cromwell in *A Man for All Seasons* at the Lyceum. Not the role I'd care to be remembered for."

"But you regarded Murray and Dianne as no more than acquaintances at that point?"

"That's right. It was only last year that Dianne and I met up again and . . . and hit it off. Odd how that happens. You know a person for years, you register the fact that she's charming, but the magic simply isn't there. Then, suddenly — *kazoom!*"

Another long silence ensued while they both assiduously spread butter and crunched celery. Buchanan could not decide how much to accept of Sherry's story. There was not the slightest hint in Sherry's demeanour to suggest that he might be gay, but if he were honest with himself, Buchanan would have to admit that he had been taken by surprise more than once when guys he'd known for years suddenly came out. And these guys were not actors. Therefore, if he wanted to know whether Sherry were gay or not, he was going to have to ask him, which was definitely not on.

He looked at his watch. "Sherry, I must go. I'm meeting someone at half two. This has been delightful."

"We must do it again sometime," Sherry said urbanely, pushing back his chair and rising to administer a firm double-handshake. "And Tam . . . I know I mustn't ask you to break client confidentiality, but if there's anything I should know . . . if it should turn out that Dianne was in some way involved, I'd appreciate it if you would let me know. In my position, you understand, these things . . . well, any notoriety can be devastating, so one likes to be ahead of the opposition if one can possibly arrange it."

"Of course. I understand." Buchanan nodded, not specifying what it was he understood or committing himself to anything. Besides, if his wife had been involved in some questionable activity serious enough to lead to her murder, a fat lot of good it would do Sherry to be the first to know about it. As far as that was concerned, he had just wasted an hour and a half. It hadn't been all that profitable a meeting for Buchanan either, other than gastronomically, but he would have to think over what had been said before he could estimate its true worth.

Fizz spent the morning doing a hand-washing and hanging it out on the "green" that wasn't a green but merely the tarmacadamed roof of the shop on the ground floor. Her date the night before had been less of a bore than she had anticipated, which was just as well, since she had found out little regarding the police view of the case, which had been her original intention in accepting — and indeed, contriving — the invitation. Dougie turned out to be a keen hill-walker, and they were able to share their experiences of the high places Fizz loved. He had done most of the better-known peaks, including the Inaccessible Pinnacle, which was on Fizz's agenda in the not-too-distant future, so she was able to pick his brains about that, as well as about Dianne's murder. He was also a good listener, and didn't expect her to jump into bed with him at the drop of a hat, so she had agreed to meet him again on Sunday afternoon for a drive out to Arrochar and a walk up the Cobbler. Maybe by that time he would have some worthwhile news to impart about the Crucifixion Case, as it was being dubbed in the press.

Around about the time Buchanan was embarking on his fillet of Angus beef, she sat down, with a glass of milk and a banana, to take another look at *Our Kate*. She didn't honestly hold out much hope of extracting any information from it pertaining to the red-haired Kate because she could see at a glance, as Zoe had done the previous afternoon, that it was no different from any other copy one might pick up second hand. No names on the flyleaf, no cryptic messages scribbled in the margins, probably no attributable fingerprints either, barring a miracle. However, she used only one finger to hold it steady as she went through the pages one by one, just to make sure.

The small rectangle of heavy paper was tucked so well into the spine of the book that it needed a small tug to dislodge it. Fizz was aware of no surge of hope as she turned it right way up to read it, and indeed took a minute to register the impact of what she read.

It was a dentist's appointment card with NHS information on one side and a date and time on the other. No name, no address, just "Monday 1st May. 4.45p.m." in a hurried-looking scrawl. The name of the dentist was Hilliard, and his surgery was at 110 Dalry Road — an area which was familiar to Fizz because it was just around the corner from the community centre.

She sat looking at it for a second or two, and it was as if she were deliberately refusing to recognise its significance. Maybe she had been so convinced that there was nothing to find that it took time to accept that she had found something — and something pretty mind-blowing at that! Okay, the year wasn't mentioned, but that was the one piece of information she could herself supply when she asked Mr Hilliard's receptionist who'd had an appointment at 4.45p.m. on Monday the first of May.

It wasn't far to the community centre and she usually walked it, but today she grabbed a bus and to hell with the expense! She had more than an hour before she had to meet Buchanan, but getting information out of receptionists was not always easy, and she didn't want to have to rush it. It was all she could do to take a minute to phone Beatrice and let her know about her change of plan.

The surgery was a ground-floor flat with its own entrance and a sooty strip of lawn separating it from the street. The windows were blank with Venetian blinds, and a sign above the bellpush said, "Dental Surgeon, David Hilliard, BDS. Please ring and enter." Fizz rang and entered.

She found herself in a square, terrazzo-floored hallway with a waiting room opening off to one side. Both were empty and smelled strongly — not to say eye-wateringly — of Spring Blossoms, doubtless in an

335

effort to mask the even more pervasive aroma of ether, disinfectant and nervous diarrhoea which Fizz imagined she could detect in every dental surgery she'd ever entered.

There were voices issuing from a room at the back of the hall: a low, bad-tempered rumble going nag, nag, nag, and an apologetic squeak in a minor key, both of them too indistinct to be intelligible. Presently, just as Fizz was about to go back out and ring the bell again, the conversation was superseded by the whine of a drill, and the door opened to admit a ginger-haired teenager in a white coat. She looked as though she'd just about had it up to here.

"Can I help you?" she said in a bright singsong that didn't match her scowl.

Fizz ignored the question and tipped her chin in the direction of the closed door.

"I've got one the same back at the office. I can give you the phone number of the Samaritans if you need it."

Ginger's face brightened fractionally, but she wasn't going to commit herself to a smile. "Have you an appointment?"

"No." Fizz wandered into the waiting room, which promised a little more privacy. It was the old-fashioned hard-chairs-and-posters variety, but, she was happy to note, it had a reception desk and computer behind a counter in one corner. "Actually, I just want to check some information."

"What sort of information?"

Fizz put her bag on the counter and fished out the appointment card and also Buchanan's business card. "I work for this lawyer and we're trying to trace somebody. All we know is that she had an appointment here, with Mr Hilliard, on the first of May four years ago. I suppose you'll have that information in your records?"

Ginger's eyes ricocheted between the appointment card and the computer for a few seconds while she thought about that. "Not on computer, no," she said, as though that were the end of it.

"Someplace else, maybe?"

Ginger smiled dismissively. "Well, yes, but it could take ages to find it."

Fizz looked painfully sorry about being a nuisance. "It's terribly important."

"I'm not even sure I'd be allowed to give out that kind of information. I'd have to clear it with Mr Hilliard." Ginger got herself behind the counter as though she subconsciously felt the need for protection.

This was bad news. Fizz's experience with medical practitioners was that they usually wanted all sorts of assurances, including a special dispensation from the Pope, before they would even open their filing cabinets. Alerting Mr Hilliard to her curiosity would be fatal.

"This is something I should have done weeks ago," she said, allowing a note of panic to creep into her tone. "If my boss asks for the information and I don't have it, I'm in deep shit. Frankly, if Mr Hilliard won't play ball I'd have to get my boss to phone him, and that would be me out of a job, and I don't mind telling you, if I lose my job right now . . . God, I don't know what I'll do." She made a serious attempt to look pale with worry and left the details to Ginger's imagination.

Ginger hesitated, looking at the card for inspiration. "See, I'm only on probation myself. I don't want to get into any trouble."

"There's no way your boss is going to find out. Honestly."

Well, of course he would find out if the evidence proved usable, but there was a fifty-fifty chance that it wouldn't. Besides, by that time Hilliard might have dropped dead, or Ginger might have dropped dead, or she might have found another job or been sacked for another reason, etcetera, etcetera. "Actually," she said, with a flash of inspiration, "all we have to do is to write the name and address on the card and I'll say that's the way it was when I found it. No need for your name to come into it at all."

"Well . . ." Ginger began to look seriously undecided. Her darting glances now took in the doorway as well as the card and the computer. She said, "Is it a criminal thing?"

"No, it's a legacy. Thirty-six thousand pounds. Only we can't trace her because she changed her name after she got divorced last year and we think she must have reverted to her maiden name and gone back to live with the guy she was shacked up with four years ago."

Ginger didn't even try to make sense of this explanation. The mention of the money swung it. "Okay, but I'd have to tell Mr Hilliard."

338

Fizz's spirits, which had leaped at the first word, had crashed again by the end of the sentence. "Well," she said, slapping on a look of deep depression. "that means I'm out of a job, but if that's the way you feel you have to play it . . ."

Ginger spread her hands. "There's nothing else I can do. The old records are kept in the cupboard in the surgery. I can't start raking through them with Mr Hilliard at my elbow."

"What about when he goes out to lunch?"

"He doesn't eat lunch."

That seemed to be it. Fizz couldn't see any way round it, but she just kept on standing there, looking at Ginger with tragic eyes and waiting. It was a trick that had paid off before.

After a minute of this treatment, Ginger hauled in a deep breath, glanced at the doorway, and half whispered, "Maybe . . . if it's so important to you . . . maybe I could get it for you on Sunday morning."

"Thank you so much," Fizz said quickly, as though Ginger had already made a firm commitment. "I can't tell you what this means to me."

"Well, I only said maybe." Ginger started to look jittery.

"I know, I know, but if I could just have that information by the beginning of the week, it would save my life. I mean that. It's that serious. Would it put you to a lot of trouble?"

"Not really." Ginger's unwillingness was visibly wilting. "Mr Hilliard rents me the flat upstairs and I have the spare key to the surgery. I suppose I could just pop downstairs and take a quick look."

"You couldn't do it tomorrow?"

"No," Ginger said with a look on her face that said she meant it. "He doesn't often come in on a Saturday but I'm not going to take the chance. Sunday's different. He goes sailing every Sunday morning, rain or shine, so I'd feel a lot safer."

"Right. No point in taking chances. I wouldn't have dreamed of asking you to do this if I hadn't been so desperate," Fizz said, keeping the pressure on till the last. "I wish I knew how to thank you."

"Leave me your phone number and I'll give you a ring if I turn anything up."

"Haven't got a phone — no, wait a minute, I'll give you the number of a friend of mine and I'll go round there and wait for your call." She wrote Zoe's number on a scrap of paper and Ginger folded it quickly into the pocket of her overall. "What time will you be phoning?"

"Not before ten — maybe ten thirty — Mr Hilliard should be out of harbour by then. I'm not promising I'll be able to find the information you want, but . . ."

"It doesn't matter," Fizz told her, putting on an expression of wistful trust. "I know you'll try."

She couldn't wait to report to Buchanan, but there was no sign of him outside when she emerged. Beatrice had promised to pass on a message for him to pick her up at the corner of Dalry Road, but she now realised that he might not have contacted the office after his lunch date with Sherry and could now be looking for her at her flat in the High Street, in accordance with their previous arrangement.

She spent an anxious four or five minutes pacing up and down before his Saab slid into the kerb beside her. "Greetings, oh Star of the Universe," she said, getting in. "I'm glad to see you. I thought you'd gone to the High Street."

"No. Beatrice said you were at the dentist. What did you have done?"

Fizz gave a snort. "I didn't say I'd gone for treatment. I went for information."

Buchanan paused with his hand on the ignition key and turned to look at her with his eyebrows all squidged up, like he did when he was angry. "Information? I thought we had agreed that you would resist going off on projects of your own without first clearing them with me?"

"Well, how could I clear it with you when you were busy stuffing your face with Sherry?"

"It could have waited." You could hear him grating his teeth.

"Listen, we won't even be getting any results till at least Sunday morning; meanwhile the killer could strike again!"

He had this nasty way of half dropping his eyelids and smiling on one side of his mouth that was particularly insulting. "So, tell me about it."

Fizz produced the appointment card. She was in two minds whether to tell him to use it as a suppository, but restrained herself and gave him a brief rundown on how she'd come by it and where it had led her.

Buchanan took it and looked at both sides. The frown gradually cleared from his brow, and when he looked up at her his eyes were sharp and clear. "Can they check out who had this appointment?"

Fizz nodded, trying not to bubble too effervescently. "The receptionist is going to try to track it down on Sunday morning — she has to be in the surgery then for some reason — so I've arranged with her that I'll go round to Zoe's and she'll phone me there when she has the details."

Buchanan sat for a moment tapping the card on the dashboard and staring blindly out through the windscreen, while Fizz glowed quietly beside him.

"The plot thins," she couldn't resist saying.

"What?" Buchanan roused himself and seemed to catch sight of something on the other side of the road. Fizz followed his eyes and spotted McGuigan, uncharacteristically smart in a sharp black suit.

"That's McGuigan," Fizz said. "He's waving to you."

Buchanan peered through the passing traffic. "McGuigan? Are you sure?"

"Sure I'm sure. I'd know those teeth if I saw them in Mr Hilliard's spittoon."

"What the hell does he want?"

An unnamed fear grabbed Fizz by the entrails.

"Pretend you don't see him," she said.

"Too late, he's crossing over."

Fizz watched with sick apprehension as McGuigan wove his way through the stream of buses and cars and approached. Buchanan wound down his window.

"Tam, dear boy. Do you have a minute? I'd like a brief word." His gooseberry eyes flicked unsmilingly to Fizz. "In private."

Buchanan said, "Could it wait till Monday? I'm in a bit of a rush right now."

McGuigan intimated something obscure with pursed lips. "The sooner we get it cleared up the better, I think."

"Oh well, if it's that important . . ." Buchanan glanced up and down the road for traffic wardens and gave Fizz a what-the-hell-next look before getting out of the car. He followed McGuigan a few steps away and stuck his hands in his trouser pockets while he listened to the rat's turd putting the boot in.

Fizz didn't deceive herself for one moment that the conversation was about something that didn't concern her. If she had been in any doubt, Buchanan's quick frowning glances in her direction would have put her straight. As McGuigan ranted on, waving his hands in furious chopping motions, Buchanan's face got grimmer and his chin tucked itself down against his collar as if he were waiting for McGuigan to take a swing at it.

There was one brief moment when things looked almost promising. Buchanan leaned forward and said something to McGuigan that made him take a pace backwards and flush purplish-red all round the brow and cheekbones. But when Buchanan got back in the car just seconds later you could feel the rage coming off him in waves, and it wasn't directed at McGuigan.

"Well, that looked exciting," Fizz commented brightly as Buchanan let in the clutch and pulled out into the traffic. He made no reply. She thought at first that he was headed for the McCaulays' as planned, but he merely drove around the corner and stopped, either to get off the main road or because he didn't want McGuigan to have the satisfaction of seeing him berating her.

"That's it, Fizz," he said, making a reasonable stab at keeping his voice level. "If there's one person in this world I hate having to take a ticking-off from it's McGuigan, and it's not going to happen again. I can't run an office with you playing merry hell behind my back — stealing computers —"

"I only borrowed it —"

"— making international phone calls, filling your desk with stationery you'll never use —"

"How did he find out about the phone call?"

"Donna admitted you'd been in the office, evidently, after he spotted you leaving, and he used the redial facility to trace the call. So you've managed to embarrass her as well as me. You don't have much regard for other people, do you, Fizz?"

"It's an area I'm working on."

"I knew the day you walked into the office that I'd regret letting you into my life. You've caused trouble in every department. It was you who got me embroiled with Murray's troubles, you who devastated my social life, you who destroyed my credibility at the community centre —"

"Nobody's perfect."

"— and you continue, despite all I say, to go off half cocked on any ploy that occurs to you, regardless of repercussions." His voice shook with repressed temper. "Well, I've had enough. That's it. Finish."

"Okay, I made a phone call," Fizz allowed, "but the fact that I happened to —"

"No plea-bargaining, Fizz, you're out. I don't want to see you back in that office, I don't want you turning up at my door, I want you out of my life now, today, and for good."

"Okay, okay, I can take a hint."

"And as far as you're concerned, Murray's case is closed. I don't want you nosing around on your own, causing more harm than good and putting yourself and possibly others in danger."

"Now just a minute." Fizz snapped upright in her seat, abandoning all hope of keeping things cool. "Just one goddamn minute, Buchanan. What I choose to do for Murray is between him and me. I've done more legwork and honest-to-goodness detecting on this case than anybody else, and I've found out more concrete evidence than you have, come to that. There's no way I'm going to pack in at this stage in the game. As long as Murray wants me to help him, you don't have any say in the matter."

"No?" One eyebrow escaped his control and jerked angrily upwards. "We'll see about that, Fizz."

"You bet we will!" She slammed out of the car and turned to shout back through the open window, "Damn you, Buchanan, you arrogant bastard, you won't tell me what to do!"

345

He leaned across the passenger seat and started to say something, but she flung away from him and stomped off, her Docs ringing militantly on the pavement.

Bastard! Bastard! Bastard! Bastard! Bastard! Bastard! she thought, all the way home.

CHAPTER
TWENTY-THREE

Saturday was a bummer from beginning to end. Knowing that she wouldn't settle to anything less strenuous, Fizz decided to get out of the city, which was like New Orleans during Mardi Gras, and pay Grampa another visit. Normally she dropped in on him about once a month, not because she was particularly worried about him, since even though he was knocking eighty he was a tough old bird, but because she felt she should show willing.

It wasn't a chore she enjoyed. Am Bealach, which wasn't even big enough to be called a village, was two miles from Killin, at the end of Loch Tay. The journey, which would have taken under two hours by car, could stretch to double that if she was unlucky with bus connections, so she usually stayed overnight and returned the following day. This time, because she had to be back for Ginger's phone call, she did it in a oner, and didn't get back to Edinburgh that evening till nearly eleven thirty.

She woke early on Sunday, impatient to get to Zoe's, but decided that there wasn't any point in getting there much before ten, since Zoe seldom showed a leg till then unless she had to. It was much too nice a morning to spend indoors, so she walked across the Meadows to a Sunday-opening fruit shop, and then took the long way round, down the Pleasance and round Calton Hill to Zoe's place.

At that hour in the morning the streets weren't all that much busier than on a normal Sunday. Most of the Festival-goers had been partying till the wee small hours and were now sleeping it off in preparation for another fix of culture or Fringe in a few hours' time. Apart from some street theatre groups, who had to get in there early to bag the best sites, there wasn't much activity. Fizz paused to listen to a barbershop quartet outside the St James's Centre, and then dawdled about looking in shop windows and watching the police making crowd control preparations for the afternoon's Festival Parade.

If she had been in a better mood, she would have considered asking Zoe if she fancied going along to watch the parade, but she was still angry at the cavalier treatment Buchanan had meted out to her and she didn't feel like joining in the fun. Nor was she, if she were honest with herself, feeling all that optimistic about getting anything promising out of Ginger, and there didn't appear, at the moment, to be any other line of investigation to pursue.

She got to Zoe's place at about ten past ten, just as a group of students who'd been trying to put fliers for their Fringe performance through the letterboxes were being seen off by the janitor. Fizz accepted a flier and read it as she went up in the lift. "*Turkestan*, a play in three acts, by Jonathan Harvey."

348

Zoe was not only up and about, she was fully dressed and had three coats of mascara on each individual eyelash. Her leggings were Jaffa orange, and the loose shirt that she wore open over a black camisole top was royal purple. Her expression showed more surprise than actual delight, but at ten past ten in the morning, surprise was about as good as could be expected.

"Well, look at you!" Fizz remarked. "All dressed up and nowhere to go!"

"Actually," she said, following Fizz into the lounge, "I do have someplace to go. I was on my way out."

Fizz dropped her bag of shopping on the floor, fell on to the couch and spread her arms along the top of the backrest. "Well, cancel all plans, Zoe, and wait till you hear what I've got to report."

Zoe put a hand on each hip and looked at her steadily. "I can't, Fizz, not now. I've got something on."

"What?"

"Something important."

"What?"

"Something *private*, Fizz!"

It gradually dawned on Fizz that Zoe really was in a hurry. She was refusing to sit down and you could see that she was itching to be gone.

"Well, this is important too," Fizz told her. "Somebody's phoning me back this morning and I gave them your number. If you absolutely have to go out I'll just have to wait in on my own. You don't mind, do you? It's a new lead I'm following up. Sit down and I'll tell you all about it."

"No, wait a minute," Zoe said, removing a hand from her hip to hold it out like a stop sign. "Couldn't you phone this person back and give them another number to reach you at? Tam's number, maybe. Then you can go over there and wait for the call."

"Bastard gave me the elbow," Fizz told her, shaking her head in contempt. "He found out on Friday about the phone call to New York . . . and one or two other things. I suspect it was bloody Donna in reception who pulled the rug out from under me by telling McGuigan, and, of course, McGuigan tore into Buchanan, who got himself into a right old taking. You should have seen him! I thought he was about to have my liver with some fava beans and a nice Chianti!"

"I'm sure he just fired you in the heat of the moment," Zoe said, momentarily forgetting her impatience. "Don't lose any sleep over it, Fizz. Give him a few days to simmer down and he'll change his mind."

"Not without a pre-frontal lobotomy," Fizz said with mock seriousness. "It was really ugly, Zoe. At one point he very nearly lost his temper!"

Zoe mimed shock-horror. "That bad, huh?"

"And the really pissing-off bit about it was that I'd just got a good strong lead on the mystery playgroup helper."

"You're kidding!" Zoe abandoned all hope of being on time for her date and sat down on the arm of an easy chair. "How strong?"

"Mega," Fizz told her, overstating the case just a little to keep her hanging around. "There wouldn't be a cup of tea in the house, would there? I'm parched right down to my belly button."

Zoe pushed up her sleeve and looked at her watch. "Okay, but you'll have to promise to drink it fast."

She wobbled out of the room in her crazy heels, her orange bum jiggling like it had been set in a jelly mould. Fizz was struck, not for the first time, by a desire to roast the inventor of leggings over a slow fire. She thought about taking off her Docs, but Zoe was back with a tea tray in what seemed a matter of seconds.

"The kettle was boiling," she said, handing Fizz a mug and carrying her own to the armchair.

"Great," said Fizz. "And by the by, if Buchanan asks you if I'm still working on the case, you'd better tell him you don't know."

"Well, I don't know, do I?" Zoe said reasonably. "So if you are, you'd better not tell me. What you found out on Friday doesn't count, I assume?"

"No, that was before he told me to bugger off."

"Right. Or words to that effect. So, what's the new lead you've turned up?"

"This is going to slay you," Fizz said, and perceiving that she had Zoe's full attention for the moment, she kept her waiting while she loosened her jacket. Zoe watched with a little tense frown that didn't ease when she heard the details about the dentist's appointment card and Ginger's promise to track down the patient's name and address.

She looked blank for a long moment, then said softly, "So, she's phoning you here when she has the information, is she?"

"Yep. Any time now, I'd imagine. I don't suppose it would take forever, would it? She said she'd start looking some time after ten, and it must be . . . what?"

"Ten-thirty."

Zoe had now, apparently, given up on the idea of dashing out, at least for the present. She had stopped jittering about and was sitting very quiet and still, staring into her tea cup, apparently trying to read her fortune without having first drunk her tea. There was a faint film of sweat on her forehead, as though she were feeling the heat, though the morning didn't seem all that warm to Fizz.

She leaned back against her cushions and relaxed. She was fairly sure now that Zoe wasn't going to chuck her out.

Bloody Fizz!

Buchanan was equally disgusted at himself for (a) ever letting her into his life, and (b) being markedly less than ecstatic to be rid of her.

She was a pain in the neck. Let's face it, she was horrendous. She was an inveterate liar, a manipulator, selfish, opinionated, miserly, and didn't give a hoot in hell about anyone but herself. Her philosophy, as propounded by herself, was: everything I have is yours and everything you have is mine. Which was fair enough till you remembered that she didn't have anything you'd want.

On the other hand, when she was in a good mood — which, okay, was almost always — she was quite nice to be around. She was different. She made you see things in a way you hadn't seen them before. Also, she had a strange kind of innocence about her, even though you couldn't trust her with the gold fillings in Grandma's teeth. But she was honest. That was the funny thing. Way down deep, where it counted, she was as honest a person as he'd ever met.

However, be that as it may, he was rid of her now, and he wasn't about to change that, regrets or no regrets. Common sense dictated that he learn his lesson and steer clear of her from now on.

But it was bloody depressing.

Bloody Fizz!

Murray and Dolores between them had done a thorough, if belated, spring clean of the entire flat. It was proving difficult to dislodge Murray, but Buchanan had to admit that it was nice to see the windows sparkling and everything in its place. Except the laundry Dolores had brought back on Thursday and left for him to put away. That was migrating from the top of his chest of drawers to every other flat surface in the bedroom, and would soon have deteriorated into dirty washing again before he'd even worn it. He decided to make time to tidy it away after lunch. Unless he decided that Murray would benefit from a stroll up to Princes Street to watch the parade.

"I don't think so," Murray said when he suggested it. "I can't stand crowds these days, they make me nervous. I'd just as soon stay in and have a quiet talk, if it's all the same to you. I haven't seen much of you, these last two or three days, and I wanted to talk over what progress you've been making."

Buchanan would have liked an hour's peace and quiet with the *Weekend Scotsman* and the *Financial Times*, which he hadn't had time to finish yesterday, but he could see that was not to be. He had to admit he'd been avoiding spending much time in Murray's company over the last couple of days. Thanks to the golf match yesterday, Murray had been on his own all day and, in fact, he'd seen Buchanan only in passing the night before, since Friday was the night Buchanan had a standing dinner-and-theatre date with an out-of-town friend. Had Murray still shown signs of severe depression, Buchanan would have cancelled both arrangements, but there was every sign that he was making a steady recovery, so Tam had no qualms about leaving him. In fact he was quite sure that it was time for a parting of the ways and intended to put that view quite forcibly whenever the opportunity offered.

"Sure," he said, bowing to the inevitable. "But I think I've told you all that's been happening."

"Yes, but only briefly," Murray said, sitting tidily on the couch to avoid disarranging the scatter cushions. "I miss hearing the taped interviews. You said that you didn't learn much from the McCaulays on Friday?"

"Didn't expect a great deal," Buchanan said. "I just wanted to make sure that they didn't hold you responsible for the death of their son."

"*Me?*" Murray reiterated, as if the thought had never occurred to him. "He was killed in Ireland —"

354

"Yes, but he would never have been in Ireland if you'd given him a decent reference for the job he wanted. He'd have been a nurse."

"Bloody right, and a right bullying swine of a nurse he'd have been too, if he ever made it through his training. Nobody but a fool would ever have recommended him for a job where he was dealing with vulnerable people. The chap had no patience at all!"

Buchanan nodded. "I think his parents accepted that he wasn't cut out for a career in nursing. They didn't hold it against you anyway, I'm sure of that."

"Well, I could have told you that," Murray muttered with a trace of sullenness, just as though he expected Buchanan to take his word for everything, regardless of his having been interpreting the truth rather loosely from day one. "And Sherry, you said, wasn't giving much away?"

"I suspect he had very little to give away. I was more interested in what he had to tell me about Dianne's early days as a TV dramatist. He appeared to think the work she was producing in collaboration with Zoe was as good as, if not better than, anything she did on her own."

Murray nodded, albeit reluctantly. "It's true. They were magic together. Given another few years, a bit of experience, they'd have made it big. Zoe could come up with the dramatic situations and she had the patience to sit down and work out the details, think up unusual twists, create the characters. But she needed Dianne to flesh out her characters, to put words in their mouths." He lifted a shoulder, staring bleakly out at the waving trees below. "They needed each other, really. Dianne found that out when her second play flopped. She didn't have Zoe's flair for plotting."

Buchanan started to get the picture. It was glaringly obvious that Dianne, having come across the enthralling story already sketched out in Adrian Ballard's manuscript, must have thought she held success in her hand and saw no reason to share it. Probably she'd have waited till she had a conditional acceptance for her screenplay before ditching Zoe, and from that day, she had gone up and Zoe had gone down.

He said, "Sherry said something yesterday about their split-up. 'Bloody tragic', he called it. Was it a messy business?"

Murray pressed his lips together. "A bit, yes. Not legally . . . they hadn't been very practical about it because, oh, because they were just getting on their feet and it never seemed all that important. I suppose Zoe lost out a bit when they decided to go their separate ways. She was very bitter at the time. Went over the score, I thought. She fell out with several of the producers who'd used their stuff previously, and made a bit of a fool of herself." He smoothed the material of his cord trousers over his knees with both hands. "Silly girl."

Buchanan could feel his pulse speeding up, but he wasn't quite sure why. "And, to all intents and purposes, she never worked in television again?"

"I'm not sure. I think she said she'd sold a few things." Murray's eyes widened with speculation. "You think she . . . *Zoe?* You think she still had it in for Dianne after all these years? You're losing perspective, Tam. Zoe would never . . . she's not the vindictive type."

"Did she know about the manuscript?" Buchanan said, wondering where the hell he'd put his notes. He had a feeling they were locked in his desk at the office. And the tapes? Dammit, Fizz still had them.

"No way, Tam. Nobody knew about that manuscript except Dianne and me." He stopped and seemed to be thinking about something. When he got tired of waiting, Buchanan said:

"What are you remembering, Murray?"

He blinked and looked up at Buchanan with a dazed frown. "The time my flat was broken into . . . I had the feeling at the time that someone had been looking for the manuscript."

"You had it in your flat? The handwritten version?"

"Yes . . . and I'll be honest with you, Tam, I wondered . . . just fleetingly . . . if it had been Dianne."

"Dianne?" Buchanan found that he was sitting on the edge of his seat and leaning forwards, as though he couldn't wait for Murray's words to reach him but had to go to meet them. "You told me you'd given her a copy of the typescript."

Murray was gripping both hands between his knees now, and his face had returned to the shade of grey it had worn when he first came to the office. "She wanted me to give her the handwritten version. It was the only proof there was that she hadn't written the play herself."

"And you wouldn't give it to her?"

He shook his head.

"Why not, Murray?"

It seemed he couldn't bring himself to answer. He stared at the carpet, at the window, at his trapped hands, and couldn't get the words out. Finally:

"I suppose I felt . . . I don't know . . . maybe it gave me a feeling of security."

"Security against what?"

"Against her leaving me." He rubbed a hand hard across his eyebrows, screening his face. "She was so . . . she was out of my class, Tam. I don't know what she ever saw in me, or why she stuck by me, but I woke every morning expecting her to be gone. You don't know what that's like, Tam. She . . . she was everything in the world to me."

"But the manuscript wasn't stolen in the break-in?"

"No. I've still got it, but it's in a safe deposit box now."

Buchanan got up and started to walk up and down, scarcely aware of what he was doing. His mind was away ahead of Murray, racing to a conclusion that left him dizzy. "You thought that if she knew you had it in your power to expose her —"

"I'd never have done it. Never! It would have ruined her career."

"As she had ruined Zoe's."

Murray's face knotted in bewilderment.

"You've lost me, Tam."

Buchanan stopped pacing and leaned on the back of his chair, gripping it hard. "You say you'd never have

358

exposed Dianne, but tell me the truth, Murray: what was in your mind that night you confronted her in her hotel room? You never even considered violence, did you? You didn't have to. You had the means of revenge locked up in that safe deposit box all ready to show to the media."

Murray glared at him, red-eyed. "Okay, I thought about it! If I'd really thought she'd done it . . . But she hadn't framed me, Tam. She couldn't have been in Edin —"

"Dammit, Murray, must you be so thick? You were just a tool! Somebody used you to get at Dianne, isn't that obvious? You had the power to hurt Dianne, to ruin her career. Somebody who had no power to hurt her primed you and pointed you and pulled the trigger. The fact that Dianne was able to dodge the bullet was just sheer bad luck. If she hadn't been able to prove to you that she was in a clinic at a time when she'd have needed to be around to plant the clues, you'd have destroyed her!"

That took a second to sink in. Buchanan watched as Murray slowly accepted the implications and started to react. "*Zoe?*"

"Who else would have chosen that way of hurting Dianne? Who else was close enough to Dianne to be able to find out about the manuscript? And who else," the thought had been hovering at the back of his mind for minutes, "knew that the stratagem had failed, that night, and went straight back to murder her, knowing you'd be blamed for it?"

"No — no, Tam, you've got to be wrong." Murray's head hung forward as though he were too tired to hold it up. He shook it slowly. "How could she have known about the manuscript?"

"She and Dianne were working closely together at that point," Buchanan returned impatiently. "There must have been plenty of opportunity for her to snoop around among Dianne's notes and to listen to your conversations when you weren't aware of her being within earshot." He saw that shot go home and pressed on. "Debbie hadn't seen her since babyhood, so she wouldn't have recognised her. Zoe could have had weeks in which to coach her in what she wanted her to say."

"But she's helped us every step of the way, Tam. She's done everything she could to help me prove my innocence."

"Of course she has!" Buchanan could almost feel admiration for her persistence. "But only because she had to prove that you'd been framed — and by Dianne. She wasn't expecting you to have Fizz and me in your corner when you got out of jail, but I'm ready to bet she'd have turned up around that time to make sure you uncovered the evidence that pointed to Dianne."

Murray was shaking visibly. He swung away and walked a few paces to the window, gripping the sill with both hands. "She put me away for three years just to get back at Dianne . . . She used my kid . . ."

"We have to phone DI Fleming," Buchanan said, and then it hit him like a tidal wave — *Fizz — dentist — phone call — Zoe's flat — this morning — NOW!*

360

"Jesus, Murray! Fizz is with her now — waiting for a phone call that's going to blow the whole thing!"

He catapulted into the bedroom, grabbing his jacket and shaking it to hear his car keys rattle, yelling all the time. "Phone Fleming, Murray! Get him out there fast. *Fast*, do you hear? I'll be there before them but I may not be in time!"

Murray was already dialling as Buchanan took the stairs in two leaps, but the sound failed to calm him. He knew that even if he were on duty this Saturday morning, Fleming would want all manner of long-winded explanations before he would send out a police car, and Murray, even at the best of times, was never the most articulate of proponents.

The car, thank God, started first time and roared up the hill to Princes Street like a Ferrari. There was something across the junction that, in his present state of agitation, took a few seconds to impinge on his consciousness.

It was a police road barrier. Beside it a polite notice informed him that, due to the Festival Parade, the road had been closed to traffic, and he was, for the next hour and a half, recommended to take a twenty-minute diversion which appeared to include a historical tour of the New Town.

It began slowly to dawn on Fizz that Zoe wasn't well. She kept closing her eyes and tipping her head back to rest it on the back of her chair, and it looked, also, as if she might be running a temperature. However, when asked if she felt ill, she denied it and made the excuse that, in spite of the morning being somewhat chilly, she was just feeling the heat. She stood at the open window for a while, but then started to shiver and had to make a rush for the toilet whence, presently, came the sound of retching.

Fizz was mildly alarmed, not because she felt any compassion for Zoe but because she, herself, had a horror of being ill. Her solitary, wandering existence over the past few years had taught her that you were okay as long as you could keep going, but you couldn't head-butt a virus. Accordingly, she got as far away from Zoe as possible by going into the kitchen and rustling up another pot of tea. When she got back, Zoe had returned from the bathroom and commandeered the end of the couch beside the telephone, so she had to take the armchair.

"This'll make you feel better," she said, pouring out a cup and handing it to Zoe at the full stretch of her arm.

Zoe looked a little brighter already. "I'm fine now. It's just a tummy upset. Probably the pizza I had last night."

Fizz furtively slid her chair further away from her, just in case. "Maybe you should phone the doctor."

"No, honestly. It's nothing. This tea will do the trick."

"Oh well, I'll be out of your hair shortly anyway, and you can have a lie-down." She squinted at the clock. "It's almost half twelve. If that receptionist's going to phone, it'll be in the next half-hour or so."

Zoe set down her cup in a hurry and made another dive for the bathroom. The noises that emerged were barely human.

"Listen," Fizz told her when she came out, "you should be in bed. I'm going to put your electric blanket on and phone the doctor."

"No, really, Fizz, I —"

Fizz ignored her and marched to the door.

"Fizz — I don't want you to —"

Clearly she was worried about somebody seeing her bedroom in a mess, which was just silly. Fizz threw open the bedroom door and stepped to the bed, which was tidily smoothed.

On top of the duvet lay an open suitcase filled with neatly folded clothes. Fizz was quite surprised, since Zoe had said nothing about going away.

"You're not taking a holiday, are you?" she called, and then jumped when Zoe answered from the doorway behind her.

"Just clearing out a few things for Oxfam."

Fizz looked back at the case and lifted a corner of the top garment with two fingers. "Your new red silk dress?"

"It was too tight. Money down the drain." Zoe moved to the other side of the bed, closed and fastened the case and slid it to the floor. As she straightened, the phone rang.

Fizz beat her to it by a short head.

"Hello, Fitzpatrick here."

"Oh . . . hello, this is Julie from Mr Hilliard's practice. I've got that name and address for you."

A wave of pure satisfaction washed over Fizz like warm sunshine on a spring morning. She turned and gave Zoe a big grin and a thumbs-up sign.

"She's got it!" she mouthed silently.

CHAPTER
TWENTY-FOUR

Buchanan did the only thing he could. He left the car in the middle of the road with the door lying open, and he started running.

As he vaulted the barrier across the opening to Princes Street he saw that the pavements were lined with crowds of people who were waiting for the parade to begin. Yellow-jacketed stewards were patrolling the kerbs, keeping the crowd back off the road and taking a fair bit of good-natured bantering from an audience who were getting bored with the long wait and were glad of any diversion.

Buchanan's explosion into this hiatus in the day's festivities was like manna from heaven to a starving people. Suddenly, after standing for what felt like hours with nothing to look at but a couple of stewards and the occasional copper with a walkie-talkie, here was a free spirit, scorning the authority of police and stewards alike, haring up the middle of the road like a madman. They loved it.

A ragged cheer greeted his appearance, swelling into a full-throated animal roar as he body-swerved past a policemen's outstretched arm and slammed into top gear. Already he was the star of the show, and they loved him. They cheered him on enthusiastically, they tripped up stewards, they howled advice and encouragement, they pelted him with empty juice cartons, programmes, crisp packets and balloons. In less than a block he was adrape with coloured streamers and trailing a long cloud of toilet roll.

The police were easy to evade. Clearly they didn't want to look as though they couldn't take a joke, so they were careful not to employ tactics that might put a damper on the holiday atmosphere. He was almost at the Scott Monument when a shirt-sleeved constable took a dive for his knees and would certainly have floored him had not a press photographer chosen that precise second to step forward with his camera and record the moment for posterity. The resultant unpleasantness escaped Buchanan for the moment, since he was by then twenty paces nearer his objective, but he saw the photograph later in the *Evening News* and thought he looked rather impressive, considering.

The incident alarmed him, nevertheless, since he simply hadn't the time to stop and explain the situation. When a second policeman entered the fray, thudding up behind him to within half a pace of his shoulder, he whipped out his squash club membership card and, without breaking pace, brandished it authoritatively. At that distance it could have been anything, but it had a photograph on it and it looked official. It was, at any rate, enough to make the copper slacken his speed for a moment, which gave Buchanan the chance to increase his half-pace lead to at least a pace and a half. That was okay. The copper could stay right there where he might come in handy.

The crowd was ecstatic. Now it wasn't just some nutter making an exhibition of himself, it was a police chase, a real-life drama, like you'd see on the telly. They looked like the Roman populace in *Ben Hur*, all blurred faces and gesticulating arms, and the noise was a huge, all-enveloping wall of sound.

Rational thought was beyond Buchanan, but the picture of Dianne's crucifixion with Fizz's face superimposed on hers screamed in his mind and thrust him forward like a piston.

When the heat got to him he stripped off his jacket and threw it away, which turned out to be a mistake because the copper tripped on it and, according to eyewitness accounts in the evening papers, skidded ten yards on his face. Buchanan was sorry to lose his support but had, at that moment, other matters demanding his attention. Beyond the cheering, beyond the sound of his own heart and the wheezing of his lungs, there was another noise: a steady, low-pitched thumping.

In the second he identified it as the sound of drums, there was a swirl of colour at the corner of Waverley Station, and the parade wheeled into view in front of him: a prancing, cartwheeling, high-kicking, rollicking maelstrom of humanity, filling the roadway from kerb to kerb and heading straight for him.

Fizz had no recollection of putting the phone back on the hook. Maybe she hadn't. Maybe it was Zoe who had taken the receiver from her nerveless fingers and replaced it, keeping her covered, meanwhile, with the gun she was still holding in an SAS grip.

She looked utterly ridiculous, standing there like a plump Sigourney Weaver with her eyes popping and her face white with panic. Zoe with a gun, for Christ's sake! A *gun*!

Fizz's mind went on saying "*Zoe!*" and "*A gun!*" for a long time, but she couldn't make the two concepts match up. It should have been funny.

What made it really scary was that Zoe was shaking as though she was plugged into the mains. She was totally out of control, and Fizz had no idea how to deal with that.

"You stupid bitch," Zoe was spluttering furiously, scarcely able to form the words because her cheeks were quivering and her teeth were rattling together. "You had to keep on nosing around. On and on and on. You never let up."

Fizz was afraid to move, but she tried to relax her posture a little. "It's no big deal, Zoe."

"Shut up!" Zoe yelled. Her eyes were flicking around the room. She seemed physically to be looking for a way out of the situation.

"Zoe, don't do anything rash. We can —"

"Shut up! I told you to shut up!"

She was waving the gun around all over the place. Fizz watched it aiming at her chest, her head, her guts, and felt the sweat break out on her like cod liver oil capsules.

"You're overreacting, Zoe. You don't have to do this."

"Yes I do!" Zoe's face screwed up as if she was going to cry. "I've got to do it now, thanks to you, you silly bitch! I didn't want to but it's your own fault!"

"No, you're wrong. You're not thinking straight. There's no rush, Zoe. You can deal with me now or in half an hour. Makes no difference. Take a minute to think about it before you make a mistake." One minute at a time. If she could just get her past this unstable state, where she might explode at the slightest touch.

The gun muzzle drooped just a fraction, but as Fizz was wondering if now was the time to jump her, it lifted again. Zoe hesitated, shifting from foot to foot, watching Fizz from under drawn brows as she tried to think.

"Sit down!" she said sharply. "No, not there. Over there beside the table."

Fizz moved slowly to the chair Zoe had indicated and sat as loosely as she could, with her hands folded in her lap. She said, "You assume I'm not on your side."

"Don't give me that! You know what I've done. You're not stupid!"

"What? Dianne? The bitch had it coming. You think I'd drop a friend in the shit for a slag like her?" She had no idea what she was talking about or what Zoe's motive had been for defenestrating Dianne, but it had to be something personal.

A sob escaped Zoe's clenched teeth. "She ruined my life. I hope she rots in hell!" She pulled herself together. "I didn't mean to do it, Fizz. I never wanted her dead. I wanted her to live and suffer, the way I've lived and suffered every day since she took away all I had to live for."

Fizz's mind was racing, but the wheels weren't gripping. She said softly, "What did she do to you?"

Tears burst out of Zoe's eyes, but she dashed them quickly away, blinking fast to clear her vision. "Just took away my reason to live, that's all. Finished me as a writer."

"It was that important to you, huh?" Fizz tried to imbue her voice with all the compassion and tenderness she could simulate.

"I was *somebody*. Together we were . . . we were achievers . . . people took us seriously . . . listened to us . . . She took all that away from me. She made me a nobody again and there was nothing . . . *nothing* I could do about it."

She seemed just a fraction calmer, although tears were still running down her face and the gun was pointed, just as firmly, at Fizz's middle.

"You couldn't write without her?"

Zoe shook her head. "Not the stuff I was good at. She fixed it for me in TV. Nobody would look at my stuff. She was flavour of the month suddenly, because of that book she'd stolen, so she could pull strings to keep me out."

Fizz doubted the veracity of that, but nodded as though she agreed. "You knew about the book?"

"Oh yes." Zoe's lip curled nastily. It wasn't an expression she had let Fizz see before, and it made her look like a stranger. A homicidal stranger. "I knew there was something fishy going on with Dianne and Murray,

370

and I could put two and two together. I'd read bits of the screenplay on her computer, but I knew damn well she'd never written it herself. I'd had a key to her flat for years, so when she took off for an overnight stay in London, I searched the place."

"But you didn't find the book?"

"Not at her place. So I had to search Murray's house."

"Murray's burglary." Fizz was beginning to see the light. "That was when he lost his camera. That was you, was it?"

Zoe almost smiled. "I broke in while Murray was at the writers' circle and Debbie was sleeping at the neighbours' house, and I took a few things to make it look genuine. If I could have found the manuscript I'd have had all I needed to drop that bitch in the shit, but if it was there in his house Murray had it well hidden. He did have it, though, somewhere. I found enough to be sure of that — he had it and he wasn't going to part with it. It was all there in the letter files on his computer. Erased, but still in the memory. All the excuses, like he felt it would be 'the ultimate betrayal of Adrian' if he destroyed it." Her face twisted with bitter cynicism. "Sick, pathetic bastard! He knew it gave him a hold over her. From the minute I introduced her to him, all he cared about was Dianne, Dianne, Dianne! Didn't give a damn about what he had to do to hang on to her. Didn't give a damn about helping her to drop me in the trash can, or anything else."

Fizz had the full picture already, and she had to just sit there and let it wash over her for a minute while she sorted it out.

"You couldn't get back at Dianne on your own, right? But you knew that Murray could. Only, he loved her too much ever to hurt her."

Zoe nodded. It was quite clear now that she was proud of her plan and wanted to talk about it. Fizz wondered if she would point the gun the other way for a minute if asked very nicely, but decided not to push her luck.

"I had to make him hate her first. I knew exactly what he would do if he thought she'd been pretending to love him just so that she could use him." She laughed silently, her wet eyes gleaming with self-congratulation.

"Uh-huh. And you were dead right, Zoe." Fizz forged an admiring smile. "And you knew just how to go about it. You got next to Debbie so's you could put words in her mouth and false memories in her head. Told her so many stories she couldn't tell fact from fiction, I bet. You altered her drawings, you arranged for the porno magazines to be found in his office. But other people said that Debbie complained of a sore bottom."

"Itching powder." Zoe smirked, and at that second Fizz knew that she was going to kick the shit out of her. If she died in the attempt she'd make that fat cow regret she'd ever laid a finger on Debbie.

"Clever," she said, smiling back. "But Murray's semen was found on the kid's pyjamas. You couldn't have arranged that, surely?"

"That was what gave me the germ of the idea." She was a lot calmer now, and the tears were drying on her face. She propped herself, half sitting, against the back of an armchair and let her self-satisfaction shine forth. "When I broke into Murray's place that evening I saw a used contraceptive in the bathroom bin. It gave me the idea that maybe I could use it to blackmail Murray into doing what I wanted. Claim he had raped me or something like that. I didn't waste time on working out the details, I just took it away. Then, when I realised the rape allegation wouldn't work, I switched to the idea of framing him for child abuse. It would take a little longer, but I could wait."

"But, surely, the break-in was weeks before the semen was found on the pyjamas?"

Zoe looked smug. "There are such things as freezers, Fizz." She shifted her grip on the gun. "In any case, it wouldn't have mattered if there wasn't enough evidence to put Kingston away. The fact that Dianne had apparently *tried* to frame him would have been enough."

Fizz looked at her round, harmless-looking face and tried not to show her loathing. Zoe the writer. Zoe the plotting wizard. Zoe the painstaking cook and patchwork cushion maker. Patient. Persistent. Going for perfection every time, rather than the quick and easy solution. Small wonder that, after more than three years of anticipating Dianne's downfall, Murray's last-minute failure to deliver had tipped her over the brink. She must have realised right away that if she acted quickly, she could wreak her vengeance on Dianne, and Murray would get the blame.

"Some plan, Zoe." Fizz loaded her voice with commiseration. "It deserved to work. Nobody could have foreseen that Dianne would have managed to talk herself out of it at the last minute. That was a piece of bloody bad luck."

Zoe looked suddenly dangerous, scowling in a manner that made Fizz wish she had held her tongue, but it wasn't Fizz she was mad at. "I wasn't going to let her get away with what she'd done to me, not after all that time, not after all the kudos she'd had for work that was either stolen or amateurish crap!" Zoe's voice wobbled in fury. "That slag — that arrogant, thieving hack! — had the gall to tell *me* I couldn't write a shopping list! Me! She'd never have sold a word if it hadn't been for my plots. She didn't have a clue about developing a storyline — I told her so to her face and I could see she knew it was true. She couldn't deny it."

Belatedly, Fizz realised that Zoe was no longer talking about the distant past but had now jumped to the confrontation in Dianne's hotel bedroom. The memory was having a powerful effect on Zoe and it was perfectly clear, even to Fizz, that in belittling Zoe as a writer, Dianne had made a fatal mistake. You don't kick away someone's last crutch with impunity, not if it's someone as jaundiced as Zoe.

"I didn't mean to kill her." Zoe's voice dropped to a barely coherent mumble. She seemed, almost, to be talking to herself. "If she hadn't come back at me when

I slapped her . . . if she hadn't had the window wide open . . ."

Silence settled round them like a funeral pall. They sat there looking at each other, unmoving, each with their own thoughts, like two actors in one of those existentialist dramas.

Fizz was furious with herself for not realising way back at the beginning that Zoe's appearance on the scene was too pat to be accidental. She had made immediately sure that she would be in the thick of things, offering her flat as headquarters, providing the tape recorder so that she knew exactly what the witnesses were saying, giving them a little nudge now and then so that they didn't stray off course. Now, with twenty-twenty hindsight, she could see that it was Zoe who had provided most of the evidence against Dianne. Practically every lead, with the exception of the one that led them to the playgroup and from there to the appointment card, had been handed to them on a plate. The information about the writers' circle had come from Zoe, and so had the damning — and probably untrue — evidence that Sherry was bisexual. Fizz would have liked to know the truth about Sherry, but —

Zoe stood up, bringing Fizz's attention back to her with a jerk. She was still white as a sheet but her hands were steady on the gun.

"I don't have any choice, you see that, don't you?" Her voice fluttered a bit but sounded horribly determined. "I can't go away and leave you behind me. That would be stupid."

"We can go away together, Zoe." Fizz spoke gently but fast, keeping her hands in her lap with an effort. "Don't you see? I'm a godsend to you right now. I know places where we could disappear for ever — where we could live like oil barons. I'm what you desperately need, Zoe, and I'm on your side. You've got guts to do what you did. Let me get you out of this."

Zoe removed one hand from the gun and wiped the sweat off on her thigh. She was beginning to get agitated again. She had obviously worked herself up to pull the trigger and was now not certain that she would be doing the right thing.

"What places?" she said, very unwillingly.

Fizz looked out of the corner of her eye at the flier the students had shoved into her hand and which she had left lying on the table. The title of the play was written in two-inch letters and was all that could be read clearly from a distance. She swallowed with difficulty and said, "Turkestan, for a start. I picked up this advert for a cheap last-minute flight on my way here."

Moving slowly, she lifted the paper between thumb and forefinger and floated it towards Zoe. It fell a couple of feet short and lay, face up, halfway between them.

Zoe glanced quickly down at it, holding the gun steady.

"I know that area like the back of my hand," Fizz lied feverishly. "Magnificent scenery, mountains, fantastic climate. You could disappear for years in a place like that. Give it a try, Zoe. It's better than being hunted all over Europe, and you can silence me any time you like. Don't do something so final without thinking about it. Look at what happened with Dianne. You regret that, don't you? You let your frustration at the failure of your plan push you into that, and now you'll have to live with the consequences for the rest of your life. Don't make the same mistake again, Zoe. Think things through before you eliminate the one person in the world who can get you clean away."

Zoe dragged in a long, sobbing breath. She was staring at Fizz with red, mascara-blotched eyes, and her whole head was shaking as though she had St Vitus's dance. Suddenly she took a step forward, re-aimed the gun at Fizz's guts, and bent forward to reach for the flier.

Her eyes dropped away for less than half a second, but that was all Fizz needed.

It was one of the most satisfying sensations of her entire life. She felt it build from her hip, ripple down her thigh, and explode in sheer ecstasy through the toe of her Doc Marten as it took Zoe under the chin and threw her back against the wall.

She lay there motionless, her head twisted sideways as though she were trying to focus on Debbie's drawing on the wall above her.

The parade, for weeks afterwards, figured in Buchanan's dreams as a single entity, a cross between a demonic monster and a Spielberg spaceship: something totally invincible and incomprehensibly huge.

In the vanguard was a Dixieland jazz band, fronted by a cake-walking coloured gent with a red umbrella and a smile that almost met at the back of his neck. Buchanan went straight through the musicians like a chicken biriani and found himself in a maelstrom of Japanese dancers, few of whom were keeping to a straight line or taking sensible precautions with their whirling fans.

Bleeding from a slight head wound, Buchanan dodged through their formation into the waiting arms of a seven-foot bunny who waltzed him determinedly in the wrong direction and took his violent reaction — namely an elbow in the solar plexus — in very bad part.

By that point, the rest of the parade was upon them, cancan girls and pipe bands, jugglers and hula dancers, cowboys with spinning lassoes and Zulus in leopard skin and feathers, none of whom were prepared for the advent of a wild-eyed madman in their midst.

In some sections of the procession the disruption was fairly comprehensive, primarily among the troupe of stilt walkers and unicyclists, though much of that havoc was not caused by Buchanan. He felt responsible only for the downfall of the first stilt walker. The others should have been looking where they were going.

After that Buchanan registered nothing but a whirlpool of colour as though he were being swallowed by the vast psychedelic maw of the parade. It chewed him up, digested him and excreted him, panting and swearing, at the head of Leith Walk.

The crowds diminished after that but seemed to thicken again outside Zoe's block of flats. Shouting something, he didn't know what, he fought his way through and hurtled into the hallway. It took only a second to note that the lift was at the fourteenth floor and to realise that it would take minutes to come down. He couldn't wait that long. By now he was in such a state that he couldn't have stood still even going up in the lift.

He was already half a flight up the stairs before he heard a door slam below him and a voice yell at him to stop. He didn't even break his stride, but a minute later he caught sight of a blue uniform sprinting up the stairs below him, confirming his suspicion that he was about to be arrested for disrupting the parade.

Grimly, he increased his pace, using one hand on the banister to haul an extra inch into his stride. Slowly the numbers on the landings ticked by like hours on a clock face. Seven, eight, nine, ten.

As he whirled round the last bend on to the tenth floor he ran into a group of people. Police.

Hands shot out and grabbed him by the arms. The bobby behind him catapulted round the corner, scarlet of face and sweating furiously.

"Tried . . . to stop him . . . sir," he panted, glaring at Buchanan like a one-man lynch mob.

Buchanan beat off the restraining hands and fought for breath. "Fizz . . . she okay?"

"She's fine," said a face, and a hand on his shoulder turned him so that he could look down the length of a corridor lined with doors. At the very end, talking to a policewoman, stood Fizz.

Suddenly all the strength ran out of his legs and he sagged back against the door of the lift. There was an agonising pain in his chest and black spots danced in front of his eyes.

"Mr Kingston said we might run into you here," said the face with a faint smile that made it recognisable as that of DI Fleming.

Buchanan nodded, still unable to speak. He bent over to put a hand on each knee and hauled scalding air into his raw lungs. A long red streamer with a yellow feather on the end dangled in front of his eyes, but he didn't have the strength to brush it aside.

"Right, Constable," said Fleming above his bent head. "I don't need you here now. The rest of you can get back to the station too."

When Buchanan straightened up, the uniformed contingent were filing into the elevator and Fleming was heading down the corridor towards the group beside Fizz. It was very quiet after they'd gone. Buchanan wanted to talk to Fizz, to ask her what had happened, but his legs were like jelly. He watched Fleming reach her and speak to her, then he and the policewoman disappeared through the open door beside her.

Fizz, still leaning against the corridor wall, turned her head and looked at him. She looked very small and slim, and her neck stuck up out of the neckline of her jumper like a flower stem.

"What took you so *bloody* long?" she yelled, straightening from the wall and starting to stride down the corridor like a charging rhino.

"The parade —"

"I don't want sodding excuses!" As she closed on him, her hips twitching from side to side with barely suppressed fury, he could see her ravaged face. It was grim now, but it was clear she had been crying. "I need to be hugged, Buchanan! And hard, dammit!"

She crashed into him like the nine fifteen, thudding him back against the lift door, and his arms went round her like a vice.

Suddenly, everything was okay. The feel of her slight body in his arms was confirmation that, even if she'd had a fright, she was safe. That was all that mattered. The police had got there in time and she wasn't the inert heap with blank eyes that he had been picturing all the way here. She wasn't the crushed and bloody pile of bones ten storeys down below that would probably haunt his dreams for the rest of his life.

"God, Fizz," he muttered. "What an insane situation to get yourself into! Just think what would have happened if the police hadn't got here in time."

She removed her face from his shoulder. "By the time the police arrived I had already made my own arrangements, thank you very much, Buchanan. Don't give me your 'silly little woman' crap. I can look after myself."

"You really believe that, don't you?" Buchanan snapped, all the fear and mental agony of the past half-hour suddenly swept away by a tide of sheer frustration at the impossibility of ever making her see sense. "You were within an inch of ending up like Dianne! You don't even seem to have any conception of the danger you put yourself in. It was a crazy thing to do!"

He heard the lift stop behind him and had to step aside, loosening his grip on Fizz at the same time. No one got out.

"Really?" she snapped, pushing him away from her with a strength which surprised him. "Well, crazy or not, I knew who the killer was before you did, smartass!"

"I told you to keep out of that business." He was now within an inch of losing his temper altogether. "Dammit, Fizz, the trouble you cause to everyone around you —!"

She stepped into the open lift and saluted him with a stiff finger.

"See you around, Buchanan," she said coldly, as the doors slid shut between them.

Buchanan sagged back against the wall and closed his eyes. He felt utterly depleted.

"See you around, Fizz," he whispered to the empty landing, and the words blew away like dry leaves into the silence.

But even as he said it, he knew with absolute certainty that he wouldn't be shot of her so easily.

After a minute or two he started to laugh, and couldn't stop.

ISIS publish a wide range of books in large print, from fiction to biography. Any suggestions for books you would like to see in large print or audio are always welcome. Please send to the Editorial department at:

ISIS Publishing Ltd.
7 Centremead
Osney Mead
Oxford OX2 0ES
(01865) 250 333

A full list of titles is available free of charge from:
Ulverscroft large print books

(UK)
The Green
Bradgate Road, Anstey
Leicester LE7 7FU
Tel: (0116) 236 4325

(Australia)
P.O Box 953
Crows Nest
NSW 1585
Tel: (02) 9436 2622

(USA)
1881 Ridge Road
P.O Box 1230, West Seneca,
N.Y. 14224-1230
Tel: (716) 674 4270

(Canada)
P.O Box 80038
Burlington
Ontario L7L 6B1
Tel: (905) 637 8734

(New Zealand)
P.O Box 456
Feilding
Tel: (06) 323 6828

Details of **ISIS** complete and unabridged audio books are also available from these offices. Alternatively, contact your local library for details of their collection of **ISIS** large print and unabridged audio books.